# SPIKES

# SPIKES

## a novel

## MICHAEL GRIFFITH

Arcade Publishing • New York

FIRST EDITION

This is a work of fiction. Names, places, characters, and incidents are either products of the author's imagination or are used fictitiously.

*Library of Congress Cataloging-in-Publication Data*

Griffith, Michael, 1965-
    Spikes : a novel / Michael Griffith.
        p. cm.
    ISBN 1-55970-536-1
        1. Golf—Tournaments—Fiction. 2. Golfers—Fiction. 3. Southern States—Fiction. I. Title

PS3557.R48928 S65 2001
813'.6—dc21                                                    00–35455

Published in the United States by Arcade Publishing, Inc., New York
Distributed by Time Warner Trade Publishing.

Visit our Web site at www.arcadepub.com

10 9 8 7 6 5 4 3 2 1

Designed by API

EB

PRINTED IN THE UNITED STATES OF AMERICA

*For Nicola*

*Rara avis in terris nigroque simillima cygne.*
(A bird rarely seen on earth, and very like a black swan.)
—Juvenal

# SPIKES

CHAPTER ONE

# Thursday, 4 P.M.

I'VE JUST DUCKED THROUGH THE CANVAS FLAP of the scorer's tent, on my way out. My shoes squish accusingly with every step; my visor wears an unheroic beard of sweat on its bill, and there are half-moons of dried salt under my arms; my slacks are mottled up to the pockets with marsh muck; the halves of my putter nestle in the bottom of my bag like a snapped wishbone. A nightmare. A disaster. A turfy Waterloo, in golf cleats, with occasional pauses to belt another rotten shot — or better, closer, today was like Corregidor: I got shoved off the Ile de Paris Golf & Beach Club and into the sea. All I want is to creep back to the motel without having to rehash my round for anyone. Regroup. Plan. Find my cups, climb in. Put my sheets to the wind, every one of them. See a flock of moons. Bend an elbow or twelve.

The nineteenth hole awaits.

But Hatch is lying in ambush, the dapper bastard, barely six feet from the tent. I can feel his hot, happy breath at my temple as I stoop to shoulder my clubs. He blots the sun like a smog. I straighten up, irons rattling, and pretend not to have noticed him — I don't have the energy to cope with *that* blowhard —

but he cuts off my path. As I try to sideslip, he seizes the furry gopher headcover on my driver.

"Give us a number," he coaxes. "Let's don't be shy." His tongue tip — a smutty purple button — teases the corner of his mouth. He continues to palm the gopher.

There's nothing on earth so smug as the smile of a man who's just carved up par. It's his right, I suppose, spoils of the victor, but it rankles anyway. And Hatch is still clutching the blade he's done the carving with: Now he's backed off a couple steps and is leaning on his putter, legs crossed, the cap of his right shoe pointed into the turf as though he's pinning the vanquished earth with it. He's a man with a solid grip on the ground, a man in perfect balance. His posture is poetry. His pants pleats are crisp as cashier's checks. His two-tone cleats gleam. He makes me sick.

"What'd you shoot, Brian?" he asks.

I've spent the afternoon dredging ponds, watching banana slices arc over condos, gouging smiling Titleists from under stands of sawgrass. Hatch can read the signs. I've been up to my ass in woe and bogey; I look like I might not have cut ninety. Silence is the closest cousin to dignity I've got right now, and I cling to it.

Hatch teases the grass with his toe, head bowed, like a shy country suitor who's just asked for the first dance. His sham innocence irritates me, so I smoke a pencil at him, the one I've just used to attest (or in this case confess) my score. Hatch doesn't flinch, thinks I'm joking — and he's right not to fear me, I'm no threat to my targets. Sure enough, the pencil skims between his feet without so much as nicking a cuff.

I owe him ten dollars on our side bet, so Hatch has come to collect and to rub my nose in it. If he kneads his palms or does his gangster schtick ("Pony up, *paisan;* don't make me croak the gopher"), I'll dismember the bastard. Look at him. Richest guy on the tour, and he can't resist crowing over ten lousy bucks. He must have shot lights out. Sixty-six, I'm guessing from the popinjay routine, maybe even lower than that. God-damn him.

"What did I *what?*" I ask.

"Card. Score. Post. Ring up. Conjure. How many licks did it take . . . ?"

"Leave me be, Hatch. Can't this wait?"

"Nah. It's only fun while the wound's fresh. Suck it up; take your medicine. What'd you shoot?"

I attempt to rally. "Nothing. I just walked today, decided not to tee it up after all. We put too much emphasis on winning in our society. I'm learning to stop and smell the roses."

"What I smell ain't roses," Hatch says, gesturing to my mud-spattered pants, to the greenish bilge pooling at my feet. "Spit it out. You did keep it in double digits, didn't you? *Hello.* What did you shoot?"

He's as dogged as herpes, is never going to let it slide. So I give in. "Myself, in the wallet," I answer, but it comes out falsely jovial, like telethon patter; as if failure's not enough, I've got to heap on the fraud, too. I clear my throat, stare between Hatch's shoes and see the pencil I flung standing on end in the matted grass at his heels. Miracles never come in the shape and place you want. They're blind and stupid and accidental, and you can count on the assholes who trip into the good ones to call it justice, to call it a meritocracy. The only thing dumber than luck is the schlump who thinks he deserves it. There are no days worse than this.

Rosa's right, I know she is; I should hang up my spikes. How much worse could accounting be, chicken farming, firefighting, chimney sweeping — or ringing up X-outs and titanium-alloy seven-woods at Gonzo Gary's Golfland? Even living at home full time, football on the tube, a pull-start lawnmower, a kid or two underfoot — would it be so bad? There would be benefits: shampoo from a regular-sized bottle, towels I can't see through . . . and the mail, I've always liked fetching mail, it would be nice to bring in the mail more often, right?

"You ought to be doing standup," Hatch says. "My sides ache. Ouch."

"You know me and Thursdays," I tell him. "I shot a wad. You won. Now take your money and go away." I reach for my wallet and come up empty. It's still in my golf bag.

My annoyance softens Hatch a little. He knows that if I walk away he won't get the pleasure of rubbing in the humiliation. He keeps twirling his brass Bullseye, keeps talking: "You always were strong out of the gate, Bri. Come on, son, it's OK. You can tell Mother."

No, not Mother. Hatch has the wrong parent — this is turning into the kind of interrogation I'd expect from my father. Dad's done his share of lurking behind scorers' tents, his share of smirking, his share of needling inquisition. And then it occurs to me: I have a card to play, something that will make this chirpy son of a bitch swallow his tongue.

"Listen to this," I say. "Bird shot Geiberger."

Bird is Jim Soulsby, one of my playing partners, this guy from South Africa who looks like he's eleven years old and plays with an eleven-year-old's utter lack of conscience. Soulsby doesn't understand the game, which is why he's so good at it — can't recognize the perils. It's not that he's stupid; he's the most bookish guy on tour, in fact, and you never know what he'll mention next, phlogiston or the Scottsboro Boys or the preparation of blowfish sushi or the bill markings of the lesser yellowlegs. He's plenty sharp, if facts and such are how you measure sharp — it's more like he thinks golf is beneath understanding. He just puts on a blank smile, aims himself down the first fairway, and the birdies roll out in front of him.

Three weeks ago we were paired together at Norfolk. It was Sunday afternoon, and Jim was three shots off the lead with eight to play. I was a couple further back, but into the money enough to be anxious. We were standing on the tee at eleven, pondering the terrifying 240-yard carry, almost 800 feet of moil and marsh between us and safety. Jim stabbed a finger at a passing bird and said, "That's a marsh harrier. Pretty far south for him. A bogtrotter, rambling, on the bummel. *Circus hudsonius*. And would you check out that plumage? Wow. He's a beaut."

The bird alighted in the sedge about thirty feet away. Just a homely, beaky thing, as far as I was concerned, the kind of feathered irrelevancy you see wheeling over a gutted possum at roadside. All I know about birds is that they're stupid, mean, and they smell bad, and one time my father slit open the crop of a dead dove to show me the assorted seed and gravel it uses to digest, and there was a bulbous chunk of green glass in there that I could recognize as part of a Mountain Dew bottle. There you have it: They shit on cars, heads, statues; they use gravel to chew; they don't know better than to eat Mountain Dew bottles. What more does one need to know about a class of animals to dismiss it from consideration?

So, listening to Jim Soulsby warble, my pulse throbbed somewhere behind my nose, rage blooming like a sneeze. This is my job, I wanted to explain to him. Yours too, in case you don't realize it. If I fuck up this shot I have to make do all week with pimento cheese and Pepsi, and hear Rosa's same old complaints — make her some hay while the sun yet shines, serve the Lord God not the Lord Par, we've had the going forth in spades, Brian, all over the country to play that childish game, three long years of it, so when do the fruitfulness and multiplication begin?

Or, worse, I endure her pity.

Anyway, the drive at eleven in Norfolk was a crucial shot. A huge carry, tight driving area bounded by a grove of hardwoods on the left and a comma-shaped pot bunker on the right. Big money at stake. And there was Jim Soulsby, in the same situation, cooing over some scrawny crow with a white butt and a hook beak. I ripped the headcover off my driver as though I were unsheathing a battle-axe. I paced. I glowered.

"Be still, Brian," Jim chided. He was crouched like a catcher in the reeds, index finger to his lips. His driver leaned, forgotten, against a wooden sign, one of those four-color schematics they set alongside the teebox for tourists: distances in red, white, and navy, fairway in green, traps in white, and the marsh pond, that blob of horrid blue — the danger that lurks, doing its lurking.

The fingers of Jim's red golf glove poked from his back pocket like a coxcomb. There was no shiver of weakness in his legs, no hint of angst. He gazed into the spartina.

Ahead, the group in front strolled up a sliver of isthmus to the green, the gauntlet negotiated. I could see one of the players — it was Jelly Roll McHugh, judging from the heft of him — hitch up his pants, Arnie-like, as he climbed the gentle rise to the putting surface, his mind returned at last to the trivial task of looking good. He tugged at his straw hat, twirled his putter, dug for a dime to mark his ball. OK. Safe. He'd make a decent check this week; it was all downhill from here.

I turned back in silent horror to the hole schematic. The robin's-egg blot behind the shaft of Jim's driver seemed to pulse, faster and faster. Jim continued his Dolittle monologue. "Quit jerking around, Brian. He's probably a bit skittish. The marsh harrier, reputation aside, is a nervous bird. Raptors can be surprisingly unfierce."

A nervous bird. A nervous goddamn bird. I sat down on a bench and flexed my fingers like a con doing curls.

After the hawk finally flapped into the sawgrass, Bird knelt and rummaged in his bag for his yardage book. He wrote a leisurely field note, all the while mumbling about undertail coverts and depleted habitats. Then he dusted off his knees, retrieved his driver, pegged his ball near the ridiculous Ole-Virginny andiron that served as the left tee marker, stepped up, and whacked a perfect drive. No practice swing. No shot preparation. No swing keys. No wind check. Grinning all the while. I can't swear he wasn't whistling. Bird never even glanced at the schematic.

I peered over the waste around me — the dead reeds floating in the slough; the gray, brackish water; the skittering hermit crabs all waving one little arm as though hailing cabs; the low, filmy horizon — and then I let my eyes rest on the tiny ribbon of paradisal green across the marsh, at Bird's ball in its close-trimmed heart. I took several practice cuts, steadied my breathing. I visualized a high drive with just a hint of draw, enough to push it past Bird's and over the brow of the hill. From the bottom of the slope it would be only a flip wedge to the green. After the drive, the hole is a gimme. Birdie would put me right in the thick of things. Steady, smooth, keep it on plane. Sweep and turn. OK. Take it easy.

And then I nearly sawed off my left ear with my backswing, half topped one into the sump *Circus hudsonius* had just vacated. In a rage, I dug a battered brown nugget out of my bag — a ball I'd plucked out of an algae-choked lagoon on the back nine of a practice round. I set it, furiously, on the tee my first swing hadn't even disturbed . . . and rope-hooked it into the slough. As I stood there listening to four days' work plunk into the muck, Bird cleared his throat: He hated to be a stickler and all, but if that second ball wasn't a hundred-compression Titleist, well, technically I was out two strokes, and he was very sorry, but a rule was after all a . . .

"Coals to Newcastle," I interrupted him. "Pile 'em on."

I made a fat eleven on the hole and consequently a check for $575, not enough to cover my entry fee and expenses for the week. Bird, meanwhile, beamed and wowed and stickled his way to a two-shot win and the twelve K that went with it.

And today he's managed the impossible. Fifty-nine . . . Geiberger. Just the second time it's ever happened in competition, and the first gave it its name.

"Geiberger," I repeat, rubbing it in. Hatch sags a bit at the news; triumphs never last. His heart rides a little lower in his chest, his spine unhinges like a sprung rhyme, his pleats wilt, his legs uncross. There's a sweat stain around his collar, I notice, a nickel-sized spot at his navel. Beneath his blond bangs I can see the faint pink glint of scalp like a watermark; Hatch better enjoy his hair while he can.

The grounds for pride, my father has always told me, are soft enough to bog a buzzard's shadow — you'll sink soon enough.

As I watch, Hatch's feet are disappearing into the ooze. I can't say I don't like it.

"Are you kidding me?"

"Thirty-one out, twenty-eight in. Lights out. We may as well start packing our bags."

Hatch rallies a bit. "It's only Thursday, man. He'll be wearing the choke chain. And there's two sixty-threes on the board. Bird's takeable." He pauses. "Christ, man, fifty-nine. How do you scrape it around in fifty-nine? Did he skip a couple?"

And then it occurs to him that there's no need to let me see him fret. *I'm* not Bird; *I* shot a ton. The light comes back into Hatch's eyes. "So . . . what did *you* score?" he asks. "And cut the crap, now. I want a number, not a tap dance."

"You first." Let's get this over with.

Hatch leans back — the question he's been waiting for. A raft of geese floats over, and he sights down his putter and squeezes off a fusillade. The putter bucks in pantomime.

Hatch lowers his gleaming gun. "Five under," he says coyly, pinching down the corners of his mouth. That would make sixty-six, and the first thing I've got right all day. "The old wand" — he brandishes the putter — "was good to me today." He lifts its blade to his lips, slips it some tongue. Waiting, Hatch practices his putting stroke. The shot is fired; he can take his time. He's like an assassin in his window eyrie, brushing off the knee he used to brace himself and calmly stowing his scope and rifle as the melee begins below. All over but the shouting. The practice stroke sets a stand of bahia grass aquiver, and black spores settle on Hatch's shoes like specks of vanilla bean. I hate this game. I truly hate this game. Its pleasure, its soul and purpose, is to lay us bare, naked, weak — to reduce us to animals.

"Six over," I mumble, giving in. "Seventy-seven. Stick a fork in me." The number says all that I can't.

Hatch has the decency not to dispute it. I *am* done. It's humiliating — Bird has already lapped me, a shot a hole, and the word I got from the scorer was that it'll take 140 or thereabouts to make the cut. Which gives me precisely no chance.

It's been weeks since I negotiated even sixteen holes in sixty-three.

Hatch holds his fingers in front of his eyes, rubs his greedy thumb against them. "Ante up," he orders. "*Diez dólares.*" He uses his left hand, the one he shields all day with a glove. It glows, white as Cinderella's shapely foot; my ten-spot will fit it like a slipper.

I don't kill him, of course; even my threats are lies. I just kneel next to my golf bag, dig out my wallet, and hand him the money. "Nice doing business with you," says Hatch, waving the bill by its corner. "And keep up the good work, Chop."

From the practice green, forty feet away, I hear a chorus of voices: "Give us a number, Hatch." There's blood in the water; my hangdog look and my sack-side genuflection have made that clear. In their flashy togs, the guys look like bright sails on a lake — about to be filled with the sweet breeze of my failure. My friends, presumably. But beneath the upper-crust politesse, pro golf is an alley fight. We all pull against one another, thrill to one another's fuck-ups. We have to: on the Snapper/Gold Club Tour (the name of our little dog-and-pony show), kindness is not affordable. There's not enough money to go around. Only the pitiless and the unthinking survive.

Which means you take what you can get. And there's a free beer waiting for me on the flagstone veranda beyond the practice green, a beer I need. Some tomato-faced high school kid in a gold tux jacket is up there manning the tap. A relief worker, measuring out succor in careful cupfuls, making sure no one takes more than one. Beer. A free nudge toward the oblivion I need.

But there's no sense in taking unnecessary abuse. Those day-glo assholes are patrolling the green, spoiling for a taste of my shame. I sling my clubs over my shoulder and make a beeline for my car — got to get back to the motel, to safety, before I do something stupid. I've been feeling the insanity mounting all week. I'll stop for a six-pack on the road.

Behind me I hear Hatch yell, "A nice fat Red Grange for

Brian, and — get this, also-rans — *fifty-nine* for Bird Soulsby, the baby-faced chicken killer of the Transvaal." I turn around to watch the reaction. There are whistles and hoots, shuffled feet, open mouths, a few groans. A moment of spiteful murmur, then silence — a thrilling and total cessation of banter. This is the hush of rationalization, music to my ears; my colleagues are doing the desperate math that will explain being a dozen shots in arrears after a not-bad round. Let them eat disappointment. It consumes all of us, day after day: play or quit? I am not alone. There's solace in that somewhere.

"See you back at the room," Hatch calls, "as soon as I lighten a few more wallets and grab some food. Say around eight."

Still in my spikes, I click across a bed of hot white seashells, then squeeze, in sour anticipation of a sting, between two yucca bushes and into the parking lot.

The blacktop is crammed with sports cars and European sedans and jeeps, many of them with punning vanity plates and "I'd rather be driving a Titleist" bumper stickers. Fuchsia crape-myrtle blossoms are strewn across the hoods of the row on my right. A service cart chugs by on its way to the front nine, a quiver of bunker rakes in its bed. Its driver waves without lifting his hand off the wheel; his passenger is expertly juggling striped range balls.

A golfer I don't recognize, probably a local whose delusions have just gone up in eighty-four or so puffs of smoke, is wedged in his open trunk, sockfeet dangling over his bumper, gouging a speck of orange cracker from between his horsy teeth with a strand of floss. He waggles an elbow at me in halfhearted greeting. As I trudge through the lot, my reflection haunts me intermittently in car sheen, a disfigured set of angles, lurid and ugly.

When I heave them into the trunk, my clubs clatter like a sack of bones. I roll the coffin, looking for the side pocket that contains my keys, watch, wedding band. Just as I reach into it, there's a commotion behind me.

"Mr. Soulsby. Just a sec, Mr. Soulsby." I turn to see a woman hurrying across the macadam and a shaggy guy with a minicam in hot pursuit. They're headed my way, and I spin to look for Bird, who is — as far as I know — still in the scorer's tent sweating over his card. The lower your score, the longer it takes to count. There's basking to be done, savoring. For the moment, he's nowhere to be seen.

"Mr. Soulsby," she says again, ten feet away now. Her hair is bobbed, henna, lovely. Her earrings are miniature onyx golf balls complete with tiny dimples; they glitter like strobes. "I was afraid we wouldn't catch you." The reporter lifts a shapely hand to her throat, as though to grasp with her fingers the pulse that throbs there.

Suddenly I realize she means me.

Suddenly I understand that I've pocketed my wedding band with the rest of my things.

Suddenly I know I've just said something.

"Color me caught, miss," comes the impossibly cheerful echo. I extend my hand, grinning. "Call me Bird," I tell her. "Everyone does."

I couldn't say what's moved me to this. Or maybe I could — the sudden bad crazies, come home to roost at last. Something like this had to happen; I knew it all along. What can I say? Golf is madness.

CHAPTER TWO

# Thursday, 6 P.M.

IN MY CELL AT THE IBIS INN, I survey my ruins. Five empty longnecks stand in soldierly phalanx on the bureau, but I'm not drunk yet, not by a long shot. There's no need for that now, I keep telling myself — the miseries are behind me now, with luck for good. Tonight there are charades to be played out, freedoms to be rung. Ashes to be hauled, if I play it right. Tonight, for the first time in years, I have a date.

But there is reason to keep drinking. Stupefy the scruples, beat down the guilt, hold doubt's head underwater till the son of a bitch quits kicking. Tonight I'll be kissing several friend-ships good-bye, torching useful bridges; and my golf career, I know, won't last the night . . . to say nothing of my marriage.

Rosa has been good to me. She's thrown good money after bad golf these last few years, paid all our bills; she's kept me in groceries, in gas, in line, even in love. My wife has worked hard to keep me on tour ("on track for your dream," as her lovably fuzzy phrase has it), and — at least until recently — she's rarely complained about having to pull my weight too.

Which is not to say I've been just another pet cause, another Fun-in-the-Son Christian Bookmobile or Save the Armadillo Society for a wife whose altruism needs outlets the way a

Mountie needs maidens lashed to tracks. I have done what I can to make her happy; in my way, I've tried. And there's been passion, too; I don't deny I've loved her. I've trailed her through countless backyard bazaars, watched her, my lovely Hun, sack sundries tables; I've crawled below covers on winter mornings to knead warmth into her warped little toes; I've napped for hours — stilly, lustlessly — in the fragrant hollow between her breasts; I've even sucked trapped scraps of juice pulp from between her teeth after breakfasts in bed (grimace if you will: exoneration isn't pretty, must be tracked into the fissures where it lives).

But living with a dynamo eats your strength; it saps you. Rosa's love is a vise. She grabs hold of every moment, every drowsy, unsuspecting moment, and squeezes until sphincters loosen. Hers is the tender autocracy of the duty nurse: There's no control more pure, after all, than that of the saint who erases one's trail in this world, the soul who's seen the vulgar lie of your dignity yet who's let you — for the moment — hang onto it. The world isn't Rosa's oyster; it's her bedpan, and she bears it away, in whispering white shoes, with a look of silent beatitude.

But don't take my word for it; ask the Lord, or the armored rat, what it's like to be loved to death.

Rosa thinks "our life together" (a phrase she employs often, and always in the singular) should be a string of epiphanies punctuated by brief bursts of sleep. The situation is made worse by the fact that I'm home, during the ten-month-long season, just a couple of days a week. As soon as I haul my gear out of the trunk, shed my shoes, and throw myself onto the couch, Rosa's waving tickets to the Metro Linoleum Show or rolling in a new lawn aerator or threatening me with a self-esteem seminar at the Knights of Columbus Hall or dragging me to Atlanta to see a drawling troupe of minor leaguers tackle a production of *Romeo and Juliet* in which the Capulets and Montagues have been marooned in Civil War Chattanooga. If I limp home on Saturday, having missed another cut, and want to watch the

Braves on TV and forget, Rosa will always — always — flounce in and stretch out on top of me and say, "Let's catch up, hon. It's been five whole days." She blots out the screen, where a shellshocked Braves reliever is dodging line drives — my chance to bask, for a reassuring moment, in somebody else's debacle. Rosa's knee digs into my thigh; her breath warms my neck. What I want to say is this: "I've been failing, dear, and failing plumb tuckers me out, so please . . . look, the game's on." But I always scrape up another rueful smile, stroke her pretty cheek, and say something like "Another sixteen tons, my love, another day deeper in debt. That's it from here. What have *you* been doing?"

This last question has been the savior of our marriage. Rosa's life is endlessly exciting to her, and I have to admit that I get a kick out of her flamboyantly disorganized anecdotes, not because they're interesting (they're not, if you're a strict judge of such things) but because the joy she takes in rehashing her days is infectious: I never feel so married, or so content, as when she's filling me in on the gossip, the adventures. I won't believe, she says, the sofas this sleazeball rep is trying to unload on her — they look like velour No-Pest strips; her office manager is trying to quit smoking, and she snaps that vile nicotine gum all day, has gone from being a two-pack-a-day smoker to a three-pack-a-day chewer; Rosa's reading a vanity-press novel by a college friend in which a woman says to a squirrel, "Well, my rodent chum. Spare me the tedious details of your peregrinations"; someone at the office photocopied his penis and left it on her desk, which is appallingly rude, and anyway it was a puny, veiny little thing, so I don't have to worry.

For Rosa, every moment is as alive as the now. She tells her stories in a manic present tense, and the colors of personal history never lose, for her, their heraldic blaze. She can relate the same anecdote a hundred times without the passage of time, repetition, or a grumpy and jaded listener fretting away its glamor. I've known her, during a weekend, to give six renditions of a story without realizing what a haggard old saw it's become, without grasping the impossibility of finding someone as riveted by the drama of her life as she is. No detail can be too banal, no audience too busy with anxieties of his own. She burbles on; I shuffle off. *Flowers won't bloom,* as the song goes, *in the heat of je-June.*

It gnaws at Rosa, she tells me in what passes for a philosophical moment, that she has to experience the events of her life in sequence. Deep in her bones she *knows* that everything, all history, all God's creation, all our lives are happening at once, simultaneously, now, always NOW. The whole world is taking place under our noses — "like a circus," she says with a loopy, cultish gleam in her eye, "with a zillion rings" — and, of course, I'm one of the saps who's missing out. The evolutionists aren't exactly *wrong,* she allows, they're just hung up in the lie of human time, they don't understand. This makes her feel sorry for them. When Darwin was puttering around on coral reefs (and I on fairways), we could have been, as she puts it, "haarkening to the Laard." Barnacles and golf — the legendary dodges of God's love.

So as for anecdotal style, Rosa specializes in reenactments; past and present spill into one another. I'll give an example. Once, six months into our marriage, we were lying in bed among the slats and lattices of morning sunshine. I was asleep. Rosa sunk her lips into my side.

"Brian," she murmured, "I want to show you something." The sound bubbled through my rib cage, and I came wide awake. It had been a rough night, and there was no reason for me not to sleep into next week. But we were newlyweds, and I loved her. So I flipped over eagerly, a ship surging at anchor; I figured I knew what she wanted to show me, was sure I wouldn't be averse to seeing it.

But Rosa lay down again, made a trough in her pillow by burrowing into it with her temple. She turned back to me. "Closer," she whispered. "You'll have to come closer. Now listen."

Rosa pressed her face gently into the pillow. She shut her eyes as though going into a trance. And then, slowly, she opened them, closed them, opened them, closed them once more. Again and again, like a girl hitting her hair a hundred leisurely licks, Rosa brushed her eyelashes against the pillowcase. Every blink tugged her brow down a hint, then let it spring back; tiny blue veins traversed the eyelid I could see. The performance was nearly silent, sounded like the snick of distant matches. Rosa's concentration was complete, and never once did she look my way as she swished out her faint, inscrutable music.

It must have gone on for thirty seconds before my patience ran out. I was baffled and sleepy, horny. My head was full of a night's accumulated snot. Blink, blink, blink. Swish, swish, swish. As far as I could tell, this wasn't morning sex, wasn't even a prelude to it. She woke me up for *this?*

"What time is it?" I demanded. "What are you doing?" No answer. Swish, swish, like a muffled metronome. "What are you up to?" Still no answer. The blinks continued, and I turned mean. "Should I call for an exorcist?"

Rosa sighed, fixed her gaze on me. After a minute, and with an eerie ghost-story tone, she began to narrate. She was thirteen, and a luna moth had been beating its wings against her bedroom window for what seemed an hour. Rosa was sure about the age, she said, because the moth appeared at the same time as her first period. It was after midnight, but Rosa was still burning a light, writing in her diary — wondering about her new womanhood and mooning over her current crush, a junior-high slash guitarist named Fred. She stopped to watch the moth try to batter its way through her window.

The story was full of unnecessary, fraudulent detail: the moth had pale, luminous wings with eyes on them; the bedside lamp was hollow glass, contained bleached sand dollars her mother had collected and cloroxed the previous summer; Fred was the only guy in school with a real Les Paul, and his wardrobe consisted of three pairs of jeans, a leather thong necklace with a phosphorescent fish charm, and scores of black Zeppelin t-shirts; Rosa was cramping and spotting.

She rambled for ten minutes, and then the story dead-ended.

No closure, no satisfaction; there was no room for them, given all the biblical hokum she had piled on. "Gossamer," she'd said. "Light under a bushel." "Oh God it is a fearful thing / to see the human soul take wing." The moth's pale-green color, she insisted, symbolized her "baptism into womanhood." "The messengers of God," she claimed, "always wear wings." She teased meaning out of that moth the way my father used to tease meat out of crab claws. How could there be so much? How could any reasonable God be such a simp?

And we were right where we started. The blood still flowed; the crush still stung; God was in His heaven; the luna moth kept trying to fry itself on the unreachable bulb.

"Anyway," Rosa concluded, "all this came back to me in my dream just now, and I thought you'd care. Though I've been wrong there before." She pouted — actually crossed her arms and stuck out her lower lip.

Her eyes loomed large as walnuts, and guilt withered my anger away. I kissed the nearer eyelid, said I was sorry I'd been cross.

"What happened to the moth?" I asked, thinking I'd gone straight to the heart of the matter, thinking I'd redeem myself by showing an interest in how things turned out. "Did you let it in?"

Rosa grimaced. "That's not the *point*. You're so thick sometimes. What would I do with a big bug in my bedroom? That's silly. Besides, all my best sweaters were in there." She gazed up at an ancient quilting hook embedded in our ceiling, as though it might be able to account for the idiocies of men, how we drag down fragile things with our grubby little questions, our nasty little facts. Who? What? When? Where? Why?

And God's winged creature at the window still, begging to be let in.

"You see," she went on, like a Sunday-school teacher trying to get through to some dope who wants to know why the whale's digestive enzymes didn't break poor Jonah down, and how did he breathe in there, and how did he stand the stench of putrefying krill, and . . . "it was one of God's signs. Moon, *luna*, do you get it, honey? And I was beating my wings, too, do you see? That moth was me."

Rosa flapped her arms a little — I swear it — to shore up her argument. Her breasts bobbed beneath her thin cotton gown, and I felt the stirrings of renewed desire.

"Oh," I said, feigning pensiveness. "I get it." God's got to be a better hand at symbolism than that, I thought. But there was no point in arguing; and besides, I was still holding out hope for sex. Allegory makes Rosa hot. "Very interesting," I continued, assaying a clumsy sideways nod from my side of the bed.

When I looked back to Rosa, she was scowling. She's one of those people who insist everything has to *mean* something. When I make an off-the-cuff remark she chides me: "At bottom, Brian, there's no such thing as kidding. All the experts are with me on this, you can look it up." If I forget to thaw the tenderloin then I'm trying, in my passive-aggressive way, to starve her; if I let a quarter-anniversary slip, it's because I regret having married her. If I don't plunge my hands into boiling water and scrub them with pumice before I come to bed, it's because I'm hellbent on giving her the cooties.

She picked out the colors for our wedding by grinding over a massive volume called *The Compleat Guide to Color Symbolism.* There were days of fevered consultation with her bridesmaids and her mother amid a jumble of dress patterns and fabrics and a mountain of ugly open-toed shoes. Rosa's father and I were watching television when the conclave finished its deliberations. The bedroom door flew open with a bang; Mrs. Fersner's cigarette smoke billowed around Rosa like a parody of the Vatican's white plume — the Cardinals' decision had, at last and praise God, been made.

Rosa chose azure and white, fidelity and purity, and I looked like a pimp's Pontiac in my sky-blue tux. Two groomsmen backed out from embarrassment.

*That moth was me.* Jesus.

"But what," I insisted, "happened to the moth?" The answer to this seemed important. A moment of reckoning for my gender — we weren't going to let her get away with that open-ended pawn-of-God crap. There were plot points we needed settled. (Sex would have to wait, I realized, but I'm as capable as the next guy of sacrifice in a good cause.)

She ignored me.

"What," I pronounced mincingly, "happened . . . to . . . the . . . moth?" I was getting pissed. What happens to signs that have served their purpose? What becomes of used-up symbols? What? Once God sticks you back in His toolbox, do you continue to exist? Rosa doesn't consider these things.

"I turned off the light," she said.

"Uh-huh? And then what?"

Rosa shrugged. "I went to sleep."

"And the moth?"

"Quit interrogating, Brian. The moth flew away, Fred moved to Richmond, the bleeding quit for a month. I think the lamp's still in my parents' attic."

To keep from killing her I tasted my bottom teeth, which were sour with sleep and venom. Rosa turned away and curled up, reenacting the final sentence of her story. I stared at the knob of bone at the back of her neck, trying to decide whether to kiss it or club it.

It's hard to explain, like everything about — well, about our life together. In marriage the rawest, most violently opposed emotions live in cramped contiguity, and one's speech tone is a slave to chance. You plunge a blind hand into the cabinet not knowing what will emerge, the bludgeon or the bouquet. Lying there in the glow of morning I was livid, but at the same time I've never been more in love with my wife than I was at that moment. She understands what I never have, how hard you can press down on life; she knows how to dive to healthy depths, knows then the precise moment to spin and head back to the surface. When she's used things up she lets them go, and counts on them to be there if she needs them again. Rosa knows how to live. Laugh if you want, but it's a gift, and it makes her beautiful to me.

I feel rotten, corrupt. I wasn't thinking. I was pinned against my bumper, my arm sunk halfway to the elbow in my golf bag; I wanted only to disappear. I wasn't looking for trouble: After all, who expects — who *wants* — to find temptation in his trunk? But Ellen was beautiful. Her earrings were hypnotic. She asked a question, and it was only right that I answer it. That's what you do with questions. That's what they're for.

The things I said were unrehearsed, unmeant, even unwelcome, if you can believe that. But I have no choice now; the evening's got to be played out. It's like another tournament begun with a sorry skein of sixes — you play on, take your lumps, look for a swing or two you can weave into the semblance of a silver lining. Then you pack your bags and load up for next week.

I may as well admit it — I can't show up at Ile de Paris tomorrow morning. Golf is nothing to me now but scarred and pitted earth, and there can be no going back. What possessed me to pose as Bird? All the tour honchos will tune in the news — making sure they get the media coverage they've energetically courted, noisily sucked up for. Some of the players will, too: in their rooms spooning Spaghettios from the can or peeling pickles off a Big Mac, putting over wormy shag toward plastic motel cups, scraping the grit and grass out of clubs' grooves with the tip of a tee and a dollop of toothpaste. My end will be televised in Room 141, too, while the guys play poker. In fifteen minutes someone will fold a hand, then glance at the screen and say, "Hey look! That's not Bird, man, that's Schwan. What is he up to? And tell me, did that no-brain SOB just *wink?*"

And then they'll turn up the sound and watch me self-destruct with the same blank fascination they'd feel seeing a monk immolate himself on the steps of a Tibetan temple. There's no understanding the fanatically, distantly aggrieved, after all: some lotus-sitter torching himself because of the absence of cable, who knows? We always knew Brian would throw a bolt, right? Let's play cards, let God sort 'em out, pass the jug and deal.

They never knew me. Which is strange, since I've played poker with them a hundred times in the last three years, laughed, drunk, belched, smoked rancid cigars as big as nightsticks. I'd be there tonight, maybe, but Rosa has nixed gambling on "games of chance." When she handed down her ruling, four weeks ago, I almost joked about whether she meant to include golf in the category — but the words caught in my throat. Humor's not Rosa's long suit these days. Her right hand was on her outthrust hip; her left clutched my checkbook like a chicken neck. She hovered over my chair as she laid down the law. On my face I felt the tiny, savage wind from my shaken checkbook. In the *Golf Digest* article in my lap, the great Finnish player Bit Bival stood up to his shins in Rae's Creek, on his way to an eight. He had gotten there by being overbold, and the lesson wasn't lost on me; I played well wide of the trouble.

"OK, sweetness," I said. "No more cards." I held up three fingers. "Scout's honor."

Rosa nodded doubtfully and let the light back in, and I knew I'd done the right thing. In a life together, jokes too can be a dangerous game of chance . . . best keep them to yourself.

I never felt at home in the poker games, anyway. Those cheap cigars spew smoke thick as a smudgepot's, and in a bed-top game there's no place to put your feet, no place to stow your thoughts — you've got to sing along, joke along, fart along, get along: There's a sloppy, boisterous, bestial peace in Room 141. They are men, together. Young, healthy, rich, white, soused. Their bellies are full, their bottles are cold, their cards are worn soft as chamois, their minds are as empty as sky. It's a peace I'd gladly sue for. Golf is a wonderful life for those equipped to live it.

Oh, save the oboes. Forget it. Most likely nobody will even notice my public suicide; that stuff before was panic talking.
There must have been three local TV crews at the club, and
Ellen's van may have been parked more discreetly than the others, its paint job may have been a hint less gaudy. Her station's
way up the dial, cached between Mister Rogers and the Beverly
Hillbillies. Maybe Ellen ran across Bird after I left, in which
case my imposture has been dismissed as an unfunny prank and
consigned to a bin of videotapes to be recycled. All the tour officials may be out digging clams or marking tomorrow's pin positions or sneaking in a quick nine before dark. Bird won't see
it; he's up to his ass in cattails in pursuit of the tufted tanager or
something. Hatch is out eating, which shuts down one pipeline.
And the guys in 141 have their eyes glued to *Hard Copy* or
Vanna White or a skin flick on pay-per-view. Lighten up. Beer
highs are too fragile. Relax. It's time to pop that last one open.

I set my fresh beer on the unsturdy bedside shelf. Charts are
ranged around me on the bedspread: greens hit in regulation,
putts, fairways, sand saves, birdies. Second-rate pros, looking
for some angle from which defeat looks less abject, go at statistics like alchemists at plummets of lead. But nothing avails, not
incantation, not baths in acid, not even the transformative heat
of hope; the lump stays lead, and no trick of algebra can melt
my seventy-seven down to par's sweet gold.

I catch myself thinking — even, on occasion, saying — things
like, *If I hadn't missed seventeen putts inside ten feet this week,
I would have shot, let's see, two-seventy. Would have lapped
the field by five.* The people who want to believe in you —
wives, fathers, and the like — will buy these numbers (these excuses, these promissory notes of a success that will never come),
just as moms always see, in the accidental abstracts of their

kindergartners, the stamp of infant genius. Loved ones have to believe or they're no better off than you. Statistics are the cant of pretenders.

And, too, stats are our way of bleeding the game of its core of mystery; we pretend that golf is reducible to formulas, that it's just a question of driving it straight and hitting greens and sinking putts. But the game abounds in weird contingencies: spin, swing arc, lie, loft, wind, shaft stiffness, dimples, green-grain, grooves, humidity, compression, bounce, God. It's as arcane, as complicated, as quantum physics or marriage. What to do?

Say you're standing in the fairway, 160 yards out. Club selection isn't, it seems, very hard — a smooth seven-iron. But the ball's sitting down in a half-healed divot, just a little, and there's a starburst-shaped tuft of *poa annua* behind it. A breeze seems to be blowing diagonally from the left; a tossed offering of a few blades of Bermuda confirms this. But up on the green, the flag is flapping left. Your stance is awkward because the ball's three or four inches above your feet, which will make you tend to draw it. There's a pot bunker left of the green, and beyond it a lake, so you're best off aiming at the meat of the green and letting the ball spin down left after it hits. But there's a dip just to the right of the hole, and the pin's set on a plateau. The ball won't bounce left unless you land it left of the pin, in which case its spin and the lay of the land will take it straight into that hellish sand trap, whose ten-foot lip has already sneered at you once this tournament. Maybe you should punch a six. But what if the bastard flies on you, as the weed tuft behind it will tend to make it do? Behind the green is jail, a stand of bushy firs as black as an enchanted forest. The air's heavy with worry and humidity. The turf is firm. Are your club's grooves clotted with grass? And what if you get a bad bounce? Hell, what if you mishit it?

Yesterday, in a practice round, Hatch and I were playing a couple of guys for some spending money, clowns we should have been lighting up for all they were worth. I was just off the tenth fairway in the first cut of the rough (and down thirty bucks), and I asked, "Hatch, do you ever think about how hard this game is?" He shrugged. I said, "No, seriously. I mean, consider this," and started to analyze my shot, aloud, as an example. Hatch interrupted — being down money to a pair of Munsingwear bojacks will make even a rich man peevish.

"You think too goddamn much," Hatch scolded. "Just beat the little nugget around the pasture and chase it till it sinks. Nothing easier in life than that." He climbed out of the cart, snatched a club. "Hit the fucking thing," said Hatch. "I'm getting old out here. And it's my money you're pissing away, thinking."

⊙

The phone bleats next to me, loud enough to make it bounce in its cradle. It's dirty white, an ancient rotary whose shattered dial has been bunged together with tape. It rings again, that shrill, explosive ring phones used to have when I was a kid, before they lost their urgency. Can't be anybody I want to talk to. It's best left alone.

Rosa makes me keep these charts. "Accountability," runs her refrain, "is the key to a successful career." She keeps close tabs; accountability is central to her idea of a successful marriage, too. I should be calling her now. Part of the terrible thrill of tonight is that the phone in this empty room will ring every fifteen minutes or so; at the other end Rosa will be tugging at her cowlick and whispering tense questions into the void. She'll get no answers. She deserves better.

Maybe Rosa's not altogether wrong about why I fail to set meat out to thaw, about why I caress her hair at night with germy and impure hands. I can be hurtful. There's cruelty, of a kind, in a life together spent apart.

Goddamn it, hang up. What's that, ten rings? Fifteen? Nobody home. Go away. Only one person I know who'd hold on that long, my mother, but why would she be calling? How would she even get the number? That's not the way it works.

☽

When I met Rosa, my freshman year at Georgia, I was majoring in art history. Several things made "the technicolor slide" — as it was known — the perfect hideout for me academically. My mother had urged (not far shy of exhorted) me to go north; she plied me with sweatshirts and a book called *From the Kudzu to the Ivy,* even pulled me out of school during the winter of my junior year for a trip to scout what she called, with dreamy pomposity, "the halls of higher learning." As we slogged through soapy gray slush behind Alexander Hall at Princeton, she interrupted her sermon about the majesty of Collegiate Gothic architecture. "What you've got to do," she said, tapping a hard-bitten fingernail against her forehead, "is devote your life to the apprehension of the beautiful. This is the place for it. This is the place." She stamped a decisive foot, an astronaut planting her flag. I started to laugh; only my mother's advice could sound so much like badly translated Latin. Next she'd be telling me to be sure to strive; striving is the thing to do; don't leave excellence unstriven for.

But I had to recognize, as I let my eyes roam over the austere oaks, the salted flagstone walks, the somber and lovely stone of the dorms, how attracted I was by her vision. Here, among people smarter than me (or was it *I?*), among monuments to a history longer and larger than mine, I might find a life outside the bounds and binds of home, without expectations, without *golf*: a life of the mind.

But it was cold, after all. The slush invaded my clothes, my skin, and new granules stung my face every second or two. I wanted to find a warm place to eat, to split a beer with Mom, have a cigarette, listen to her gush: "Gosh, Brian, it says here Princeton's often called the northernmost school in the South and the southernmost school in the North. In the War, they lost exactly as many students in butternut as in blue. How about that?" At home she rarely drank, never smoked, but up East we were to be sophisticates, Ivy League material, not refugees from some Dixie cowtown. She wanted me to see, too, that this trip — and my impending "decision" — marked a passage into adulthood. I was a big boy now, my own man . . . at least until we crossed back into the South, into reality, into my father's realm and purview. I knew, as we settled onto stools in a be-lowstreets tavern, that on our way home Mother would remind me that *Some things are best kept to ourselves, and certain omissions, in a good cause, needn't count as deceit.* (Near Richmond, three days later, she said her piece . . . and then flipped the last of our cigarettes, along with a disposable lighter, into a dumpster behind McDonald's. We put on our parkas and stocking caps and drove the next forty miles with the windows open.)

But it pleased me anyway to sit in a bar with her, smoking, nursing an English ale on draft — Mom having misled a shrug-ging waiter: "He's my son, flesh of my flesh. You don't think I know how old he is?" — and listening to her prophesy how I would thrive in what she kept calling "a stimulating environ." I knew we'd go home eventually, knew this illusory "adult-hood" would evaporate, knew my father and golf would loom up again, stake their old, their prior, claim . . . and my grades wouldn't have cut it, most likely, and anyway my parents' little bit of money was tied up in my travel, equipment, entry fees. I'd go to a school where I got a full ride, crip classes, and year-round sunshine. We were pretending, and Mom saw that as well as I did. But we sat there still, fingering the shiny taffrail, spinning cardboard coasters printed with semaphore flags, blow-ing smoke, talking and listening . . . equals. Is there anything lovelier than an amber ale in bar light, underground, amid brass and black wood and nautical curios, on a winter after-noon? We knew it couldn't last, but we averted our eyes from the truth, kept up our chatter: Omission, after all, needn't count as deceit. Not always. Not in Princeton.

So art history was the best balm available for Mom's disappointment, and perfect for my purposes: high-toned but low-key, ether enough for her, gut enough for me. It had other advantages: What better place to apprehend beauty than a department where four-fifths of the students are women? In what other skate major could I nap in class without having to battle the lights? The college trip was a fading memory by then; I was in Athens to play golf, not to learn. I had left that behind. It could wait, always had.

Golf had been my focus since I was seven, when my father sawed down a set of clubs for me: Tommy Armour Silver Scots; their shafts were still warm to the touch when he steered me into the backyard to get me started on a short game. By the end of the next summer I was playing forty-five holes every day and shooting under forty a nine from the women's tees. On my way, Dad told me, to something great. We'd get there, he assured me; he'd have done it himself, if only he'd been gifted with "the advantages you've had." I would swing the club, not a thought in my head, and he'd take care of the rest: graphite drivers, smooth-bore irons, travel, coaching, thinking. Together, we'd make it.

I became a very solid junior player, won a passel of state and regional events and a handful of national ones. I loved the winning from the beginning (who doesn't?), and eventually the golf leached its way down into my soul, too, a creeping poison. My rivals, mostly country giants who swung out of their shoes at every shot, had to stand by and watch me knock three-woods stiff from seventy-five yards behind them, and they couldn't take it. Trying to outdo me, they would flail at their wedge shots like woodcutters, lay a shroud of sod over their barely budged balls. The dreaded chili-dip. Having walked ahead, I stood on the edge of the green, putter against my scrawny leg, hands on my sawhorse hips (making sure to point my thumbs

to the front, like a pansy). I watched the fuming brutes fetch
divots thick as their forearms, then kick them savagely back
into place. I watched middle irons get buried up to their hosels
in fairways; I watched wedges windmill into ponds; I heard
curses of impossible virtuosity. No finesse, poor things. All the
strength in the world, but no finesse at all. In defeat, their hand-
shakes were always sweaty and limp, and their congratulations
were inaudible.

Far from the greens — in itchy shrubbery, canebrakes, abandoned deer stands, and even, once, in the bed of a construction-
site dump truck — my father, his view of the action partially
eclipsed, pumped his fist in the air where only I could see it.
Later, in the car, we replayed my victories shot by shot, over
and over. As we sped home past clapboard groceries and dis-
emboweled stock cars and fields of broom sedge, the gold trophy I'd won sitting in the backseat like a passenger, I was
happy. My father mussed my hair; the wind roared; the trophy
gleamed; he let me work the gear shift. We were a team . . . as
long as I kept up my end of the bargain, as long as I kept winning.

When I finished high school the scholarship offers rolled in,
though my scores had leveled off during my final two seasons.
After trouncing the competition at the state championship as a
freshman and again as a sophomore, I slipped to third — then,
senior year, I shot a fat eighty the last day and fell all the way
out of the top ten. I blamed my punchless play, not very nervously, on senioritis — by then I'd signed a letter of intent.
Nothing to worry about: the future was already written.

I chose the best golf situation I could find close enough to
home for my father to see me play. Georgia had a solid tradition, good practice facilities, a well-organized, hands-off coach,
a decent home track, and four graduating seniors; if they happened to have a library equipped with books — and Mom assured me, trying to make the best of it, that they did — that
was gravy as far as I was concerned. (As for Mom, the only sign
of discontent I could see was in the way her hopes for me had

wilted. Grand aspirations can't take the climate down here, it seems. Too hot, too stupid — we don't have amber ales or mind-clearing cold or Collegiate Gothic, the prerequisites of respectability. "Be good, Brian," she said, as I sat in my packed car, idling, raring to go: *off to college.* I shifted into gear, set my foot on the brake: *Get it over with, Mom. Tell me you love me. Tell me to excel.* "Be good," she repeated, almost sadly; I edged forward. Tears were welling in her eyes, and I turned away to drive. I expected her, as she usually did, to rally at this last moment, to lift her head, wave briskly, and shout something about performing to my intellectual capabilities. Instead her voice grew soft, plaintive. "Play well," she mumbled, and I went.)

I was a dull, inept, inward kid — the kind who's liked (meanly) because he consents to being the butt of pranks: the good sport, the quiet sufferer. Even at the golf course, where my skills exempted me from outright abuse — flat tires, wet willies, noogies, rattails, wedgies, pull-my-fingers, being stripped of shorts and shirt by a mob — I tended to have rivalries rather than friendships. Hatch was as close to a friend as I had, and all we had in common were golf (my kingdom, and he didn't want to talk about it) and hormones (his kingdom, and I couldn't bear to think about it).

I'd like to say I didn't date in high school because I was shy and afraid, didn't rebel out of a lack of imagination, didn't toke or snort or trip because I was sleepy and incurious; and all that's true, up to a point. Mostly, though, I was indifferent; I wasn't interested in people my age. I didn't care, didn't have to. Dad had cut a snug niche for me in the world; we had poured my energies, my skills — all I had to offer — into golf. I had every assurance I needed: I was a winner. Coming down our street in the rain, you'd pass a dozen houses, two dozen, without seeing a single car exposed to the elements; but my father's convertible dripped ostentatiously in the drive, displaced from the garage by my trophies. It was a sleek red billboard: Winner Lives Here.

Dad had enclosed the carport, installed backlit lucite cases, Astroturf for bad-weather putting, a workbench for club repair — he'd made a shrine to the idea that I was special, that I was immune from the world's petty insults, its distractions, its ways of wearing one down. He kept the trophy room immaculate, the cases Windexed, plaques polished, lights bright. One stormy day in junior high I decided to monkey around with a Crenshaw-style swinging-door putting stroke, so I sequestered myself in the garage. On my father's bench, spread over sheets of newspaper in ragged rows and columns, were nearly a hundred of the miniature plastic drivers that crown trophies the way angels bestride Christmas firs. I scanned the room, saw that every trophy's clenched hands were empty, then looked back down at the drivers. Around each was a halo of gold touch-up paint: Triumphs, my father believed, must not be permitted to dull. He's a scary man. Had I been an adult, I might have pitied him. I'm sure other parents on the junior circuit had a good chuckle at his obsessiveness, his on-course peculiarities; maybe I *wasn't* the only person to see my old man crouched in the forks of low trees, peeking from between giant heads of fountain grass. But I had no basis for comparison. He was my father; he loved me; he wanted my wins to stay golden.

So when I got to Georgia, I was convinced that my life had been laid out and that my destiny was simply to traipse through it, uncovering the glories. I'd been lucky enough to find, at an age when I needed it, a talent. My life was on the links. School was just the purgatory where I worked off the excesses of joy. I was naive: I suppose I assumed that everyone had a gift, a vessel into which to pour a life. I guessed everyone sleepwalked through the rest of it, the unworthy hours devoted to other things. Mediocrity didn't exist, so far as I knew. I had found something I did better than anyone else in the world. That would never change, and every person must have a similar skill, a preserve, a reason for living. It never occurred to me to question — Dad had told me a thousand times: Winners win. Losers think.

I arrived in Athens assuming I would put in my four years of golf, attending class, as always, as a counterweight to bliss. I would collect my All-America plaques, my NCAA Championship cups; I'd pass them wordlessly to my father, whose eyes would be moist as he installed them in their allotted spaces in his garage. Then it would be on to the PGA, to wealth and stardom.

The team practiced on several courses around Athens, including one way out off Highway 129 — a rough track called Cob's Glynn. Cob's attractiveness as a practice site had nothing to do with golf; its bunkers were bottomed with gluey red clay, its greens were pocked with *poa annua,* billy goats grazed in pastures that abutted (much too closely) the fairways of the back nine, and in its layout were all kinds of gimmicks: blind shots, hidden fingers of creek, old oaks in landing areas, even a greenside bunker in the shape of Georgia (cut with all the punctilio you'd expect from a speed freak on a backhoe).

Cob's was a dog track, but practice there was followed by a sojourn to Hawg Heaven ("Where All *Good* Pigs Go"), a legendary barbeque joint in the sticks. The proprietor was a huge booster of Georgia athletics, a bald fireplug named Seamus O'Lughnasaigh. On fall Saturdays Between the Hedges you could see him in his seat behind the Bulldog bench, jabbing the air with a whiskey flask, a red-and-black logo painted atop his pink pate. Mr. O'Lughnasaigh could be counted on to give all Bulldog athletes — even those who played lowly nonrevenue sports like golf — free plates of Q, slaw, hash, and rice.

I'd heard all about Hawg Heaven, and I was primed for the free meal after we played Cob's early in my freshman fall. It wasn't that I'm a barbeque nut (I don't, truth be told, much like the peppered mustard-grease that passes for sauce in north

Georgia). More than the food, what I was ready to dig into was the feeling I'd hit the big time: Rules were being finessed for me, risks run (piddling risks, true, but risks all the same). At Hawg Heaven I would collect, on a wafer of styrofoam, the first modest perq of celebrity. I skipped lunch in preparation.

But things didn't work out as I'd hoped. Hawg Heaven turned out to be a white cinderblock shack with the caved-in look of a mouth devoid of teeth. Dangling from the side of the building was a gnarled air conditioner; the niche for the unit had been cut too big, and someone had stuffed the resulting space with oilrags and plastic grocery sacks and scraps of corkboard. The gray wreckage bore spray-painted swastikas, bullet holes; its vents had been pinched like a pie crimped lovingly shut. It was covered on one side with bumps, swellings, nodules — an unreadable rash of braille that made it look like someone had tortured it, from inside, with a tack hammer. The window unit was one of those things so sublimely damaged, so dumbly ugly, that it had depths of expression: I felt for it, somehow. And despite the disfigurements, it chugged away — the deafening suck drowned out all other sound.

On the wide front window, "Hawg Heaven" had been stenciled in silver script, and painted above was a bulbous cartoon pig complete with halo and harp; otherwise the shack bore no decoration. The window was broad as a service bay; in fact, the restaurant looked very much like a superannuated filling station, dragged into the woods to live out its golden years in peace. The hot tang of sauce filled the air, strong enough to bring me to the verge of a sneeze.

We walked in. Hawg Heaven's floor was cracked cement crammed with picnic tables set end to end. Checkered sheets of plastic had been fastened to the tables with an industrial stapler that hung on a hook beside the cash register; iced-tea pitchers and loaves of white bread were spaced along the tabletops. Outdated calendars — Norman Rockwell, power tools wielded by women in bikinis, chimpanzees on toilets — lined the walls. Behind the counter, absently shooing flies away from the potato salad with a ladle, was a girl in a sauce-smeared apron. No Mr. O. No customers. It was four o'clock.

I was near the back of our group, a freshman — I think there were probably ten of us. Like the other guys, I hadn't bothered to put on my street shoes after I shed my spikes and socks at Cob's. We wore shorts, and our legs were deeply tanned, but our feet gleamed like bone. One way we could be recognized by Mr. O'Lughnasaigh as golfers, I supposed, was the way we'd track clay into Heaven on our pale, homely feet.

The first guy to the feed trough was this asshole named Wass, our only senior. He wasn't a good player — he'd never made the traveling squad for a tournament — but as our loudest, brayingest veteran, he rated the front of the chow line. "Coach left me in charge," Wass bellowed in the parking lot, "in his absence. Watch and learn, youngsters." Forays into Hawg Heaven were the only benefit Wass got out of his affiliation with the team; he was planning to take full advantage. I had played with him at Cob's (Coach believed in spreading the misery; no one — especially no freshman — was exempt from being paired with Wass). For a change, he didn't spend the day bragging about how, in his spare time, he starred in porn movies under the name Iron Johnson. After every bad shot, instead of screeching about his ratshit luck or helicoptering clubs as was his habit, he'd only rubbed his belly, smiled a rapturous smile, and said, "Good groceries comin', friends. Good groceries comin'."

Most of what Wass said was legitimately awful, but *everything* he said, even the rare innocent remark, was rendered a bit creepy by his aspect. He'd had his eyebrows singed off in a high-school lab accident, and at some point, fueled by bourbon and vanity, he'd hired a tattoo artist in Atlanta to draw him new ones. He'd gone to a grimy parlor uptown with a bottle of Jack Daniel's to cut the pain and a dishrag to stifle his screams, conceiving of the operation as a sort of old-time waterfront-movie adventure. The result was grisly: too high, too dark, and with an impossibly steep, quizzical arch. The new brows made

him look like a cross between Lon Chaney and Divine. Wass
was sensitive about his replacements, and he often wore a wide-
brimmed white plantation hat tugged down over them.

But he'd doffed the lid when we came inside Hawg Heaven,
in accordance with some quaint Christian custom his parents
had taught him, a habit that (unlike every moral tenet) he'd
never quite got around to abandoning. The too-snug hatband
had left a bright red track across his forehead, from brow to
vaulted brow, and Wass looked scary. As he approached the
counter, he fisted flat the crown of his massive overseer's hat,
then reinflated it with the fingers of his other hand. He faced
the poor girl and growled, in about as friendly a tone as you
ever heard from him, "Where's Big O at, sweet?"

"Out."

"Where out?"

"Not here out. What can I do for you?"

The girl was staring frankly at Wass's forehead. His tone
grew chilly. "Well, we're the golfers, and we're hoooongry.
Dish us up some Bulldog specials, would you?"

The girl pointed at a hand-lettered sign on the cash register,
smiled wanly. "No shoes," she read aloud, "no service." She
backtracked to the top. "Hawg Heaven regrets."

Wass snorted. "Glad you didn't leave anything out, miss," he
said. "You know who we are?"

The girl shrugged. "No," she said. "But I know you don't
have shoes on. Sorry."

"The Big O is gon' be pissed if you don't feed us," Wass went
on.

The girl shrugged again, looked straight at his brows, and
said, with no hint of sarcasm, "Gracious. Is that paint? Are you
maimed?"

Wass was too startled to be mad . . . yet. "Pardon?" he sput-
tered. "What did you say?"

The girl didn't back off. Her eyes never left those ghastly ink
arcs, and her tone was all syrupy concern. "On your forehead.

Where your eyebrows ought to be," she said. "You look like you've been *vandalized*. Do you need to use the phone?"

I thought he was going to leap the counter. "Listen!" Wass exploded. "We're the Georgia golf team, and we can come in here buck goddamn naked if we want, and our food is *free*. You're paid to keep your bitch mouth shut and sling hash. So sling. Now."

The girl's face clouded. She set her mouth. "I'm sorry," she told him. "You'll have to take that up with Mr. O. I don't know anything about free food for anyone."

"Which is why I'm telling you," roared Wass. "Dish us up some grub."

The girl was marvelous. Her hair was tied into a ponytail and looped through the back of her Hawg Heaven baseball cap. There was an orange daub of sauce under her ear, and tiny droplets of sweat stood out on her face. She was staring at Wass now in what looked to me like genuine bewilderment. Hadn't he been in some sort of horrible accident? Hadn't she only been trying to help? "No shoes, no service," she repeated, firmly. "No exceptions. I couldn't be sorrier."

Wass turned to his confederates, the other hangers-on of the team; he shrugged, as if to ask whether frat-boy noblesse oblige had any hard and fast rules against killing barbeque girls who jeer your eyebrows and refuse you the tangy pork of your dreams.

There was a hush that must have lasted fifteen seconds — during which the girl stood fast, Wass fumed and rocked threateningly, and the rest of us made an uneasy peace with our cowardices: What could I do, after all? I was at the back of the pack; Wass was bigger than me, older; the girl was taking good care of herself.

Just when the silence was becoming unendurable, a candy-red Caddy barreled up the access road, kicking up spumes of dust, its horn blaring the Bulldog fight song. Seamus O'Lughnasaigh.

"Hold on a minute, Wass," someone said, as though he hadn't been. "It's the Big O cavalry."

Everybody except me turned to watch. I pressed forward until I was almost beside Wass. Who was this girl? What was she up to? I cast around for clues. A stack of textbooks, the top one propped open with a yellow highlighter, lay on a card table next to the walk-in freezer. A student, then. A pair of gold sandals had been slung over a chair by their knotted anklestraps — I could see (by leaning toward the plastic sneeze-shield) that there were duckboard flats laid across the floor behind the counter for footing, and the girl wore blue canvas Keds to navigate the greasy skids. Her ankles appeared slender, but I backed away, scared she'd catch me appraising, before I could make a conclusive judgment.

The girl never looked at me, never budged, merely kept stirring the hash, two brisk swirls and then a solid clack of the ladle against the side of the metal bin, over and over. Her rhythm was slow and perfect, reminded me of the solemn rumble of war drums in the movies: swirl, swirl, click; swirl, swirl, click. I could see her facial muscles tense as the doorchime sounded, and I wanted to help her. Laugh if you want. I thought she needed me.

Mr. O strode in, and golfers parted to let him through. I retreated. The boss man grinned and said, "Hey, fellas! Welcome to Hawg Heaven, where the hogs is dead and the folks get fed. Who wants a little something to stick to his ribs and make his tail twitch?"

"Afternoon, Big O," said Wass, suddenly calm.

"Good to see you again, Mr. Wassink. How's your grandpop?"

Wass's grandfather was a much-decorated general of the Vietnam war, a hero in these parts . . . and the reason there was no getting rid of young Iron Johnson. Ironically, the general was famous for his formidable black brows. Those thick, fierce, unmoving lines could be counted on: Fighting dragged on, body counts mounted, atrocities worsened, but Papa Wass's twin tarantulas never wavered — again and again they announced that U.S. policy was just and consistent; her boys were fighting the good fight against those sly slopes and their Russian domino. Those brows were a bulwark amid the chaos. (I'm borrowing, you might have guessed, from my mother's testimony.)

Wass spoke up. "He's fit and fine, Mr O'Lughnasaigh. Sends his regards. But it gets to him sometimes — the country's going to hell in a handbasket, you know. Fags in khaki. Baby-killing. Japs buying up all the best resorts, even Pebble Beach. Gooks fucking up the curve in math classes."

"Amen," answered Mr. O. "Amen."

Wass went on. "I'm afraid we have a . . . situation here. This girl of yours says we ain't welcome. I was sure she'd gotten it wrong." He grinned expectantly, raising his awful brows. His yes-men, all the upperclass hacks and squirrels, murmured their agreement. Wass kept pushing. "By the way, Big O, you got a complaint box? This employee was rude to me. Hurt my feelings. Worse than that, she insulted our whole team — she insulted the *U*-niversity of Georgia. She treated us like a bunch of niggers." He brandished his hat, a visual aid.

Seamus O'Lughnasaigh's face darkened. "Is this true?" he demanded, turning to the girl. Slowly, she sunk the ladle in the vat of hash. She looked up at her fearsome pink employer, tears in her eyes but steely. This was the battle she'd been girding herself for. I could tell she needed the job badly, could see her calculating what it was worth. She didn't answer the question. I looked around, but no one was showing any sign of stepping forward. Least of all me.

Mr. O cleared his throat, and wattles swayed. "I asked you a question, sweetheart. Did you treat my guests with disrespect? Don't cry now. Just speak up. Did you treat these fine young men like *nigras?*"

The girl stared at her feet, drowned the ladle one last time in the tub of hash, and through the sneeze-guard I could see her fingers snake around her back — she was going to untie her apron. No job could be worth putting up with these rednecks. No job could be worth occupying a stinking shack in the boonies, alone, fending off packs of barefoot peckerwoods with crayoned facial features.

"No," I broke in, and my voice surprised me; it sounded like something rusted clean through. "She was fine. It wasn't her fault. Wass was giving her a hard time." The girl stared down at her red hands and started to wring them in her apron. I couldn't tell whether she was pleased with me or annoyed.

Wass and his boys glared. "Fucking hotshot," Wass muttered. "She wouldn't serve us," he explained to our host. "She busted my chops in front of my friends."

Now the girl spoke up. Her voice was soft but calm. "It was an accident, Mr. O'Lughnasaigh. I didn't mean to be impolite. He just kept insisting that he and his friends didn't have to pay. You never told me anything about that, and I was trying to stand up to him. I'm the only one here."

Mr. O shook his head and said, "That's OK. That's a good girl." He turned back to Wass. "Sorry about this, boys, I suppose I'm to blame. I forgot to mention our little arrangement . . . which is why I dropped by. I hope you'll accept our apology, Mr. Wassink." He clapped Wass stoutly on the back and spoke over his shoulder to the countergirl. "Aren't we sorry, Rosa?" *Let's make nice; he comes from powerful people.*

She nodded miserably. "Hawg Heaven regrets," she whispered.

"Right," echoed her boss. "Right. Hawg Heaven regrets." He began talking to Rosa now, but without looking at her. "These boys are fixing to kick some SEC ass this season, so let's take good care of them, OK?" Rosa nodded again.

"All right, then," Mr. O announced, suddenly beaming. "All better. All better." With that he spun and waddled back to his car, which he'd left running; when he swung open the front door, I could hear the Mills Brothers on his tape deck: "You always take the sweetest rose," they crooned, "and crush it till the petals fall."

Rosa began heaping food onto compartmented plates. Wass kept making her add a spoonful of this, a dollop of that, trying to humiliate her. His plate was overflowing when he tired of the game and slid over to the ice dispenser. "Thanks, darlin'," he said. "How about a hummer for dessert?"

Wass's friends kept the vitriol coming, unspeakable things, but Rosa bore it silently, with a terrible dignity. I felt rotten for her; she must really need this crappy job. "Look," said Wass as she started to dip out hash for me, "if it isn't Lancelot. Why don't you two get it over with and fuck right now? We'll clear a spot on the grill. Sizzle, sizzle."

"Shut up, Wass," I said, searching for a clever retort, hoping indignation might supple up my lame tongue. No dice. After a few seconds of strain, I settled: "You're a big old turd," I spat. "A *big* old turd." To Rosa, I rolled my eyes.

"Thanks for sticking up for me," she whispered. "I guess." Her left eye, I noticed, was higher than her right, and she held her head at a tilt — adorably — to keep the world in alignment.

"I'm not sure this job was worth keeping."

"Better than nothing," she said, "though you do get your share of freaks out here." Rosa smiled, smacked the ladle against the side of the trough to clean it. We had already run out of things to say. She really was pretty.

"Could I have a little more slaw, please?" I asked.

"Sure."

I groped for conversation. Nothing came. She kept piling food onto my plate — more slowly than before, it seemed, trying to buy me time to cook up some passable repartee. The well was dry; I'm not sure it had ever been wet. Golf was all I was good at. Finally I thought of another question. I mustered my courage, smiled my toothiest smile; this was it.

"Happen to have any sweet gherkins?" I asked.

Rosa flashed her gorgeous, uneven teeth. To be bestowed a look like that, and just for asking, stammeringly, after pickles: It was a dream come true, it changed me. "In the back," she said. "Hold on a sec."

She went to get them, and I began to rummage through my
wallet for a tip. I'd spotted a jar on the counter. All I had was a
ten, but that seemed about right, all things considered, and I
started stuffing it through the hole in the lid. I didn't want her
to see me and think I was trying to buy her good graces. But
about the time the bill cleared the slot I noticed the faded snap-
shot affixed to the jar, of a young couple with bad teeth squatting in front of a cheap silver Christmas tree, the woman
holding a squalling baby up to the camera like a fish on a
stringer. Beneath the picture was a slip of paper: "Ray and
Marlene lost their trailer in a tornadoe and dont have nowhere
to live. CAN YOU HELP? God bless you!! (They are Chris-
tians!!!)" I was trying to extract the bill from the slot when
Rosa returned. She stared at me, stealing from good church-
going people with a gutted trailer and a colicky new kid. I
twitched.

"Umm," I said, "I was trying . . ."

"I saw," she answered, "and it was sweet, but they need it
more than me." She tamped the jar lid with the butt of a fork —
my fork, a gherkin speared on each of its three tines. The ten
dropped to the bottom. Then she handed me the utensil.

"Thanks," I said. "Thanks a bunch. I really like pickles."

"I'm glad," said Rosa. "Anytime." She gave the bin a vale-
dictory clack, sent me on my way.

A few weeks later, when I spotted Rosa in the foyer after an
art history class, I tapped her on the shoulder. Would she, uh,
be averse, uh, to maybe going out with me sometime?

"Sure," she said, in a tone of blandest unsurprise. She sor-
celed a datebook out of thin air (or maybe pulled it out of her
backpack), then uncapped a pen and looked straight into my
face. "Say Friday afternoon. We'll score a bottle of sweet
pickles and find a nice place to eat them. Does that suit? How
about I pick you up at four. OK? Where do you live?"

Friday afternoon we laid a gingham cloth in deep centerfield
of the baseball stadium. Rosa was chattering away worrilessly,
brazenly — as though, if caught, we could claim it was by sheer

and inexplicable accident that we ended up here, on the matted sod of the outfield, battening blue-and-white corners with a menagerie of animal paperweights that Rosa produced from her bag — accident, too, that we'd scaled a hurricane fence and climbed from the right-field bleachers onto the cinderblock wall and then dropped onto the field and were sitting, now, in the late sun, talking, amid the wreckage of our peculiar picnic — our jar of gherkins (now seriously depleted), one of those rubber-gripper jar openers (brought just in case and not, thanks to Rosa's powerful fingers, needed), and a pair of cock-tail forks, face up in the sun, still speckled with little green drops of brine.

Rosa kept her job at Hawg Heaven for another ten months, until she found something better. The air conditioner kept up its chug, she claims, until the day she left . . . and though I'm not sure I believe her, I want to, which is near about the same thing. That year there was an irremovable orange ring around her fingernails, and we fell in love.

By the time I used up my eligibility, Rosa had made sure I got myself a "practical" degree — in accounting — and her an engagement ring. I earned the art history diploma on the side by taking a heavy course load, even eked out honors to make Rosa and my mother proud; I was named an Academic All-American each of my last three seasons. Even now Rosa thinks I studied hard because I was obeying her injunction to have something to fall back on, but I never figured I'd have need of a net: My golf was solid, and my destiny had been writ. Once Rosa swept into my nongolf life and occupied it (the thing had been, God knows, only lightly defended), I studied because she told me to. I was following the path of least resistance: I wanted to please her.

Meanwhile Rosa collected her fashion merchandising degree, *magna cum,* went immediately to work as a buyer for a department-store chain. I headed home to beat my game into shape for the tour grind — looking forward to October qualifying. We were married at the end of the summer. Almost four years ago.

My skills atrophied during the wedding rigmarole, the cocktail parties and compatibility quizzes and china choosing and ferrying of relatives, the ceremony and then a two-week trip. Though we were in south Florida, home to some of the best golf in the world, Rosa wouldn't let me take my clubs along. "I won't be a golf widow during my honeymoon," she insisted. I gave in.

When we got back I tried to recapture my edge, but it was gone. I was guiding the ball, making a scared swing, and my putting stroke turned jumpy and inconsistent. In the first round of the Tour qualifier I posted a butt-ugly eighty-one, and the skid was on. Later that October, in the consolation tournament for those who failed to get their cards, I never even sniffed making the new Hogan circuit. I trickled all the way down to the Snapper/Gold Club Tour, water finding its own miserable level, and I've stuck there. Since then I've had three tries at the PGA, three tries at the Hogan, six flameouts. I've been to Canada, Australia, Europe, the Far East, trying to catch on somewhere — feeling at first betrayed, then bewildered, then merely bitter. And now I'm sitting on seventy-seven at the Ile de Paris, eighteen shots back of Bird Soulsby. The lights are out in the trophy room, and destiny's taken a powder. Dad's car could be dry, safe, out of sight, like everyone else's.

Beautiful.

The charts on the bedspread, back here at the Ibis Inn, are there not as analytical aids, and not only so I'll have (in the absence, Rosa insinuates, of a paycheck) "something to show for your week," but because she demands that I keep my bookkeeping skills sharp for when I retire. Until recently I'd thought this insistence was just another indication, like her thirty-year bonds and our burial plot and the boxes of secondhand baby things in the back of our closet, of her compulsive planning for the future. But on Monday afternoon, three days ago, she moved up the schedule.

I was up to my elbows in dishwater, scrubbing a crusty pot. When I'm at home I try to do as many domestic chores as I can — appease the household gods. Rosa crept up to me from behind and pressed her lips into my shoulder blade.

I've always taken pleasure in conjuring my wife whole from tiny details — the merest trace of her voice, several rooms away, can yield her telephonic posture, the pale thigh slung over the arm of her easy chair, the moody arc of her eyebrow (made of real hair!), the doodles blooming under her right hand, the impatient way she taps the receiver against her chin when she's listening to a story that's gone on too long. There have been times when my knowledge was less burden than blessing.

In this case, the evidence pointed in an unpleasant direction. There was precious little tenderness in her lips, I noticed — it was as much a collision as a kiss. Only the rustle of parachute shorts to announce her. No hands — they must have been clasped behind her back. Barefoot, I surmised by the height of the impact, the noiselessness of her approach. She lingered behind me, scratching her forehead on my back, waiting for an invitation to begin the siege.

All the signs were there: My beautiful bride was about to embark on one of her crusades. I braced myself.

"When are we going to have a baby?" Rosa began. She has this habit of damping hard words by speaking them into my skin; my shoulder blade zizzed like a kazoo, and I twitched away, banged my head on the cabinet above the sink.

"Sometime," I said, massaging my scalp with my soap-slick left hand. I reached for the steel wool. "Later."

"After golf, you mean," said Rosa. "When you're finished chasing balls up and down the coast for fruit-picker's wages.

When you're finished being ego-absorbed. When my biological clock quits ticking."

I scoured, and scowled. This sounded rehearsed. Ego-absorbed? Biological clock? Lord deliver us from the tender mercies of self-help. "Um," I replied, staring into the grimy colander. "Please, honey."

Rosa leaned around me. She is blunt, broad of forehead, looks like a pretty hammer. The steel wool had abraded my palm, and lukewarm dishwater prickled the new skin. "You listen here," she commanded, giving me no choice. And then she started in.

She said, I've let you chase that dream. She said, I've worn plastic visors and green skirts with hippos on them and lived out of suitcases and ruined my skin in the sun and prayed till my palms are callused. She said, With God's help, I've been a patient and forbearing wife, I've been a rock and a helpmeet. She said, I'm tired of excuses and statistics, how many tournaments have you won? She said, You've netted nineteen thousand dollars in three years, I'll let you do the math, you can still do division? She said, We haven't spent more than ten days in a row together since we've been married. She said, I want a baby. She said, I want a baby, Brian — Brian, I want a baby.

Patience, I answered. I'm thirty-fourth on the money list, which isn't, you know, half bad, dear, think how many guys are more hopeless than me. I said, Of course some of the other players are married, what is that supposed to mean? I said, Hold on just a while longer, I've got this game on the run. Besides, I joked weakly, maternity clothes are ugly. You won't like them. Big old gunnysacks with clipper ships on them. And clipper ships are worse than hippopotami, if you think about it: Hippos can communicate underwater, and they have wondrous nostrils. They're cute and wise. Really. It's true what I say. Patience. We'll make babies in time. Good time. Soon, or at least soonish.

I meant what I said, more or less, but it sounded thin to me.

And after a while I couldn't say anything more. I took my medicine. I kept my eyes in the sink.

She finished. I picked up my towel and wiped a skillet dry. Rosa was perched on the counter next to the sink, sniffling. Her knees looked huge and bare and white, like misshapen moons. Looking at them, I felt their tidal tug. I could have cried. "I'm about to break through," I told them, fearing to let my eyes rise higher. "I know it. I can beat this game. This week I'm going to do something special. For you. Count on it. Charleston's the kind of place where magic can happen, just ask my mom. This tournament will be for you, honey. A test. I'm going to win it for you."

Rosa blotted a tear with a knuckle, like a ragamuffin in a Depression musical. "'By their fruits shall ye know them,'" she quoted. "Not by their excuses."

"I'm done with excuses," I pledged. "It's just me against golf now. One on one. The final cage match."

"You're not playing against the game, Brian," Rosa said softly. "You're playing against yourself and against me and against God. And you're playing against our children. That's something you'll have to face up to someday. You're a selfish, selfish man."

This was too far. "Goddamn it!" I shouted, yanking my left hand out of the water and smacking it against the skillet. Rosa was bounding away before the water, or the sound, even hit her. And before I could summon her back to say I loved her or explain how much I've invested in golf or spell out one last time how clearly and how needfully I'd always seen my future in it, a wisp of sud, stirred to flight by my pot-wallop, drifted slowly past my face like a bubble of cartoon dialogue. It landed on my dishtowel, began to dissolve.

Mockery everywhere. I had lost, again, and I was alone. Rosa's sobs vibrated through her shut door as through a membrane, and my shoulder blade twitched again.

I saw an image of myself as my father: standing behind the

eighteenth green at some junior tournament, out of sight but not earshot, feet spread wide, arms crossed, cigar gnawed through in torment — screaming at my boy. "Your life is a fucking lark, son! All you do is play golf. You have every advantage on this earth because I work my duff off fifty hours a week. And this is my reward, coming out here to see you stick your head up your ass. If you can't handle a wedge any better than that, we'll see if you do better with a pickaxe or a lug wrench. What in God's name is wrong with you? You can *bury* every one of these punks. *Bury* them, goddamn it. Look at me when I'm talking to you!"

I finished the dishes in silence. When I wiped my hands, I noticed the lacy cursive legend across the towel's frayed bottom: "Golf is a four-letter word."

And with the pressure on, having promised Rosa the sun, I went out today and bumped it seventy-seven times, after which I posed as Bird Soulsby and made a date with a television reporter. What am I doing? Who am I?

"What are you like?" Ellen asked me, once the tape had stopped rolling. "You give good interview, which means you're lying, right? I've seen *His Girl Friday* — I know these things." She smiled.

"What am I like? You tell me." I was buying time, assumed the interview had bled me dry of bullshit.

"Don't know yet. Too early to tell. Different."

"Not what you expected?"

"I expected a glib airhead in pastels. Sound familiar?" She looked skeptically at my eggshell shirt, my beltless salmon pants.

"Well," I replied, catching my wind again, "I suppose I'm like a pig on a sofa, a lonesome polecat, like fat in a house afire." I smirked. I was warming to this mysticism rap. It was exhilarating, like being Kesey, or Kerouac. It was all tone . . . the words hardly mattered. "If you know what I mean."

"Oh," laughed Ellen, "I do, I do." Her cameraman made a choking sound. Enough.

"Do you date the glib airheads who dress in *drab* colors?" I asked. "I can probably scare up some gray trousers in a good cause. You look like a woman in need of a night out. Minor-league golf probably isn't the plum assignment you were hoping for when you got to the station this morning; it doesn't have the drama of a hostage situation, say." I knew immediately I'd punched the right button. I felt disgusting, and invincible. I winked.

Ellen unclipped her microphone and showed me her eyelids, dusted with a bronze as delicate as that on a butterfly's underwing. She tilted her face like a lolita; her onyx earrings swayed.

"What makes you think I'll buy an awful line like that? What makes you think I'm not happy here? And by the way, hostage situations are overrated, just a bunch of cowering out of the line of fire and waiting in camera trucks."

Ellen's nose, like Rosa's, is small and slightly upturned. Her nostrils are long, narrow, pinched in at the middle. Hips like a pageboy's, unlike Rosa. I looked down to her lower lip, whose plumpness gave her a bit of a perma-pout, like a polar cap of disappointment; then farther, to her long, unblemished chin.

I reached out and pressed my thumb lightly into the hollow over Ellen's trachea, as though pressing an elevator button. She didn't flinch. "What a beautiful throat you have," I said. I am nothing like this, I swear it; *I like pickles a lot.* How could I have known it would work?

"Ah, a wolf," said Ellen. "In schlep's clothing."

Her cameraman rolled his eyes, snorted again, turned to leave. He'd had more than enough. "OK then, Sleazy," Ellen continued. "I'll see you at the Meeting Street end of the old slave market at eight, sharp. Drinks, dinner. I'll wear a high collar. You wear a credit card."

Oh, how I love a woman who takes charge.

I'll watch the sports before I go . . . only four or five minutes left, the weather goon is prancing and pointing at a smiley sun he's pasted in the center of the blue pie wedge that is South Carolina. And I *will* go. Drinks are harmless, dinner, a little conversation. Finish what's been started. Way of the Tao. You find yourself a road, you go down it. What else is there to do?

Besides, I have to get out of this motel room. Hatch might come back and gloat about his round. The ice machine is on the blink. TV reception is fuzzy. Reading lamp is burned out — the three-way control makes the light over Hatch's bed blink like a bar sign on the seedy side of town. Above my "headboard" (a graceless plank of plastic glued to the wall), a Winslow Homer print — of a cinnamon man riding mean seas on a box top — is taunting me.

And in the dresser drawer are two of Mr. Gideon's books. Not one, two. That extra New Testament is jangling my nerves. Six months ago Rosa took a part-time second job in one of those strip-mall Christian bookstores ("the Work of the Savior," she calls it, and hands over the four dollars an hour to her church mission); this second Bible strikes me as somehow her work. Every time I go anywhere she manages to stash three or four morsels of godly wisdom into my luggage — maxims tucked into my shoes, homilies scrolled around my toothbrush. Once she even taped an Old Testament verse to the face of my five-iron.

So far this trip, I've come across two. Yesterday morning, shaving, I found a strip taped to my can of foam: "With God there are no bogeys," it informed me. Thirty minutes ago, getting dressed, I unknotted a pair of socks and a fortune-cookie sliver of paper fluttered to the floor. I left the note in the shag while I pulled on my socks and shoes, while I pulled out my stat charts, while I flipped on the television. I didn't want to read it. It read: "There is no sight so precious to the Lord as a child."

I'll go. I won't have to be me for a while.

But first I'll watch myself on the news, see what other appalling things I said. There could be trouble. Impostors are dealt with harshly. But I've been counting on that all along, I'm beginning to realize. I've been daring my luck to go bad on me, like firing at tucked pins on a day when I'm not sharp, figuring instant disaster beats an afternoon-long agony of treading water. Make something happen . . . at any cost. It's been a long time coming.

I suppose I could still call the station, ask for Ellen, confess, fix things up; there may still be time. But I won't. Once you've chosen a club, stick with it. Hit the ball, hard. Chase it around the pasture. Until it sinks. I haven't stayed out here for three years without learning anything.

I glance up at the screen. Banter at the anchor desk. Cut to a bucket-headed sports guy in a shit-brown suit, hint of a harelip under his Rusty Jones mustache. Here we go. I'm looking forward to it.

# CHAPTER THREE

## Last Tuesday, 8:50 A.M.

ATOP A CEMENT PICNIC TABLE, his midsection lumped ac-cordionlike around the stanchion of the umbrella that shades him, Hatch is asleep. The table's one of those circular, half-ton concrete monstrosities with fake filigree around its border to make it look light, and the tin umbrella has been painted in gaudy stripes now mercifully faded; the original shades seem to have been white and Howard Johnson's turquoise, but they've been baked away to cream and cafeteria-tray. Hatch's face is dappled with the sunlight that leaks through the rust-eaten rents in the tin above him. One of his flip-flops dangles at a right angle to its foot; the other lies sole up in the dirt. His golf clubs lean against the bench, next to a crocodile duffel bag and a toaster-oven stuffed with towels and trussed with its cord — an uncooperative prisoner. It's ten till nine in the morning at a rest area along I-26 near Bambury, South Carolina. I've been on the road three hours.

"Up and at 'em, Hatch," I call. "Let's go to work."

Snoring. Hatch is conked. Asleep on a slab of cement along a forsaken stretch of highway. Coiled around that iron mast. Barefoot, more or less. Wearing hundred-dollar khakis, a gleaming Rolex. A thick wad of twenties in his wallet — which is riding high and tawdry, like a Belgian whore in a display window, on the hip he has raised in sleep. An invitation to cut-purses, cutthroats. The tools of his livelihood — the clubs, the leather luggage, the toaster-oven — are stacked beside him in a parody of the migrant's bundle. Has Hatch never heard the phrase *homicidal drifter,* never seen hitchhiker movies? Does he not understand that this is a murderous world? What's wrong with him? Where is his fear?

*Gro-o-onk,* Hatch explains. *Gro-o-onk.* Behind me a trucker chuckles.

"Hatch, let's go!" I shout, louder than I mean to. There's a bubble of spittle the size of a pencil eraser at the corner of his mouth. I grab his golf bag by its strap and rattle his sabers; I wouldn't mind putting a little scare into him. Give him a sense of the risks he's running, the dangers he's taking no note of. The unexamined life . . .

Hatch slowly uncoils himself from the pole, sits up, pinches up his fallen flip-flop with prehensile toes. He rubs his eyes with balled fists like a tot, wipes his mouth with the back of his hand. "Well," he asks cheerfully, "why didn't you say so, Brian?"

"How long you been out here?"

"I guess that depends on what time it is."

"Almost nine."

"An hour and a half."

"You knew I wouldn't get here until now."

"Yeah, but little did I know when I swept the lovely Marlys off her feet last night that she would have to be on them again at seven."

"Marlys?"

Hatch closes his eyes, tilts his head back. The cheerful satyr. "Choicest biscuit, my boy," he coos. "Met her last night at a new karaoke bar up in Spartanburg. She seemed a little cold at first, a little suspicious, but a couple Spinners tunes, just the smidgiest skosh of Barry White, and next thing I know she's fixing me breakfast in the buff. Waffles, bacon, Kona . . . and you should have seen that back porch twitch while she beat the batter. Bring on Mrs. Butterworth." He wakes up spouting this stuff. AIDS, knife-wielding cuckolds, unwanted entanglement — Hatch has no fears. We scoop up his gear and head to the car.

After the fight last night, my morning was somewhat less romantic than Hatch's. Buffless. Syrupless. Rosa didn't say a word, though I could tell she was awake as I dressed. Her breaths, ragged and stertorous when she's asleep, were perfectly regular, and she had tugged her nightshirt down — in a gesture either of modesty or erotic revenge — to cover the sexy arrowpoint of her pelvis. She usually sleeps on her back, sleeps big, arms and legs splayed and staggered as though she's climbing a rope curtain on some dreamworld obstacle course; but this morning she was clenched in an armored ball, knees huddled snugly under her breasts. Like Hatch on the picnic plinth, but harder. More visible ribs, more angles, more clefts and joints and topographical charms.

As I left, I gave her a peck goodbye — lifted the fine hair at the top of her head and kissed the little bald spot there, remnant of childhood sutures. Holding her by the shoulder, I was amazed as always at how sleep softens her skin, warms it, steeps it in her doughy scent. A lovely angry bun, my wife. "I love you," I said, able to mean it again. "I'm sorry." She groaned and rolled away. "I'll be back on Sunday, bearing checks." Nothing. "You're a lousy sleep-faker," I added. She didn't budge.

◦

Hatch and I are on the way to Charleston for this week's event, to be played at a new resort named, inexplicably, the Ile de Paris Golf & Beach Club. Hatch has managed to mooch yet another ride. His method is foolproof. He calls Rosa, ties her in knots with flattery and tour gossip and a rude, rough wit she'd never put up with from me, then arranges an out-of-the-way rendezvous like Bambury. The man has an unerring instinct for when I won't be home to nix the deal. I always know he's called — when I come in Rosa's cheeks are flushed, and she hands me an envelope scrawled over with instructions, maps, code words.

The directions are always convoluted, as though Hatch is a drug cache or spy secret to be collected on the sly; the envelope on which Rosa has recorded road numbers and landmarks is a welter of red. Every week, it seems, Hatch uses his extraordinary wealth to land somewhere between me and the week's tour stop — but never to get all the way there on his own. I'm constantly picking him up in unlikely locales: truck stops, reptile farms, drag strips, Waffle Houses. Once I was told to collect my ward — after an anfractuous rounda-route that involved a lap around a legendary tire fire ("Smoldering since 1978") and then a stop at a rural Alabama monument to the boll weevil — at betting window seven of a dog track near Montgomery . . . there I was to be careful to call him "Colonel McVicar."

The directions often involve feints and switchbacks, as though I'm being tailed; I ignore all the unnecessary fucking around, of course. No time. It's not even honest paranoia — the cloak-and-dagger charade is Hatch's idea of *fun*. He wants to be my scavenger hunt. Usually I'll wander into the appointed dive to find Hatch propped up at the lunch counter like a sultan among cushions, with baleful stares and bared bad teeth at his back. He smiles at everyone as I usher him out, leaves a twenty as tip: "Best hen bullets I've had in many a moon," he calls. He's wearing some cheesy disguise that makes him look like a child molester — a Peterbilt cap, a Texaco jumpsuit, once even a novelty mustache, gluily askew. It's like a field trip for him, or a game: Rubbing Elbows with White Trash. What I want to say is, "These are people's lives." He wouldn't get it. He's too busy hitting up desperate, hard-drinking, badly married carpenters for estimates on blond paneling, or maybe feigning an interest in coon hunting and the Tony Orlando Club in Branson, Missouri.

This time, though, he's made fetching him convenient. Rosa

and I live in Emma, Georgia, forty-five minutes east of Atlanta, so the Bambury rest area isn't out of my way. Hatch and I are boyhood friends. In fact, Hatch has been in Lamartine, our hometown, these last few days to look in on his parents; their house — their estate, I suppose — is only twenty minutes from the rest area. This stretch of nothing is home to us both.

We met when I was nine and Hatch was eight. My father had finally, after years of conspicuous thrift, squirreled away enough money to join the Country Club of Lamartine and to buy a secondhand convertible (it wouldn't do to drive through the club gates in his El Camino — "You don't meet the queen in bowling shoes," he explained). Dad practiced his golf all the time, but rarely played; signing on at the club was a sacrifice, I realized much later, made solely so I'd have a golf course — "a track with a little *character*," he called it — to learn on. I had outgrown the barren muni on the northeast edge of town, the Bird o' Paradise.

At the time, the CC of Lamartine was a magical place to us. The course was older than my dad; it was fussed over by a greens superintendent who had, mind-bogglingly, spent *four years of college* studying nothing but how to superintend greens; rumor had it that there was a red telephone on the ninth tee whose purpose was to allow famished fatsos to call in lunch orders to the grill. They had valet parking for Sunday dinner, a full-time crew to weed and water the flowerbeds around the clubhouse. There was even something lofty about the name: not "Lamartine CC," but "The CC of Lamartine." *The* Country Club — others need not apply. And that stately *of* — prepositions are classy.

Early on the morning of my ninth birthday, Dad drove me down Pill Hill to the club. The Hill's official name was Racine Drive, but nobody called it that. The street was lined with the colonnaded mansions and manicured lawns of our town's doctors and lawyers; blackface jockeys (painted over in pink by the rare liberal family) lifted lanterns to show the way up the flagstone walks; sleek German cars dotted the driveways. We'd all heard stories: There were houses here where they still had slaves, or even elevators — one kid I knew swore up and down he'd been in a home that had a drinking fountain in it, mounted right in the middle of the entry-hall wallpaper.

My father and I had been to the CC of Lamartine before, but only on Mondays, when the course was closed, or late on rainy afternoons — to find a deserted hole where I could work on short irons and bunker shots. We had always sneaked onto the course: using an obscure back road, parking in a cul-de-sac in a housing tract where construction hadn't started yet, pushing our way through foliage, our heads on watchful swivels.

My father's posture was always a little stooped on those occasions, and the snap was gone from his step; his eyes roved the landscape nervously. Once, we were scooping up shag balls on number sixteen when my father spotted — in the distance — someone bouncing toward us in a cart. We headed into the undergrowth, my clubs clicking against my father's back as we ran, the shag balls clomping in their satchel. With my scotch-plaid kiddie bag strapped over his shoulder and his forefinger to his mouth, my father looked like a low-rent Robin Hood.

After a few minutes, the man stopped stomping around and shouted into the swamp, "This is Grant Lipscomb, PGA Professional, speaking. If I catch you scumbags trespassing again I will prosecute to the fullest extent of the law. Bank on it! I won't warn you but once." He paused. "Do you hear me? I know you're in there." He squatted to pick up a ball we hadn't shagged. "You boys missed one," he said snidely. "Ooh, and it's a dandy — a Kro-Flite. I wouldn't want you going home without your Kro-Flite."

With that, he lobbed the ball into the woods and waited, hands on hips, as though we'd be flushed from our hiding place by the bait of a twenty-five-cent, out-of-round Kro-Flite. After a few seconds we heard a chuckle from Grant Lipscomb, PGA

Professional; we'd turned out a hint smarter than he'd given us credit for. "I think I said this was your only warning, gentlemen," he continued. "I meant it."

Sweat stood out on Dad's upper lip. His face was pale. Crouched among the cypress knees, a finger to his lips to keep me quiet, there was nothing heroic about him: He was just another craven interloper, another can't-pay stiff holding a chintzy Kmart kiddie bag, hiding in the woods from the sheriff of Shangri-La. My father's legs were strong (he's always had the biggest calves I've ever seen, like torpedoes encased in skin), but his crouch that day was weak and quivery; he had to brace himself. When we finally came out, our feet were wet, and Dad kept his eyes low to the ground, as though he was looking for a ball we'd missed retrieving. When we reached the car, he touched me on the shoulder. He seemed to be looking through me. "I can do better, Brian," he said, "I can do better." We didn't go to the club much after that.

So it was with genuine shock that I watched my father turn onto Pill Hill on my ninth birthday; it led directly to the front entrance of the club. No side streets, no turnoffs, nowhere to hide. I had thought we were going for a ride in the new car. I shrank down in my seat, pressed my face into a button: The new wheels had made him overbold, and humiliation was waiting for us at the gate. But we made it. Dad began whistling as he pulled between the fancy brick half-columns at the entry, nearly sideswiping a mortar pineapple perched atop one, and I peeked through my fingers. We passed the driving range. A few well-dressed hackers were pounding balls; they turned around in bland curiosity, and my father waved.

I was amazed to see that the members' golf bags were, by some miracle of affluence, standing at attention behind them instead of lying on the dewy ground like the bags at Bird o' Paradise. Off to the right I could see the tenth tee, the eighteenth green, and the graceful, glassy black pond they shared. The grass was impossibly green, and pine trees three times the size of the ones at the muni lined both holes. The flags of the nation, South Carolina, and the United States Golf Association whipped in the wind high above the Tudor clubhouse. Here was the Promised Land.

My father parked the car, plunked his heavy key ring with a finger so that it clicked and swayed. He turned to me and smiled. "Son," he said, "this is your club now. You can play here anytime you want. Anytime your heart desires."

I swallowed thickly, nodded. Here?

"This is," my father announced solemnly, "a layout by the Great Robert Trent Jones." I knew, I knew. Robert Trent Jones was held in higher esteem at my house than Jesus. Water into wine was parlor magic, no great shakes; Robert Trent Jones had turned scrub pine and swamp bottom into Elysium. My father invoked his name with veneration, and never without the adulatory adjective: Ivan the Terrible, Richard the Lionhearted, Andre the Giant, the Great Robert Trent Jones. He was the club's crowning glory, the source of its magnificence.

"If you can learn to whip a Jones, son," my father continued, "you can flat *bulldoze* any golf course in the world."

"You mean," I stammered, "we're not trespassing?"

My father permitted himself a smile. "We belong," he said slowly, oozing satisfaction; and then he led me in to introduce me to the pro, Grant Lipscomb, that former figure of fear who now turned out to be just a turtle-bellied man in blinding white shoes. There were no Kro-Flites under his counter, no scotch-plaid kiddie quivers to smirch his shop.

Hatch was there that day, at eight years old already the cock of the walk. He'd won the Peewees' Club Championship, thrashing all comers eleven and under, and was something of a celebrity among his peers. He even had an entourage — a tow-headed kid named Ryan and this gangly, double-jointed goof whom Hatch called "Antenna." I didn't know them because they went to school out on Five Chop Road, at one of the academies founded when the Feds finally began enforcing desegregation. There hadn't been any other juniors at Bird o' Paradise, just lunchpail foursomes, old couples with pullcarts, the occasional hustler with tattooed forearms and a sunburned face.

Hatch (back then he was called "Oz") was sitting on an abandoned greens mower drinking a Coke, and his flunkies were nearby, putting on the practice green beside the first tee, when I made my way down to tee off. My father had told me he'd be back at sundown. I was eager to explore my new domain, to discover the snares and hazards the Great Jones had laid out for me.

I was toting my new golf bag, the biggest one I had ever owned. It was as tall as I was, and my cut-down clubs floated around the top of it, hung up by their necks on the dividers. I was proud of my new sack. It was bright chartreuse, trimmed in blinding orange, and bursting with secret compartments . . . a beauty. It had a tee-holder, a scorecard clip, umbrella loops; its zippers gleamed goldenly. And — best of all — the bag was covered, in crisp royal blue, with golf axioms: "Keep your head down," "Replace all divots," "Drive for show, put for dough."

I strode past Hatch and his confederates without a look, switching my bag to the shoulder where they'd have the best angle to admire it. Preening a little — I belonged, after all.

Ryan and Antenna bent double with laughter. "Looks like the Mystery Machine on Scooby Doo," offered Ryan, loudly.

"Public-school butthead," the gawky kid chimed in.

I looked down at my white knee-socks, my red golf shoes, my formerly gorgeous new bag, and had to choke back the tears. There would be no belonging here. In desperation, I spun away from my tormentors — and spotted a plot of new sod on the teebox. Just in order to be doing something, I stuck my tee into that inviting patch of grass, set my ball on it. I glanced behind me and saw the three of them still sniggering. I stepped up and let fly.

As the drive landed, 160 or so yards down the fairway, I heard Hatch say, "That public-school butthead can kick y'all's asses."

I kicked Hatch's, too, but he didn't seem to mind. We played five or six nines a day that summer, and we've kept in touch (well, vaguely) ever since. Hatch went away to Woodberry Forest during my last two years of high school, but he played his college golf at Clemson, where we were rivals again during my final three seasons.

Hatch's father is a cardiac surgeon who's made a fortune clearing plaque out of the arteries of textile tycoons up toward Spartanburg; more important, he married into the oldest of the old money, which is how Hatch came to be so filthy rich and filthy reckless. . . .

"Hey," Hatch interrupts from the passenger seat, "you mind if I light up?" He holds up his slender cheroot and the smart silver guillotine he uses to trim it. "Cuban, my man. Taste the quality."

Hatch may be the only twenty-five-year-old in America who smokes hand-rolled fifteen-dollar cigars. He's prone to broad gestures, high volume, ostentations — like he's playing his life to the most distant balcony. Being trapped in a car with Hatch is like watching Party Day at Nuremberg in 1934 from three feet away. You count yourself lucky if you don't get clocked in the cods by a goosestep that got away.

On cue, he purses his lips and shoots the smoke out of the side of his mouth and through the window. "You seem awful quiet," he says. "All well with the old ball and chain?" Hatch is the kind of guy who tells quadriplegic jokes. But nice, of course, real nice, the soul of gentility; Rosa wishes I were more like him.

"I'm OK," I say, but I'm dismayed to hear a puling note in my voice. I can't possibly want to talk to him about this. Pearls before swine . . . plus he might report to Rosa. I have my suspicions there. Sometimes she knows things about tournaments that *I* haven't told her.

"The doctor is in," announces Hatch, casting aside his newspaper, folding his arms. "It's time once again for Dr. Oz's Shrink Rap. Hit me, sir, lay it right on. No sin too low, no shit too deep."

I wait for a minute to see if he'll lose interest, but his cigar ash glows at me, an implacable eye.

"Yes?" asks Hatch finally, stretching the vowel beyond its breaking point.

"She wants me to quit."

"Uh oh," the wise doctor proffers. "Nasty." This I already know.

"She wants a kid."

"Oh," says Hatch, brightening, "is that all? It's obvious, then. What she *wants* is a rugrat — that quitting stuff is just to get your attention." He grins. "Problem solved."

"And how are we supposed to manage that?"

"Well hell, Brian, that's easy enough; you've been married for years. Do I have to lead you to it?"

"You can kid around all you want, Hatch," I say. "You're single, and loaded. I'd have a family to consider. Keeping a kid in carrots and milk isn't cheap, and it's hard to change diapers long-distance."

"Don't get bent out of shape," says Hatch. "I'm only pointing out that you act like everything is so fucking hard. Last year there were forty zillion kids born. Just stick it in and wait nine months, then do what you have to do to get by. You can be dumb as a box of hair; that wall-eyed kid down on the square with the shunt coming out the side of his head is a daddy, for Christ's sake. So are Pat Robertson, Leon Spinks — how hard can it be?"

"Fatherhood is a full-time job," I insist. "A trust. A minefield. It's rife with respons —"

"Blah blah fucking blah," says Hatch loudly. "You have no worries. You've got a great wife, a house, parents who offer every other day to spot you funds. You play fucking *golf* for a living. You even get to hang with me, from time to time. Life is sweet, but you're too antsy to enjoy it." He waves his hands dismissively.

"Easy for you to say. It's not your — not your burden to bear."

Hatch convulses with impatience. "Check that," he says. "I

take it back. You *are* right to be worried about Rosa dropping a kid. But not because you're poor, because you're cinched up too tight to be a good anything. They could harvest diamonds from your colon. You're a championship-caliber flake, Brian."

This is the kicker. Being called a flake by Oswald "Hatch" Clement, King of the Flakes — that's too much to take. Having heard that golf balls whose cores are warm fly farther, he drags that stupid toaster-oven around with him. In motel rooms he plugs it in, sets it to *Lightly Toast,* and wraps his Titleists in damp towels to heat them overnight. In the morning he has to pull them out with oven mitts, and he can't put bare hand on balata without raising blisters until he's finished six holes. He fusses over the damn things like they're liable to hatch — hence the nickname.

Once I walked into our motel room on a Saturday afternoon and found Hatch standing motionless between the beds, peering at the closed curtain. On television the Celtics were playing the Hawks, but Hatch's attention was fixed on a sheet of paper taped to the drape, a sheet on which he'd drawn a giant black dot. Leaning far forward, like a ski jumper in flight. Face in a grimace. Staring.

"What are you doing?" I asked.

"Shh . . . I'm enhancing my concentration skills. At my plateau of near-yogic intensity, it requires absolute silence."

I watched for a few seconds. His eyes never wavered.

"Who's winning?" I asked.

"Celtics," answered Hatch, not missing a beat. "Eighty-six to seventy-nine. Dominique sucks; the Human Jheri Curl is constantly costing me money. Now let me be. Improvement at this level doesn't come easy. So saith the man."

And he's calling me a flake?

"Just make some money this week," Hatch continues, puffing on his cigar. "Show Rosa you can play the game. Don't be such a goddamn deep thinker. Have some fun." He pauses, tamps his ash on the window frame. His irritation has passed. I'm supposed to be well now. This discussion is over.

Hatch is a pain to travel with, but there are advantages to having him along, too. He insists on paying all fuel costs, cuts my lodging expenses in half. We've known each other for fifteen years, so we're comfortable together — kind of. He's never boring. And Hatch is one of the most popular players on tour. He gets me into things: poker games, nights out, pro-ams, home-cooked meals, big-money cakewalks against locals with delusions. The first year out here I was a loner, like Bird, and had a reputation as a clubhouse intellectual — on the Mower/Stripper Tour, all it takes is being spotted in the company of any book thicker than a yardage chart. Keeping to yourself out here makes people suspicious, engenders myths. It can be a solitary life.

As we speed through the Sandhills (through Columbia, past St. Matthews, past Orangeburg), Hatch emerges now and again from his newspaper cocoon to read me a snatch of some offbeat story or other: A gravediggers' strike in Ypsilanti has left them stacking corpses in aluminum sheds donated, for publicity, by a local hardware store; a frat rat at Bowling Green smashed a liquor-store window with a forklift and drove off with thirty cases of beer, was tracked by a trail of shards, empties, and blotto alleycats; Ed Ott, Hatch's favorite baseball player, suffered two passed balls in an inning last night against the 'Stros. My team, the Braves, is already fifteen games out, and it's not even June. "Mathematical elimination fever," smirks Hatch. "Catch it."

◎

I remember watching Roadrunner cartoons as a kid. Whenever Wile E. Coyote ended up over a chasm, his feet dug into the empty air as though it were solid ground . . . until that moment, always a little delayed, when it dawned on him that there was nothing below but space. Only then did gravity call its bets. Wile E. turned to the camera, waved forlornly, and sank like a stone.

You run into that "Perception is reality, gravity holds no sway" argument a lot in art history classes, and I've always been attracted to it. I even spent some time my freshman year (before Rosa finished renovating my life) hunched over stoneware mugs at a place called the Con Leche Café, babbling about George Berkeley. The femme *bohêmes* dug me. I felt smart. Those were heady times.

It's tempting to think that if you really felt like it, you could change any detail of your world by willing it — you could blot out anything merely by diverting your attention. *Esse est percipi,* to be is to be perceived — so if you refuse to percip that snotty fuck with the Mercedes roadster, then he can't esse. It's a hell of an appealing way to think.

But it turns out to be just the prisoner's way of making his cell a home. It's better, the reasoning goes, to look the chasm in its eye than to cave in to idiot gravity because it's the Law. You get to preserve at least the husk of free will that way, and maybe you don't feel quite like the pawn you are.

But I'm not a freshman anymore. The Bishop's beliefs take more imaginative energy than I have, than anyone over twenty-one has. It's flat-out work, being the creator, remaking the world from scratch all the time. Better to believe in the enduring power of inertia, it seems to me. Better to believe things stay the same unless something comes along and changes them, something you can measure. I like for the rules to be observed. Gravity is less frail and flimsy and contingent than perception; it's more reliable than emotion. I believe in it.

The downside, of course, is that my way robs you of useful illusions, of necessary myths. If you don't believe on a given morning that you can wax every golfer there is, why bother to peg it up? Why leave your bed? Ignorance beats the hell out of the clear-eyed perception of danger: If Mr. Magoo could see, the old geezer would be a basket case.

When I walk off a cliff, it never occurs to me to disbelieve in gravity. I accelerate at sixteen feet per second per second, like a tangerine or a waffle iron. Sentience is no help to me.

Meanwhile, the bankrupt live like kings; cancers wither into remission; Hatch goes his merry, clueless way; the oblivious float above us like unblinking stars. In every theology, the entry into knowledge is a fall.

So I do the worrying for two. I have to.

During the first year of my marriage, I fretted every time Rosa left my sight. If she was five minutes late, I panicked. I'd tell myself she had until a count of a hundred to get home before I assumed the worst. Her faith was too simple. She didn't watch her back, trusted completely in her laggardly God. It was up to me to keep an eye open. So I'd mouth the numbers, each syllable a beat, to a hundred and beyond, until the rhythm was no longer enough to stave off terror. It was like going mad in slow motion.

Once the counting was done, I would imagine every kind of disastrous death for her. I thought if I outcreated Fate, if I kept a step ahead of its plotting, I could save her. No detail could be spared: I had to conjure the sandy shoulder lying in ambush along a curve; the rapist with running facial sores tugging on his mask and black gloves while humming a Viennese air; the cracked oak branch measuring its plunge to her windshield; the dowdy doctor's wife backing her Lincoln out of the driveway — slowly, Fate whispers to her, slowly, a little faster, depress the accelerator just a little harder, NOW — just as Rosa turns the corner; a heart attack in the cash-only lane, Rosa collapsing across the conveyor atop her leafy greens; an aileron crimped by the wind's icy fingers and a fiery crash in a stand of pines.

I had to see Rosa lying there, powdered glass sparkling on her face, body twisted like Hand-pulled taffy. It was the only way to save her. And when she pulled into the driveway unscathed, singing, I resented her for not recognizing the dangers that lurked. Exactly like Hatch.

"Aren't we a worrywart?" Rosa would say, nipping my ear as she brushed by and bounded onto the porch. "You look *awful*. Need a drink? I picked up some wine. Well. Are you coming in?" The door would slam.

I was crazy with concern. And when I confessed, when I told her all about it, she said only this: "I have two responses, dear. One — trust unto the Lord. Two — by all means, seek professional help."

I got over it. Inertia works two ways.

○

"You know who you play with Thursday?" asks Hatch, looking over my shoulder. On the northbound side of the interstate is a billboard advertising honeymoon suites at South of the Border: "Pedro sez, 'They're *heir* conditioned.'" We've just passed a black-water river called the Maniscaloon. This is the Lowcountry.

"Yeah, I called down. I tee it with Ripper and Bird. We're the last group Thursday and the dew-sweepers Friday. You go off around one Thursday and nine Friday, with Cyclops and Mellichamp."

"Great," huffs Hatch. "The Personality Twins." He's honestly miffed. Hatch thinks he's out here to be entertained. He may not have to make a living, but most of us do.

Cyclops is a nice enough guy. He's the only one-eyed golfer I've ever met, a forty-year-old hustler from Florida with skin as leathery as a gator's. He spent fifteen years on the old minitour circuit, living out of a trailer attached to his van, bankrolling himself with a variety of hustles having to do with his dead eye. I've seen it; it's a milky, glowing, awful thing — looks like those pictures of the galaxy you used to see in *National Geographic*. It makes him look crazy, like the rot extends back to his brain.

'Clops usually hides his diseased orb under patches his wife, Regina, sews from swatches of scrap cloth — she caddies, cooks, lives with him in the trailer. He's a brooding, silent player, too busy translating what he sees into three dimensions to chitchat with Hatch. He *needs* to make a check, so he grinds. On the course, Regina pitilessly enforces quiet around him; she nearly always has a dirty finger to her lips. She's a tiny woman, barely half her husband's size, and her habit of going braless under tube tops resulted in a new caddie dress code a couple of years ago.

When I first joined the tour, Cyclops tried to befriend me. He was, pathetically, the closest thing our tour had to an elder statesman: an overcooked, chain-smoking gambler who made his home in a tin can. One day when Regina was away — hunting fabric at the rummage sale of a dying motor court, or maybe lurking in the local library's stacks to shush frightened children — Cyclops asked me over for coffee. It was maybe my third week on the SGCT; we were in Valdosta for the Okefenokee Open. His trailer had long been banned from tournament sites for esthetic reasons, so I drove to the ragtag campground where they'd hitched up. Cyclops and I climbed into the trailer (I could feel it sink a few inches as we stepped in) and settled into captain's chairs. The low table between us was tiny, maybe fifteen inches square, and we gawked at one another's knees and drank; he smoked. I complimented the chairs, and Cyclops demonstrated their ability to spin 360 degrees. "Yours too," he suggested, and I complied with a thin smile. I couldn't believe how grim the scene was: the campground, the dingy trailer with its aluminum floor showing through worn carpet, everything stained seedy sepia by cigarette smoke, the cases of tuna and deviled ham stacked beside Regina's sewing machine. The coffee was surprisingly good, but the cups were chipped and discolored. My eyes strayed to the rumpled bed, and then I spotted a pair of gravity boots mounted and carefully braced on the ceiling. They were bright, new, optic yellow. Cyclops grinned, grew suddenly loquacious. "Ah," he said, "you've seen the old marriage bed. Here's some advice, Schwan: If you ever decide to live in a van, find yourself a woman who's small and limber." He winked. "My Regina could be a goddamn acrobat. She can near about kiss her own ass." He took another sip, raised his cup. "Anyhow, welcome aboard. Don't hesitate to ask for help if you need it. Hit 'em good, buddy. And if you ever need wholesale canned meats, I'm your man."

I was nonplussed by all this, a little. I got into my car and left the campground, making a point not to notice the cinderblock shithouse, the prowling cats, the underthings drying on shrubs, the ring of toppled bedsprings and game freezers around the caretaker's double-wide. Why notice? This had nothing to do with me, after all. Cyclops's life had nothing to do with mine.

I drove back to the motel, and then, thinking it would make me not a prick but a raconteur — one of the guys — I retailed the whole thing to Hatch. He had a good snort, and before long — guiltily, shamefully, but with a rush of relief — I joined in. I couldn't help it. It seemed laughable, at the time, almost. I still believed in myself then; I'd suffered a brief setback, but the world would soon be set right.

I admit it; I laughed. *If you ever decide to live in a van . . .* sure, Cyclops, I'll seek your wisdom. I wouldn't want my misinstalled gravity boots to cave in the ceiling. *Don't hesitate to ask for help if you need it . . .* if there's a deviled-ham famine, I'll know where to come.

But that life doesn't seem so ridiculous now. Bully for Cyclops and his practical engineering; bravo for the flexible Regina. May their trailer rock long and loudly; may there be pleasure in every position, and may that ceiling never fall. One day a few weeks ago I found myself paging through the *Swap & Shop,* pricing used camper tops. Putting my accounting skills to good use, Rosa, just for laughs — do you know what my annual motel expenses are? I thought maybe you'd come along on a trip now and then; it'd be an adventure, a way to see the country. Wouldn't you like that? But when I flashed back to that day when I'd spun in the captain's chair and peered into the Old Marriage Bed, I got a queasy feeling, and I stuffed the newspaper into the bottom of the garbage.

Hatch started calling the two of them Dell & Travers, after a roving carnival he went to as a kid, and every time he saw Regina, he'd say, "She looks a hell of a lot better upside down, I bet." I chuckled along. That was the easy way, and easy was what I wanted.

Glenn Mellichamp, on the other hand, is one of the few guys on tour who's defied Hatch's gift for nicknaming. He's a gaunt Dakotan who chain-smokes Camels, pounds range balls after every round. Can't hit it out of his shadow, hits every iron thin, but around the greens can get it up and down out of a cement mixer. The result is that he's always around par, never much better, never much worse. He's been out here five years, since the SGCT began. I've never heard him speak except to answer someone's question . . . usually the second or third time it's asked.

"They've stuck me with the two deadest beats on tour," Hatch is complaining. "Tweedle blind and Tweedle dumb."

"They're trying to spread you entertainers around, make sure nobody gets gypped out of a floor show. Would you rather have Ripper?" Ripper is an Alabama country boy with a bright red face and one of those skimpy caterpillar mustaches. He grunts mightily on every shot, swings hard enough to corkscrew himself into the ground. He never talks, but he has a country boy's lack of self-consciousness about bodily functions. I've seen him sidle up to trees not ten feet off teeboxes, not thirty feet from back patios, and whip it out. His farts ring out like rifle shots, and after them he looks over at you, smiles, sighs contentedly. He expertly spits balls of snot at innocent trees, tee markers, passing chipmunks. You can find him, mornings, in the locker room, bloodily excavating an ingrown toenail with a penknife and wearing the grin of a boy blowing up frogs with firecrackers.

"Aw, you don't give Ripper enough credit. He's fun to watch at least. The Human Whoopee Cushion. It's Bird I'd be worried about, the loony Limey. Do you two have something going? It seems like you play together every week."

"He's South African, not English."

"Same difference. He's got the hot pants for you."

"Come on, Hatch, give me a break. It's not like Bird has any control over pairings."

"This makes four tournaments out of five. Are you saying that's not weird?"

"No, I'm saying it's luck of the draw."

"Black magic, man. The guy is up to creepy *E-vil*."

"He's not so bad, most of the time."

"You're the one who almost stove in his skull at Norfolk, Clutch, not me. Don't act like I'm dreaming this up. Mother-fucker is spooky. For one thing, he's got some kind of voodoo thing going. Somebody told me he was waving grass in the air and mumbling witch words before the Toe ham-sandwiched that ball O.B. last Sunday that handed the tourney away. This source, who must remain nameless, told me he heard the words *banana slice Satan*."

"Oh, for God's sake," I protest. "You can't trust the Toe." The Toe got his name because he never seems to get a bad lie. His footwork is fancier than Astaire's.

"I never said it was the Toe."

"Hmmph."

"No, really, I mean look at him. A face like a hatchet, hair like the Shark. I say it spells black magic. The boy is a witch."

"Warlock. A man witch is a warlock."

"A Manwich is a meal." Hatch rolls on, the Ban-Lon juggernaut. "He's got his head either in a book or up some bird's ass at all times. Nobody knows where he stays, where he stuffs his face. Nobody ever sees him out. Far as we know the guy has never eaten, or taken a dump, or even . . ."

"I've seen him take a slash," I say. "I can put that rumor to rest. The man contains a working bladder."

"OK," Hatch allows, "but only liquids. The other's still in doubt. Besides, nobody ever laid eyes on him before he started playing the Blade-and-Titty — even though a bunch of guys played Division II in college, just like he claims. You don't get that good without somebody taking notice, Brian. And I hear his father is up to his *cojónes* in diamond mines, but Bird drives that piece-of-shit Pacer. There's the watch-the-birdie crap, all that deep-thought mumbo jumbo — and his backseat is like a goddamn lending library for freaks."

"He can be annoying," I agree, "but he means well. I'm sure there are explanations."

"You sound like a chick defending her deadbeat boyfriend to Daddy. You better be careful. That guy wants something out of you." Hatch lets his wrist flop.

"Oh, so now you really think he's gay."

"He may not suck it, but he'll hold it in his mouth till the swelling goes down. Shit no I don't 'think he's gay.' I *know* he's a flamer, and you're the lucky pincushion he's got his faggot heart set on. He's somehow setting it up so you play together every week."

Bird is peculiar, and he did piss me off in Norfolk — but Hatch's homophobia is such that he thinks every guy he's never actually seen astride a woman is gay. Sex isn't it, though I admit that the playing-together thing has become a little odd — it's beyond simple coincidence. We've been in the same group for nine of my last eighteen rounds, and Bird does seem pretty tight with the tour director. But why me, of all people? What could he possibly want from me?

Two weeks ago, at Southern Pines, there was a hellacious thunderstorm. As the klaxon sounded to suspend play, Bird fatted a simple wedge into a bunker with an eight-foot lip — left himself a fried-egg lie, very little green to work with. We made our way to a wooden lean-to at the edge of the woods. It reeked of cheap disinfectant; the floor was a crumbling slab covered with worn Astroturf; in the bathroom, the urinals were rusted through. Other guys straggled in, soaked to the bone, keyed up, vexed by the weather or their play or both. The shelter was tiny and rickety, and we were lined up shoulder to shoulder against one wall, packed like immigrants in steerage. We stowed our clubs in the women's restroom, the driest repository we could find. Every thunderbolt rattled the roof.

I was standing next to Bird, who should have been angry and apprehensive — the horn had shrilled at the top of his backswing, and he'd noticeably twitched, chubbed his shot something awful: Bogey would be a solid score from the jail his ball was in. It wasn't his fault. But even in this reeking madhouse, amid the plaints of a dozen damp and discontented peers, he was calmly reading a book he'd unzipped from the pocket of his bag — Nietzsche's *Genealogy of Morals*. The margins were thick with notations. Bird's right arm and my left were jammed together so tightly that every time he flipped a page I could feel his elbow digging into my triceps for purchase. He had a pencil behind his ear that he would occasionally haul down, cupping his fingers over the lead to avoid spearing me with it, to mark a passage.

Near us, the hue and cry went on: So-and-so's grips were damp now, color him done; somebody else couldn't play worth a rip when the barometric pressure was too low, something about his thin southern blood; a third unfortunate had a three-foot stack of fresh towels in his car but had brought only one on the course, and that practically the size of a Kleenex. Bird kept reading.

When the storm had finally passed and the klaxon sounded again, as the other players prepared to resume their rounds, Bird turned to me and said, out of the blue, "Brian, are you alarmed or a bud of pry?"

I stood there goggling at him. His accent had thrown me off. What? Was I a what? I pretended I hadn't heard. Around us I could hear the hum of commiseration. That seemed the safest topic, so I started into my litany of protest: "It's going to suck out there now. The greens are waterlogged; the fairways are lakes. They ought to call it quits for today."

"Brian," Bird repeated, "would you consider yourself a lamb or a bird of prey?"

I shrugged, trying to look thoughtful instead of puzzled.

"Well," he continued, tapping his nose, "we shall see. We shall see. The bird of prey takes advantage of changes in conditions."

He smiled an inscrutable smile, fetched up his bag, and went back to work. (Bird carries his own clubs because a caddy would cramp his style; most of us out here eschew spear-carriers because we can't afford them.) He quickly dug his feet into the soaked sand, glanced carelessly at the flagstick, hooded the face of his wedge a little, and knocked his bunker shot stony — another kick-in par. Meanwhile I three-putted from fifteen feet. Another bogey. Another stroke closer to the end of my rope. Was I a what?

CHAPTER FOUR

Tuesday, 1:30 P.M.

WHEN I WAS A BOY, among the curing sheds and the package stores, the dogpens and clay fields, of what my mother called the Backcountry, Charleston seemed a City of Light: home to cobbled lanes, campaniles, baroque iron gates, statues cloaked in verdigris. Charleston, Mom never tired of telling me, was class: "This sofa," she'd say, backhanding the expanse of tatty plaid between us, bringing up a russet cloud, "would get us the heave-ho from Charleston. We'd be outcasts. And without a word said. It's instinct there, bred to the blood: A Charlestonian sees crushed velour and her veins seize up. Tacky is not put up with. Now I know full well a plaid will hide stains, but there are things it'll show, too. I'm not blaming Daddy, Brian, if he's a sow's ear he's a fine one, the best I know, but there's still no making a silk purse out of him. Do you get my meaning? Can you see this couch for what it is? This is tartan, Brian. Velour. Do you think they bother with Scotchgard in Charleston?"

"Yes, ma'am. I mean, No, ma'am." I didn't know why she was agitated, but I knew what was expected of me.

My mother is from Charleston — "Well, very near it, *very*," she would concede if Dad, roosting nearby, stirred, groaned,

and arched a doubting brow — and she's never tired of chron-
icling her girlhood, its splendid backdrop. The stone churches,
the assorted boats: pleasure cruisers cutting the gray chop of
the harbor; dredges; tugs; yachts; destroyers. Tour ferries, each
attended by a cortege of gulls. The low trees, the high sky. The
air clotted with wisteria and history's tenacious afterscent —
an aroma that becomes, as memory yields through the decades
to imagination, ever more precious and more dangerous: It'll
put a place to sleep.

My folklore professor at Georgia, a cranky halitotic whose
corduroy jackets gave off a whiff of brimstone and bananas,
contended that Sleeping Beauty's hundred-year trance was to
be read psychologically. The "putative nap," as he put it, was a
radical form of vanity, of self-involvement, and she needed
("Hmmpphh") love ("Hmmpphh") to bring her back to the
world. "Beauty wasn't," he claimed, "merely sleeping the sleep
of the just. Where's the anguish in that? The worthwhile evils
rot you from the inside, make you lose touch with the world.
Sleeping Beauty wasn't snoozing; she was, as they say, way into
herself. There's a common misconception that it began when
she pricked her finger on a spindle. But let's not forget: Sleep
overtook our beauty when she placed that injured digit in her
mouth, when she tasted her own blood." Charleston's that
way, a city whose long self-love — born of an incurable taste
for itself — could be taken for a coma.

That's not the way Mom sees it. In her mind Charleston is a
utopia, the last outpost of caste in a world beaten level by so-
cial erosion. It's a city where substance takes its rightful backseat to style, where everyone knows his station, high or low,
and nothing ever changes.

All of which is ironic. Until Mom was fifteen she never set
foot in the city, and then — "Country come to town," Dad reports, "in a big, big way" — only to help an older sister pick
out a wedding dress. My relationship with my mother centered,
all through my childhood, on a "hometown" in which she had
(and has) spent less than twenty-four hours in her life.

Mornings, Mom and I would often sit together before she packed me off to school (my father had to be at work by six), and she'd tell stories of Charleston. In grand detail she'd spin the tales of debutante balls she had never attended. "There were trellises bursting with tea roses, and the mothers had taken care not to buy their daughters gowns — by 'buy' I mean have made, you understand — that would clash with the décor or the flowers. The young gentleman who escorted me — his name was Jubal Manigault, and he was a certifiable dream-boat — came to the door behind a bouquet half as big as me, I mean *I*. I remember it had a calla lily in it, irises."

As she rhapsodized, Mom would squeeze her coffee cup in both hands as though trying to bleed it of heat. She was trans-ported by her invention, set free from brick box and Backcoun-try, from plaid sofa, linoleum, the son underfoot; hers was the unburdened smile of a Charleston girl on coming-out night.

She had left me in the front room, among the comic golf prints, the slipcovered chairs, my father's cedar sideboard lined with souvenir shot glasses from Pinehurst, Pebble Beach, Shin-necock . . . by myself now, though she hadn't budged from her place on the couch cushion. Through the swinging kitchen door, wedged open with a house shoe, I could see an open tub of pimento cheese, source of my lunch. I could hear, outside, the sprinkler's heavy thwick, could hear the spray change in pitch when it pounded the martin house Dad and I had rigged from a hollowed gourd. I looked again at Mom, still basking in Jubal Manigault's dreamboatish regard, and took my chance to stare. Her pretty hair in its morning riot. Her eyebrows, the outer ends upturned so that she seemed enthralled by whatever anyone said. The wrinkles beginning to gather around her eyes, the nose a pleasant, unfancy arrow to her blissy smile. The point of her chin, gone now slightly to flesh. And, below, her hands throttling the cup of tepid decaf.

My mother should have been dandling a china cup, tobacco

leaf, in dainty, manicured fingers. Instead, her nails were cracked and scarred, her knuckles blunt and knobbly. We had brought home the mug they whitened against from a plant picnic: "Hughes Hose," it read, "We'll Put It Out Quick."

She always came back shortly. The smile paled and shrunk, and with selfish relief I watched it devolve — lips closing slowly over her teeth — into the sad, small, musing grin that was characteristic of her. My mother — returned to me, mine again — pecked me on the cheek, mussed my hair. "Time to skedaddle, Brian," she'd say. "Now show Mama your teeth. Mmm-hmm. You take another swipe at your molars while I finish fixing your sandwich."

I adored her stories, and it didn't bother me (though my father thought it should) that she'd made them up out of whole cloth. I understood, more or less. Charleston was the city of her dreams, as it was of mine.

At night, drifting into sleep, I often thought of her as a girl, pressed between sisters in a salty, humid bed, stinking of the sea, hands ribboned with cuts from shucking the oysters her father had harvested — and thinking of the life she'd have in Charleston, all pekoe and Virginia reels and crinolines and harmonium lessons. In Charleston her hands would be milk, and when she slept she'd tuck them under the down pillows of her four-poster bed. She would never be jolted awake in the small hours by the roving elbow of a fellow dreamer: In Charleston my mother would be an only child, would be like me.

Whenever I wasn't at the golf course because of rain, Mom would chase me out of the trophy room/garage. "Quit practicing," she'd say. "Scoot now. God's telling you something when He makes it storm." I'm not sure I thought Jehovah opened up the heavens to scotch my putting drills, but I never minded going with Mom. She'd sit me in a beanbag chair in her sewing cubby and give me things to read. Often as not they had a link to Charleston: coffee-table books full of color shots of the Battery, Rainbow Row, the Citadel; *Southern Living* magazine, with its articles on "Balustrades of Lowcountry Plantations" or

"The Paris between the Ashley and the Cooper"; state histories bound in musty maroon; novels of manners. She made me memorize poetry: courtly verses by Archibald Rutledge or William Gilmore Simms (our bards), "The Cremation of Sam McGee," "Casey at the Bat," hucksters' songs from *Porgy and Bess,* inspirational schlock like "Somebody Said That It Couldn't Be Done." She enhanced my vocabulary with lists acquired by mail from the National Spelling Bee. (She didn't seem to see that usefulness in conversation isn't the spellmasters' first criterion in picking words. So I was the only kid on my block to know a supererogatory orrery when I saw one, or an antediluvian flibbertigibbet; meanwhile, I couldn't even talk decent weather.)

Often Mom looked up from her dress pattern, a needle between her lips, and smiled: "My little scholar," she'd coo. The needle made it come out more hum than speech, but the tune I knew and loved — a mother's pride. She went on: "Golf is well and fine for a boy, but there's more to life. You'll be a *Renaissance Man,* Brian. This world needs Renaissance Men."

This was her most cherished phrase, her loftiest ambition for me, and she devoted all her energies toward my achieving it. I had to squire her to every piano recital and road-show musical, every Footlight Players production of Shakespeare (they only did Falstaff plays because the one passable actor in town was the grade-school principal, a sodden pink ham of a man who was too loud and fat to play tragedy). One of my most vivid memories is of being propelled down dark aisles by my mother's heavy hand — planted, as always, between the shoulder pads of the blue blazer she trussed me in when we attended Art.

Her special obsession was that I should be able to identify native plants and trees: "The best men call things by their proper names," was the way she explained it. Mom harried me through yards, parks, and public gardens, making me commit to memory the names of flowers . . . and taking care to highlight those named after South Carolinians: "Brian, this fragrant

blossom is the gardenia, named to honor Dr. Alexander Garden, a fine gentleman and fellow Charlestonian." She said this
as though Alex had rambled with her along the banks of the
Ashley just last spring, swinging his cane, crowing about the
progress of his hydrangeas and summer-sweets or gallantly
keeping up his end of the dialogue; the good doctor had by
then, for two centuries, been mulch for cemetery jimson.

"Your father is a fine man, Brian," my mother informed me,
"but rough around the edges. He does love you; it's just that his
temper gets away from him. He wants you to play better golf
than he could, and it makes him crazy. Now he may think that
game is the be-all end-all, but a pastime does not a life make.
You have to be exposed to art, music, literature. It's a shame to
know more about elliptic grooves or dimples or whatever —
nonsense — than about history. But you can't blame your father altogether. He never had the chance to attend concerts or
plays, visit galleries; golf was as close to class as he could go.
No Renaissance Men in *that* family tree. Drunks and jailbirds,
jailbirds and drunks. Country lawyers. Scamps and rabble-
rousers. I want you to be more than that. You'll go to Chapel
Hill, Washington & Lee, or Princeton. Maybe even Sewanee,
where they still wear ties and robes."

I wasn't sure (as old Huck used to say) whether I'd rather be
civilized or boiled — and what boy wants to hear that his
mother's most exalted hope is that he should roam rural Tennessee in a floor-length gown? — but I treasured, in my way,
the hours with Mom in the cramped sewing room. A gooseneck
lamp beamed down hotly on my head. As I flipped pages, the
beanbag chair crackled. Mom sang quietly as she stitched,
tapped her feet on the dusky throw rug beneath her table; the
machine's intermittent whine served as accompaniment. Rain
drummed the strip of window. She looked beautiful there,
serene, though I realize now that she must have been bristling
underneath at the closeness of the walls, at having to live in the
prosaic upstate with a husband more ear than purse, a good
man but without the scantest hankering for the Great, a man

who might be born again, for Easter week, but who would never be *renaissed*.

Once, years before, she had made the mistake (an oyster girl's mistake, a naïf's) of thinking that my father, the articulate, handsomish, college-educated son of a small-town lawyer — a man who played *golf*, who drank port — was an aristocrat. She had traded, then, one crowded bed for another, one set of finger calluses for another. And though she wasn't really prone to regret (it being a slippery, slippery slope), she had never forgotten her misjudgment. Still, at close to forty, she was dreaming furiously of milk hands, a fresh birth, a bouquet half her size — of Charleston.

As a kid, my favorite story from state history was the failed British invasion of Charles Town in 1776; I couldn't get enough of it. When I was in fifth grade, the school librarian, Mrs. Hungerpiller, grew so tired of renewing one account of it that she checked it out to me for three months: "At the end of that time," she warned, "you may *never* sign this book out again. *Verstehst*, young man? Do you unterstent?"

I had persuaded myself (I don't remember why, but manias of the sort were commonplace with me) that just one copy of the story existed. Not only was the volume in my hot little hands the only one in Lamartine, it was the last copy *anywhere*. On no other cover was there this lurid illustration of a drowning British sailor, his mouth open in a death scream or last gasp, reaching from the spume with an imploring hand while behind him the Union Jack dangled from the splintered mast of a doomed (and badly foreshortened, as I recall) battleship. No other book contained the scurrilous attack (pp. 69–71) on the Brits for their inability to swim: "Empire indeed," scoffed the author, "whose mariners could not so much as execute the Deadman's Float!" The breathless phrase "Davy Jones's Locker," which appeared every three or four pages, I imagined to be the invention of *my* writer, whose rights to it were exclusive and absolute.

Faced with the inevitability, once my months were up, of losing the story forever, I vowed to learn it by heart. I labored, rainy afternoons, in the sewing room with Mom, and by the time I handed the book back to Mrs. H, the pages of Chapter 7 — "Showdown in Charles Town Harbor" — were badly dog-eared, stained with chocolate and concentration. But I knew the story line by line, inside out.

In early 1776 the British planned to attack the unfinished fort on Sullivan's Island and use it to bring the town to heel. Their numeric advantage over the colonial militia, commanded by William Moultrie, was staggering. It looked like a walkover. But General Henry Clinton was thwarted in every conceivable way, by both a determined band of colonials and, the author implied, a righteous God. A force of redcoat footsoldiers, set down on an adjacent island, couldn't wade across the deep channel; three warships ran aground on a devilish shoal; others, trying to escape a similar fate, had to limp in a dead calm through the American (American!) line of fire. Most remarkable of all, a heavy cannonade by British broadsides achieved nothing — the spongy palmetto logs of Fort Sullivan, chinked with thirteen-foot-thick layers of beach sand, held solid. The walls, it was said, swallowed cannonballs whole.

I thrilled to the words *swallowed cannonballs whole:* the rush of seeing justice thrust rudely down the throats of oppressors, of seeing infidels routed. Charleston, saved by soft trees, dune sand, and the hand of God.

After all that, the book informed me, a young hothead named Francis Marion fired a forty-two-pounder at one of the retreating ships, "for good riddance," and the offending frigate, its hull shattered, "sank with sullen joy to the bottom." For weeks I turned that phrase in my mouth like a sucking stone.

I nagged Mom into buying me a set of plastic boats, poked holes in them with an icepick filched from my father's workbench. Then I carried the punctured vessels to the pond so I could see them tilt, bubble, and spiral down through the black water with slow, slow dignity, full — I imagined — of the sullen joy, etcetera.

My favorite figure in the siege was Sergeant Jasper (a man too wonderful, too legendary, to suffer the indignity of a first name). When a lucky shot by the Brits splintered the fort's flagpole, the sergeant "leapt boldly over the bulwarks, amidst a fog of bullets and *anopheles,* to rescue his standard." The flag he saved was simple, a tiny silver crescent in a field of blankest blue; with the addition of the palmetto tree that had served so heroically, it became the state flag. The fort's name was changed to Moultrie. Jasper got his own county, farther downstate, whose year-round plague of mosquitoes is a kind of tribute, I suppose, to its namesake. Francis Marion grew into the Swamp Fox my high school was named for.

I haven't thought of the "sullen joy of sinking ships" in years. Strange: only now does it occur to me that the joy is out of place. I can spot the sullenness, the sullenness jumps right out at you — a ship would be sullen at sinking; the sailors grasping spars and beams or trapped in the hold might well be sullen. But the joy, where's that come from? Whose is it? There's no joy on the ship, certainly, or in it — what frigate wants to find itself cruising, of a sudden, among startled fish?

The answer is obvious. The pleasure has to come from outside; it has to belong to someone glad to see her go down. The verb is transitive, I guess: of *sinking* ships. The joy requires a firebrand with a cannon, an amateur historian with a chip on her shoulder, a kid with an icepick, a husband who can't stand happiness. The joy is the joy of destruction. We're cruel. We're selfish.

Rosa deserves better.

Hatch and I are approaching the coast. It's early afternoon, another scorcher. We're skirting the Cooper now, passing Goose Creek and Summerville, entering the spit of land that tapers, pinched between converging rivers, to almost nothing — to Charleston. This is the first time I've been here since Hurricane Hugo roared through less than eight months ago.

Last September, Rosa and I watched CNN all night as John Holliman adopted a wide, sturdy, bent-kneed stance in various windy locales, wrapped in a yellow slicker like the lobstermen of social-studies books. His bangs were plastered to his forehead, the thinning hair on top bunched like a cockeyed mohawk. Water crept across his face at peculiar angles, as though across a windshield. Awnings flapped deafeningly above him; the wind whined; the rain swirled behind like a test pattern. Rosa tracked the eye's progress on a grid she picked up at the grocery store — buy a clutch of bananas, a can of peas, and they'll throw in the means to chart a distant misery. From the quiet dark of our bedroom we kept vigil as the eye pushed inland and churned, more or less along the route of the interstate, toward the Midlands.

Even this far — twenty miles or so — from landfall, the trees look flayed and beaten; severed limbs and uprooted slash pines are piled along both sides of the highway. The bulldozers that have heaped them seem abandoned for the moment — lunch break, most likely. All the dozers are new, unlike the battered fossils you usually see road crews lounging around. These are shiny federal troops, part of the bailout effort.

I'd never been to Charleston till I joined the SGCT. My mother's parents lit out for Boca Raton about the time I was born, and whenever our family went to the beach in-state, my father insisted on the flashier charms, cheaper room rates, and "stuff to do" of Myrtle Beach and the Grand Strand. "Charleston is a goddamn mausoleum," he sniped. "And when your business is storing stiffs, you can't afford to be snotty about it." My mother didn't let his insolence pass, but her defense of Charleston was always bookish, formal, false. "Honey," my father interrupted, "*Then:* Huguenots. *Now:* bums, wharf rats, junkies, and navy squids. Are you with me?" This would provoke a spell of histrionic sighing from Mom, but she never tried to insist that we lump Myrtle and go to Folly Beach or Kiawah instead. She didn't want to visit Charleston either. Dad's grousing aside, she has always known, deep down, the distance between her brilliant figment and the washed-out city she painted it over.

Dad spent our vacations with me, playing golf and skeeball, riding rollercoasters, poking through (despite Mom's complaints about it being the "Halfwits' Museum of Dumb, Dumb, Dumb") the popsicle-stick Taj Mahals and the nose-ringed headhunters at Ripley's Believe It or Not. Meanwhile my mother walked the beach with her guidebooks to shells and shorebirds, read classic novels, crabbed in the tidal inlet. We'd be driving up the causeway from Highway 17, my father and I, on our way back from the Pavilion at Myrtle, and Dad would say, "Son, do you see your mother out there, up to her ass in muck?" I'd scan the featureless landscape until I caught sight of her, invisible up to her straw hat in the marsh grass she called nimble Will, dragging a chicken neck on a string along a narrow sluice of retreating water, a wide green net in her hand.

"What's wrong with her?" Dad would ask, chuckling. There was, beneath the usual crust, admiration in his voice; this was as close as he came to effusion. "Your mother has a screw loose," Dad would say, and lick the streaming goo from his ice-cream cone off his fingers. "She got seafood up the yin-yang all her childhood. She doesn't even *like* crabmeat; she's out there for the battle of wits. Trying to outsmart a thing that runs sideways, eats garbage, and wears its eyes on stalks."

When Mom came back to the house, the handle of her bucket bent by the weight of its haul, she let me rinse the crabs — thumb over the hose's snout for extra pressure. Then she had me upend the pail to drain the water, net pressed over the bucket mouth to prevent escapes. Once I'd popped back in any blues that managed to entangle themselves in the twine, I would lean over and watch.

A few feisty ones skittered on top, backing as far as they could, pincers arched and open. Below, others awaited their fate more calmly. Tiny bubbles formed around slits in their abdomens, and their gills crackled softly. "They're talking to you," Mom claimed. "Listen close." I always poked a stick into the bucket and drummed a fighter's carapace until it pinched my weapon. Then I swung it into the air — I wanted to flip it, determine its sex.

The first few times I ran away, shrieking; but my parents taught me how to take hold of the crustaceans, behind their rear claws — "Thumb and forefinger," Dad said, "like you're dipping snuff" — and after that I'd pluck the crab neatly off my stick and swing it (clicking futilely) over my head.

"Sook!" I'd cry. "And she's pregnant." Her abdomen was swollen, and orange as a sweet potato.

"No wonder she's mean," my mom would say. "Throw her back."

Afterward, in the kitchen, Mom let me dump a miniature croker sack of boil-spice into an iron pot. Then she'd lift me onto an idle stove-eye to watch her drop the wriggling crabs, still alive, one by one into the scalding water. Their green-blue shells went instantly orange. "One!" I counted. "Two! Three!" My mother laughed aloud as I ticked them off, her straw hat with its baby-blue sash crowning the counter beside her . . . both of us enjoying this seafood taken on her terms, the fruit not of commercial pots but of green string, putrid meat, and patience: the muddy pastime of the upper-middle-class vacationer. "How'd you like a little she-crab soup, Brian?" she'd ask. "Charleston style. It just so happens I know how to do it."

This year we're playing at a new resort that sits, among razor grass and scrub palmettos, midway between Charleston and Georgetown: the result, as usual, of greed, lax water-use rules, and a pliant loan officer . . . and not long for this world.

The Ile de Paris is only ten miles north of McClellanville, my mother's real hometown, which I've never seen. She was excited to hear I'd be passing through her neck of the backwater. "Be sure to look up the Jeffcoats and the Wannamakers and the . . ." she droned at me the other night on the phone. "They're good people, and they'd be more than happy to fix you a nice big pot of shrimp stew." Eventually I pretended to acquiesce, a bit crossly — knowing full well I won't make it to the Jeffcoats' et al. I have other worries: a marriage to save, a career. Bigger fish to fry.

South Carolina's coastal development has gone like the building of the transcontinental railroad; golf-and-tennis villas have spread south from Myrtle Beach through Georgetown and north from Hilton Head through Beaufort and Charleston. At Ile de Paris, it seems, they've finally pounded the Golden Condo into the marsh. You could drive the coast from Wilmington to Savannah without straying more than a smooth six-iron from an Ile de Paris or a Quahog Creek Plantation or a Wilde Pocosin Golfe & Racquette Clubbe. There's no escaping the game.

The courses are packed cheek by jowl, and they advertise like Vegas casinos — billboards, magazine spreads, even tip-ins with rental-car keys, all including package-deal prices. They have preposterous rococo names, tile-roofed condos, streets named after indigenous trees or the shrines of golf, pricy landscaping, gates like walled cities. Even carnival gimmicks. My father and I teed it up at one track near Georgetown, Heathergorse Linksland, which has a sky tram to whisk golfers from the parking lot over a homely bayou (the "Firth of Filth," my dad called it later) to the pro shop; there's a glorified carny in a Scottish-caddy getup to hoist your clubs into racks and slide home the safety bolt. "Play bonny well, gentlemen," he sings in his Dogpatch burr. "Hit 'em good. Enjoy. Tipping is appreciated — it's a right poor land, Scotland, and we do what we can."

Some vacationing rummy had vomited in the tram car, and the floor was covered with the kitty-litterish grit I recalled from grade school. Once we began bouncing over the spartina in our sour-smelling cage, Dad spoke up. "Just like the county fair," he said. "What kind of horseshit is this? The goddamn Optimists probably have a dunking booth on the back nine."

The SGCT is making its swing down the Atlantic seaboard from the Chesapeake to Jacksonville. Most places we play are new enough that you can still find sod seams on the greens; the saplings are tagged with surveyors' ribbon; as often as not, the turf is sparse enough that we get to roll the ball in the fairways (which goes a long way toward explaining why scores are so low). Many of these coastal-plain courses are like Dutch polders except reclaimed from scrub and sandspurs instead of the sea, and nature is held at bay not by dikes but by million-dollar sprinkler systems the courses don't get enough play to justify running. Most of these resorts are in the boonies and need to drum up play, to lure suckers to buy time-shares. All of them are strapped for cash.

Thinking a Mower/Stripper event will bring paying customers in its wake, even that it will scare up publicity in any appreciable amount, is a desperate gambit. We're small-timers; there are more important tours to pay attention to. So we often function as Chapter Eleven's avant-garde — and we rarely play the same course two years in a row.

In this case the developers may be in grimmer straits than usual; Hugo ripped through, I'm told, just as they were finishing the golf course. Since the storm's eye made landfall just fifteen miles southwest, and since a hurricane's intensest winds are said to be north and east of the eye, I'm expecting something not far removed from a lunar landscape.

Hatch is dozing, an Amana visor over his eyes. One foot sways in the onrush of air outside the window, and one hand is clamped over his gonads like he's warding off a blow. Ten miles to Charleston, maybe thirty to the golf course. Let him sleep.

I need a plan for the week. If I'm going to pull the fat out of the fire this time, I need a plan. The odds are stacked, of course, against me. I've never seen Ile de Paris, but I know. My game is tailored to the classic golf course — Merion, Pine Valley, Harbour Town — tight driving areas, swaybacked postage-stamp greens, harsh penalties for inaccuracy, not overly long. I'm best where par is at a premium, where caution and shotmaking guile are rewarded.

But that tends not to be true of resort links, especially before they mature, before they grow into their architecture. Even if a club has ambitions about hosting professional events, the design premium is on so-called playability, which means that the architect is in every case to leave an easy route for the unskilled player: no sizable carries, no banked driving areas or overhanging trees that would require bending an approach shot one way or the other, no mounded sea-serpent's-back greens, room to run up Roto-Rooter iron shots. If the turf is in bad enough condition that they let us move the ball in the fairways, but the greens are decent . . . somebody might shoot zero. It doesn't matter how long the layout is — the Ile's moneymen and the tour powers-that-be will do what's needed to keep scores down the first two days, hoping they can draw some fans from among vacationers sick of thrashing their way around rival courses in 110 whacks. There will be immature doglegs for the long knockers to sail it over without a thought, manicured bunkers filled with sand as soft as goosedown, dance floors big as carrier decks.

And the guys don't need much help; there are some marvelous players out here. The Snapper/Gold Club Tour is composed mainly of young bucks fresh from college, of hardened minitour vets like Cyclops, and of former hangers-on from the Show. We all missed out on the second-tier tours — Hogan, Canadian, South African — some by bad breaks, some by cracking under pressure, some, like me, by an abject country mile . . . and we're trying to stay afloat until next fall, when it's time to try to qualify for the PGA Tour again.

A good many of the college guys come, like Hatch, from privilege. Golf's a full-time hobby for them, and any winnings are lagniappe. For the rich boys, a missed cut means two more days to scuba-dive, a weekend junket to Nassau or Sea Island in Daddy's Cessna. Most guys out here, though, weren't so gently born. They don't have a pot nor a window — or, like me, have pots and windows beyond their means, and mortgages to go with them.

The tours with bigger money and more prestige conduct their events by invitation only. The SGCT, on the other hand, is essentially open. They keep the purses up by starting gargantuan fields — up to 210 guys — and letting just about anyone with four hundred dollars and a pulse tee it up. It's the deep-pocketed locals and dreamers and pretenders, hundreds of them, who make the tour possible. They shoot their pair of eighty-twos and go home smarting, but their entry fees go into the pot.

The tournament purses are basically our entry money, shuffled and redistributed by a middleman: the SGCT, Inc. Out here there are no corporate sponsors, no endorsement deals, no corporate tents, no million-dollar payouts. You fork over your fee, and you get it back if you make the cut — maybe with a little chunk of interest. You stay in marginal motels, eat bad food, take advantage of whatever meager extras the host club can afford: soft drinks, range balls, occasionally a plate of cold banquet chicken and waxy green beans. The tour is like a member-guest Calcutta where the only team you can buy a stake in is yourself.

The winner of an event pockets ten or twelve grand, but shares dwindle dramatically from there. Sixty players (plus ties) make the thirty-six-hole cut; the twentieth-place finisher makes only about eight hundred, and last will net you four-fifty. The reason for the odd purse structure is twofold — they want everyone who makes the cut to take home more than his entry fee, and they want to encourage aggressive play on the weekend, to satisfy any gallery (usually no more than a hundred lonely souls) they've managed to gull into coming out at five bucks a head. Most Sundays, the difference between seventy and eighty-five might be fifty bucks; the difference between seventy and sixty-five can be six or eight K. So you try to knock down every pin, no matter where you find yourself. It's a birdie contest.

My only hope is if the wind kicks up. These limberbacks can play it only one way — nuts out, don't leave anything in the bag, close your eyes and belt it. If there's an advantage to keeping the driver in the bag and boring the ball under the wind, running it up to greens, playing a little cute, then I can compete with anybody out here. Maybe I can pull a Fort Moultrie, fire my dimpled 1.62-ounce missile and nab for myself a pinch of glory. . . . A big check. A reprieve from Rosa.

But who am I kidding? The best I can hope for is to stall her a couple of weeks; I'll miss another cut sometime, Rosa will squawk again, and next thing I know I'll be doing spreadsheets for Special K's Kash and Karry and huffing through Lamaze.

A history lesson, Mr. Visionary: In 1780 the British returned to Charleston. They trounced the militia, occupied the town, won a victory bigger than Saratoga; Sergeant Jasper got run through with a bayonet. The city has been in decline ever since, even if it hasn't noticed.

It's over already, all but the shouting. So shout already. Shout and go home.

Charleston is, of course, a grand anticlimax. We're herded through at high speed by traffic. Hugo's spoor has been sprayed and scrubbed and deterged away, for the most part; we catch a whiff of it in the number of trucks hauling shingles or glass, in the sight of roofs covered, still, by blue tarps ballasted with brick.

"Jesus, I'd love to be a roofer in this town," says Hatch,

brought out of his slumber by the sweet smell of commerce. "Those guys are making a killing."

We rattle over the Cooper River Bridge, past Patriots' Point, where the USS *Yorktown* is moored, through Mount Pleasant on US 17. Occasionally there's a plyboard shelter at the side of the road, occupied by a lone black woman weaving — amid heat, blowing sand, gnats, exhaust — plain straw hats and baskets. We pass stands advertising clingstone peaches, boiled peanuts, berries, even turtle soup. At one, someone is touting "Fresh Tamotos" on a cardboard box flap; the sign appears to have been lettered in either nail lacquer or fresh blood. A man sits alone in a lawn chair under the shadow of a listing old oak, sipping beer from a forty-ounce bottle and waving, with unnerving placidity, at every car that rushes past. Along the roadside black men on bicycles made for children teeter past smashed dogs.

"Isn't this great?" asks Hatch. "Americana. What do you figure that chick gets for a boater hat?"

"Not enough," I say.

"Naw," he continues. "She's raking it in. She bought those lids and picnic baskets for two bucks apiece; she's just fiddling with that other to make you *think* they're handmade. It's scams like this that make America great."

"Oh, yeah," I reply. "Racial injustice always puts a spring in my step."

Hatch is peeved. "Save the documentary crap," he says. "You don't get to be everybody's voiceover. It's scary enough you get to be *yours*."

"I'm serious, Hatch. These people are victims. We exploit them. We play golf for a living."

Hatch glares at me, exhales. "Sure, they could have more, but they know how to take what they've got. I keep thinking you'll realize that the fatasses scooched into the booths at Waffle House are happier than you. All it takes is hot coffee, a slab of ham, one of those goopy pitchers of syrup. A key ring swinging off the belt. A little innocent flirting with the counter-girl. So you can spell better than they can — a lot of fucking good it does you. Quit feeling sorry for people who are better off than you are. It's insulting."

I want, badly, to dispute this. After a silent mile I say, accusingly, "Easy for you to say. You're white and loaded."

Hatch smiles at me. "As you like it, Brother Bri. As for me, I say honky guilt is an unclean thing. There's too much pleasure to be had. . . . What asshole ever told you anything was fair?"

We lapse into silence again.

◌

"What is that?" Hatch asks, pointing through the windshield, pulling me out of my morbid haze. Over the trees to our right is the tip of what looks like a bright-green oil derrick. As we round the curve I catch sight of the sign we've been looking for, "Ile de Paris Golf & Beach Club." The name stretches, in calligraphy so classy as to approach illegibility, over an arched sandstone gate you might see at a thoroughbred farm; no more than fifty feet behind it, the behemoth Hatch pointed at splits the sky, and what it is suddenly occurs to me. I slow the car.

"That," I tell Hatch, "would be the Eiffel Tower." The damned thing must weigh thirty tons. It's brand-new, sixty feet tall, made of what appears to be sloppily welded steel and spray-painted that grisly metallic green I remember from the miniature Christmas tree I had to make in grade school (macaroni on a cylinder of styrofoam with Elmer's paste, circa 1973, part of the permanent collection of the Schwan Museum, Lamartine, SC). The Eiffel is surrounded by a six-foot wall of razor thistle intended, I suppose, to discourage climbing. On our side of the barrier grass, "Ile de Paris" is spelled out in a bed of ornamental cabbage built up at the back for visibility. The road forks around, past a plat board promoting homesites for sale. The board bears a legend in a cartoon bubble, and alongside it, encircled by lightning bolts, a worm in a fedora — the brokers' anguilline shill. "Hang On Tight," reads the sign. "This Is One *Electric* Ile."

"I'm not," Hatch says, taking in the tower, the flowerbed, the eel, "a religious man, but I feel like shouting hallelujahs."

"Talk about your turd in a punchbowl," I say.

"The punchbowl's no great shakes, either," corrects Hatch, gesturing at the carnage around us. There are downed trees everywhere. Beyond the kitsch monument the wreckage of a massive live oak rests half on, half off the road. Too big to drag away without heavy equipment. It's a squat, denuded, graceless corpse; its roots hang obscenely in air like ripped-out wires. In eight months, all anyone has done for it is to tie a red ribbon at its crown, where it juts farthest into traffic — as though it's a jointlet of pipe overhanging a pickup's tailgate.

"For lo, though we romp through the alley of the shadow of pith," says Hatch, "we will fear no oval. All praise the big Redhead for our safe passage."

"Bill Walton?" I ask, getting into the spirit of the proceedings.

"Don't blaspheme, here of all places." He gestures *à l'Eiffel*. "This is a shrine."

Gawking at the damage, we drive the quarter mile or so to the clubhouse — which turns out to be a charmless square of stucco, but intact. I park at the near end of the lot, next to Bird's Pacer. While Hatch collects his clubs and shoes, I inspect the car. Hatch's chatter doesn't bother me, truly, but it wouldn't hurt to find some small confirmation that Soulsby and I have been thrown together by luck and not design. I'm in search of an honest augur, and any detail will do: any hint that Bird's life, like mine, is arranged and disarranged by bootless chance.

The Pacer appears held together by force of habit. The muffler dangles, prevented from dragging the asphalt by a soiled and frayed shoestring anchored through a hole in the bumper. Bird's backseat, where most wrinkle-conscious pros have mounted a shirt rack, is piled high with books and shreds of paper, and I can make out a few titles: *The History of Magic from Paracelsus to Mandrake; 77 Dream Songs; Exxon's Yearbook of Filling Station Design, 1957; Madame Bovary; Birds of Dixie; The History of the Damnable Life* of someone or another; *Hop on Pop.* There's a plastic tumbler full of suckers on the front floorboard. The driver's seat has one of those wooden covers that looks like a sheath of abacus beads. A pine-tree air freshener droops, fadedly, from the rearview. It's the car of a California guru, the kind of man who anoints his feet and subsists on shepherd's bread dipped in olive oil.

"What an asshole," opines Hatch, now looking on. I sidle past him and gather my gear. "Freak," he pronounces sadly, shaking his head. "Freak, freak, freak. But look on the bright side: If the fucker ever has to carry a six-foot hoagie sideways, he's got the wheels for it."

We've entered the clubhouse to register. "Down the hallway, two rights and a left," says the surly young waiter Hatch shanghais for directions. The kid turns and scurries through the empty dining room and into the kitchen. "Thank ye kindly, Salad Boy," says Hatch as the swinging door vibrates shut. We head down the hall. It's carpeted in trendy teal, lit at ridiculously close intervals by chandeliers. Every two chandeliers there's a big poster reading, politely, "No spikes, please." On each one somebody has written underneath, in angry red caps, the words *THIS MEANS YOU.*

There's a hubbub in an alcove to our left. A hefty woman is giving booming instructions to an audience we can't see. She's wearing a yellow visor of stiff plastic, a white shirt, and a tentish green skirt dotted with yellow Eiffels. Her breasts are a forbidding shelf. She's topped off the outfit with pompon socks and, in flagrant violation of the rules, Lady Daisy golf shoes; she's probably the reason for the pissed-off addendum.

"Now all you forecaddies listen up," she bellows. "I'll not

chew my cabbage twice." As we pass, Hatch cranes his neck to
get a look at the woman's auditors — a gaggle of bare-legged
schoolgirls wearing lime-green berets. The volunteers. The
gofers, bearers of standards, concessionairesses, scoreboard op-
erators, forecaddies. Nymphets all. I imagine they're about to
hear a speech about fraternizing with players, those slimy, here-
today-gone-tomorrow wolves who are too old for you, not to
mention drunken liars and disease risks to boot. We get an unfair rap, or at least only a partly fair one . . . or, well, at least a
*few* of us are chaste and kind.

Hatch quashes my try at indignation before I can even half-
mean it. "Ooh la la," he sings. "Yes, yes, yes. Welcome to Paree,
City of Love. Looks like I'll have to buy me some *hard* candy."

I'm suddenly weary. It's been a long trip, and I've overdosed
on Hatch. But I can't help realizing that there's triumph in my
exhaustion; I've stopped worrying for the moment. I'm at rest,
more or less. We're here, at the end of the line, on our way to
register. There we'll collect our start sheets, bag tags, yardage
books, scorecards, sponsor coupons, maybe a beer cozy or a
key chain. And after that, having shaken the hand of the vol-
unteer who's minding the table, having caught a glimpse (on
paper) of the allures and challenges of this new golf course,
having entered this new week where (at least until Thursday)
I'm tied with everyone else — having arrived at Ile de Paris,
there's nothing to do but go outside and tee the son of a bitch
up, play golf. It's time to go to work. Aim it at the Eiffel and
swing away.

It's a complex emotion, because what might be a *tabula rasa*
is tainted, already, by dread: a fresh start, yes, but the nagging
knowledge of what you've done with others. Every tournament
is a new opportunity to fall on your ass; every week brings a
resurgent joy, but also — yin's unshakable yang — a fresh pre-
sentiment of failure. Still, my mood isn't wrecked by knowing
the end it'll come to. Joys are necessarily fragile; they have to be
compromised, have to be tinged with sorrow or fear. Only a

fool's cup runneth over — if you can run it over you can run it dry, and that's a chance I'm not willing to take. Happiness is a form of balance; it needs its black *despite* or it's worthless.

It occurs to me that my anticipation has another element, the satisfaction of journey's end. Here I am, more or less in Charleston, at the end of my drive with Hatch, of my rope, of Rosa's patience. And my half-bred joy . . . maybe it doesn't take malice; maybe it doesn't take two. Here it is, mine, the feeling of a crippled ship contenting itself as it sinks through the silt of ages with the knowledge that its struggles are at an end — how much lower can you go, after all, than rock bottom? — and thinking *You can't*. You can't, Brian.

This is what nowadays passes for happiness in my life, the sullen joy of sinking ships.

But it can always get worse . . . and does. The first person we run into after registration is Bird, slouched in a wicker wing chair outside the pro shop, reading.

"Vaya con Dios, fellas," says Bird. He looks like the Sun King perched there, blond hair tousled, halo of wicker. But just a kid. Twenty-five, tops. He's wearing chinos, a plum-colored shirt, an irksome air of innocence. He lays the fingers of his right hand inside his book to mark the place, slides the spine to his beltline.

"Hello, Jim," I say. I'm feeling pretty good now, better. Bird's just young, that's all. He, too, will be a washout before you know it. I should take it easy — leave the young to their follies. I had my own hopes, once upon a time.

"Looks like Paris has been sacked," says Bird, gesturing behind us.

I'm waiting for Hatch to pull his conversational weight, but he's busy studying his feet, muttering "Freak."

"It's a mess," I agree. "How's the track look?"

"Not as bad as the road in. Greens are bumpy, fairways patchy, but not bad, all in all. They're going to let us lift and place in the short grass."

"Are you sure?" Damn it. Scores will be low.

Bird nods. "Read it in the pro shop." He goes on, without transition: "I've been boning up on local history" — he thumps the book with his left hand — "and I'm thinking of tootling down to Isle of Palms this afternoon for a little sightseeing. Thought I'd take a gander at Wild Dunes and then hop over to Sullivan's Island to see Fort Moultrie."

"Tootling," parrots Hatch, behind me, too low for Bird to hear. "Gander. Jesus Christ on a popsicle stick."

"Site of a grand humiliation for the British Navy," embroiders Bird. "I suppose you know all this?"

"What?" I ask, a little alarmed.

"You two *are* Sandlappers, aren't you? Born and bred? Look away, look away?"

"Uh-huh," I manage, barely above a whisper. "But Upstaters."

Bird smiles. His sun-burnished cheekbones slide back as smoothly as a trombone glide, and his lips part to reveal several hundred teeth. "I thought you two aborigines might like to tag along. Site of a heady victory for you Yanks, and all. Historic. Pretty day, too."

Hatch demurs with a loud, clear "Nope." I look his way for help. The chubby asshole winks at me, lecherously. I feel like someone is scissoring off my scalp.

I turn back to Bird. "I can't," I tell him, though — to my shock — I'd like to. I've been so preoccupied that I haven't even considered it, but going to Moultrie is exactly right. The perfect thing, the next step. Mapping out the battle, formulating a plan, laying in the palmetto logs. But not with Bird, not now. He's become too spooky.

"I've got to bring home some bacon this week," I blurt. I feel like the front-row doofus the comedian has picked to rag on. "The wife, you know. Wants me home. This week's . . . ah . . . the moment of truth."

Bird laughs as though I've said something witty beyond compare. His mirth is as moist as a kiss. How does he know so much? What is he after?

Bird speaks. "A woman is only a woman," he pipes, "but a hefty drive is a slosh." He grins insanely, cocks his head.

"Well," I stammer. "Well."

"Wood house," Bird clarifies. "The oldest member. Do you know it?"

I'm in over my head now. I hear a snort of laughter from Hatch, and I nearly knock him down as I bolt. "Sorry, Jim," I mumble over my shoulder. "Catch you later."

"Christ," Hatch growls. "Ready whenever you are, Grace."

"Your loss," sings Bird as we retreat. "I hear they've got trees over there that'll swallow a cannonball whole."

My legs half-buckle when I hear this, and I have to strangle a wail in my chest. How can he know the things he knows? Is he boy or demon? Monster or ingenue? Am I to believe that this, too, is an accident, a phrase he's plucked out of the sky? I can feel insanity blooming in my blood like a bubble of air. If it reaches my heart, I'm a dead man.

I might kill someone this weekend; I might . . . anything is possible. What can stop me? Does the code of the sea still govern the ship that's bitten into basalt? The ocean floor marks a dim, silent, solitary freedom. The old laws, the old constraints, seem absurd — why should the downed boat, held fast by rock and water, recognize any other power as binding? So I'm free, in a way, newly free. The end of this life, this golf, and I might do anything.

What is wrong with me? And how does he know?

At the practice green, ripping open a new sleeve of balls, Hatch turns my way. "Aw," he says. "Dat wud so weet. I'm telling you what's the truth, Bri, you two are a love story waiting to happen. He'd like to swallow your cannonballs whole, you adorable ab-o-rigine you."

There's a pain behind my ears. I'm sweating, aching, twitching now. All the signs. The sudden bad crazies ride again.

My mechanic in Emma, a Vietnam vet named DeWayne Wills, did a ten-month stint at Milledgeville a few years back for trying to run down a family of berrypickers. He attributed the incident to "the sudden bad crazies." DeWayne said he was driving home one evening, daydreaming about a muscular mid-'70s Pontiac whose engine he was retooling, pondering whether to swing by the Big Chix for their famous thigh dinner, when he swerved off the road to pot a few fieldhands. No plan, no thought, no warning: one instant he was halfway home, the next he was out of his mind. He ended up buried to his door panel in the vestibule wall of an African Methodist church, had to be cut free, much later, with a blowtorch. His intended victims rolled, unhurt, under a picnic table; DeWayne had (accidentally or not) laid on the horn when he veered. They were still there when the cops arrived, DeWayne told me, pressing their stained blue fingers together in prayer.

DeWayne claimed to have been in the grip of something bigger than him: "I just got overcame," he explained to me, "with the sudden bad crazies. I'd had 'em before, even before 'Nam. When I was in junior high, I tried to sell my sister once. Got this funny feeling in my throat and the next thing I know I'm talking up her good teeth, her childbearing hips. The crazies come on you like a night sweat, and you know you're gonna do something fucked up, maybe today, maybe tomorrow, but you're gonna do it, and you can't stop yourself. I saw them pickers walking the road, and I had me a vision, like in the Bible, of fruitmen scattered like tenpins. I didn't have nothing against them, didn't even know 'em to talk to. Just watched the wheel spinning under my hand and thought, *Uh oh. Here we go again.* You better keep your eyes peeled," he warned, "for the sudden bad crazies. They'll eat your ass alive."

I doubled over when I told Rosa that story; she scolded me, said it was in bad taste to laugh at misfortune. Where was my Christian charity?

"What misfortune?" I asked. "The church had insurance. Nobody got hurt. You ought to be pleased; a good scare sets some people to praying. And it probably took DeWayne six months to realize he was in the loony bin."

"Mr. Wills," she said sharply, as though to a child playing dumb. "Mr. Wills," she repeated, "that poor, tormented soul. He served. He served his country."

"Ah, hell," I said, "he's a wigged-out mechanic. They're a dime a dozen. You want a cause, I've got one right here. Your husband — victim of rotten bounces, uphill breaks. The poor man never knows what hit him."

"That's enough," said Rosa, snuffing out the conversation. "That is quite enough, Brian."

And now I have them, the sudden bad crazies are here, and they feel just like DeWayne said they would. This weekend I could do something I may never get out from under. I'm unstable. Out of control. Plain crazy. I'm only glad I don't have a sister to sell.

"Let's line up a couple of stiffs," Hatch interrupts, having rolled a few practice putts to gauge the speed of the greens, "and make a little pin money." So I sigh and choke it all back and lace up my shoes. Hatch couldn't be more right. It's time to go to work. Nothing to do now but tee it up, one last time, crazies be damned, and play golf like I've never played it before.

## CHAPTER FIVE

# Thursday, 6:20 P.M.

A s THEY TURN IT OVER TO THE HARELIP Rusty Jones for sports, the phone rings again — setting off an accusatory vibration among the tees and coins on the nightstand. Who can it be? Surely the tour bloodhounds haven't sniffed me out already; my sham is as yet unaired. Maybe I should pick it up. This could be the last call I can answer safely for a while. But I don't want to miss my performance. Let it lie. The world can wait.

I remember seeing this movie once, during Rosa's foreign-film binge back in Athens. She had us down at the Hermann almost every Monday night, honing our intelligences by watching films about razored eyeballs and enigmatic Parisiennes with hairstyles that hid parts of their faces. (There's never been a woman in my life who didn't hustle me down darkened aisles in pursuit of improvement, but the cinema's a step in the right direction: I prefer my improvements with a tub of popcorn, generously larded.) And this movie was pretty good, for a change, basically a crime flick with accents and funny camera angles. Rosa had been fooled by its title — one of those one-word, Scandinavian-angst deals, I think, *Pity* or *Agony* or somesuch; she despised the film, she informed me later, because it "skimped on metaphysics." Which was precisely what I liked about it, I suppose: I'd propose a metaphysics ban if I thought the world would pass it.

The movie was about this guy who planned to fake his own death by finding a ringer and greasing *him*. The guy spent the first half hour rubbing his hairy hands together and proclaiming the genius of his scheme. How could anyone unravel the brilliant skein of his thought? How could anyone even follow it? A double: he would kill a *double*. The only stumbling block was that he was a nut; the drifter he snuffed looked nothing like him, and the killer dumped his own identification at the scene so the police would think he was the stiff. As "farcical gendarmes" closed in on him in distant France, the thwarted mastermind was left to wonder: Who would care if it had been an ape he killed? And what if it was kind of a bright ape? Or a swarthy, bald ape, one that could speak passable Danish? And if, the killer reasoned, one ascended the evolutionary steps carefully enough, couldn't he off even Shakespeare or Adlai Stevenson with perfect impunity? "Where," he queried, "is the border beyond which the sophist gets into trouble?"

Where indeed? I'm beginning to feel a bit cocky. I've got this conscience thing near licked. I'll put it plainly: How can I commit adultery if I'm not me? I can't. Hang *that* sin on Bird. He's the guilty party. I can't be touched.

The phone rings for the eighth time. Rusty is saying, "They're jockeying for start positions at the Brickyard this week, and the action's been hot and heavy. Tonight's focus: those controversial new tires." My interview won't be on till Rusty covers the afternoon baseball, the NBA playoff matchups, the angling outlook. There's time. And it can't be Rosa — she has choir practice at 6:30; she's gliding into the chancel about now in her burgundy robe, clutching her sheet music. I roll over and snatch up the phone.

"Yup?"

There's a longish pause at the other end. "May I speak to Brian Schwan, please?"

"Who?"

There's a pause, a heavy sigh. "Don't be rude, Brian. This is your mother."

I sigh, too. "So I gathered. What do you want?" This sounds meaner than I'd like.

"Well, how are you today?" she asks — a little hurt, but making a game try at blitheness. What did I pick up for? I'll be on the line till the millennium.

"Mom, I'm in a hurry. What's up?"

"What do you mean?" she asks, defensively. "Does a mother need a reason to call her son? And where are you going in such a rush?" Something's distressing her, but I don't have time for fellow feeling, for tenderness. Tonight is mine.

"How'd you know where I was staying?" Cut to the chase, Mom.

"Well . . ." There's a hitch in her voice — I can envision her clearly, at the kitchen table under her imitation-Tiffany fruit chandelier, gutting the utility bill with a letter opener. "Rosa called a little bit ago." Great. Just great. "She was upset, Brian. She worries about you. She said you'd shot a seventy-seven, and she and Oswald feel you're behaving, um, erratically. You didn't really hang up on her last night, did you?" Hatch's given name is Oswald, the secret source of his nickname mania. Why did he call Rosa . . . and when? Erratic how? There are spies everywhere; these are rough times for trust.

"Is everything OK?" my mother asks. "Have you got your head on straight?"

I ignore the last question. "No complaints. I played rotten. Tomorrow's another day." On the television some floozy in a bustle and a straw bonnet is fondling the hood of a '76 Impala. Just $795, daaaahlin'. Before they cut to commercial, Rusty promised news of the tourney. Hurry.

"Don't mind Hatch," I continue. "He's just running his mouth. And besides, where's the shame in being called erratic by a man who blow-dries his pubes for pleasure?" What am I saying? Why did Mom call? Doesn't she spend Thursday nights trying to clamber up the senior ladies' tennis ladder at the club?

And why isn't my father fulminating, as usual, in the near background? "That boy can't hit a bull in the ass with a goddamned bow . . . every advantage in the world and he's getting his clock cleaned by the likes of that punk Oswald. Seventy-fucking-seven. I can shoot that, and I'm an old man who's got to *work* for a living."

Mom always translates his cracks into saccharine encouragement: "Your father says keep after it, keep that competitive spirit blazing. Chin up. Forward ever, backward never. Good things come to those who wait. Luck evens out in the long run."

The commercial break is winding down. "Mom," I say, "what's this about? You didn't call to see how it felt to play one more crappy round, did you? Where's Dad? Is he OK?"

"Well," Mom answers, sounding a little unsure of herself, "that's why I called. He's . . . he's on his way down there."

"Down where?"

"There. Charleston. To see you."

"Tonight?" Oh, shit.

"He'll be there by the time you tee off tomorrow. I assume he'll stop at a motel tonight."

"What does he want?" There's only one thing the old man could want.

"I think I'd best leave that to him, Brian. That's *his* subject. But I did want to . . ."

"He talked to Rosa, didn't he?" No answer. "Mom? He's coming to tell me to quit, isn't he? She's sucked him in with her grandson-on-your-knee routine. Probably told him to cut his losses, maybe the *next* generation will have the golf genes he's looking for. Son of a bitch." They've always been way too chummy; Rosa should have married my old man.

But that's a lie: The agony is that I've seen this coming, and it has nothing to do with Rosa. My father, first to believe in my golf — first, last, and always, or so I thought — I've seen his ardor cool, his confidence erode. When I was spanking all comers on the junior loop (and in high school), he never missed a match. We collected hardware, plaudits, predictions of greatness. He drove to every college tournament within several hundred miles of Lamartine, still enthusiastic — though we had our share of somber meals in chain steakhouses, he and I, in Haines City, Statesboro, Santee, after yet another workmanlike 216 in a tournament where the big boys were eight or nine under. I'd reached a plateau . . . but we both felt, I think, that it was only a question of learning to play more aggressively, of learning to treat par rudely. And he surfaced — though more taciturn than before, pinch-faced, brooding — at probably fifteen events during my first year as a pro. But he's seldom come during the last year. The old man's taken up a hobby, a benign, homey, puttering cliché of a hobby — gardening! — and several times he's failed to show up at events within a hundred miles of home. He'd rather thin blackberry vines or mulch carrots than watch me coast to twenty-fifth in another RC Cola Bottlers Classic or Cox Wood Preserving Open. My flaws — lapses in course management or in nerve, flares of temper, an occasionally balky driver, a decelerating stroke on downhillers — he's begun to regard with the same auger eye that made him abandon his own golf.

After close to twenty years of ruthless boosterism, of a belief so intense that it seems the precondition of my own, his faith has wavered. He's breaking down, giving up; he's putting me, the way he put himself, out to pasture.

But this has all been his idea: Golf is his idea. What made him think it was who I wanted to be? How do I throw it away — now, after all this time — and salvage a self? *You can't make me hang it up, Dad. Without golf, what would be left? How would you know me? How would I?*

My mother scolds me now. "You know your father doesn't let anybody write his script, Brian. And watch your language. Just because Daddy has a pottymouth doesn't mean —"

I interrupt. "In other words, yes. He wants me to call it off." Just like old times, Dad. Down to see a milestone. Sonny boy's last dance. How could this have happened? How does a belief like that die?

"Doesn't Mr. Greenjeans have some tomatoes to stake?" I ask.

"Now Brian, don't tell your father I called. He wanted his visit to be a surprise. He was *very* clear about that, and I didn't want to tangle with him. He'd turned that awful color he used to get. He's too old to turn purple; purple's no good at his age. I worry." I remember that hue well, remember the way his face looked bruised and swollen while he yelled at me for skanking a chip shot or failing to put away a lesser opponent. A high-school teammate who witnessed a few of those scenes used to say Pop looked like a cross between an eggplant and Jackie Gleason.

Mom's injured tone stings a little. She's trying to help, and I've been nothing but curt, ungrateful, mean. In her mind this call is a betrayal. She's been forced to examine her loyalties, to make a choice, and after all, despite their thirty years together, I'm her boy. I must be making her proud: her dear little Renaissance Man. Pottymouth. Ingrate. Asshole. Soon-to-be adulterer. Not a skill in the world, nor a kindness.

"Do you hear me, Brian? He wants to surprise you."

"I'll say," I whisper. Here comes Rusty again. There's a big "59!" looming over his left shoulder. I'm on. "Thanks for calling, Mom," I say, as quickly as I can. "Really. It's been a pleasure. I can cover the rest myself: Forward ever; the best men call things by name; may conscience be my guide. 'Bye now. Goodbye, Mom. Thanks." I hang up as she starts to whisper, sorrowfully, that she loves me.

"And finally," chirps Rusty, "history was made today at the Ile de Paris resort near McClellanville. A young South African, Jim Soulsby, notched a sizzling 59 on the 6,890-yard, par-71 layout. That makes only the second time it's ever happened in competition; in 1977, for you trivia buffs, a journeyman pro named Al Geiberger shot a 59 at the PGA stop in Memphis.

Our Ellen McCovery was on the scene this afternoon with the astonishing story."

Cut to a shot of Ellen standing next to me, her microphone shimmering under my nose like a disco ball. "Mr. Soulsby —"

"No need," I interrupt suavely, "for formality. Please. It's Bird to you." Don't they edit these damn things? What happened to my ten-second burst of fame?

"OK then, *Bird,*" she emphasizes, a smile playing at the corners of her bountiful mouth, "how does it feel to play your way into the record books?"

The camera closes in. My visor half-shades my face, leaving a yin-yang whorl of sunlight. My shirt blazes. I begin. "Feels good," I sum up. "It's not a bad thing, all in all."

Ellen rephrases, let down a little. She wants sexy copy, an interview she can parlay into choicer assignments. Come on, you stupid jock. "Don't you feel . . . exhilarated?"

"Golf," asserts the glowering philosopher-king on my screen, "is a demanding mistress. She eats her young." He pauses to wink. "It's never a good idea to let this game hear you say you've got her. I may squirrel it around tomorrow like my friend Brian Schwan, whose luck today was as hard as mine was soft. Ellen — may I call you Ellen? — well, Ellen, it's a hard game, and mostly, today, I'm grateful."

She is happier with this. Off camera, she grins. I smile back, tug my visor back from my brow, whisk a button of sweat off the end of my nose. The face on the TV screen is hardly recognizable as mine — its every line is animated, and there's well-being pulsing from every pore. I'm pleased to see that my features, which have always seemed beakish and angular, don't look too bad. I'm tan, weathered; I resemble a leather golf bag, a little pouchy, but classy.

Ellen proceeds. "What's the key to a round like this?"

"Well," Bird/me weighs the question, "the secret to golf is that there's no secret. It's a simple sport. Hit it, chase it, sink it. Make birdies. Bear down hard, and don't let the course's throat loose till you feel the last flutter of breath expulsed."

*Expulsed?* Where does this crap come from? I sound like some loopy visionary; hell, I sound like Bird. In my motel room I think, proudly, of the German artist Joseph Beuys — standing on a darkened, empty stage. Lightly coated with gold leaf, face smeared with honey, shackled at the ankle to an iron boiler-plate, he mutters for three hours to the bloody corpse of a hare that he holds tenderly at his breast. In the audience not a cough, not a yawn: Who dares call it dumb? He seems to be doing it on purpose; the program says ART, right at the top there, in big block letters. In plush seats the critics formulate judgments for the organs of culture: "To see the void plumbed this way is enough, must be enough. What higher goal for Art than to plumb the void?" It's thrilling to be puzzle for a change instead of puzzled.

"I see," says Ellen. Time to get back to the haven of facts. "Have you ever shot a round like this before?"

"Once," is the answer, "when I was ten or so, I shot a fifty-nine in the British Open, held that year at the cradle of the game, St. Andrews, in my backyard — near Pretoria. I used a wiffle ball and a plastic driver."

Ellen laughs tinklingly. "I guess you never thought you'd du-plicate *that*." Modesty being a virtue, Bird peers down at his shoes. She presses on. "And lastly, how does this stack up with journeyman pro Al Geiberger's achievement?" Why do they keep saying that? Geiberger won a million damn dollars on Tour back when a million meant something. Journeyman my ass.

The inexplicable figure on the TV raises his hand to his chin — the international sign of cogitation.

"Geiberger's fifty-nine," he says, "was on the big tour, so the stakes were higher, and on a par-seventy-two layout, I believe. Besides, Al's diabetes and the heat of the day made his a struggle for survival. Mine is a happy occasion, to be sure, but second-rate in a not unpleasant way."

She's momentarily dumbfounded by this. It takes a cue from her cameraman (captured on the tape as a violent waggle) to bring her back. "Thanks, Mist — Bird," she says.

Only now does the camera pan back to Ellen. She is radiant. She is irresistible. "The words," she summarizes, "of a reluctant new star. That's the story from what is tonight an *electric* Ile de Paris Golf Club. Now back to the studio."

"Ba-dom-POM," says Rusty. Ellen's recycling the jingles of real estate, the jokes of subdivision flacks. Ellen my minx, my fizgig, my heart: she *is* irresistible, isn't she?

I hate to hear anyone claim he's stunned by something he said. It's the kind of sideslip you expect from a politician. Confronted with video surveillance tapes of calls to 1-900-MLK-MAID (his face a swollen cabbage rose, his wick an avid purple), the senator blames alcohol, prescription painkillers, stress. The unctuoso tells his blue-eyed lie. . . . But I *am* stunned. That wasn't me, hardly resembled me. The impostor was carefree, glib, on the verge of handsome. He was a man with golf securely in his pocket, with the world well in hand. And though I knew I'd been guilty of a good bit of nonsense, I'm shocked to see how far it — how far *I* — went. I've never talked like that before. And, unaccountably, it worked. All my life I've been a fledgeless fraud, but tonight — just this once — I've done it. I've left gravity's stale suck beneath me. I can fly.

I'm not afraid of reprisals now. I'm feeling, in fact, pretty close to "exhilarated" (Thanks, Ellen). Untouchable. Free. I know I'll be called in front of the board tomorrow on charges of unprofessional conduct, but so what? Golfers, with their sentimental esteem for "gentlemanliness," are suckers for earnest bunkum, and that'll be my strategy: *My actions were amateurish, your honors, but in the purest sense of that term: after the manner of a lover. Golly. Whatever rash things I did — and, love being blind, I remember only vaguely — I did them for the love of the game. Shucks. Hey . . . what would you do if golf were being taken away from you? Jeepers.*

It's as though I've been set loose from a captivity I didn't know I was in. The old Brian — the drab, mute, muddied, married Brian — I can see him, down below, pinned to the earth like a moth to its board. I've left the sorry motherfucker behind, thank God. Tonight I'll be Bird; we'll see where that takes me.

Now that it's no longer mine, I feel up to facing Brian's round, picking it over, recording it in the ledger. Six-thirty-two. It'll take forty-five minutes to get downtown, which gives me another forty-five to blow. Plenty of time, and I'm in Charleston, after all: The forms must be observed, and let substance fall where it may. Hatch won't be here until he finishes stuffing himself with shrimp and hushpuppies, so I'm assured solitude.

And besides, logging the round will keep me from thinking about my father's — or Brian's father's — impending . . . Damn it. Ecstasy is always fleeting. The world never looks so dark as ten seconds after orgasm. But I can't help it, can't help seeing the differences between the TV apparition and me. He's Bird; he busted sixty; the world is his oyster. And me? My slacks are brindled with sludge; my wife says I'm erratic, and my father is coming to fetch me from foolishness; for years I've thrown good money after bad, good work after rotten . . . and nothing to show for it. I'm all vague shame, sour stomach, the ache and bloom of hay fever. While Bird's head is full of *les Mystères,* mine is full of snot. I'm allergic to grass, trees, molds, dust, even my own skin as it sloughs away, have to carry a syringe in my shaving kit. The ideal affliction for a golfer: an allergy to grass. Betrayal is everywhere, and there's no staying out of its way for long.

I was in a good frame of mind when I strode to the first tee this morning, fully recovered, I thought, from the borderline insanity of Tuesday.

Yesterday was a good day. After a rocky start Hatch and I

cleared forty dollars on our practice-round wagers — to go
with fifty from Tuesday. In yesterday's match I birdied the final
three holes (with absolutely staked iron shots) to account for
the bulk of our winnings, so I was even feeling sanguine about
my game. Hatch and I had found a cheap but clean motel only
ten minutes up Highway 17. The Bulls whipped the Bad Boys
in their playoff game. Bird never darkened my path. A good
day indeed, and a needed reprieve.

I even had a pleasant conversation — I think — with Rosa.
We gabbed about the fashion biz; about her bookstore inven-
tory ("I have devil-worshipping teenage shoplifters," she re-
ported. "I'm not joking. Somewhere in Emma are seven 'Jesus
Saves' bumper stickers stolen from *my* stock — who knows
what they do with them, Brian, maybe cut them up for ransom
notes or burn them on dead-kitty pyres, you know how sa-
tanists are"); about the Eiffel Towerette, the aftermath of the
hurricane ("Have they mucked out all the pluff yet?" she asked,
laughing, echoing the haughty aristofart we saw on Oprah
when the show visited the Port City after Hugo; "Not a pluff in
sight," I told her, "must be all mucked out"), her dinner Tuesday night with her parents.

Rosa's lived in Emma since she was a girl, and her parents
have helped generously with the house — her father is a master
carpenter and her mother runs an interior-design business, so
we got materials on the cheap (and a hefty chunk of labor for
nothing). Actually, the Fersners were the ones who discovered
the house in the first place. It was part of a probate auction, and
it firmly resisted sale — though it's a beautiful old two-story
Victorian, right near downtown, huge magnolia tree, pin oaks
flanking the front walk, hydrangeas, picket fence, hardwood
floors, vaulted doorways, high tray ceilings, the works. The
oldest standing home in town, but the bank couldn't scare up
the minimum bid.

Reason? The place looked like the embers of Atlanta in Sher-
man's rearview mirror. Just before he kicked off, the former
owner had meticulously, lovingly ripped his house apart, in-

tending to remodel — the scorched-earth school of do-it-yourself. He laid waste to the place from baseboards to roof joists. But only two rooms were finished when he died, and most would-be buyers were put off by the prospect of funneling thousands upon thousands beyond the purchase price into finishing the renovations. There were so many things yet to do, ranging from ripping out floors and shoring up walls to replacing warped window sconcheons and installing locks — for 113 years, the owners had made do with spinnable blocks of wood mounted on the doorframes.

In case the turmoil inside wasn't enough, there was a snafu with the driveway easement; Attila the Handyman had bankrolled his depredations by selling off the land at one side of the house (including the driveway) to a condo complex next door, and the complex had given him leave to pull through their lot. But the easement — these things happen — died with the man.

Rosa's parents spied the house on one of their Sunday rambles for antiques and yard-sale bric-a-brac . . . for anything varnish or paint or scumbling might make more valuable (reclamation projects are a Fersner specialty). Loretta and Bert conducted a grueling three-hour inspection; I still wonder what the agent thought when they arrived, Mrs. Fersner towing a child's wagon full of radon meters and carbon monoxide detectors, Mr. Fersner with his nasturtium kneepads and his miner's lamp. Afterward they sold us on the virtues of the noble ruins, then ponied up the down payment to seal the deal — our wedding present. They were dynamos: They greased the wheels at the courthouse on the easement problem, worked their asses off finishing the renovations, even brought in fresh sod for the yard — a hundred emerald-green coils of centipede, six feet by a foot and a half. Loretta and Bert have been "real troupers," as Rosa says — including herself in the compliment, I think.

All of which is great, of course — wonderful, really, I don't mean to be ungrateful — but there's a downside, too. For as long as we stay in Emma we're securely under the Fersners' thumb, and I have to endure, through Rosa, her parents' cease-less caviling about my career: "How come Brian spends thirty-five weeks a year on the road and comes home with zip to show for it? It's time he grew up and took on some responsibility, isn't it? After all, you've got two jobs, dear, and he's got none."

Once Rosa had a fender-bender while I was in Bethesda try-ing to qualify for the U.S. Open — just a light bumper kiss, minimal damage, but when I got home I found her in the sun-room, gaping moonily at the TV, her neck swaddled in a whiplash brace. Loretta was stuffing wet clothes into the dryer. Bert was on his back under the sink, sealing a sweaty pipe. He looked like a half-eaten meal as he wriggled in the cabinet's maw; he was wearing his miner's lamp for light. "Hey, Pop," I said. "How's the canary holding up?" He didn't answer.

There were a few seconds of silence as I moved through the kitchen and into the sunroom. "Well," Loretta finally sniffed, a basket perched on her mighty hip, pointing at the neck brace with a bright red talon, "it's about time you slunk home. Your wife is *injured*, for goodness sakes. Hurt." I set down my golf clubs, my hanging bag. "Don't be looking for a warm welcome, mister," she jeered. "Rosa and I are fresh out of warmth, fed up. Aren't we, honey?"

Rosa smiled up at me, weakly, held out her arms for a hug. Mrs. Fersner stomped back to the dryer; Mr. Fersner continued to thrash and grumble beneath the borborygmic sink. Rosa told me later that her mother had made her wear the brace "to teach that millstone of yours a lesson." Not a word was spoken about my near miss at Bethesda, where I'd fallen shy of making the field by a single stroke; some things go without saying.

Anyway, last night Rosa was sweet, conciliatory. She hadn't meant to pressure me about our baby: She knew I'd "invested an awful lot of baggage in golf" (as a rule, her way of putting things is no less stinging for being half accidental). There was no reason we couldn't sit down and talk it over — "in a nur-turing atmosphere," she breathed, "of mutual support" — when

I got home. Her feel-good jargon aside, the conversation was nice: affectionate, amusing, like old times.

But then she dumped another cheesy allegory on me. About a month ago Rosa started a dream-narration kick. The first was a suspicious parable about a peach tree — itself sterile, but in the midst of an orchard cruelly pungent with creation, ovaries swelling into drupes and ripening into sweet flesh and dappled rind, blah blah blah. The lonesome tree wondered, glumly, why it hadn't yet borne fruit. Rosa's eyes swelled, descriptively, to the size of June Elbertas. "A sad, sad peach tree," she concluded. "Barren and alone. But knowing, deep down, that it won't always be that way. Knowing that the sunshine and the rain and God's benevolence will pollinate it someday."

I had started out amused, seeing self-parody in this — in the contrivances of her plot, her shameless overemoting, the hand laid swoonily across her eyes. But Rosa, ever a stranger to restraint, had not held back in any particular; as she draped herself across the foot of the bed, her dream's opening bars were nearly drowned out, through the open door, by the stereophonic swells and throbs of the "Ode to Joy." Every film needs its soundtrack. Finally she peered up at me, let her ogival brows ascend: her own cathedral architecture, pointing prayers the way to heaven. "What do you think it means?" she asked. "I'm not too good at this sort of thing, but I thought maybe you could help."

By now any trace of amusement had vanished. And being an untested Sigmund, I misread the thing. I guessed Rosa was trying to break the news of a pregnancy. So I asked her.

"Hon, are you, um, by any chance, expecting?"

She said no, a bit hotly. I heaved a sigh of obvious relief; Rosa looked like she'd bitten into a quince. "That wasn't what it *meant*," she whined. "Really, Brian, you're supposed to be *smart*."

"Well what, then?" I asked. "You said you didn't know."

"I don't," she said. "But I know it didn't mean what you said."

"I see. Maybe we can handle this by elimination. I'll guess, and you let me know if anything strikes a chord. Got fertility woes you haven't let on?"

"No. Not that . . ." she trailed off.

"Well, what then?" I asked again. Sometimes stupidity is the smartest available course.

"It was just a dream, I guess," Rosa huffed. "Forget it."

Later I discovered that her bedside Bible was open to the passage in Genesis where Joseph, held by the Pharaoh, construes his fellow prisoners' dreams: "And they said unto him, 'We have dreamed a dream, and there is no interpreter of it.' And Joseph said unto them, 'Do not interpretations belong to God? Tell me them, I pray you.'" Whereupon Joseph somehow teased a reading of imminent freedom for one of the dreamers from the skimpy testimony of a grapevine and a goblet. He then twisted the paltry clue of birds pecking at basketed bread into a sign of coming decapitation for the other. I suppose Old Joe's tricks of oneiromancy had made Rosa overestimate my ability to unravel *her* dream. But — and what the hell, Rosa? — do not interpretations belong to God? Don't go looking at me.

By the time Rosa sprang another maternity dream on me a couple mornings later, even someone as resolutely clueless as I had to put the pieces together. And the allegories haven't stopped, though she's running short of emblems. Fruits, eggs, bread, storks, marsupials, and fields of wheat — they appear again and again. Rosa's no Scheherazade, would never have lasted 1,001 nights; she's barely limped through a month, and the story well is dry.

This is her idea of subtlety, of gentle persuasion. "Want to hear?" she asks, and she's off without a breath (or a reply) into her dream polemic. It doesn't stop. She's like — have I said this already? — a pretty hammer.

Last night on the phone, after our chat had started so promisingly, she settled into her irritating ghost-story-around-the-campfire tone and told me this one: "I'm at the shore, in the moonlight. It's late, and I'm sneaking out to see the turtles —

you know, those big oceangoing ones that look like ottomans. And I sneak through the dunes and part the sea oats and the mama is digging with her flippers. Digging with all her little turtle soul. She wants to lay her eggs, but the sand keeps falling into the hole. Flippers are not ideal trenching tools, you know. Anyway, I look down and notice a garden trowel in my hand. It's made of gold; it's a golden trowel. So I start to dig, and suddenly this giant stork wearing a surgical mask flaps out of the bulrushes and shields the turtle mama. The stork's wingtips are jagged like rakes, and as it speaks, the fabric of the mask moves in and out. It says, 'What right have you, Miss, to spy on this miracle?'" And so forth: It went on from there.

At the end of her performance Rosa stopped, as always, and asked in a small, expectant voice, "What do you think it all means, honey?"

"Search me," I snapped. "That in a world whose God was paying attention, turtles would have spades instead of flippers?"

"But don't you see what he's trying to tell us?"

"Who? The stork? What is the stork trying to tell us? I don't know. Maybe he wants us to know how he keeps his surgical mask on. Do storks have the ears for that?"

My fit of meanness shook all the artifice out of her — not that it was well hidden in the first place. "You know," she said, "that I hate it when you act like this. Isn't it clear what God's plan for us is? Can't you see it? Don't you care?"

I broke the connection. A stork in hospital blues, for God's sake. A golden trowel. Bulrushes. This miracle. Spare me, baby: I had golf to play. For that may God be thanked.

       ◎

But despite the call I was feeling chipper when I strolled to the tee today. I couldn't help it. There's nothing quite like the feeling of marching across macadam through the clatter of your own cleats, a feeling that you're somehow . . . well, purified.

You've cast off silent comfort, stowed it in the locker room with your cedar shoe-trees, your watch, your worries; you've traded the mellow tread of daily life for these big, fierce, noisy stilts. You can hear yourself coming.

And, too, golf holds at least the satisfactions of habit, of familiarity: the edgy murmur on the practice green; the weirdly purposeful clicks and thumps and grunts from the range; the megaphone screech that signals the next group to shoulder their sticks and tap across the path — to begin. Bird was already on the teebox when I arrived, marking a handful of Titleists, six of them, with a green felt-tip pen. He webbed four between fingers, cupped the other two in his palm. It was like seeing a sleight-of-hand man limber up backstage.

"Six?" I asked. "Planning on a bad day?"

"Be prepared," said Bird sunnily. "That's a titbit of Yank wisdom, isn't it? Better safe than sorry." Adam's apple bobbing, a moronic grin spanning his face, Bird returned his attention to the task at hand. He said nothing else. Like a miniaturist he squinted and daubed, tongue teasing the corner of his mouth; he pinched one eye shut to inspect his handiwork.

Watching him filled me (I hate to admit it) with pleasure. I was ready to give up my theory about his arranging the pairings; I could live with this paint-by-numbers Boy Scout, this titbit nitwit. Bird was no different from the rest of us, no more enlightened, no less at sea. As I did my stretching I couldn't help feeling good about the day to come. The auspices were piling up: a new day; a laconic Bird; a well-tuned short game; shoes that took good hold of the ground. Things were looking better.

The starter at Ile de Paris has had his voicebox removed, and as he announced our names and credentials over the electric megaphone he pressed a wallet-sized gray box to his flabby throat. The effect was a prodigious croak, a cross between Yahweh and Johnny Most: "Next on the tee is Brian Schwan, a former North-South Junior Champion, an Academic All-American out of the University of Georgia and the lovely town of Emma. You may fire when ready, Mr. Schwan."

I pressed my tee into the turf, tilted it forward for extra top-spin. In the great tradition of getaways, the opening hole here is a forgiving par four. A wide-open driving area, only light rough, the single hazard a stand of pines to the left — gaunt, scraggly survivors of Hugo. A warm-up, a lid-lifter. I spun the ball in the tee's dainty cup until I had it right: It's bad luck to strike a virgin ball on its lettering. Stepping behind, I waggled my driver a few times, identified the dimple I wanted to scar. I drew a breath, gave myself a pep talk: *You are a warrior, now don't let that hip spin out early you stupid bastard.* I settled in, feeling my spikes grab, tapping the clubhead behind the ball to assure myself, in a last spasm of panic, that the earth would hold. And then I swung.

I started with a rope-hook boomerang into the pines; Bird piped one about two eighty that never left the center sprinkler line. Ripper belted his drive a mile and a quarter, but a full thirty degrees to starboard, into the far side of the adjacent ninth fairway. He took off after it like a bird dog, both hands steadying the bag behind him, face lifted, clubs clicking in time with his steps — a man who's used to living his life upwind, uphill. Ripper's a Blade-and-Titty lifer, will never move up a rung; he hasn't made any money playing golf, never will, and it doesn't faze him. If he wasn't butchering Ile de Paris, he'd probably be at the ass end of a mule.

As I descended from the teebox Bird caught up to me, butted my bag with his. He emerged at my left side. "Hello, Brian."

I looked away. "Mmmph," I said.

"Together again, eh?"

"Looks that way. Looks that way."

I swung my bag as aggressively as I could from my outside shoulder to the one nearer Bird, to fend him off. He started up anyway.

"Well, I always enjoy our rounds together. Thanks for going to the trouble."

"What?"

Bird shrugged, grinned.

I snapped. "Look, Soulsby, just stay out of my way. I don't know what you're talking about, and I don't want to."

Bird stretched his hand out easily, indolently, laid it over the flange of my wedge. "Yes you do," he said, smiling. Glancing down, I could see his knuckles whiten.

"Fuck you," I said, and jerked out of his grasp. What had happened to the feebleminded Webelo with the marking pen? What had happened to my optimism? Where the hell was my ball?

I could still hear Bird, a few steps behind me now, his tone returned to lightness. "Did you know that Charleston was bombarded 587 days in a row during your Civil War?" he asked. "Or that submarine warfare began in her harbor? The *Hunley*, 1864, sunk the Union sloop *Housatonic,* then rolled onto its back and disappeared, no survivors. They're talking about dredging her up. Learned that on Tuesday. You should have come along."

He had followed me to the verge of the trees. Fifty yards to my stop, Mr. Conductor. "Look," I said, "cut the crap. Go mess with somebody else for a change."

I started — more than a little torqued — to poke for my ball in the coppery straw. Pines are excellent golf-course trees because they choke out undergrowth; it's usually a cinch to find your ball in a stand of loblollies. So where was mine? Bird set his sack at his feet, just outside the tree line, and went on, paying no attention to my search.

"You know, that starter put me in mind of a story. Would you like to hear a story?" I was threshing straw away from the bases of trees like a machine. My five minutes would be up before I knew it, and it was beginning to look like a freakish retee on the first hole. I couldn't afford a six. Not again. Not this week. And Bird standing by, useless . . . chattering.

"It's a corker," said Bird. "A riot. I know you'll want to hear it." I just glared and threshed, glared and threshed, until I looked back and saw the starter sailing down the fairway in his cart. He had donned a madras Rules Committee blazer, traded his megaphone for a walkie-talkie. I was threatening to put him off schedule, and that wouldn't do. When trouble comes, she don't come half-stepping.

When the cart got within a hundred yards Bird turned to the old man and gave a brusque backhand wave. The starter braked, held up his voicebox questioningly. Bird waved again, with a flick of the wrist that managed to be mild and peremptory at the same time, and the starter turned back. Then Bird took one decisive step forward, shoved aside a mat of grass clippings with his toe, and pointed at my wayward ball. "I'll tell you the story later," he said. "I suppose you have work to do." He ambled off across the fairway, whistling. One shot, and already I was in over my head. One beats the bush; another gets the bird.

I got greedy with my recovery, trying to bend it around a tree and coax it to the front collar of the green; smacked an old-growth Goliath in its forehead, one of the few aged singles left intact by the storm; watched the trunk fling the ball back past me. I had to sink a twenty-footer to salvage bogey. Bird made a tap-in three.

I carded another sloppy five on two — blew the simplest sand save in history. Bird made uneventful par. Ripper hit two so deep into the grahdu that they'll never be found, made a snappy snowman — 8.

I was pissed; I never blow an opportunity to handicap myself at the start. But only two over, plenty of holes between me and the clubhouse . . . and it would have been worse but for that putt at one. There was hope yet.

Three's where I lost it. It's a diabolical three par, 185 yards across an arm of tidal marsh to a shallow, two-tiered green. Wind in our face. A hole you don't get cute on, just collect your three and move along. Bird had the honor, as usual, and he pulled out a four-iron. As he settled his blade behind the ball, ready to play, there was a loud "crunk, crunk" to our right. It sounded like the noise docked boats, tossed by wakes, make when they chafe against styrofoam pylons. Enough to make my back crawl. A big white bird with black wings came flapping across the ripgut grass, its neck extended. No, I thought. Not again. Hit the fucking ball, Bird. Please.

But he pulled back. "Wow," he said. "Do you fellows know what that is? First time I've seen one in the flesh, but I'd know it anywhere. That black-beaked beauty is the flinthead, the *Mycteria americana,* the wood stork. A rare bird these days. Strange, you don't often see them alone, and they keep their beaks shut unless there's something pretty heavy going down. Storks are held sacred in Sweden because they're said — against their reputation for quiet — to have raised such a ruckus when Jesus was crucified."

This was too much. Besides the ornithology crap, Bird speaks that brand of pidgin American that's half movie slang and half PBS. "Enough," I said. "How about let's play golf?" Ripper, eager to get a few holes between him and his eight, nodded his support. Bird looked hurt. "Fine," he said. "Fine. But keep in mind that this isn't neurosurgery. I'm just trying to be companionable." He hit a decent shot, forty feet away but in the meat of the green, continued talking as though there'd been no interruption. He barely even watched his ball land, do its backspin dance. "You'd think you might trouble yourself to learn something along the way to the grave." For a moment I was afraid he'd say he was disappointed in me. What is it about me that brings out the lecturer in people? Why do I listen to this same garbage from Bird, my parents, Rosa, even Hatch?

I took a five-iron, having decided to hook it in. The stork (missing his mask this morning) settled on a stalk of grass fifty yards or so away, directly beneath my line of flight. "Shoo," I called, "scram, vamoose." The bird didn't budge, so I aimed over its head, hooded the clubface a little to set up for the draw. But I skinned the shot badly, and the ball rocketed off the club right on line, but low. Buzzing loudly, my ball ripped through the grassculm the stork was perched in — mowed it straight through. The beast bleated, dipped out of sight for a moment, then flailed gawkily away. The ball disappeared into the sump.

Bird yelled, "You hit the stork! You hit the stork! That bird is endangered, you asshole. You did that . . . you did that on purpose. You swung that club with malice aforethought."

"You're nuts," I fired back, "if you think I care enough about some stupid fisheater to spend two strokes to waste one. I can't throw one in the goddamn ocean. What makes you think I could plug a crane at fifty paces with a five-iron?"

"It's not a crane, you stupid bleeding rube!" raged Bird. "It's a *stork*."

"And I missed the damn *stork*."

"See," hissed Bird, "see. You've just admitted . . . I ought to have you pinched. You're a menace."

"Dave Winfield beat that rap," I said. "I can too."

Ripper piped up. We had hit on his one area of expertise, sports trivia. "That was up in Canada," he noted. "Mid-'80s. Seagull."

"Thank you, Ripper," I said.

"Sure thing." Excepting belches and score reports, we didn't hear another peep out of him all day.

I hit an indifferent third and two-putted for double-bogey; Bird got his par. As he set the pin in the hole, I apologized. I had gone over the line — not that he hadn't provoked me — but I've never been one to perform well amid tension or anger, and this round was going to continue, like it or not, for fifteen more holes. It was time to make peace with someone, anyone, and Bird was the available apologee. "Look, Jim, no hard feelings, OK? I wasn't trying to brain the bird."

"He does appear healthy," answered Bird, pointing with his putter to the stork, which stood placidly beside the green, no more than thirty feet away, watching. "We're all of us no worse for the wear, I suppose." Then he looked away, toward the next tee . . . and I would swear he called out the words "Scrub suit, eh?"

It took me a second to regain my senses.

"Me? Four," said Ripper, apropos of nothing.

I parred the next three, number five with a delicate flop shot from behind the green, and Bird began his run with a birdie on six. Seven is a shortish par five, easily reachable in two shots; Hugo knocked over the lone oak that sheltered the hole's belly, left the green open to approaches from anywhere. The stump has been sawed to the ground.

If I was going to save my round, seven was a must birdie. But off the tee I came over the top again. Into the palmettos. Another pitch-out, another routine bogey. Bird hit a frozen-rope two-iron to within twelve feet and drained his eagle putt to go four under, nine up on me. After his putt he unwrapped a Blow Pop and started sucking on it.

"Watermelon," he announced, the sucker wallowing obscenely in his mouth. "Watermelon is tops."

Bird parred eight, and I cut him one — held a nice smooth six-iron under the wind and got it to check up just two feet behind the stick. Birdie, the first time I'd clipped him all day. Hope — the foolish, dauntless weed — sprouted again. I was only four over, I thought; if I got hot now, I could get into a groove and springboard myself into position tomorrow.

But it was over before I hit my drive on nine. At the tee we had to wait on the group ahead — some kind of lost-ball snag. I had the honors, so I pegged it up and started pacing. Bird lay back on the matted grass, using his bag as a pillow. Ripper produced a beef-jerky billy club and tore into it.

Bird started up. "Oh yes, Brian, the story, the story. Did I ever tell you about my trip to New Mexico when I first came to the States?"

I muttered "No," scanned the fairway impatiently.

"I was hitching my way west, and I was picked up in the middle of Texas by a bloke without a larynx. Like the starter. Only I didn't know this was a larynxless bloke. He was driving a red Ferrari. The man pulled up beside me and signaled me to get in. I noticed, of course, that he didn't talk, just smiled and swabbed at his ears with a Q-tip dipped in a bottle of peroxide he'd wedged between the seats. And he drove like a bat out of hell. I thought he was just a shy man who liked fast cars and clean ears: I was new here, as I said. So far as I knew, America was a land of opportunity and action, its people banded together against idle talk and earwax. After a while I noticed a box on the console that looked like an electric razor, and I asked what it was. The American picked it up, spun it in his palm like a six-gun, raised it to his throat, and croaked, 'My voice, son. This here is my voice.' He smiled at me with big, white teeth as he flipped the box back onto the console.

"He didn't say anything else, just kept driving, faster and faster. An hour later we wrecked. He flipped that Ferrari in an arroyo, doing about ninety. It was strange: One minute there was endless horizon, and then there was sand in my lungs and the world had collapsed to the size of a bucket seat. We were wearing safety belts, and neither of us, amazingly, was seriously hurt."

Still no movement in the ninth fairway. The group ahead was waiting for a ruling, and not a committeeman in sight. Bird kept on. "So we hung upside down, suspended by our harnesses. All my blood was in my head, trying to make a break for it through any available orifice. I could see powdered glass on my clothes. I was hawking up silica and fossil dust. I was stunned. And the whole time the old man was rummaging calmly above his head. I thought he was trying to claw his way through the top of the car or something. For five full minutes, I coughed and he fingered the roof. When he finally dragged down his voicebox, he held it up like an acorn he'd found, and he grinned. This leering, idiot grin — there was a smear of blood on his teeth. He put the box to his throat, and he said, 'Fu-u-u-uck.' That was it. 'Fu-u-u-uck.' Then he let the box drop, closed his eyes, and crossed his arms, upside down, to wait for help. I suppose if your voice runs on batteries, you say only what's necessary. Fu-u-u-uck. And he was right. That about covered it."

Bird lifted his head off the bag and snorted; Ripper, doubled over with glee, dabbed at his greasy fingers with the ballwasher towel; the threesome ahead finally inched out of range. I stepped up grimly and took my futile whack. Scores: bogey for me, another three for the hitcher. *Fu-u-u-uck* about covered it.

On ten, things turned even hairier. I shoved a two-foot second putt. As my ball sat smugly on the high-side lip, peeking into the hole, I could swear (as if Bird and his stork weren't phantasm enough) that I heard Rosa's voice behind me: "Give it up, dear. Pack it in. It's not God's will." I jerked around and heaved my putter into the sky. It windmilled across the green, still rising, making that glorious thrown-club sound: *fwup-fwup-fwup.*

The putter smashed into a greenside oak, and, with a sound like a damped bell, its shaft snapped in two. An angry mockingbird came out to investigate, chattering. I scrambled down the embankment, stumbled among the roots, and gathered the remains in my arms.

*"Mimus polyglottus,"* I heard Bird say to no one, ducking into his bag for the notebook. I held the blade of my putter and heard a noise emerge from my throat, a strangled, soulless wail. It was like something out of Hieronymus Bosch.

But when I climbed back over the brow of the hill, I found Bird and Ripper standing exactly where I'd left them: a tableau of unconcern. Ripper was leaning on his extended-shaft Zebra, snapping gum and checking out the star-shaped hole my buzzbomb had cut in the oak's foliage. Bird squatted behind his marker, licking a grass stain off his ball. Where was the notebook? Had I imagined it? Had I imagined Rosa's voice, too? And what was I going to do for a putter?

I was so discombobulated that I didn't realize till I got to the hole that my ball no longer occupied its place — the stone had been rolled aside. My ball had dropped.

"Nice putt," remarked Bird. "That's a good four from where you were."

For the next five holes I bunted the ball around the greens with a one-iron, made dull pars. I hit a few decent shots, played conservatively. Meanwhile Bird was in a zone. He's one of those guys who can make birdies in bunches, five or six at a stretch without even thinking about it; to me, on the other hand, par is such a sacred figure that if I string two birds together I sit back and wait for fate to exact revenge. Fate is always prompt; it does its exacting without delay. Double, triple, quad.

Ile de Paris has several immature doglegs, and Bird was blowing his teeballs straight over them. On fourteen, already seven under, a huge draw over the treetops left him only twenty yards from the green . . . but he stubbed his pitch badly. The ball barely trickled into the fringe, leaving him sixty feet of bumpy, undulating, spiked-up terrain. An iffy two-putt at best. It was the kind of half-spastic shot you expect from a twenty 'capper, and I allowed myself to think that Bird might be succumbing to the pressure. The first sign of anxiety. At long last, feet of clay.

Bird reared back and guffawed. "Did you see that?" he howled. "Did you see *that?*"

He ambled to his painted Titleist. From shoulder height he let his clubs drop to the thick apron in front of the green. An iron made contact with a sprinkler head; there was a crack like a rifle shot. Bird paid no attention. "Take it out," he ordered, squinting up the slope at the flag. Ripper (safely on in regulation) had shuffled into the woods, ignoring a strict tour policy aimed at him, to take a leak; I could hear his manly splatter amid the yuccas. So I went to fetch the flag.

Bird didn't line up his putt, didn't pace or plumb-bob or check the grain. He didn't even wait until I'd dragged the pin out of his line of sight; he just popped it, and as soon as the ball left his putter face he said, "That one's in." It wasn't a boast or a wish, just matter-of-fact: That one's *in*. The ball crept steadily up the hill, holding its line, breaking in a gentle, slow, inevitable bow toward its target. With every revolution I could see Bird's identifying mark — that blotch of viscid green — leering at me like an eye. The ball topped the plateau, and a moment later I heard its cruel rattle in the cup. My own eyes were clenched tight.

We were waiting to hit at sixteen tee when I spied another specter in the barren along the right side — a burly figure picking his way among fallen myrtles and crowns of bull thistle. Dad, I thought. Just what I needed. I had thought, before I talked to Mom tonight, that he might make the trek this weekend for fun, for support, for old times' sake. I wasn't inclined to trust my eyes, though . . . not again, not today.

But this phantom wasn't a wife's voice heard dimly through a roar of rage; this one didn't depend on reading Bird's lips. Whether the figure was my father I couldn't tell — but ghosts don't for the most part trip over logs, don't set heads of thistle to nodding with their missteps. No apparition could be so inept.

When I was playing the juniors circuit, some kids and parents called my dad "Pan the Goat Man" (actually, it was Hatch's father, the cardiologist — a block off the old chip — who coined the name and disseminated it most eagerly). I see now where he got it: Dad was thick-haired, bowlegged, bottom-heavy; he wore a tangly, hircine beard; a cigar depended from his lips at all times, the aromatic stub of a flute; panic was his state of nature. But most of all he earned the moniker for his habit of spectating from nooks he'd carved out of the underbrush. Dad always waited for my tee shot near the landing area, hidden among ferns or briars like a skittish woodland god. Shielded from sight by a limb, a pennant of moss, a cinderblock shithouse — and with the aid of a versatile wardrobe of forest green and charcoal — he waited for me, invisible.

When my drive landed safely (as it usually did in those days), Dad — without even a mannerly show of interest in my partners — would hurry toward the green, weaving through trees, to prepare for my next shot. Every now and again the flow of play on an adjoining hole would ensnare him momentarily, and he'd freeze like a buck in a clearing — counting on majestic disdain to hide him. There he'd be, caught, in his familiar spread-legged stance, chin in his left hand, nub of cigar between his teeth, aggrieved look on his face: What were these snot-nosed hackers and wailers doing here, cluttering the course that belonged, rightfully, to his own little genius of a ball-striker? What kind of angle was this to watch my approach?

Throughout my round he'd puff away, either furiously (bad shot) or anxiously (next one could be bad). He was as skilled as the mantis that mimics a stalk of grass, as a moth undetectable among lichens; often he'd follow for three or four holes before anyone but me noticed. Lurking in a grove of young trees; halfway up an unscalable bank; across an unjumpable creek; even standing brazenly at the edge of a patio with a hose in his hands for a prop, posing as a homeowner lured from his chores. But always present.

His attention took a weird form, sure, but mostly I was grateful for it. How many kids can make their parents *run?* My father in the woods was a plump Natty Bumppo, scampering through snags and snarls without snapping a twig, and his nervous agility was a gift from me; I was responsible. There could be no higher pleasure than to see him pump his fist and then jog ahead again. And what but love would move a middle-aged man to pinch a lineman's hardhat and belt and perch halfway up a light pole? Why else would he carry a tarnish mitt everywhere, in case I won another bowl or chalice that might need a fresh gleam? OK, so he might mime hara-kiri when I left a putt short; he might writhe and seethe and, now and again, holler himself purple. But what he yelled was true, I couldn't deny that — he *had* sacrificed, *had* given me every advantage. There were lessons, camps, custom-fitted clubs, and he and Mom had driven me all over creation to play this game. I owed them. I still do.

And there were parents on the juniors circuit who were cruel, mad, monstrous; he was nothing like *them*. I saw bad rounds punished by public whippings, a whimpering kid splayed against the family Mercedes, hands on the trunk, while a red-faced father whaled away with a razor strop; I saw rival mothers brawl in a bunker, their bright nails flashing, while their kids stood by holding rakes, eager to smooth away the shame. Denny Giacomo's father responded to errant shots by decapitating ballwashers or beating tee markers to a jelly or tearing down tree limbs with his steel-tipped walking stick; he was hauled off once in cuffs for caning a Canada goose to death after Denny dumped an approach into a pond. There was sour Mrs. Gilyard, who roved the course with binoculars, hunting someone to accuse of cheating — trying to bring the field back to her boy Walt.

But the most painful to watch was Mr. Mikuno, who spoke no English and never smiled and stood behind meek Yoshi on every shot, twisting a red umbrella in his powerful hands. Mr. Mikuno's wrath seemed to follow no pattern; you never knew what would set him off. Did Yoshi march off a distance in a laggardly way? Steal a smile at another player's low joke? Make a lazy practice stroke, carve a sloppy divot? Did he dishonor his father with a failure of posture? Or was Mr. Mikuno just so precisely attuned to him that he could sense any lapse in Yoshi's focus? Could he read his boy's *mind*? Whatever the case, playing with Yoshi was an agony of anticipation. You knew at some point you'd hear the sudden whack of umbrella against head, and you'd look back to see Mr. Mikuno staring blandly into middle distance, wringing his weapon, and Yoshi on the ground at his feet, stunned, hat askew, knees stained, and wondering — like the glazed-eyed tornado victims on the jar at Hawg Heaven — what had brought this sudden storm. What can account for acts of God? You pick yourself up; you move on; you listen in terror for that whoosh in the sky.

Dad was once a skilled golfer, the five-time champion at Bird o' Paradise and a scratch player. He was addicted to the game. When I was very young he'd stop off on the way home from work, at three o'clock. After playing nine (or a quick eighteen if course traffic permitted), he'd breeze into the house and have Mom pour him a stiff gin and tonic. Then he'd take his stadium cup onto the porch, slip back into his FootJoys, and swing him-

self over the rail fence into a neighbor's pasture to poke exper-
imental wedges until dinner. He'd take five balls, hit them at a
target, then scoop up his drink and wander down to fetch them
and hit them back. He'd try all kinds of lies, all kinds of plays:
feather shots, open-face explosions, punches, flips, blades, co-
zies.

At least once a week, after he'd been dodging the cowpies
awhile, you'd hear the crash of the screen door and the click of
cleats on linoleum: "Yes," he'd sing out, "YES!" And Mom,
keeping her eyes on the cutting board or the stew pot, would
warn, "Don't you dare prance into this kitchen wearing those,
those . . ." I could tell her annoyance was only half meant by
the way her shoulders twitched in back as she talked: She loved
my father for his exuberances, could never manage to resent
him for long. She was just playing her part.

"Spikes," my father said. "Spikes, baby."

"Things," Mom finished, pointing at his black-and-white
saddle Oxfords, the ones he always wore to tinker with his
short game. "They pit my floor. Don't you have any sense?"

Dad flailed his hands. "Madeline, this is a watershed. Big.
This will make me famous."

"It's *always* big. Three nights this week it's been big. I've had
enough big for a lifetime."

"I have the secret, Mad. I've figured this game out. It'll never
beat me again. The *secret*, baby. It's a final: Russell Schwan one,
golf zip. Hey, sport," turning to me, "what do you think? Your
old man's solved one of the great mysteries." He mussed my
hair. "Come on out and watch me stomp the beast that's beaten
men down for centuries."

Mom swears that once, when she and Dad were newlyweds,
he made her drive him to the Bird o' Paradise with his driver
held out of the open passenger window. It was a raw October
evening, and the wind whipped and whistled. My father was
too agitated to talk. He stared at the block of varnished persimmon, trusting luck and Mom to keep him from shearing off
a mailbox or a head in the gathering darkness. His discovery

that evening had been about his grip, and he feared he wouldn't be able to re-create the epiphany if he took his hands off the club (lab conditions can't always be duplicated). At the Bird o' my mother trained the headlights on a spot of turf, and she was asleep at the wheel when my father finally slipped back into the car, deflated: another key that failed to turn the tumbler, another secret dispersed by time, wind, an inexplicable lapse of concentration.

The key always dissolved with a couple of mishit shots, usually before Dad could get it onto the course; secrets are perishable. But every time a would-be philosopher's stone didn't pan out, my father tried something new. He still (though less and less often) tiptoes around the chips in that field, meddling with his game; he still props his dwindling gin and tonic among tufts of bitten grass; on rare occasions he may even come clattering into the kitchen, a momentary victor. But he hasn't played a round of golf, to my knowledge, in ten years.

Once I started competing, Dad's play tapered off, then stopped altogether. He diverted his energy into seeing me succeed. By the time we joined the club he had essentially quit the game, and he piddled in the cow lot only on evenings when I was there, too. He funneled all discoveries to me, watched me hit countless balls — he had to superintend every practice shot, offering half-baked advice, analysis, semimystic swing keys. He entered me in tournaments, had Mom ferry me all over the South during summers, looking for top-notch competition. On Saturdays he often left home in the early-morning dark and drove for hours to see me tee it up in Pinehurst or Dothan or North Myrtle Beach.

My father has a new pair of shoes now, with waffle soles instead of spikes; they're more comfortable for spectating. His saddle Oxfords have retired to the back-porch utility closet, where they molder among chipped clay planters, expired pesticides, sprung rakes, and dusty deposit bottles. The uppers are dried out and fissured; half the spikes are missing. That part of golf — *his* golf — is forever gone; my father can't stand people who are cheerily average, can stand mediocrity least of all in himself. When he realized he'd never be among the best in the world, he put golf away. He didn't want to keep playing for leisure, didn't want to see his joints stiffen and his handicap creep up with every passing year, to take the duffer's solace in a lucky good shot now and then, in the fresh air and the green lawn and the sunshine — he wanted to be the best, and barring that he wanted nothing at all from golf. I don't mean to say it would have been easy for him to drop it, but the fact that I had a knack for the game, that he could reinvest his enthusiasm, made it easier, I think.

So Dad doesn't play anymore, but at least until tomorrow his son, his ball-striking prodigy, is still out there: shooting seventy-sevens, berating birders, arranging adulteries. Until tomorrow, when my father — since I'm not man enough to do it myself — puts a merciful end to my mediocrity.

Chastened into concentration by the specter of the Goat Man, I birdied sixteen with a great approach shot. That, I figured, would take a little sting out of the round for him. I didn't know how much he had seen.

But as I left the green I spotted the fraud squatting beside his bass boat in a nearby yard, messing with a trailer hitch. He'd pushed his feed cap back so that the bill pointed straight into the air — a sign of pissed-off bafflement. The cigar was a Tampa Nugget, unlit and dark with saliva. The man's legs appeared to be made of ham loaf, and he was loudly cursing the uncooperative hitch. Not my father after all, but close, close — another man wound too tight, another man grappling with troublesome pleasures, wondering if they're worth the effort.

I gave the stroke back with a weak pitch at seventeen. It figured; I had taken it under false pretenses.

By the time Bird snaked in a thirty-footer at seventeen to go eleven under, even I was getting caught up in his round. It irked me to discover that I was rooting for him; clean-eared and closemouthed or no, we Yanks are Marlboro men, rugged individualists, and I've never met a success (not mine) that I couldn't begrudge. But you had to admire his cool. Beneath the devil-may-care veneer I could see the signs of skill, fastidious planning, even passion. Bird was playing smart, hitting the ball to the side of the fairway that would afford him the best angle to the pin, firing at flags on flats, leaving himself uphill rolls on more swaybacked greens. He pounded iron shots, watched them eat pins alive, then collected his divots and kicked them in; it was like watching a savage tango, all fury and rhythm. Meanwhile I churned up manhole covers, left them where they fell — my divots are wounds inflicted on an enemy, and I'll leave the first aid to others.

When we reached eighteen, I was amazed to discover that I wanted Bird to notch his three, to have his run at Geiberger. He'd hung in all day under mounting pressure, had hit every shot crisply, made every putt die at the hole. He'd held that enormous no-brainer on line at fourteen by force of will. He'd played without wasted motion, like he was laying pipe; if they'd been measuring the course today, the surveyor would never have strayed from Bird's side. I had to admire him, a little.

Eighteen is a brutal finisher, a straightaway par four of 458 yards. There's a jungle of subtropical deadfall to the right, a series of deep, soft fairway bunkers lining the left. The green is flanked by another half-dozen traps, and it slopes severely — except for a sedan-sized plateau at the rear — from back to front. A hard hole to birdie under any circumstances, but especially so today, with the pin nearly falling off the back edge and a stiffish breeze from right to left. Any approach shot struck too cleanly would spin all the way down to the front fringe, leaving a seventy-five-foot uphill nightmare and a likely bogey.

Bird worked his tee into the scabby hardpan, laid down his

Titleist with exaggerated ginger. He spat on his glove, stepped back, pantomimed a half swing to check his rhythm; I'd never seen him sweat over a shot even this much. Then he let fly. The drive started out perfectly, toward the South Carolina flag above the clubhouse, but it had a hint of hook spin that the wind made worse. The ball landed in the left edge of the fairway and took a hard kick into one of the bunkers. Jail. There are no birdies to be had with four-iron shots from fairway sand, particularly on a hole where too much backspin will yoyo your ball right back at you.

"Oh, man," I whispered, not meaning to. "That kick sucked."

"It'll work out," Bird comforted me. "It'll be fine. I grew up in a briarpatch." I couldn't understand how he had heard me.

"Get it up and down and it's Geiberger."

"Am I that far under?" He paused. "Hey, if I manage it, you'll have to hit the town with me. Celebrate."

"Can't. But no reason you shouldn't get a shine on. You deserve it."

"I'll buy."

I could think of nothing to say to this. The world had somehow slipped out from under me; my will had seeped away. I was a spore to be whipped about by every draft, every loosed instinct, every whiff or whisper or creepy velleity — mine or another's.

"Don't make me beg, Brian. I'll spring for dinner, too."

"Well," I answered, not nearly as noncommittally as I'd hoped, "if you put it that way . . ." No harm, I figured: I was tired of arguing about it, tired of bucking him. And after all, birdie looked impossible. Bird was mired in the Ile de Paris version of Oakmont's church pews, and the fairway bunkers here are filled with heavy beach sand; muscling a long iron out of one of those back-benches is like running a ten-second hundred across a dune.

I shrugged. "You shoot fifty-nine, I go. Deal?"

"Deal."

Bird dug himself into the bunker. He aimed way right — at least twenty-five yards wide of the green. He picked it clean, hardly disturbed a grain of sand, and hit a graceful, rolling hook. The shot cleared the front trap by inches, skipped twice, then ran up the hill, onto the Chevy-sized steppe, and trickled to a stop eighteen inches short of the hole. The dozen or so on-lookers ranged around the back of the green clapped and whooped.

As soon as my card was scored, I fled the tent. Moments of fellow feeling are, happily, fleeting; the survival instinct kicks in. I had my own problems. I wanted to disappear before Bird could extract any of the information — where I was staying and so on — that he'd need to hold me to my idle promise. Besides, I was livid. That Roto-Rooter snap line was three inches from the lip of the front bunker, three inches from a sure six. Inches. "It'll be fine," he'd said. "I grew up in a briarpatch." Of course it would. It always is for idiot savants.

It's one thing to admire a man's skill, to appreciate a feathery touch around the greens, the ability to drop the hammer on the teeball, the guts to rap downhill eight-footers with authority; but there's nothing — nothing — more dispiriting to me than seeing blind faith rewarded. I hate it, hate it, hate it.

An example: I can't get onto my home track in Emma till noon on Mondays, and I usually stay home in the morning and watch television. The talk shows, for starters — Geraldo, Phil, the bald black drill sergeant, the blond with the leaking breast implants. At ten there's an evangelist on; his set is made of crepe-paper streamers, plastic ivy, a dozen soft-focus prints of Jesus, and a white lattice backdrop that appears to have been tacked together out of popsicle sticks or paint stirrers. It looks like a grade-school carnival. Which is, I assume, at least part of the reason why the show's been exiled to Monday: the Whatever-Day-They'll-Agree-To-Put-Us-On Adventists.

The Reverend R. A. Culver is an acne-scarred redneck with slicked-back hair and a sharkskin suit, and his show has twin subjects: faith healing and threats of damnation. Last week they paraded in the most pitiful band of rheumy-eyed analphabetics I've ever seen. The first guy up, it was explained, had been nerve deaf since birth. The second patient had a mysterious back ailment that had not responded to chiropractic, acupuncture, bed rest, tobacco poultices, or baths in Old Crow. The third sufferer whispered solemnly to Brother Culver, her chinless mouth nearly touching the ringlets over the reverend's ear. "This poor sinner," he explained, almost too broken up to speak, "suffers from one of the devil's vilest afflictions, the one known — God *He-p* us! — as *piles.*"

For each of them, Reverend Culver summoned two attendants whose job it was to stand behind the patient and catch him once the Holy Spirit tipped him over. Then Culver scrunched up his face, incanted a few "Demon come out, in the name of Jesus, demon come OUT!"s, and pressed his hand to Sufferer #1's ear, to the small of Sufferer #2's back, and (in what was either a touching display of delicacy or a grievous medical error) to Sufferer #3's waist. They all fell, were caught by the professional catchers, and recovered quickly enough to skip around the stage praising the Lord. The guy who'd been nerve deaf did a virtuoso rendition of "Oklahoma!" in the Jim Nabors style — not bad for someone who'd never heard it, and almost enough to make me want to swap maladies with him. I'd be deaf; he'd play golf. Fair's fair.

But it's not the frauds I feel bad about. It's the folks who have real problems and think Elmer Gantry can press his grubby fingernails to the locus of their troubles and *presto!* I wanted to say, "Look, #2, you may feel flush for the moment, but you're going to be laid out again tomorrow, with the added agony of having had false hopes. And #3, you'll be bleeding from the ass until they lower you unless you go to a doctor. Don't let this oily cracker touch you. And if you must, by all means wear a full-body antimacassar."

No, no, that's not it, either. I'm trying to duck what I really think. The problem isn't that these people are being gulled, though the Right Reverend Culver *is* a charlatan and his show *is* a scam. The problem is, at bottom, that faith does the trick sometimes. If someone comes to a Reverend Culver in good faith, believing absolutely in his connection to God and in God's desire to heal infirmity, maybe he or she *can* be healed. Piles do subside, sometimes. Tumors do shrink. Back pains do disappear. But it's not because of that quack, and it's not because of God. It's because of the faith itself; faith is the secret. People who have it can invest it wherever they want, according to their lights, but what they *do* with their faith doesn't matter at all — it's belief itself that cures them.

The kicker (and the grain of sand around which my anger has hardened like a bitter pearl) is that faith isn't available to everybody. It is a club exclusive to those who don't, who *won't*, know better. I hate them for the purity of their conviction. Because God doesn't really maim your boss in a wreck so you can have a promotion, does He? Prayer doesn't soak your crops. If you plow off a bridge in your car and, airborne, yank your hands off the wheel and shout *Jesus!*, the car doesn't turn into Chitty Chitty Bang Bang. The guy in the bathrobe who calls the ambulance and then disappears into the night isn't an angel; he's a neighbor who's eager to get back to World Championship Wrestling.

Cancers are not unmetastasized by positive thinking. Church singalongs do not reverse neurological damage. And having a boghopper in a fancy suit palpate your beltline won't unvaricose your rectal veins. I know, lady, I know what you'll say: "Tell my hemorrhoids that, young man. *I* feel great, praise the Lord."

Believe me, ma'am, I'd tell them if I could. That you can believe. I'd tell them all.

I haven't always felt this way: One of the things I adored about Rosa from the beginning was her religion, which seemed to me thrillingly uncompromised by theological content. She didn't "believe" in "God" in any emotional or intellectual way. Church was something you filled Sundays with, one of the rituals that happily, healthily, innocently circumscribed one's life. The churchyard's azaleas bloomed beautifully at Easter, always exactly at Easter — their timing, year in and year out, was all the proof of God's existence anyone could need. The windows along the sanctuary were pretty, the hymns tuneful and soaring; in the Holy Bible, bound in finest cowhide, Jesus's words were set off nicely in red. During dull moments you could check the bulletin to see whose birthdays were coming up, which elderly lady donated the flowers in the narthex in memory of the husband she survived. The offertory dish was lined in felt so as not to sully the service with the clink of coins; and one never felt better than when — in the yard, after the sermon — one shook the minister's dry hand and exchanged pleasantries ("Words of wisdom, Preacher, you were in rare form." "Thanks, Sister, thanks." "No, thank *you*. Will I see you at the potluck tonight? I'm bringing those lemon squares you like so much.")

I'm not being a smartass when I say that — in the beginning — I admired Rosa for the seamlessness, the certainty, the continuity of her world; her faith seemed to me not blind and unconsidered, but the product — it sounds silly to say it now — of an instinctive spiritual tact, a knowledge of how hard to bear down on questions and when to let them go. I thought . . . there was a time when I supposed I could crack the code of belief, when I believed that I too might learn to keep doubt at bay by putting on a suit and tie Sunday mornings and belting out a few hymns, taking in a maxim or two, donating six bits to the Fellowship Hall Fund. I went to church with her in Athens whenever golf permitted.

But since we married, Rosa's faith has taken on more of the zealot's willful blindness — and I'm to blame, at least in part.

It's just that the man from Nazareth and I are at loggerheads: He loves the little children, all the children of the world, and they scare hell out of me. I just want to win at golf. Is that so much to ask, to be good at something you've suffered for your whole life?

If you refuse to attend to the dangers — does Rosa have any idea how hard being a parent is? how consuming, how expensive, how painful? does she see what unconditional love costs? — if you refuse to attend to the dangers, they don't exist. Parenting isn't a perfectible art, and we'd fail our children somehow, no matter how we love them; all parents do. Knowing that, how can I choose to be a father?

I can't keep my eyes off the out-of-bounds stakes, the hazards, the traps. I can't. I've read the statistics, and I know that maybe ten percent of a golf course's acreage is tended — the rest is pure, unreconstructed trouble.

Meanwhile, Rosa pleads with me for a baby, and Bird never even noticed that bunker on eighteen.

Seventy-seven. For God's sake. Seventy-seven. The final tallies: nine greens hit, an anemic five fairways. Two lousy birdies. Thirty-two putts. One for three on sand saves. One snapped club. One scared stork. One ended career. Nice work. Good work.

And tomorrow's the swan song; tomorrow I die in music. Dad will be there to see his years of time and money and overblown hope spiral down the drain. That's the way he wants it. Cut your losses, son.

And Rosa, Rosa will be proud of me in at least one regard; I've kept good records. Going over my round was a rotten idea: They all are, after all. But it's done now, and the ledger needed to be kept. There's no reason, tonight of all nights, to do something dumb and fall afoul of my bitter half. I don't want Rosa suspicious. Speaking of which, I need to have a talk with that snitch Oswald, make sure he doesn't repeat his performance of this afternoon. *Acting erratically.* Tonight I'll show him erratic.

Seven-oh-nine. Time to go. It's a good thing I've got those practice-round winnings; I hope Ellen doesn't take me somewhere where ninety won't cover the damage. The last thing I need is to pull out my credit card and risk exposure . . . on both ends.

Some clown has parked about eight inches away from my car, so I have to brace myself with my left hand to snake my way into the seat; as I do, I hear the telltale tick of my wedding ring on the doorframe. Which is a good thing, all in all. *That* would be a clever move. Most of your first-rate philanderers show up at their assignations sporting wedding bands.

Hearing the click of ring on car roof reminds me of my first weekend of wedded bliss. As soon as Rosa and I could slip away from the reception, we left for Lauderdale. I'd insisted that nobody smear shaving cream on my car, tie cans or old shoes to my bumper — I hate those fertility customs — so as we sped down I-95, there was no incriminating "Just Hitched" sign to identify us. I told Rosa I'd divorce her on the spot if she burbled to anyone about our being honeymooners. "When have you ever seen me burble?" she asked. "Ever? And what makes you think that being married to you is the kind of thing that would set a girl to burbling?"

The whole way down I drummed my wedding band on the top of my car, spinning it a quarter turn with my thumb every few minutes — trying to beat away its sheen. A gleaming ring is a dead giveaway, and I was determined not to have to endure the smirks, the honks, the lifted thumbs, the leers that seem to be the lot of the newlywed. By the time we hit the Florida line that ring had passed twenty simulated anniversaries; it was as dull as nicked brass. And all the time we were in Fort Lauderdale, nobody figured us for just hitched. I consider that one of the triumphs of my life. You take them where they come.

This time I have a different set of questions to evade. Circumstances change, they say, as you get older. I'm surprised that I put the ring on in the first place. I was so rattled by running into Rosa's proverb a little while ago — "There is no sight so precious" — that I must have just slipped it on when I got dressed. Habit, what every marriage eventually breaks down to. I'll slip the surly little bond into the bin beneath my fusebox for safekeeping.

But when I pull down the lid of the cubbyhole, there's a sliver of notepaper looking up at me. Another of Rosa's bunny eggs, in there for who knows how long — long enough to have yellowed, to have curled at the edges like parchment. I unroll it and read this, in vivid red caps: "'CURSE NOT THE KING, NO NOT IN THY THOUGHT; FOR A BIRD OF THE AIR SHALL CARRY THE VOICE, AND THAT WHICH HATH WINGS SHALL TELL THE MATTER.' (Eccles., 10:20). Watch your mouth, Brian. Love, Rosa."

The note is a relic of Rosa's miscarried crusade, a year and a half ago, to wean me of my so-called habit of blasphemy. I crumple the warning, toss it onto the hood of my neighbor's car, start my own. As I back out, Hatch comes cruising into the parking lot, riding shotgun with a Chicano rookie they call Oscar. (For weeks I thought Oscar was his real name; it turns out to be a sobriquet Hatch saddled him with because he carries a sleeve of lunchmeat in his golf bag to snack on.)

As I pass, Hatch flags me to stop, but I just raise my middle finger and step on the gas. From the corner of my eye I watch his chin swivel in disbelief. The narc. On my way out, I sawed his toaster-oven cord in half with my pocketknife. Nothing to lose now.

Near the highway, under the glowing, fifty-foot Ibis Inn sign, the proprietor is watering his zinnias. They're zinnias for sure, I can thank Mom for my certainty about that; I can see their tall, tossed heads, even the fur on their stems. They fill a small brick bed that surrounds the metal signpole. The masonry has been cracked away by some traffic mishap, and the brick is sooty with exhaust; these blossoms spend their days bent double by the wind of passing trucks, and the sun punishes them. But zinnias are hardy, can stand up to most anything. And these are loved. I've seen the old man out here three afternoons in a row now, hosing them down.

The gardener/motelier is a retired mailman, a friendly Minnesotan named Dexter Clough. He wears a fishing hat decorated with lures, maroon Bermuda shorts, the navy support stockings that carried him over his route for thirty-odd years. If you took home a room key, he's the kind of guy who'd write you a letter and ask you to send it back. You'd find a stamp clipped to his request, a smiley-face inked on its back.

I creep over his hose with my front wheels, call out a soft "Sorry" through the window. I don't want to disturb him at his leisure; he's like my father out back in that cow lot, plunking wedges until supper — a man piecing his world together with the available glue.

Dexter turns and waves at me with his hose hand: "No problem," he mouths. As his salute reaches its highest point, my rear wheel releases the hose, and there's a surge of pressure. The water froths up, spills onto Mr. Clough's white sneakers. He hops backward.

I turn right, toward Charleston. I'm exactly on time.

# CHAPTER SIX

# Thursday, 8 P.M.

AT FIVE OF EIGHT I PARK ON Rev. Marshfield Ave., ten or so blocks from the market. Feeling frisky, I leapfrog a parking meter and get a dirty look from a dowager in a blue evening dress. Her son's bouncing along beside her, talking, but the lady moves so smoothly that I can't believe she's not on casters. She stares, glissades my way.

It's hard to tell, for a moment, that the stare is unkind; age has melted away her lips, and she's painted in their stead a kindly coral rictus. The woman's hair is a white poof, smooth and round as a basketball. Beneath her temples are two slashes of rouge, stakes to mark the cheekbones buried there years ago. Her face is lined like a road map that's done duty since the Eisenhower years, but the effect is almost pretty — after all, it's helping people get where they want to go that creases maps and dowagers. I almost fool myself into believing she's just a sweet old biddy out for a night on the town with her boy.

But once you know to look for it, her scorn is unmistakable. You can see it under her balding brows, where loose skin has clumped like twin thunderheads; most of each eye is concealed by the fallen and falling flesh, flesh she's shadowed an angry slate-blue to match her dress. It's a wonder she can pinch a glare out of the slits she has left, but she does. The other sign of enmity is, oddly enough, her purse. It's a fierce, fist-sized thing of chain mesh, and she holds it in front of her to ward me off.

The old woman can't bear to look at me for long. But as she floats by (I look up from digging for change, flash my winningest smile), she crooks a finger and says, "Not necessary." It sounds like an overall appraisal, a verdict on my life.

I pretend not to hear, flush a dime down the meter. She turns around, five feet away. "Not necessary," she calls again, almost affably, "NOT necessary." I wave. Thanks for the advice, Mamie, and have a nice day.

She waves back with her mailed fist. Her eyelids look like moldy cheese; it occurs to me that, as hair and fingernails legendarily do, that slack skin will continue to accumulate after she's dead until it covers her whole face.

The dowager's son hops alongside her, yammering — he's wearing a tux and whipping the air with a rolled program like a jockey trying to get the most out of his mount. There's a patch of razor burn like a love bite under his ear. He's pleading with her about something; I can't make out much, something about a river, but I distinctly hear the phrase "groping for trouts." Senseless, sure, but that's what I hear. They float down the street — mother steady and stately as a ship, son leaning into her — then sweep around the corner and out of sight.

I've been feeding the meter dimes ever since the old lady caught me (she imagines) mounting it. By the time I realize that the metermaids punch out at six, I've poured sixty cents into the abyss. Ah, well. No harm done. A gift to the Grand Old Lady, Charleston — may she use it well.

I head east. Two blocks down I pass a fire station staffed by vintage trucks soaked in the surreal red that engines get painted — three of them, lined like tinker toys along the sidewalk. One is an ancient steam contraption drawn by a tractor; it consists of bright valves and vaguely fallopian pipes and spirals, looks like a calliope. The engines have just been washed; their tires are bearded with foam, and spent water is seeping into the gutter. I can see my reflection in the paint. Their ladders are gleaming silver; their hoses are pristine.

No detail has been stinted in this genre portrait: On the threshold of the station house a fire-axe stands guard over the watermelon halves it's been used to cleave; yellow waders dangle from a hook inside the open door; there's even a sleeping dalmatian in sight. No firemen to be seen, not a sound to be heard. Which seems right: this station is meant not to be manned but to be gazed upon. In Charleston, it's more impor-tant to put out artlessness than fire.

I can read the word "Hughes" — the familiar, low-tech sten-cil — on the underside of one coil, and I wonder whether, years ago, my father watched these hoses — six-inch high-pressure fire tubing, jacketed with cotton and dacron — slide by his crew on the conveyor belt that paid for my golf.

Charleston is a great place to let your mind roam, a living mu-seum; and like any good museum, it's designed to promote not reflection but a languid history-consumption. How to fret over your prosaic problems in an exhibit hall? The scale's too big — your split-level ranch is smaller than the information kiosk in the lobby. What's a hundred-buck phone bill or a bunion among reassembled triceratopses? Think you have it bad: Your foun-dation slab's been extruded by an oak root. Well, they can't fix Bhopal or Chernobyl with a steam jack and a few sacks of Redi-Mix. And how much can that new contact lens smart when your eyes are taking in the horrors of *Guernica,* or Tre-blinka?

There are no mirrors to be found in galleries — for once, you get to pay attention to things outside yourself. Your mind has things to rest on that aren't the shabby furniture of your life. For a few hours your every failure isn't underfoot. There are facts to be plucked, weighed, labored over. Again and again you whisper, "Now I didn't know that; that I did not know," and there's relief in that, maybe even pleasure: You're tired of everything you *did* know, sick of what you can't un-know. In a museum, you're safe from the limits of your cramped little life.

In the grand entryway your eyes rove over the cutaway diagram of the gallery, where the wealth of the collections is laid out for you. You pass those eyes appraisingly over rooms of artifacts as you do a fork over a crowded plate; like feasts, museums make you logy, gassy, full. The exhibits are respectfully spaced, and no low ceilings to press you down. Walls are stashed behind pictoglyphs or Picassos or *Pickelhauben* so that they escape notice. The floors are specially designed to dampen footfalls. It's the doorways that dominate; they seem to be everywhere, imposing enough that you can call them portals if you've a mind to. They lead to the bony fishes, or the Etruscans.

In a good museum the air is warm and heavy. There's nowhere to sit. Trouble is kept under glass. Snoozing guards set you an example, and all lighting is indirect.

I take in the sights of Charleston. For the first time in forever, I have something to look forward to, and the best thing about that is that I don't have to, for once — look forward, that is. I don't have to ponder the next failure on my schedule. I can savor whatever my eyes settle on, can feel — I can't helping thinking of it this way — that I've been set free from a long imprisonment. Drinks, dinner, manumission. Ellen.

For these next five minutes, until I get to the market, I can watch Charleston parade past in evening's flattering half-light. She's an old maid, of course, but the kind (like my pal Mamie) whose former beauty can still be read from the ruins. The streets are pretty empty in this neighborhood, the sidewalks broken up every twenty yards by a threadbare sabal palm or a bum toping out of a sack. There's scaffolding on nearly every exposed wall, and I pass an old art-deco moviehouse whose marquee appears to have been lifted off by the hurricane and then set down slightly askew, like a cheap toupée.

Near one storefront a black woman in a lawn chair shucks

Silver Queen corn — a phenomenon that needs explaining, since
the shop she's in front of vends art books and the street appears
not to contain any housing. Her fingers drip silk, and she never
raises her face as I go by.

I make my way into the cheese-and-towel district, that area
in every tourist town where visitors can buy gewgaws for in-
laws or dog-sitters or grandchildren; I see cigarette boxes with
Fort Sumter in brass intaglio, she-crab-soup prints, Charles
Towne potpourri, wrought-iron umbrella stands, wicker baskets, Porgy and Bess bobblehead dolls, "I Survived Hugo"
t-shirts, Rainbow Row postcards computer-blurred to resemble
Monet water lilies.

As I near the market, the midpriced knickknacks give way to
fancier wares: Godiva chocolate, Dunhill tobaccos, Laura Ashley frocks. I pass a shop called Mayrant's Apothecary where, in
the backlit show window, there are stone pestles, phials full
of herbs and saps, and tall bright jars filled with peppermint
sticks.

It's less deserted here. There are men in tuxes, women in
gowns — looking to be in a hurry. Some are sipping cham-
pagne from two-piece flutes. The whole city seems to be turned
out in formal dress tonight. Behind me a church clock tolls
eight, and I pick up my pace. A young man with a flashily
waxed mustache, sitting on a stoop, asks if I have any letters
I'd like him to mail. He extends his hand. No thanks, I tell
him, none just now, but he doesn't retract the mitt. "So they're
about me, then," he accuses. "What lies do you spread about
Smaragd?"

Horses clop by towing carts packed tight with sunburned
tourists; the carts are festooned with ads for bailbondsmen and
all-you-can-eat seafood restaurants. Plastic sacks swing beneath
the horses' tails — some empty, some not. The animals know
the drill. Slow, easy: the pace of a tourist jaunt and of a funeral
retinue are the same. Underneath the males you can see the
pouches of scar tissue, all that remain of the stallion: *stumps of
black gutta percha wagging limp between their haunches.*

Golf balls were once made of gutta percha. The first was molded in 1845 by the Reverend Robert Paterson — who used, legend has it, the packing around a statue of Vishnu a spiritualist had sent from India. The molded ball was a rousing and immediate success; gutties were durable, cheap, waterproof, and rolled truer on the greens than the featheries they replaced. They took some of the luck out of golf and lowered scores dramatically, both of which kindled new interest in the game. As a result of the introduction of the gutta percha pellet, the Old Course at St. Andrews got so crowded by the mid-1850s that it had to be expanded to eighteen holes, which subsequently became the standard.

In short, gutties saved golf: God provides, it's said, and Vishnu's beneficence is well-known. But that's not where the occult angle peters out. It's not just a case of one plaster Vishnu, a little excelsior, an overheated imagination. Golf's weirder than that. The greatest of the gutta percha balls was called the Agrippa, after the German writer and sorcerer Heinrich Cornelius Agrippa von Nettesheim, author of the *De occulta philosophia* and purported model for Goethe's *Faust*. The Agrippa ball came in sizes ranging from twenty-six to thirty pennyweight and bore a lovely bramble marking like the one, so I'm told, on the throat of certain birds. Its name, I imagine, came from the way the ball's flight path could seem to bend to the will of a skillful player. Good golf has always implied traffic with the devil — it's in the nature of the thing.

The earliest gutta balls were as smooth as eggs and tended, until they got scuffed up in play, to duck and dive unpredictably, a tendency that earned them the nickname "quail darters." Soon the best ballmakers slit and dented their gutties with a hammer as a matter of course, to make them fly better; those random hammerings are the forerunner of the almost six hundred perfect duodecahedral dimples on the nugget I teed up today.

Vishnu, Agrippa. There's never been any separating golf and the occult. But it goes far beyond German magic and Hindu gods, crosses all lines of faith: In the dictionary, for example, golf fits snugly between golem and Golgotha. I've looked it up.

Before Vishnu gave Bob Paterson a nudge in the right direction, golf balls were made of cowhide stuffed with boiled goosedown. Feathers. I remember my father reading to me about those primitives from an enormous green book, entitled *The History of Golf* but called by him simply *The Lore:* me in my bed, Dad alongside in my puny desk chair, half-glasses near the end of his nose, index finger tracing his progress down the page. It was around the time when he sawed down my first set of clubs, and I was as excited with the game as he was. It is the only book I remember him reading to me. He recited with feeling:

> When the stuffing iron failed there was brought into play an awl, and the artisan instilled into the leather cover a volume of feathers not less than that used to fill the crown of a beaver hat. The ball was hammered into the semblance of a sphere, coated with three layers of paint. In wet weather these unround balls often grew sodden and flew apart, with disastrous consequences for the conscientious golfer, who was often unsure which remnant good sportsmanship dictated he continue play with.

That was poetry to me. I haven't laid eyes on *The History of Golf* in years, don't know if my parents still have it; its binding was letting go already fifteen years ago, and every time I finished dipping in, I had to secure *The Lore* with rubber bands to replace it on the shelf among Dad's books of tips and pointers (his "library," as my mother truculently referred to it, consisted of fifty or so of these manuals plus the thick, esoteric, greenbound volumes of *Decisions on the Rules,* which my father paid the USGA to send him every year). The point is this: Despite the lapse of a decade or more, I'm sure I got the passage about featheries verbatim. There are things you don't forget. Golf was beautiful then.

My father, for his part, always grew glassy-eyed on the subject; despite the abuse he heaped on Mom for her "silly" romance with the aristocracy, he was as bad about *The Lore*. "Charleston," he'd tell me, "isn't the only damn thing with a history. Golf has one, I have one, you too. Hell, even fire hoses have a history. They started out back in olden times with a length of ox gut, switched to sewn-up leather in the 1700s, and now . . . now we've got your modern space-age polymers. I'm talking about *fire hoses,* son: as much going on there as Charleston will ever manage. Folks at the Battery are like Chinese: They eat rice, they worship their ancestors. But they've got no more history than anybody else."

When I was eight, *The Lore* was exactly as tall as the space between my pelvis and neck; it notched there nicely, felt as natural as a cane pole might have felt in the crook of my thumb in another time, in another South. I used to nap under it like a twenty-pound blanket. I sat in my room or the sewing cubby for hours at a time, running my hands over pictures of the great players (Old Tom Morris, Horace Rawlings), the great courses (Royal Lytham, Cypress Point), and the miraculous clubs themselves. I wanted to know everything about golf: its history, its rules, its elaborate etiquette, and most of all its core of mystery. Once I learned the lore, once I mastered the skills, I would be serene; I would be sure; I would be my father on one of his rumbles into the kitchen. And my victory — unlike his — my victory would last. They'd record it in *The History of Golf*.

The clubs were my favorites — weapons crafted with as much attention to beauty as effectiveness, like maces nearly too heavy to wield. In the nineteenth century the sticks carried exotic names: bulger, spoon, brassie, niblick, mashie, cleek, baffy. The gutty was cruel on clubs, so after the introduction of the new, harder ball, brittle thorn gave way to softer woods — apple, beech, and pear — in the making of clubheads. Shafts were whittled out of the hearts of hickory limbs from Russia or Tennessee, the wood worked with a hundred vivid verbs along the way: seasoned, cut, filed, shaved, chiseled, gouged, leaded, boned, planed, scraped, blessed, and, last of all, "glass-papered down to the required length, shape, and degree of whippiness, which was the real art."

The grips were spirals of untanned hide bound with tarred twine — unattached, they looked like apple skins unwound by old-timers. The blades were forged from bars of iron *The Lore* called "mild." Hammered. Tempered. Notched. Emery-wheeled. Inset with leather. Wooden clubheads were treated with a hare's foot dipped in a stew of varnish, oil, and crushed garlic — the hare, of course, having been selected as much for its legendary good luck as for its usefulness as a varnish brush. Garlic was sprinkled into the mix as a hindrance to magnetism. Allium, so it's said, can kill off lodestones' ability to attract metal, and it wouldn't do to have your irons serving two masters: best to keep their attention aboveground. Clubmakers let nothing slip by them. Like any other science, sorcery calls for vigilance, for scholarly, loverly care.

In *The Lore* there were pages and pages of psalms to the clubmaker's art. I read them, treasured them all. "A good club," the book informed me (without — it was an old book — so much as a hint of blue), "should fit your hands like a good woman. Your grip should be firm but tender, and the rightness of the fit and feel of the lovely implement should announce itself in the minutest details." I can't recall believing anything more fervently than I believed that.

❦

Before I'm halfway across the street that fronts the market, I hear Ellen's voice, raised in complaint: "It's about time you showed. I thought I was being stood up." She taps her watch twice with a flawless nail. Click, click.

Since I last saw her, Ellen has changed into a sailor jacket with gold piping, a matching miniskirt, white knee socks. Her hair is bundled in a prim chignon that shows off a neck any greyhound would be proud of — but where did all that hair come from? I feel sure it was short this afternoon, remember thinking about it while I watched the interview. The henna coil must be a prosthesis. They sell them in catalogs these days, like vacuum attachments; they're made from horsehair, nylon. There are even women, I hear, who make a living by their scalps, growing strands of waste skin and sebum for sale to the highest bidder.

Yes, I can see the heavy pins that shore it up, the paisley bow that imperfectly conceals the stays. A good omen. The world smiles on cosmetic lies, Ellen's no less than anyone else's. I feel good. My new life is beginning, and I feel, for once, like an artisan. I am good at what I do: hammer, temper, plane, notch. I am indomitable — not to be domited by man, woman, or golf. I shot fifty-nine today. Geiberger. Me.

My date looks like a porn Pippi Longstocking, all red hair and hellcat, but fastened in for the moment, buttoned up, demure as a Tri Delt pledge. The effect is knee-weakening. I can picture Ellen as a candystriper, wheeling month-old magazines through hospital halls, calves flexing under white stockings as she bulldogs her battered tin cart around a corner; every day she swats away the roving hand of a lech in for angioplasty.

And I imagine (I can't help myself, or rather Bird can't help himself) her pubic thatch now, tonight, shaved into a Doric strip for the coming beach season — an auburn exclamation piled onto the pink point of her pudendum. I envision (now that I'm getting the hang of this foreign lust) Ellen in her bath, tracing the shaven edges to be sure her new tonsure's straight, rinsing the razor, teasing recalcitrant curls from the blade with the pad of a finger. I think of the halo of virgin skin exposed by the shave, that shocking white that heralds her sex like smoke around a magic trick. Here, Agrippa, is your philosopher's stone. *I do not think this way; I do not.*

"Think you might want to check me out above the waist, too?" asks Ellen, peevishly. "Yoo hoo, up here."

*"Bon soir, mon faire Pipi,"* I open, suavely, lifting my eyes to meet hers. "No harm meant. I was thinking about something."

"I'll bet," says Ellen, looking perplexed. "I'll bet you were." It's hard to tell how offended she is. Off on the wrong foot again, but tonight I have confidence on my side. "Where've you been?" she asks.

It's only three after.

"A gentleman doesn't make a woman wait," she chides, "especially if she's tarted up like *this*." She gestures to her sailor suit like a game-show hostess introducing a frostless fridge, brushing her hands upward along her ribcage, past her breasts (with a hint of shy acceleration), up the dainty filament of her neck, along the bow of her jaw line; finished, she drops her palms over the gold-braid epaulets on her shoulders. I'm a little teapot.

I look at Ellen's throat, at the ripples of blue beneath it, and I imagine what Rosa's doing: She's standing on rickety plyboard risers in the rehearsal room at the church hall — the adult choir having ceded the chancel to the kids — bringing in the sheaves. She's wearing her velveteen practice robe over jeans and a t-shirt, hair tied back with the rubber band that bound last Sunday's Atlanta *Constitution*. She's entirely sure of herself; she draws a tithe card slowly down the page to mark her place; the robe's frayed hem pools at her feet. Rosa's throat is corded out like a dockworker's arm.

Meanwhile, one of Ellen's upper incisors is lovably off kilter; her nose, it seems, is smaller than my thumb. *Charmant.*

"Anything to say for yourself?" she finishes. There's more coquetry in Ellen's speech, I think, than annoyance; she owes me, after all, a debt of gratitude for buying her so much airtime this evening. She wouldn't have landed it without me, and if she expects to graduate to bigger stories, bigger markets, bigger dollars, she has to log some flight hours. I'm just this side of a godsend.

I *am* late, though, by however little, and what she's looking for now is a gallant. I'm only too happy to oblige. I can be anyone she wants me to be. A gentleman it is.

"I apologize. I had to park over . . . yonder, near the, the" — how much Charleston should I know? — "Mississippi or the Pecos or whatever. I beg the lady's indulgence."

"You've never been to Charleston, I guess?" Her small talk is a little disappointing, listless, pro forma. I decide to show her the way.

"No, but I love my rivers. I'm a geography buff. This trip to your country has been, for me, a voyage of discovery. Edisto, Maniscaloon, Chattooga, Pocotaligo. At home we make do with the Limpopo."

"You're a regular Vasco da Gama," teases Ellen. She says da Gamma, like he's one of her sorority sisters.

"Fourteen-ninety-seven," I stall, racking my brain. Is that right? "Cape of Good Hope, Cape of Storms. That's us. La Africa del Sur. Pearl of the nether hemisphere. Vasco's a — how do you say it? — a homeboy of mine."

"Congratulations." She shifts her weight from foot to foot. I appear not to be exactly what she was expecting.

But I keep swinging away. "I try. You know, folks appreciate it when you show an interest in their grim little hamlets, their arid little lives. All you need to know is a landmark or two. . . ."

"Enough!" says Ellen, rolling her black eyes. They're shadowed in Egyptian bronze. Classy. Rosa wears cakes of blue like a girl playing at womanhood. "I *know* you can talk shit. Don't you know any other tricks?"

Talk about your low-hanging fruit. I think she's hoping I'll say something salacious, confirm my pigdom, but I'm too quick for her. A shrug is my only answer. A subtle, blameless, genteel sort of a shrug.

Ellen nods, feigns a yawn. She's doing a marvelous impression of someone who has no interest in me. "Look," she announces, "we'll have a drink or two, eat some dinner, then cut our losses. OK?" Her hostility is alluring. I worried that our date would go *too* smoothly. Every pursuit has to have an element of doubt, of suspicion. I've never seen a movie romance that didn't begin in awkwardness and animus. Ellen's complicated; I'm liking her more every minute.

"By the way," she says, "those are swell threads. You look

like a young Lawrence Welk. Didn't you promise to bring it down a notch tonight?" The only blazer I brought along on the trip is Masters green, and I'm wearing it with khakis and a white golf shirt. Rosa was sure the ensemble would wow my mother's cronies in McClellanville.

"Whelk? You mean like the seashell?" Ho ho HO. I'm enjoying this. Rosa, by contrast, isn't much for the old Hepburn-Tracy-style repartee; she lives her life in dreadful earnest, like the lower animals. There's no irony in her. Ellen will be eating out of my hand any minute now.

"Never mind." Americans are so ill-educated; they know the names of almost nothing. I try another tack. "I'm desperately sorry to have kept you waiting. I was pondering the verities, you know. That eats up the clock. I —"

"I thought you were parking."

"Well, that too. Parking's one of the seven *modern* verities. Now, what say we find ourselves a pub and tap the admiral before dinner?" I'm cutting a dashing figure, I believe, a devastating cross between Cary Grant and Noel Coward. Bird would be proud to have lent me his name.

Ellen reaches out, and I assume she's going to stroke the Adam's apple that's ticking out all these devilish quotes. Instead she springs the tip of my collar loose from my lapel. Then she licks her pinky, Mom-like, and scratches at a splotch of congealed gravy on my shoulder.

"Look, you smug bastard," she whispers, "I'd ditch you now, but I've made reservations it would be expensive and embarrassing to break, so we're going to stick this out. You're going to buy me dinner, and we're going to get along. But it's my turf, and we play my rules. Do you understand?"

I nod, shakily. Where did that damned gravy stain come from? I'd hate to have it drag me down.

"That glib crap plays all right on TV. I was drawn in at first. You seemed enigmatic; I assumed you weren't letting on what you really thought because there was something *to* it. But I figured your act was, like, an act. I didn't think that could be all there was to you."

"But . . ." I sputter. "But, but . . ."

"Hear me out," she hisses. "Tonight's not TV; we're in three dimensions now. Did it ever occur to you that my idea of a good time might not be holding a microphone under the nose of some bush-league whack-off from Racistland? That I'd like to do a little talking myself, to be *asked* a question or two? You might do me the favor of treating me like a person and not a goddamned straight man. Also, for your information, I know what a whelk is. Surprise! We've got eighth-grade science in America, too. It was only that I couldn't believe you had said something so asinine. And you need to brush up on your French, slick. I don't think *Mon faire pipi* means quite what you hoped."

She pauses, just getting warmed up. I can't meet her eyes. My calves ache. People are gawking at us as they stride by on the sidewalk, at Pippi and her whipping boy, the princess and the smug bastard.

"And while you're at it," Ellen goes on, "get better material. If you want to hone your lounge-lizard routine, I'll be glad to drop you at the Holiday Inn. You can work your way down the bar asking the D cups their birth signs. But don't lay this 'tap the admiral' garbage on me. If you want a drink, say you want a drink. If you want to eat, speak up. If you want to fuck, you can fucking forget it. Got me, chief?"

It all comes crashing down; I'm Brian Schwan, a kelly-green clown on a lifelong losing streak. I shot a ton this afternoon. My dad's on his way to call an end to the charade. I've just had my balls cut off and handed to me by a woman who did the right thing but doesn't know why. I'm a married man, a would-be father. A dope. And Rosa is my life.

And the one thing in this world I understand a little, golf, fits my hand like a good woman. The rightness of the fit and feel announce themselves in the minutest of details.

How many times must I be taught? All joys are ephemeral, all fancies passing, all harmonies vagrant. It's over, again and again and again and again.

"I'm sorry," I mutter. "I'm sorry, I'm sorry." My tongue sags in my mouth, a slab of waterlogged leather. I can hardly stand up. Did I say Cary Grant? I couldn't have said Cary Grant. Did Cary Grant ever puke himself?

"You're looking green around the gills," says Ellen, taking my arm. Her cheeks are splotchy with ebbing passion. "Don't let it get you down. We'll make the best of it. I didn't mean to hit you quite so hard. I thought you could take it. I just want you to be yourself. Now show me a good time, OK?"

She pats me collegially on the side, cocks her head toward a seedy-looking bar about twenty feet away, executes a half spin. I get whipped around on the fulcrum of her arm, limp as a rag-mop. I don't even have the strength to flee; where would I go? I can hear the booming echo of my lies — "Once you find a road, you head down it," "Whack the ball, chase it till it sinks" — and I know that it's nothing so grand as philosophy that keeps me attached to Ellen's elbow, not terror, not even duty. All it is — once again — is dumb, graceless, unslippable inertia.

A cracked wooden sign proclaims the dive's name to be "Under the Rose." I follow Ellen in, licking my wounds.

☙

The laminated tabletop between us has been scored with the names of defunct couples: Troy hearts Tammy, Becky luvs Yobbo 4Ever, Nikki-n-Mike. While Ellen talks, I imagine keys and files and knives drawn furtively from pockets. I see the horny boys carving, the flattered girls looking out — or vice versa. All those hopeful surgeries — like clubmaking, if you think about it, but with a different set of verbs. Dig, plane, blow, whisk, spit-darken. Luv.

I think about those kids who figured it only takes a few

swipes of a knife to make half a dozen backseat gropes and a frantic coupling or two into forever. I know all there is to know about sham permanences. I've been married. While Ellen recounts her college days, I run my hands over the scarred tabletop, reading it like braille. I'm looking for "Rosa and Brian."

Of the thirty or so people in here, Ellen and I appear to be the only customers of legal age. I'm sipping a Dos Equis with a lime shoved down its throat, my seventh beer of the evening and the most needed of all; Ellen is working on something called an "Absolut Martini Extra Dirty on the Rocks with a Twist," her second.

She's been telling her life story, and I've laughed at every anecdote, asked every question I could think of. I've nodded so often that I feel like one of those bobblehead Porgys I saw in the shop window . . . could it have been less than an hour ago? Things are going bearably now, but it's a constant torment to look across at my foulmouthed, sloe-eyed ex-Pippi. I like Ellen for despising me. Maybe I even love her a little.

A while ago I was tempted to come clean, admit everything. Maybe she'd be flattered by the depths I'd sunk to; maybe she'd be a congenial audience for rock-ribbed confession. But I couldn't, for several reasons. Deceit is a road that, once struck out upon, can't easily be retraced or undone — why would Ellen believe me now, this time? I could show her my ID, but how would she know I wasn't lying about the details of my "rocky" marriage? And why would she look kindly on the truth, if its truthfulness alone wasn't enough to win her over? I've been a jerk; if I'm looking to fuck, I can fucking forget it. Easy enough for her to be a cynic now — I've given her every reason. And I can't say I don't love Rosa, that's the one lie too low even for me.

And if there are repercussions tomorrow, the truth would put Ellen in a worse position at the station. She's better off if she can deny all knowledge of my masquerade. Knowing who I am would scotch that; she might even feel compelled to admit my ruse to her bosses and suffer the consequences of having trusted me. I've drawn her into this. It's too late for regrets, I suppose, but I do feel bad.

Because she was a telejournalist, I assumed she'd consented to be cut down to the dimensions of a screen. I assumed she was as much a fake as I; it was a game to her as well. But it turns out, now, that we're linked in another way, a more human way: She too is twenty-six, unhappy, going nowhere, looking to change careers. She wants out of Charleston, out of small-time television.

"What I'm looking for now," she confided a while ago, "is something like the cliché my mom had, the life I despised for the longest time — a house with a wraparound porch, banisters to polish, begonias, someone to sit in the breakfast nook with me, children. But with one difference: I want the duties shared. I want to work, too, to be respected, to be taken seriously. I couldn't be more different from Mom — she claims that in every marriage there's 'one chief and one Indian,' and the woman is the Indian — but the things she wanted and had when I was a kid (I mean the actual *things,* not what she was willing to submit to in order to get them) aren't that different from what I'm after. I'd get a kick from tearing canning tips out of the paper over my second cup of coffee, every once in a while. I want to know how to grout, how to spear potato eyes on toothpicks and make them put down roots in a plastic cup. I want to teach girls in beanies the Girl Scout oath. As long as it's not my *obligation.* Obligation sucks, Bird." She stops, smiles. "Pretty good rallying cry, huh? I thought of it myself."

"Nice slogan," I agree. "Pithy but true. You ought to run on it."

Ellen continues. "I think I might even want to take up golf. Something to do in the sun. Tennis *clothes* are a lot better, but there's the sweating. I'm anti-sweating. So maybe golf would do the trick. You know, a pastime."

"Instead of kids?" I think I asked out of genuine curiosity, or because I was on questioning autopilot, but Ellen treated it as the pinnacle of wit.

Her epaulets rustled when she laughed. "I can't have both?" she asked. "Golf and children?"

My area of expertise, such as it is. I shook my head, smiled ruefully. There are no boths in this world. Boths are out of the question.

"Once you turn off the bullshit, you're really not that bad a guy," said Ellen, then caught herself. She sounded surprised to discover she might feel such a thing. "I don't mean that the way it sounds, Bird."

"What way does it sound?"

"Harsh."

"I have no problem with harsh," I told her. "Harsh I deserve."

She seemed to think that this, too, was funny. Her epaulets bobbed.

◎

We're going, she tells me, to a restaurant called Country Luke's. Its name is misleading — they serve very fancy ("tony," as Ellen says) Continental fare, complete with molded scallop mousses, veal medallions in blackberry butter, tarragon béarnaises, custom-blended teas.

Every night at 9:30, Tuesday through Saturday, twenty-four lucky gourmands get to watch the proprietor, Country Luke, pretend to put the finishing touches on each element of a seven-course meal. Dressed in tails and a crisp chef's toque, Luke stations himself in a copper-fitted *faux* kitchen shaped like a tongue of stage, accepts delivery of the silver serving dishes from underlings — and while he presents the sliced roast breast of duckling in its Oriental spices and raspberry purée, he tells tales of the comically backward Backcountry of his boyhood: "He's from some dinky hole upstate," Ellen tells me, "Clementine or something, and he's got some great stories, they say. Hick stories . . . you know, about outhouse pranks and cockfighting and screwing sows. Cross Jerry Clower and Paul Prudhomme, throw in some barnyard smut, and you've got the picture."

The things that pass, in snooty Charleston, for entertainment. A Redneck-Chef-from-Clementine, filling the bellies of transplants and parvenu tourists with the fare of the Old City: fool's pride, garnished with jeers. Ellen continues. "Everyone tells me it's a fabulous restaurant that doesn't take itself too seriously. I've always wanted to go. You're my chance."

The reason she hasn't gone, I'm left to interpret, is that she can't afford it — which is, at $72 per person, hardly a wonder. She thinks all golfers are loaded. My cash winnings from the practice rounds will barely cover our bar tab. How am I going to explain a $144 meal, plus tip — charged on the credit card whose use Rosa strictly polices? How am I going to sit through seven courses of rich food and Country Luke yarn-spinning after all that's happened today? I have an early tee time tomorrow. I'll bet Bird's in bed already, preparing himself to blitz the Ile come morning. He's mapping a plan of attack: where to let it rip, where to play for fours.

I hope he didn't see my performance on the news; the official consequences don't matter, but Bird would take it personally. I don't want him and Ellen caught in the crossfire of my suicide. The authorities ought to stuff me in one of those mesh cages and have the bomb squad detonate me under cloth. No need to take out any innocents. Contain the blast.

☺

Ellen's taken off her prosthesis, said it was "distressing" her scalp. No need to impress me anymore. The chignon sits in the middle of the table like a henna pincushion, a miniature mushroom cloud, a tomato, a dark crystal bolus.

This date is over . . . and I'm glad I'm past it. In a perverse way I'm eager to get back to the brand of failure I've made my career for these last few years. I want to get tomorrow over with; to-morrow I say my goodbyes. Tomorrow, at last, I contain the blast. At the end I'll saunter over to my father, crouched behind whatever refuge is handy. I'll shake his hand, thank him for everything, and I'll move on. "It's the cow lot for me, too, Dad," I'll say. "Maybe someday I'll have a kid who can play it right."

Rosa will be happy with me for quitting, and I'll do what I can to be happy with her. I'll get along.

Until then I can tough it out; I've been on my share of doomed dates. It's not even a question of toughing it out, really. I'm be-ginning to enjoy myself. The pressure's off. Plus, it's been a long time since I listened to a woman talk, really talk, at length, about things that matter to her; Ellen's told me more in the last three-quarters of an hour than Rosa's said in three years . . . though I suppose the fault there isn't all Rosa's, or isn't Rosa's at all.

Only thirty-five minutes till Country Luke breezes through the stage doors, into the footlights and the superbly spiced va-pors, and sings out a Snopesy prolegomenon to his epic meal. I'll make the best of my time.

Ellen came to Charleston five years ago, fresh from college in her home state of Virginia, thinking she'd set the Lowcountry on fire. "A nose for news," she told me, a tinge immodestly, "and a bod for the movies. I figured I couldn't miss." But her station's news director and evening anchor is, according to Ellen, a frumpy old hag who can't stand the competition ("She hides her makeup," Ellen expanded, "in a Craftsman tackle box, applies it right before she goes on, scrubs it off immedi-ately after the newscast. For months I wondered why. Turns out it's because the warthog who used to read weather told her she was the spitting image of Tammy Faye Bakker").

Ellen's first day on the job, she approached Tammy Faye, who was chain-smoking tiparillos and typing on the aged Royal she uses to seem as much like Edward R. Murrow as possible. Ellen told her how glad she was to be aboard, how much she was looking forward to learning the ropes from her and so on. After a couple of minutes Tammy Faye swiveled around from her typing, which had gone on noisily and uninterruptedly through Ellen's introduction.

"Princess," said Tammy Faye, "if you're going to sleep your way to the top around here, you're going to have to do it through me." She smiled sweetly, spun herself back around. "Dismissed," she barked, when Ellen didn't leave instanter.

Ellen's still not sure, five years later, what her boss meant. "And I haven't understood anything she's said since, the horsy bitch."

Rosa doesn't curse at all, though once — a pipe dream from the waning days of the sexual revolution — I asked her to in bed. She explained, coldly, that my question was not only unerotic and rude but could I see Moses and Jesus and Billy Graham talking that way? *The three of them together?* I thought, but I held my tongue. Furthermore, said Rosa, on a roll, our marital bed — "our marital bed," like the rumpled trailer-park nest of Cyclops and Regina — should be kept pure: What kind of child would be the issue of such a union?

Ellen, on the other hand, is better at cursing than any woman I've ever met. To hear a beautiful woman say "horsy bitch," "assface," "cocksucker" — what higher pleasure exists?

Anyway, Tammy Faye is stingy with airtime for the women reporters, so Ellen's been treading water; she's stuck covering satellite-tour golf, bromeliad societies, people who buy junker cars and park them over their water meters to avoid paying delinquent bills. Twice she's been sent to cover births at the zoo: one giraffe, one stump-tailed macaque. Tonight is the longest piece of hers the station has ever aired. "And I'm basically invisible in that. It's all you, Mr. She-Eats-Her-Fucking-Young."

I'm sorry. Sorry is something I have no trouble being. I've put

Ellen in danger. I'm sure the tour would want to squelch any scandal, to "save" its "reputation" — so it's unlikely that word of my deception will get back to the station unless some loose cannon (Bird?) calls there tonight. But Tammy Faye is vengeful, and not without resources — I don't know what I'd do if I cost Ellen her job.

On top of everything else, Ellen's been through a busted marriage. "I was that rarity," she told me, "a twenty-one-year-old virgin. Married the first guy who got in my pants."

"How'd he do that?" I asked. I was spewing out every question I could think of, my attention hopelessly divided. I had meant to say, "Why'd you do that?"

"What?"

"Nothing."

"How did he get in my pants? It wouldn't work anymore. The idea of dying with my cherry intact has lost its fear for me. You're a day late, a dollar short."

I tried to redeem myself. "Well, what happened? With your marriage, I mean."

Ellen bit her bottom lip, shrugged. "We got hitched. He couldn't get used to being a grown-up. Things went sideways."

She drew an unpolished oval nail across her neck.

"Isn't that always the way?" I lamented.

"So they say." That was the end of that topic.

I gesture to the bartender. He's behind his counter, plunging soapy pilsner glasses onto an upright brush while he checks the baseball scores. But that's thirty feet away.

"You want another martini?" I ask Ellen.

"Sure." She slugs down the last quarter of her drink, comes up with an olive between her teeth.

I hold up two fingers, shake them. The bartender reams another glass, sticks it in a rack. "Pardon me," I call.

Nothing.

"Barkeep. *Mister* Barkeep."

"Wanna hear me wissow?" asks Ellen, chewing her olive. "I'm a very good wisswer." Her two martinis have done their work.

"That's all right."

The bartender looks up, but not in my direction. Some joker's standing in front of him in a white poplin suit, hair gelled back. Cigarette smoke plumes around his head. The guy's holding a wide-brimmed plantation hat like the one Wass wore, eight years ago, on the day I met Rosa. He's twirling it atop a finger . . . another agonizing echo of Wass. Who's he kidding? Must be a foreigner, or an idiot — a lid like that is likely to get him knifed down this way. After a moment, though, it strikes me that the squire at the bar has a familiar frame. I've seen that sunburned neck, that yellow hair. There's something about the way his pants pouch in the back that I can't help recognizing. I can feel the bile rising in my throat, a fearful tide. Then he turns, points at us.

"And two more," yells Bird, "for my good friend Bird Soulsby and his *dazzling* companion." He grinds out the cigarette and strides our way. Bird. Gliding like a god, like some carefree kenotic who'll be back at the right hand of the Almighty in no time, no worse for the wear, as soon as his work is done.

This can't be happening. Black magic again. Bird Soulsby knows things no one can know. How did he find us? Why is he playing along?

"I'm a good friend of Charlie Parker here," he tells Ellen, kissing her hand. He's handsome, I realize, even dressed like this. "Brian Schwan. I'm very proud to meet you."

Ellen's mesmerized. "You're gorgeous," she says.

"Why thank you, Ms. McCovery. You're not half bad your ownself." This is the same stuff she deplored in me. I wait for the anvil to fall, but she blushes, smiles.

"Please, it's Ellen. Don't I know your name from some-where?" She doesn't wait for a reply. "Are you going to a cos-tume party?" She giggles.

Bird has a finger raised to his lips, a look of mild alarm on his face. He twirls the hat like a six-gun. *I'm a-gonna clean up this here town.* Abruptly he reaches across me to the middle of the table, drops his hat over Ellen's doffed chignon, claps both hands onto the brim. "Never fear," he says. "I think I trapped it." He grins at Ellen. Where did he get the hat? Has he tracked down Wass? Have they conspired? Could Bird have *researched* ways to humiliate me? And what's his angle? What is Wass's headgear supposed to tell me? Is all this a preamble to expo-sure? Is Bird going to rat me out to Ellen, to the tour director, after all? Or will he play along all evening, giving me, in his teacherly way, the scare I "deserve" — setting me up for a lec-ture tomorrow? (If tomorrow comes; if I can show my face at the Ile in the morning.) Is the lid an evil he could have plucked up by accident? Is it the kind of thing he'd wear to the slave market — he's an odd man, to be sure — as a private joke? Maybe the market is just another destination on his tour of Old Charles Towne; maybe he's stumbled upon us. Can't be too many bars down here. There are explanations. There must be explanations.

Bird keeps babbling at Ellen. "To answer your questions: Bird was kind enough to mention me in y'all's interview. I played with him today. That must be why I seem familiar. As for the wardrobe, I'm settling a debt. I told my partner here on the eighteenth that if he closed out his fifty-nine, I'd wear the manhole cover" — he gestures to the planter's hat — "*à la belle étoile* tonight."

"You saw my interview?" Welcome to rock bottom.

"Oh, absolutely. Marvelous work. First-rate. Your questions were incisive, well put. It won't be long before you have your own show. These yokels be damned. They're not taking full ad-vantage of your talents. Eloquence like yours deserves a mid-major market at the least."

"Thank you." Ellen beams.

Bird looks down. "Would you two hotshots buck if I were to ask to join you for a minute? You know, every also-ran likes to rub shoulders with greatness now and again." He chuckles.

What do you say if the man you've been impersonating walks in on your date, got up like a Kentucky colonel on Derby Day, claiming to be you, and asks do you mind if he tags along? How do you shed a shadow?

"Well," I said grumpily, "OK by me, but we've got to go in a few minutes. Ellen?"

"I wouldn't dream of letting him get away," she purrs. How quickly they fall.

"And I wouldn't dream," says Bird, "of holding you up. You're busy people, I imagine." I'm busy people indeed.

Ellen stifles a burp and says, "You two pardon me a minute. I'm sure you've got plenty to talk about. Keep an eye on him, Bird. I'll be back in a jiffy." She tips the hat, retrieves her coil of hair. I see it disappear into her fist as she wheels for the bathroom. The fraud is on again, all the way around.

CHAPTER SEVEN

# Thursday, 9 P.M.

ALONE WITH THE BEAST. As Ellen weaves toward the ladies',
I stare into the tray of honey-roasted nuts on the table —
looking for a friend. The platter's in the shape of a pig, and
peanuts have been prodded to its edges, where they've caught
on the stickled lip. The shards ranged along his spine make the
pig look like a docile cousin to the stegosaurus, a resemblance
I find comforting.

I once had a book called *The Stegosaur Who Burped
Bubbles*. A gift from an out-of-touch aunt, it was that rarity, a
plaything unlinked either to golf or Charleston; Aunt Beth didn't
know the prescribed themes. The book had to do with a sweet-
tempered refugee from the Jurassic who was adopted by a kid
named Clarence. Clarence hid his friend under tarps and old
fishing gear in the carport, and Mom and Dad learned about
Steggy only when he ate a box of laundry detergent and, with a
series of massive burps, overran the neighborhood with foam.
This was where the book took a turn toward fantasy: Clarence's
parents only clucked their tongues and mussed the boy's hair
and insisted that henceforward he feed Steggy dog food or table
scraps. Clarence got to keep an armor-plated monster, but
for me one careless double-bogey meant a week of enforced

practice in the garage, making my putting stroke failsafe and brooding on the price of mental errors.

Steggy was purple, and every time he belched a soap glacier, the illustrator raised a green welt of blush on his cheek. I haven't forgotten that bashful bruise: I had a stash of books in the trophy room, stuffed down the mouth of an old golf bag, and despite frequent exiles my putting never approached Dad's ideal. (He had to suspect. Whenever I complained about lip-outs, he said, "You make your own breaks. Bad luck is the game's way of telling you to get your tail in gear. Have you been doing your drills? Boys who *practice* enough don't get the burps. Remember Trevino: 'The more I practice, the luckier I get.'")

The more I think, the more fucked up I get.

Focus, Brian. Focus.

I rededicate my gaze to the pig. The area of tray laid open by our nibbling is teal glaze stippled with salmon-colored scales; the artist appears to have had misconceptions about pork.

I've seen this hog before. Above the whirring slicer at Hydrick's, where I went as a boy with Mom, there hung a diagram of a Berkshire swine, his carcass serrated into cuts of meat. An animal well on his way from pig to pork, but placid all the same, pigly; he bore his fate bravely. This tray depicts the same animal — I never forget a smile — but over the years he's come down in the world. Now Friend Pig has been painted pomo and pressed into duty as decor; he's sprinkled with nuts scavenged from airline surplus. He'd rather, I know, be rooting kale, or nosing compost, or even — glazed — bearing an apple in his mouth, gently as a dog mouths a fallen bird. He'd rather be anywhere but here.

The universe has become a morose and shrunken thing. It's lit with a cheap red tinge, flickeringly, by bell-jar candles girdled in plastic mesh; its limits are the polished rectangle of the tabletop, the high gray walls of the bar. Bird is its dominant figure. My masquerade is finished.

Ellen's disappeared behind a lattice strung with ersatz roses; Bird must have turned back this way, waiting. Waiting. My enemy is perched on the booth bench opposite like a priest behind his grille, spoiling to hear a confession. He gets a rush out of his power of absolution — who wouldn't? How long, my son, since your last? Finger that rosary. Second chaplet, the sorrowful mysteries. Hop to it. Anything God should know about? Is there? What's the magic word? No, the other one.

Say something, Bird. I won't start this. There will be no apology until the charges are read.

So we'll wait.

I'd run my fingertips over the braille of couples' names again, but Bird's hat has engulfed them. The table is too small and frail to support that behemoth, which rides it like a farmer fits his milking stool. You'd expect to see such a hat on the overseer at an indigo plantation in 1857 — not, in 1990, on a tavern table in enlightened Charleston, a city where slavery has given way to a bazaar for yuppie tourists of soap, candle, and tobacco shops, a bazaar set down among the old holding cells and show pens.

I wish, senselessly, that Rosa were here to help: She'd take care of Bird with one phrase. The shortest distance between two points is a blunt question. She is good, she's straightforward; she could get me out of this.

I don't know what to think. What's to become of me now? Why won't he say anything?

Ellen will be back any minute.

"Look, Bird," I mumble, "I never wanted anybody to get hurt. It was a prank — you know, kid stuff. I didn't mean anything. I didn't mean to *do* it in the first place."

"You know, Bird," says Bird smoothly, paying no attention, "I wouldn't have guessed you were the type to invite me along to celebrate your good fortune and then cooze out of it. What kind of friend does that? Some, they say, success goes to their heads; maybe you're among them. But that fifty-nine doesn't seem to have made you *happy*. You look as jumpy as ever. If you don't mind my saying so: I *am* just a journeyman pro."

"I mean," I lurch on, "I know it was stupid. I had my head in my trunk, minding my own business, and . . . it was the sudden bad crazies. You know?"

Bird replies, "Why certainly I accept your apology, Bird. I'd be excited, too, if I Geibergered. I might forget, myself."

"Damn it, quit fooling around." I haven't dared look at him. I'm peering into the turret of that hat like it's a crystal ball: What to say? Will I come out of this alive, married, myself?

Bird shuts his eyes, lifts his chin, and lets a look of salacious ecstasy cross his face. "You know," he says, "Ellen's a mighty fine-looking woman. If I were the adultering type, I might be tempted to — how say? — put my ring on a different finger." He winks theatrically.

"What's that supposed to mean?"

"Step out. Swing. Sip from the cup of abomination. Trash the vows. Grope for trouts . . . in a peculiar river."

I shudder. That's what Mamie's boy said. Another pawn, plant, mole, mouthpiece. Another of Bird's eerie legion. So this is how it's going to be. Uncanny to the last.

"Of course," he says, shaking his head, "*I'm* not the type. *I'm* true."

What can I do but play along, take my lumps, let Bird do what he wants? He has the upper hand, temporarily. Ellen and I will be out of here in half an hour, less, and that'll be the end of it. What's another thirty minutes of vilification? Owls to Athens, coals to Newcastle. The hat glows malevolently.

What worries me most is Bird's wolfishness — real or feigned — about Ellen. Lust isn't like him, and she's been played false once tonight; I can't let it happen again. If he comes on to her, I'll punch his lights out. I've got to let him have his way with me, but I draw the line at bystanders — sweet, sad, half-potted-on-martinis bystanders — getting toyed with, swept up, ravished. I don't have to let Bird spirit Ellen away with his lies. It's ironic, isn't it? Her protector, her gallant: me. I'll do whatever I have to, because I know the truth: Ellen deserves far better than Brian Schwan . . . in any of his incarnations.

I look up at last, and Bird smiles, the soul of artlessness. I bear down on the words: "You'd best *stay* true, 'Brian.' Do you understand me?"

"An interesting phrase, *under the rose.*" He wiggles a finger at the giant damask bloom, eight feet tall or more, painted on the wall above the doorway. "*Sub rosa,* as the Romans used to say."

What's he digging at now? Rosa hasn't traveled with me in two years, so Bird has never laid eyes on her; I haven't mentioned her except as "my wife," or maybe (in a weak-willed, playing-along moment in the locker room) as "the old ball and chain." So how could he possibly know her name?

He continues. "You and I are peas in a pod, Bird. The other players know it; we know it. We're students of the game, oddballs, deviates. We live in our heads. I know I don't often own up to this, but it's just the two of us now, no need to deny the . . . link. We're alike; we're bookmen. There are things we'd rather chase than birdie, than skirt. So I trust a scholar like yourself, Soulsby, knows the origin of the trope: *under the rose.* Hmm?

"It's said that in antiquity, Eros — acting in Aphrodite's behalf — presented a rose to Harpocrates, the god of silence, along with an order not to let anything slip about the boss's *affaires de coeur.* The bloom was a bribe — or a fragrant threat. The Romans got wind of it, and *under the rose* made its way into their language, meaning *secret.* Eventually European meeting halls and public houses started decorating their ceilings with the flower, too, to indicate that anything said or done there should never be sounded about. Drunken indiscretions weren't to be smuggled into the sober world, where they could cause harm, wreck lives. What happens under the rose, then, stays there. The flower marks a pact. A quaint custom, eh, Bird?"

This is, I think, something akin to a peace offering. He'd like to deal; he'll keep his mouth shut, but he wants to buy my silence, too. But what *for?* What does he want me to hush up? The compact is one-sided. What's in it for him?

"And one worth preserving?"

I nod, and as I do Ellen flops heavily into her chair, almost tipping it. Before, she was where Bird is now, across from me, in the banquette. Where did the extra chair come from? When did Bird set it at the foot of the table?

Ellen steadies herself by throwing her hands skyward and flapping her legs open for balance, and I see a flash of white, like the belly of a dove. A glimpse of Canaan, home of the pubic mohawk. Ellen. I shut my eyes in shame. In some horrifying way I'm lusting for two now. When I open them, I see what took so long, remember she took it with her: The chignon is in again.

"Whoa, Ellie," says Bird. He clutches an epaulet.

And it occurs to me. The bastard wants me to hand her over. That's my end of the bargain. Under the rose, I am to play procurer . . . for "myself." No questions asked, no secrets divulged.

Ellen snorts, lays her palm across Bird's forearm, which is now bare. He's rolled his cuffs to the elbow, smartly, and his shed jacket spans the back of Ellen's chair. When did he do all this disrobing, this furniture-moving?

"You won't believe," she announces, "the graffiti I just read."

"Try me." The slimy SOB. I have to put up with his burlesque of Dixie — and that's what it amounts to, the hat, the poplin suit, the bolo tie, the cigarette case. I've got to accept the proffered bloom, keep my mouth shut. If he wants to be me for the evening, I'll stay out of his way; I owe him that. But — again — I don't have to . . . she's tipsy, for God's sake, vulnerable; she's tricked out like a Venetian sailor. *If Bird wants to fuck, he can fucking forget it:* That's going too far, charade or no, the rose be damned.

"In the stall," Ellen relates, "somebody had written 'Oh my God, I lost my virginity,' in this real shaky teenager's handwriting. Like she was so upset that the first thing she did was hop on her bike and pedal down here with her marker. Underneath it somebody had written, 'Chill out, girl. It's OK, long as you have the box it came in.'"

Ellen and Bird laugh. I glance at the convoluted damask bloom, then at my watch. 9:04. Twenty minutes more. Time is my ally. I can endure.

"Isn't that *hysterical?*" asks Ellen.

"You bet," says her eager suitor. Brian. "That's a riot, all right."

Ellen asks him, "Where'd you get your accent?"

"My mother's an Aussie," breezes Bird. "She and my old man met in college."

Ellen burps, a half beat before her hand can leap up to snuff it. Discretion is lagging, flagging. She turns to me for the first time since Bird arrived, and I get a whiff of olives. Extra dirty. "And where'd you pick up yours?" she asks. "It's bizarro. The southerner sounds like David Niven or somebody; the South African drawls like Deputy Dawg. You two ought to flip-flop accents." She laughs. "How about a trade?"

Bird cuts in, fields my question. "Television," he says. "TV's the answer. You know, *Dukes of Hazzard, Gomer Pyle, Mayberry RFD, Hee Haw.* I'm not sure about Deputy Dawg, but that's the idea. In Cape Town you can be an honorary cracker and never leave your rumpus room. Right, Bird?"

I would have thought Ellen was nobler than to delight in rot like this, but delight she does. "Where'd they go to college?" she inquires. "Your parents, I mean."

"The Colorado School of Mines," he lies. "But let's talk about someone more interesting. Let's talk about *you.*"

Ellen beams. "God knows it's nice to meet a man who'd

rather discuss me than him," she breathes, cutting those inde-
scribable almond eyes my way. "But there'll be time for that
later. At the moment I'm kind of looped, so you'll have to carry
the ball. Spit it out: Who are you? What makes Brian Schwan
tick?"

There'll be time for that later? What is she talking about?
We'll be at dinner until midnight, and damned if I'll roll over
for a nightcap with Bird after that. I can't bear it anymore. "His
wife," I growl. "Brian's wife makes him tick."

Ellen grabs Bird's wrist as though they're old pals, holds it up
like a torch . . . to show me. Bird, ever accommodating, spreads
his hand. "No ring," she says, looking disconcerted. "No ring."

Bird pipes up. "Separated," he says sadly. "A year ago. She
wanted me to quit golf, start a family, stay at home to care for
the kids. I wasn't ready." I feel like a mummy being wrapped;
I'm wearing the world like a muffler. "She works," he finishes.

"Why no divorce?" asks Ellen in a tone of concern. "Any
chance of getting back together?"

"No. She's holding out for an annulment. She doesn't want
to split her earnings, and she isn't eager to spring for alimony.
But it's not greed, it really isn't; more like moral disapproba-
tion. I'm irresponsible, selfish, etcetera, and she's unwilling —
this is how she puts it — to support my golf habit anymore."

I have heard this phrase before. This phrase is not Bird's to use.

"What does she do for a living," asks Ellen, "that pays so
well?"

"I'm still in love with her, you know," avers Bird, shaking his
head. Buying time to dream up a story, no doubt. "She's a sci-
entist."

"What kind?" I recognize the stratagem. Bird's playing the
old feminism pick-up scam. *I feel your pain. I do. It's no walk
in the park, being a woman. But then I hardly have to tell YOU
that.* How could Ellen fall for a ploy so hoary, so obvious? But
she has, unmistakably. Her shoulder tassels are quivering. I
want to leap across the table and wrestle her away from him,
but — and I know how silly this sounds — the plantation hat's

glare, mute and brutal, won't let me up. It's holding me in place like a knife at my throat, like the mummy's windings of shroud. I need air.

Best to let it go. They have a chaperon, after all, and in twelve minutes Ellen and I will be gone. How far can he get in a dozen minutes of public seduction?

"Her field is very new, and she's just patented a device and a process that will make her millions, tens of millions. Have you heard of bauxite hemoglobin engineering?"

Was my material so much worse? Is it his looks? Is it that air of invincibility?

"She studies core-temperature fluctuations of coal reserves. I don't mean to brag on her, but she's a leading contender for the Nobel, and she's only twenty-eight. She plays down her chances, says she can't see the stolid Swedes being bowled over by an invention that's no more than a sophisticated turkey thermometer. But that's just modesty. It's a turkey thermometer that promises to stretch the world's reserves another fifty years at virtually no ecological cost. Her process allows engineers to know when beds are ripe for harvest. A simple, ingenious theory. And because the technique requires delicacy and patience, it's basically put an end to the era of brute-force strip mining.

"Rosa's on the cutting edge of feminist science. She believes we have to replace the invasive, aggressive, exploitive metaphors of knowledge that male science has promoted: We have to rethink scientific inquiry as a cooperation with nature, as interdependence rather than rape."

The environmental rap, on top of feminism. If he makes Rosa a porphyric dwarfess in a breath-driven Stephen Hawking wheelchair, he'll have the hat trick. The man is a twisted genius.

Bird fibs onward. "Do you know the ins and outs of coal retrieval? It works," he whispers, "kind of like ovulation, except on a monumental time scale. You" — he leans toward Ellen with his blond, blemishless brow, so close that their foreheads seem to brush. She shrinks back, but not from revulsion; it's more like she's recoiling from a shock. Then she tilts back in, eyebrows vaulted, mouth open — a leaf inclined to the sun. "You," Bird repeats, "are fertile every month, for a day or two; but there are only a few weeks a century when a vein of coal is at its optimal temperature. Mining it at the right moment can make anthracite burn eighty percent more efficiently. The curve for bituminous coal looks even better, as you can imagine. And lignite! I don't even need to tell you about lignite, whew! Rosa's made it commercially viable to mine lignite again. She'll save the Third World billions of dollars by allowing them to retain, and later to take advantage of — in the new, symbiotic sense of that term — resources they've always had but had no way of using. It's not going too far, though she'd deny it, to say that her work will put food in the mouths of millions of children."

Ellen sighs. "Wow," she gushes. "What a woman." What a man, she's thinking, to have dreamt up such a paragon. She has to know that this Rosa is a plaster saint. Has to. The Mother Teresa of charcoal. Lady Lignite. "It must have been tough to lose someone with a mind that . . . that *alive*. I lost my husband, too. It's tough." She's acting like hubby's dead and sainted, Nobeled himself; not twenty minutes ago she called him a lowlife needledick who ought to have ASSHOLE tattooed on his forehead to save other women the trouble of finding out for themselves. The man makes his living selling rhinestones and paste gems in bulk to sweatshop costumers. She told me he dresses, on the road, like Elvis in the days of his terminal Vegas bloat. He runs through a bottle of Brut a week, splashes it on in lieu of showering because, he insists, "career-squaws" respond best to men who smell strongly: He read it in *Psychology Today*.

I can't let Bird get away with it. His falsities are corrupting Ellen; she's started lying too. So I challenge him. "You're claiming you have to mine coal at a certain temperature?"

"Absolutely."

"Hogwash. That's crap."

Ellen rallies to his defense. "What do *you* know about mining, Bird?"

"Enough to know that what . . . what *he* just told you is a crock. How do you account for there being coal in all kinds of climates?"

"That's a fine question, Bird," replies Bird, tapping a congratulatory finger on his temple. "Excellent. Bauxite hemoglobin engineering is based on a premise much like the one that underlies Mendeleev's table of the elements. There are families of optimal temperatures, and they repeat periodically. So coal would be mined at different, but equally ideal, temperatures in, say, Tanzania and the Yukon. And also at different depths in the earth."

He's left little to chance, I see. I switch tactics. "Rosa Schwan," I tell Ellen, "isn't about to win a Nobel Prize. She's probably never won so much as a Best Gardenia in Show. She sells Jesus key chains for a living, or tries to pick the season's hottest trend in armoires. Or something."

"Honest Injun," swears Bird.

"In what field?"

"Petroscience. Surely you've read about her discoveries. She was kind of a celebrity for a while. They did a show on her on PBS."

"Wow," says Ellen. "I think I saw that. She's a pretty brunette?"

"Yes."

"Wears those lab goggles?"

"That's she," says Bird. "That's my Rosa. The genius in the bubble specs."

"There's no goddamn Nobel in petroscience," I growl. "And the only brunette in goggles ever interviewed on PBS was Kareem Abdul-Jabbar."

"Don't let Bird get to you," Ellen comforts him, flashing me a surly look. "He's just jealous." She's working more slowly on this martini, like it's becoming important to have her wits about her. I slam the rest of my beer.

"You're going too far," I say to Bird. "Push any more and the deal's off. You hear me?"

"What deal?" asks Ellen.

Bird spins a finger at his temple, smirking. "Have I mentioned that *I*'m something of an inventor, too?" he queries.

Ellen shakes her head, as vigorously as a wet setter.

"A dabbler, I'm afraid, a would-be, but I try. You see," he begins, "I've always wanted to fly."

With that he launches into one of the most dazzling disquisitions I've ever heard. Ellen picks at an incisor with her thumbnail, ready for rapture; I retreat into the corner of the banquette, bring up my knees and hide behind them. My head pounds, heart aches, liver groans. The clock slows, or perhaps time ceases to move: I couldn't say.

He has nothing, Bird generously allows, against the Wright brothers, who were after all mechanically ingenious bike repairmen and not visionaries; he has no quarrel with modern, commercial, *engined* aeronautics — but his fascination has always been pure flight, powered by nothing more than muscle and will.

This is nonsense of the most outlandish kind, but Bird's face is lit with an ardency too strange to be counterfeit. The dim barlight, interrupted by fan blades, pulses across his face and gives it a fiendish glow, like in a mad-scientist movie. The red-glass votive in its mesh glows dimly, looks like a heart trying to burst from some cruel net or girdle. Alive. His voice leaps and wavers, and he has the rapturous look I recall on Jimmy Stewart's face in *The Spirit of St. Louis,* a movie Rosa brought home recently as a rental. (I couldn't figure out why until, afterward, she asked whether I knew that the Lindbergh kidnapping spurred the invention of the baby monitor. Did I know that, did I, huh? Out of every evil some good must come. Nope, I answered. Did she know that Hauptmann's mistakes made later kidnappers more careful about not dropping the kid on his head on the way out of the house? Did she know about the case's improving effect, *tank Gott,* on ransom-note grammar and spelling? This drove her into the bedroom, and I rewound in guilty silence.)

Anyway, as Bird sketches the history of human flight — with details too vivid and too full not to be in some sense true, with a passion that itself seems a subcategory of flying — neither Ellen nor I interjects a word.

His oration is both unforgettable and unrememberable. This isn't an excuse, or anyway isn't *only* an excuse: I don't mean I won't be able to recall *in future,* after the fact, what Bird has said. Time wears grooves in all our memories, of course, like handles to help us bear them. That's ordinary. But from almost the first word, it's clear that this isn't just another jaunty lie but something into which Bird has sunk years of emotion, of work, of eccentric but real erudition. His list of myths and innovators, the technical data he tosses off, allusions to research in half a dozen languages over two millennia . . . they make an impression. I realize that — its spurious context aside, its nub of impossibility be damned — this is one of those moments when I ought to listen. Bird is speaking the truth, insofar as he can; what fragment he has of it is hard won.

The paradox is that in trying to mark every sentence for memory, I lose the essence: I miss the ligaments, the sinews, the sureness that makes Bird's narrative so coherent and so compelling. I catch the facts, miss the gist; catch the feather, miss its flight. It's a curse I've known always. I'm smart enough, if barely, to recognize I'm hearing something that might matter . . . but I'm so intent on preserving the message, and so proud to have plucked it — useful knowledge! — from the drone of everyday speech, that I mislay the meaning. It washes over me.

And Bird is especially hard to follow. His account is shapeless, full of swoops and leaps. He celebrates those men (always men, it seems) who've preceded him in flight, who've made attempts: Eilmer the geomancer, a twelfth-century Benedictine monk who is said to have pulled it off, to have floated for more than a furlong from a tower and then to have set himself down if not with grace then at least without disfiguring injury; a sixteenth-century Norman laborer, forever nameless, who fashioned wings from the halves of a winnowing basket, lashed a coal shovel to his trousers as a tail, and — after what must have been a tricky climb — leapt from the crown of the tallest pear tree in the province; Wan-Hoo the mandarin, who had his servants affix forty-seven gunpowder rockets to his sedan chair and then light them (their report of the result wasted neither words nor sentiment: "Smoke, an explosion, and Wan-Hoo was no more"). Bird relates the story of Salomon Idler, a cobbler from Cannstatt, near Augsburg, who — when worried friends dissuaded him from heaving himself off a castle turret — jumped instead from a low roof onto a bridge bedded with bags of straw. He broke the wooden span and crushed several of his neighbor's hens, which were nesting peaceably under the bridge eaves. They never saw what was coming. Afterward Idler is said — dusty, dripping straw from his mouth, marked with the mingled blood of his hands and the burst hens, a fog of feathers swirling around him all the way — to have dragged his wings to Oberhausen and to have bashed them to bits. He retired to shoe repair.

There was Icarus, of course, who presumed to fly too high and was struck down by affronted gods and melted wax; the Swabian tailor Berblinger, who took out a braggarty newspaper ad, drew a huge crowd, and then was dumped into the Danube by the Devil himself, to be ridiculed ever after; the chemist and self-styled flight instructor Griffolino d'Arezzo, sentenced by Dante to an itchy, scabid hell (Eighth Circle, Tenth Pouch, First Group, the Falsifiers of Metal); and Giovanni Damianti, abbot of a Premonstratensian monastery in Scotland, who in 1507 framed a set of wings and stuffed them with eagle feathers. When Damianti plummeted from a palace wall in Stirling, describing the graceful arc of a stone let drop, he is said to have blamed his shattered leg on someone's malicious substitution, during construction of the wings, of chicken feathers for eagle's plumes: the lowly feathers, he explained, had fled immediately toward the earth they knew and loved.

And there were, as Ellen and I doubtless know, the two looming greats: Faustus and Leonardo. Of the former, Bird reports that flight was his obsession, the failure to master it his reason for bartering with Mephisto in the first place. Looking, in his outlandish poplin suit, like a demon Atticus Finch, Bird quotes — first in fluid German and then in a translation he recites with eyes shut tight — Faust's lament to his sidekick, Wagner, near the start of Goethe's version of the tale:

> Ach! zu des Geistes Flügeln wird so leicht
> Kein körperlicher Flügel sich gesellen.
> Doch ist es jedem eingeboren,
> Daß sein Gefühl hinauf und vorwärts dringt . . .

> Alas, the wings that lift the spirit
> Remain unjoined by bodily ones.
> And yet it's inborn in us all:
> Desire presses us forward, upward . . .

Our teacher reports that in Upper Austria the doomed Faustus is said, on his last night, to have climbed astride the devil's back and demanded to fly high enough to hear angelsong. When, amid clouds at last, he sighed at the blessed sound, Mephistopheles — knowing his charge was on the brink of repentance, which would undo their bargain — threatened to dump him to earth. Faustus, cowed, held his breath. He turned away from God once more, out of nothing more than fright. It was thus, the story went, that he fell one sigh shy of heaven.

Here Bird pauses, says he thinks the Upper Austrians may — no disrespect intended — have it wrong. He hypothesizes that even then Faust could have saved himself simply by dismounting the devil. Why should God settle for a second sigh, after all? Let the fool heave a dozen. Who wouldn't have regrets in his predicament? Who wouldn't, given the choice, rate *excelsis* over hellfire? But a show of faith, even that late, might have restored the professor to grace. This was Faust's opportunity to take his leap . . . to fly, finally, on his own terms. He let it pass.

Meanwhile, a great white bird kissed Leonardo in his cradle. He told the story himself, countless times; it was the childhood memory he felt freest with. Leonardo claimed to remember its approach: the riot of jagged shadow above, the attention-getting eddy it stirred, the scrape of talon on crib edge as it alighted. He recalled, too, as the bird tipped down on its knobbed legs, the fishkill smell of its breath, and then the way the beak felt against his mouth, rough, surprisingly cool. The spicule at bill's end insinuated itself between his lips, reached behind the sleek baby-ridge of gum to give his tongue the slightest peck: a raptor's kiss, an inoculation, a calling.

Leonardo always knew it was his fate to fly. He knew it from a baby, was reminded whenever he heard the whispery scritch of a fingernail across a sketch, a plan, a canvas; whenever a windblown tree flapped its shadow overhead; whenever he caught the scent of fish curing in the sun; and — to the end of his days, this the most potent spur to memory — whenever he stooped, on his own knobbed legs, to kiss a child.

"He was on the right track, as usual," Bird says. "He saw he would have to befriend the birds, mimic them, and he devoted himself to learning everything about the mechanisms by which they flew. He made studies of air pressure, density, resistance, inertia. He pored over the architecture of the wing, the tail's adaptable geometry. He made precise observations, used them to speculate about steering and banking, braking with the feet, attitude control, the use of the *alula* or wing's thumb as a forerudder. He finally prepared, after hundreds of sketches, mockups, and models, an ornithopter: a set of flexible, flappable, amazingly complex artificial wings.

"Leonardo made a mistake, though. He jumped the gun. He let himself imagine what it would be like to have solved the air. He would (forget the claims of cranks and cultists) be the first man to fly: Think of it. He wrote in his journal: 'It will strike the universe with astonishment and fill all of literature with its renown; the nest where it was hatched will have eternal glory.' He weighed himself down with pride.

"At last, around 1505, he was ready to test his flying machine. He climbed Monte Ceceri, outside Fiesole." Here Bird stops, turns to me, taps his fingertips against his sternum. "Monte Ceceri. Swan Mountain, my ancestral home. Presumably Leonardo took his crack at it from the steep hillside. He tried, as he'd put it in his notes, to 'fly from the back of the bigger bird.'"

Bird pauses again, draws a deep breath, licks his drying lips. "The DaVinci ornithopters are among the most intricate and beautiful machines ever devised; he ranks among the world's unquestioned geniuses. But literature has kindly kept its tongue about the results of his jump."

Bird leads on. He flits from subject to subject, with divagations into the arcane, the absurd, the goofy: Plutarch's assertion that loud cries can rupture the air and murder birds; Paracelsus' notion that air is the supreme element, in which the others are embedded "as a house is set on foundations"; the theory that weight is *higher* after death because the person's soul, which strives upward, has flown, leaving gravity to rule the corpse. "Does a puppet weigh more," Bird asks, "after its strings have been snipped? It does."

He tells us of the manucodiata, a bird that belonged so fully to the air that it was born without feet. "One might wonder," says Bird, though Ellen and I are now beyond wonder, "how such birds reproduced; the answer is that they didn't, for the most part, which is why they haven't been seen for centuries, since Buffon's report that, in India, the bush-tailed bodies of apodes (the other name by which they're known) were sometimes found — having plunged from on high — with their beaks impaled in the earth, stuck fast 'like tent pegs.'"

Here our guide introduces the belief among funambulists that sex is injurious to balance. "'Love destroys the center of gravity in tight-rope dancers,' the historians of the circus have written, 'and as a rule equilibrists might rank with the Roman

vestals.'" Another reason, Bird surmises, why pure, footless
birds must be chaste; another reason their kind cannot long
survive. And, practically speaking: how to get the necessary
purchase in air?

"So you see why I can't have children," he announces suddenly. "It's something Leonardo understood, too; you can de-
tect it in his telling of the kiss. And I'm so close, so close. Glued
feathers won't work; the frame doesn't matter, or the architecture. Size, shape, material — irrelevant. Succedaneous wings
are folly . . . as Robert Hooke understood, as Leonardo learned,
as we all know now. In August of 1640, Descartes wrote to the
flight enthusiast Marin Mersenne: 'One can indeed make a machine, metaphysically speaking, which will sustain itself in the
air like a bird; for birds themselves, at least in my view, are such
machines; but it is not possible physically or morally speaking,
because one would need springs so subtle and at the same time
so strong, that they could not be made by man.'"

Bird stops, closes his eyes. "The father of rationalism is, so
far as he goes, absolutely right. Human beings can't get airborne with birds' feathers; our muscle power is inadequate. It's
a matter of physics, and maybe of morality as well. Do you
remember the Gossamer Albatross? Nineteen-seventy-nine.
McReady managed to coax it across the English Channel using
only pedal power, but it nearly killed him . . . and his Albatross
was unbelievably light, simple. Made of balsa wood, Saran
wrap, and bicycle gears. It was the ungainliest, the brittlest bird
in history.

"Actually," Bird continues, emitting a small, strangled moan,
"it was Rosa who gave me my breakthrough, in a way." When
I hear these words, the spell is broken. He's returning to a familiar fakery; the conviction seems to drain from his voice. He
plumps the slaver's hat to its full size, regards Ellen randily. I'm
restored to sense, to sight: There is no Rosa, and there's been no
breakthrough. When he resumes the narrative, its magic has
fled; gravity has called in its marker. I can record every word. I
don't believe him. Not a word of it is true.

"One day shortly after she left, I was rereading a passage from Cicero in which he identified the ether as feminine, 'assigned to Juno because of its extreme softness.' It's the kind of ancient taxonomy that's dismissed and ridiculed these days because of the way it identifies femininity with softness, tractability, and so on. But something clicked for me that day. It had to do with the emptiness of the house: the furniture gone, drapes, rugs, light fixtures, her shower curtains with the seahorse stencils, virtually everything but an inflatable raft I'd patched and was using as a mattress, a twenty-cup coffeemaker, and my boxes of flight notes. There were tire tracks across the front lawn, Mayflower's scars. Rosa had even made the movers stop on the way out to uproot the mailbox — it was a beautiful piece of work, a red schoolhouse whose outgoing-mail flag was just that, an American flag you drew up its plastic pole with a tiny lanyard. They left the bare post. Anyway, I was sitting in the house with my coffee and notes and bare wires and wet bathroom floors, waiting to intercept the postman. All alone. Adrift. I knew she'd done what she had to, but that made me feel worse, not better. I'd let her down; I could no more play good golf than fly. And I knew the postman wouldn't be bringing anything for me."

Despite it all, I find myself screening this farce in my mind's eye. The long-suffering Rosa, the Brian left behind. A world without lamps or cute shower curtains, where there's nothing to do but wait for the jeep to bring your daily nothing. And ruts in the yard to let the world know you've failed her. How can I half believe this? How can his lies make *me* feel guilty?

Bird presses forward. "It occurred to me, finally, that Rosa's model for bauxite hemoglobin engineering might hold the key: Why not read Cicero as a protofeminist? Maybe his remark was born not of prejudice but of prescience — or should it be *postscience*? Was he predicting that the air wouldn't yield its mysteries to the kind of interrogation he foresaw from science? If the supreme element is feminine, flying is not a 'problem to be attacked' in the male way; the skies are not to be 'conquered.'

A new strategy is called for, a 'womanly' one. Descartes was right: Wings could not be made by *man*, via the tools of physics — but by woman, maybe, with the feints and lures of metaphysics?

"Men have built marvelous approximations of the wings of birds. But what if what's required is something else, an analogous understanding of the mind of birds? Or not exactly *understanding*. We're like Faustus. We complain that we don't have bodily wings to go with our spiritual ones. So we manufacture them; and they don't work. What we need may not be cleverer ornithopters, but retooled spirits. Do you see what I'm getting at? *Geistesflügel* aren't a metaphor; they're real. They're what can make you sigh again and jump off the devil's back. The excess weight that dragged down Leonardo, Desforges, Wan-Hoo, the Arab al-Djawharī, and the others was the weight of reason. It was arrogance, the belief that the air was a medium to be subdued and inhabited.

"I told you about Leonardo's pride; I was guilty, too. So were others. Auceps had written, in 1653, that the falcon 'makes her nimble Pinions cut the fluid air . . . and in her glorious carere looks with contempt upon those high Steeples and magnificent Palaces which we adore and wonder at.' That's exactly wrong, except for the bird's — psychological — gender. The falcon thinks no such thing. The sky will not hold anything aloft that fails to recognize the air's supremacy. Do you see? Do you see?"

Bird is pleading now. He holds his fists together, pinkie to pinkie, shakes them entreatingly. Ellen breaks out of her trance. "I do," she gasps — as though she's been the one talking for the last two hours or so, as though she can hardly bear, now that she *sees* it, to do air the banal cruelty of breathing it.

My God, what time is it? We've missed dinner; it could be morning, for all we know. I check my watch: *9:24. Six minutes have elapsed. Six minutes.* Bird's black magic has expanded, has taken over even time. How can he have packed all that into six minutes? It is the plainest impossibility, the most flagrant fraud yet — how high does this conspiracy reach? — but Bird and Ellen seem not to notice. They have eyes only for each other.

I can't bear it. It's up to me to restore the world. "So all you have to do to fly is steer clear of sex, commune with air, and think like a lady pigeon. Well, you're two-thirds there, I'd say. But the last stretch is the hardest."

"I see what you're saying, Brian," Ellen chimes in scornfully. "Some people will *never* fly. Some people are sour and earth-bound. Some people have no metaphysics in them at all."

"I suppose DC-10s recognize the air's supremacy," I interject. "They're smart that way."

Bird flashes his enigmatic yogi smile. I try another tack, work on Ellen: I am the great debunker. "Don't you see what he's saying? Men are logical; women are intuitive. Isn't that offensive? Isn't that the oldest offense in the book?"

"It can be done," Bird asserts quietly. "Flying is possible."

I'm beyond exasperation now. "Pull it off, Brian, and you could be a two-Nobel family. You and Rosa. You'd have to add on to the house to store all the hardware."

Bird swivels his downcast head, trying to pinch out a tear. "Not a family anymore," he intones. "If I'm going to solve this, I'll need my womanly input from elsewhere."

Ellen ignores the transparency of this. "I don't think you'll have any problem," she says, reaching into her purse to replenish her lipstick. "You're a remarkable man."

"Time to scoot," I say. "Past time. We'd better move it, Ellen. You must be starved."

Ellen peers up from her purse, the lip-color unwinding, in her hand, from its golden hole. She looks startled, cuts her eyes at Bird. "Check," she calls to the bartender.

Meanwhile, Bird fixes his eyes on me. He mouths, "This is the way it's done, Clutch." And then he winks again.

☙

"Clutch" is a taunt, Bird's way of telling me he knows all my swings will be whiffs. Not enough to make an oeuvre of the air; now he has to annotate it.

Some of the guys on tour (at Hatch's urging, of course) call
me "Clutch" or "Cousteau" because of a pair of spectacular
flameouts. Last June I led two straight tournaments at the mid-
point of the final round. Nine holes from victory — in each
case a smooth homestretch, with greens too grainy and too
piebald for anyone to make a major run — and I was tight as a
two-bit windup toy. In each case I dumped two teeballs into
water: in Lafayette, Louisiana, I shoved them way right, into a
spillway pond on the tenth; in Natchez, Mississippi, on number
twelve, I yanked the first into a backyard swimming pool, then
bore down and cranked the second fifty yards farther along,
into the next pool down the line. A kid was diving for canned
goods and Hot Wheels in the second, and his mother, after
shaking a snorkel at me, took my name and address. (If I happened to win a big event in future, she'd sue me for scaring
Baby out of a lucrative career in marine mechanics or niblet salvage.) Anyway, I shot thirty-nine and forty-one, respectively,
finished back in the pack . . . went home muttering excuses.
Lafayette wounded me; Natchez did me in. Bird's reminding me
that I'm a choker.

All his talk about chastity, all the priestly fuss and fudge: another trick. Ropewalkers my ass: it's just an old golf supersti-
tion, translated and adapted for color. Slammin' Sammy Snead,
among others, used to eschew sex before tournaments because
he thought it screwed up his putting. "When you sole that
blade," my college coach used to say, "you're a tripod: three
points on the ground. And that putter better be the only third
leg you got working. You hear me?"

"Well," sighs Ellen, turning back to the table. Her lips are
aglow. "Well."

Bird smiles at me, and she smiles at him, and their hands
slink steadily closer, and I know what I should have realized before: I'm being ditched. *He*'s going to eat with her at Country
Luke's. That's what the bargain has devolved to. I've been
carved out of the triangle.

So I snap. It's the only option left. "You hypocrite!" I yell. "Why don't you tell her where you're *really* from? Tell her who you are, you fake! You can stick your rose, do you hear? I don't care anymore. I'm calling it off."

I turn to Ellen, pleading. "Look," I explain. "*He's* Bird. *I'm* Brian. You wondered before why our accents are backward. Don't you see? I'm the Yank; he's the Boer, or whatever they are over there. I'm sorry I misled you, but I wanted the chance to get to know you, I had my reasons, they were pure in their way — and you already thought I was Bird, it's not like I made it up myself. . . ."

Ellen consults Bird. "Is he crazy?"

"Looks like. He's had too much to drink. I don't mean to make excuses for him, Ellen, but you have to understand: A round like that ratchets up the pressure, the expectations. His career won't be quite the same now. It's hard to prepare for a slice of immortality, even a small one. He wasn't ready for success. Sad," he whispers.

All this time, I've been thinking. Even under pressure, against expectations, I'm a thinker. "Hold on!" I yell. "Hold on one minute! Check my driver's license. Brian Schwan, Emma, Georgia. Five-foot-nine, one-fifty. Eyes blue, no lenses, organ donor. Organ donor, do you hear? *I'm* the humanitarian here. I'm the good guy. Free Mandela! End apartheid! Look! Look!" I grope for my wallet, but just as I find my pocket the bartender delivers a rabbit punch, short-armed but potent, to my right kidney.

"You reaching for a piece?" he asks, and hauls me up by the armpits. I shake my head. It feels like he left his fist in my back. I try to crumple to the floor.

"Let's go, captain," he says, twisting my arm behind me and holding me up. His hands are still wet from washing glasses. "And don't be talking shit 'bout Mandela in here, buckra."

"He's *lying!* Bird's lying! I shot seventy-seven today." I scream it to the room. "I shot seventy-seven today!"

There's a smattering of sarcastic applause.

"Good for you," the bartender whispers hotly into my ear. "Now are you going to go peaceful, or are we going to have trouble?"

Bird rounds the table. "Sorry about the hubbub," he says. "He'll go quietly. I'll take responsibility. I'll escort him." After all this, he has the chutzpah to play the white knight. I've been bested, beaten. And what's new about that?

Bird's sealed me off from Ellen, blocked me out, so that if I go for my wallet again, he can — with his henchman's help — subdue me. She'll never see the evidence. She won't believe me. It's over.

"You sure?" asks the bartender, relaxing his grip.

"I've got it under control," says Bird, handing him a ten. "He's had a stressful day."

"I've got dinner reservations in about two minutes," Ellen says to Bird, "at this swanky place, and the guy I had planned to take kind of didn't work out. Would you be sweet enough to fill in?"

"Gladly," answers Bird. "More than gladly. But pardon me while I get Bird a cab. I'll only be a second. Keep an eye on my hat?"

The lid is a giant coin he's used to mark his ball; he'll be back momentarily to finish out.

Bird nods to me like a rough but good-hearted TV lawman. The prisoner's delusion of dignity is to be encouraged. Let him ascend the gallows under his own power: He'll think he's going out "a man." Under the watchful eye of our bartender, I lead Bird under the rose and through the door and into the street where Ellen started me on this miserable spiral. The market stalls across the way are deserted, their scarred tin shades drawn. A hundred yards along, a couple emerges from a restaurant. Otherwise the street is empty.

When Bird talks, his tone is normal, even solicitous; it's as though there's never been a charade. "Brian," he asks, "are you drunk?"

"You miserable son of a bitch."

"You'll thank me. Now . . . are you drunk?"

"I think your goon ruptured my kidney."

"Brian, are you drunk?"

"Not enough."

"Can you drive home?"

"Yes," I say. But I won't drive home. I'll follow them all night if necessary. Ellen needs protection, whether she knows it or not. Brian Schwan will sleep with her when . . . pigs fly. That's a joke. A kind of comfort. And why didn't I throw the nut dish into his face? Maybe embed one of those spines in his forehead? Knock him out with a pig let fly. An irony; that would be an irony. God, I *am* drunk.

"You lost focus for a minute," says Bird. "Yes what? Can you drive home?"

"Yes, I, can, drive, home, ass, hole."

"OK, then," Bird says. "It's best this way, Brian. Don't be sore. I'm the one who was wronged here, in the big picture. We'll laugh about this in the morning."

Ellen's the one who was wronged here, I think, and I'll never laugh about tonight. I say nothing.

"Better get back to your hat, Casanova," I say.

Bird taps his foot on the sidewalk. "By the way," he says, "I watched your interview tonight. Enjoyed the show. And I figured something out that's been bugging me for months. Know what your problem is?"

*Know what your problem is?* No, Mr. Wizard, and I need you to tell me. The last thing I want from Bird Soulsby — rake, sorcerer, Geiberger, coal-vein hematologist, man aspiring to the mind of a bird — is amateur psychoanalysis; I can get that at home. I know where to find out what's wrong with me, don't even have to ask for the diagnosis. I turn to leave.

He calls after me, "Brian, I'm only trying to help."

I spin. "Help someone else. So far your help's got me a ruined career, a shaky marriage, and probably blood in my piss. I've had all the help I can stand. Butt out, all right?" I start to walk away.

But Bird can't resist the last word. "You don't know the difference between mystery and mystification," he announces. It sounds less like a parting shot than a debating point. "There are plenty of real mysteries in the world without pumping the simple things full of air. When you do that, you get *yourself* in trouble. What's wrong with you is you."

I turn around, thirty feet distant. Bird's under an old brass streetlamp, the gooseneck kind that lit my mother's way to imaginary deb balls, and his white suit is bathed in white light. As he shouts this nonsense into the salty night sky, his hand is raised in benediction. He looks like the Reverend R. A. Culver about to touch the wound of a supplicant: Demons come . . . OUT! HEAL! HEAL! *When you do that you cheapen the genuine mysteries. What's wrong with you is . . . you.*

"Leave me alone!" I shout. "For once, leave me alone!"

"Golf's no mystery," Bird hollers back. "None at all. It's just a game."

"If you so much as touch Ellen," I spit out, "I'll kill you, I swear it."

This time when he speaks, he does it in a low and affable tone, and I can barely make out the words. "The only good adultery," Bird seems to say, reaching for the door, "is adultery by proxy. Night, Brian. Sweet dreams. I'll see you at Ile, bright and early."

◯

The door bangs shut; its handle is an ugly brass rose, tarnished by use. Besides the blinding pain in my back, I can still feel the barkeep's damp handprint on my hip. It'll be there for the next half hour. It's been a long while since someone other than Rosa laid a hand there; the hip is, after all, one of the last preserves, accessible only to dance partners, tag-football pursuers, tailors and their tapes, lovers (and golf pros: I remember during my first lesson, back at the Bird o' Paradise, the way my teacher, Rocco Mediamente, knelt behind me — first spreading a towel so as not to muddy his slacks — and rolled my hips between his massive fingers to demonstrate the proper rotation during take-away. Rocco was constantly cracking anise seeds between his teeth, and he moved within an acrid envelope. To have your hips torqued by such a man, amid a peppery haze of licorice, is to know what it's like to serve in a harem. I was humiliated by his touch, but I loved the results; and who has ever been able to untangle gratitude from shame?)

Even doctors steer clear of hips . . . except, of course, for the specialists who lift, clean, and replace them, and (I guess) gyne-cologists. Funny, I can hear *pap smear* or *speculum* or *stirrups* and not feel even remotely troubled; but to envision the doctor palpating a woman's hip, maybe using it, casually, as a fulcrum or a handhold . . . it's incomprehensible. One of the dehuman-izing aspects of cities, in my way of seeing, is that the urban-dweller's hips are annexed to the public domain, brushed and butted and ground against in subways, elevators, airports, taxi-cabs. I'm a prude, I know, but I draw a line at the hip: It's the last private joint.

So now mine is damp, handled; my name is stolen; my career is over. I am in the midst of adultery by proxy. Bird will . . . is that what he said? . . . see me in hell. What to do?

After I've been standing in the street for thirty seconds, mas-saging my dented kidney, a black man wearing a plum fez emerges from the shadows alongside the market. On his fez the word "Jamil" is stitched in ungainly cursive with yellow thread. There are hats everywhere tonight, tassels, threats. I step back.

"Want some pussy, buddy?" he asks. His incisors are jew-eled. He's wearing a tank top, and I can see that his torso is sculpted like a bodybuilder's. There's a triangle of scary muscle extending from the bottoms of his ears to his shoulder blades; he looks like he swallowed a billiard rack. The guy can't be older than eighteen.

"No, thanks," I say.

"Tight white I got too," he says, "unless you wanting a sis-ter. But mixing's five extra, we got to keep an eye out for our sisters, you know. Got to keep the race," he chuckles, "pure. Whitey know all about that, I guess. You know what I'm saying?" Idly he flexes a bicep.

"I know," I tell him. "I read you loud and clear. But not tonight." I need to follow Bird and Ellen to the restaurant; then I can get my car, park it out of sight, and wait for them to waddle out, bloated and horny and defenseless. Seven courses are bound to take until midnight or so. Go away, please.

He insists, "They clean, too, these girls. I even got one with baby-milk, if you're looking for something kinky."

"Sorry," I say, "sorry. You're kind to offer. Maybe tomorrow." I walk briskly away. The pimp doesn't budge.

"May be," he repeats matter-of-factly, from the darkness at my back. "May be."

I hide behind a dumpster, among broken bottles and tomcats and puddles of urine, just before Bird and Ellen come out of the bar.

"He's under a lot of strain," explains Bird. "He's not a bad guy, all in all. He . . . well, he's not as dumb as some. And he means well. Or at least he *means* to mean well."

"He's an asshole," says Ellen; her words are clear enough, but her gait is shaky. "Garden variety."

"I've got a theory about Mr. Bird Soulsby," announces Bird as they stroll past, less than ten feet from my alleyway. He slips his hand into hers. "May I try it out on you?"

Ellen clasps the pale paw. Her chignon is perched atop her head like a parasite, a hair remora. "Oh, please. I just adore a good theory."

When they're fifty feet farther along, I make my way to the sidewalk and follow at a discreet distance. Country Luke's turns out to be only three blocks away, on a street called Cotesworth that's lined with law offices and art galleries and fern-filled café-luncheonettes. A doorman in full livery waves Bird and Ellen through the iron gate. As I lope past, I doff an imaginary cap and wish him a good evening; he fingers his whistle thoughtfully.

I retrace my steps to the car.

First I stop by the Biddie Banquet Chik-n Shack for a mess of wings, a tub of dirty rice, slaw, and biscuits. I set the greasy bag on the passenger seat and drive back to the market. This will be my first taste of stakeout food. I'm warming to the task ahead; justice roils my blood, and the chicken smells great. My one chance to strike a blow for the pure of heart.

I cruise down Cotesworth, casing. Three blocks from Country Luke's is an Italian joint called Pappagallo's, and there's a cluster of expensive cars outside it. A guy in a Hawaiian shirt and beach thongs sits smoking a cigarette on the stoop of a clapboard kiosk. He's holding a flashlight large as a hunting thermos — it's more club than lamp. Security. He looks at me dully.

Otherwise the street is deserted. No police, no foot traffic — only the omnipresent roof tarps, dark façades in varying degrees of disrepair, hydrants painted to look like prominent Charlestonians from myth and history (Good evening, Dr. Garden; How do you do, Mr. Pinckney, Mr. Rutledge; them's right fine strawberries, Porgy), sickly palmettos shielded from dogs by the dinky wire wickets old folks use to fence tomatoes. Just three in five streetlights are lit — a legacy of Hugo or thrown stones or simple municipal neglect — but the lack of illumination is to my liking. I drive a few blocks past Country Luke's, then turn around, switch off my lights, and creep to a stop a hundred or so yards from the doorway — facing it, but not visible from it. Under a streetlamp whose eye has been put out. I uncrimp my bag of food and set to.

When I finish eating it's only 10:25. I rifle the car for reading material, but all I can find is a year-old *Golf World* wedged under my seat — not coincidentally, the one that details my collapse in Natchez. The paragraph about me reads, "Brian Schwan, who paced the field through sixty-three holes, spent his final nine strafing backyards with teeballs and dropped all the way into a tie for seventeenth. He left his chances among chlorine sticks and drowned toys in a swimming pool alongside the twelfth." Cute, boys. Frilly. I'm sure the editors — eight to fifteen handicappers all, unless I miss my guess — got a kick out of that "strafing" bit; and how does the asshole reporter, who never left his desk in Pinehurst, know whether the pool (or, technically, pools) had chlorine sticks? (Do they even use those nice chalky cylinders anymore? And canned goods aren't toys, so far as I know.) Funny, funny stuff. The guy who wrote it probably has his own smartass column now: "Choke of the Week" or "Rub of the Groan" or something.

There's no need to check the accuracy of the quote; I have, as I've said, an infallible memory for humiliations. So I don't even open the *Golf World*. Instead, under my map light, I inspect the advertisement on its discolored back cover. The ad is for Absolut vodka. It depicts one of the legion of tan, forgettable ex-Tarzans, Ron Ely, relaxing with a vodka martini in a sterilely opulent Manhattan apartment. He's clutching a stout jungle vine that's suspended from the ceiling. His dimples look like holes in a mask. "ABSOLUT ELY," reads the copy tag.

The magazine has been interred beneath petrified french fries, blackening wheels of pickle, Nab wrappers, coffee mugs, and chain-store circulars because I intercepted it before it got into the house, where Rosa might run across it and use my misadventures against me. I admit that I fudged the numbers, told Rosa I'd been "a couple" over on the homeward nine Sunday because of plain old buzzard luck. That's one of the Blade-and-Titty Tour's silver linings — the sports pages include us only in slow periods (in March, before baseball begins in earnest, and then in the summer, from the end of the NBA season to the start of the NFL — on those rare weekends stranded between golf or tennis majors). We have, therefore, room to maneuver, to wriggle. Privacy. Our hips are our own.

So I stuffed the evidence under my seat and tried to forget. So I fibbed a little. What did it matter? It's all of it lies. Ron Ely's dapper grin hasn't faded during the eleven months of the time capsule (but, once again, his career has); and for the guy who's reading this issue in the locker-room john at some publinx, my two choked drives are still in the bottom of that single pool in Natchez, among anachronistic chlorine sticks and imaginary drowned bears.

I throw the magazine into an overflowing trash bin on the curb, fish it out again to rip off my address label, then wonder why I'm going to such lengths to be furtive — I'm the good guy here. I'm preventing a crime, not committing one. If there's going to be any sleeping around in my name, I want to do it myself. A man has rights, maybe even a shred of honor, whether he's a garden-variety asshole or not.

Bird's probably laying out his "theory" of me right now over Black Forest toadstools, thrilling Ellen with his account of my life-despising soul, my scorn for the wonders of nature, my preference for mystification over mystery. "There's something in him that hates happiness," he's saying, and I can see Ellen's chin bobbing coarsely, like a cork tugged under by a fish. It's not true, Ellen. It's just not true. Don't wag your head in agreement, don't dip it in awe. None of it is true.

I'm sick to death of theories. *The enemy are sick, and so is us of.*

Three weeks ago Rosa first leveled the accusation: "There's something in you that hates happiness," she said, and then tacked on, as though she hadn't shoved the dagger in cleanly enough, "there's something in you that can't stand joy."

The evening had started innocuously. She was watching a

pseudodocumentary called "Jesus Contra Darwin" while I
fiddled with financial records. Now and again some morsel of
soulful illogic would catch my ear, and I'd glance up to see another Bible verse (in a hip '70s translation) confound the fossil
record. Rosa lay on the floor like a child, face propped in her
hands, feet swaying gently above her, taking it in. I found myself wondering why production values on the Christian chan-
nels are so shabby. Can't God whip up cameramen who don't
have the DT's? Has there ever been a Christian film that wasn't
overexposed? In which the boom mikes didn't bob into every
shot? And the crap these people say: "Christ," asserted the
squeaky, weak-chinned host (who appeared himself to be a not-
distant descendant of the gibbon), "was the Son of God, not the
Nephew of Apes. He said, 'I am the Way and the Light,' not
'Oo-oo-oo-oo-ah-ah-ah.'" Well, who can argue with that?

When the docuphilippic finally ended, Rosa crawled into my
lap. "Mmmpphh," I said, battling a little upswell of scorn.
"Dear, you're sitting on my motel and gas receipts. You'll
wrinkle them."

"I'm sitting," she replied, playing hurt, "on my husband's
lap, who's supposed to love me."

"Oh, I do," I assured her, "but auditors are cranky that way.
They want legibility, and love's no excuse. Up, now . . . please,
honey."

She lifted a cheek, and I extricated the records. I smoothed
the ruffled pages, set them on the floor. Rosa settled in again.

"You know," she started, "natural selection is just a theory,
and yet in our secular humanist society, we teach it like it's fact."

I grimaced. When the words "secular humanist" come out of
Rosa's mouth, the best recourse is to flee the temple, get out
while the getting's good: Your moneychanging table's about to
be overturned. But I was feeling ornery, so I said, "Look, all
useful theories are constructed out of facts, Darwinism no less
than any other. They glue in the gaps with theory until better
evidence comes along. And flaws or not, natural selection beats
the hell out of its so-called competition. The *facts* support it."

"That's not so. Facts can be bent in any direction you please. Theories have to stick to a deeper truth, the truth you feel in your heart. I mean I know we can't *scientifically* determine that events in the Bible happened just so, but we know they did. We *know* it. The evolutionists don't understand God's time scheme. The facts can all be reconciled to Genesis, if you know the truth in your heart."

"We who?" Never contend with the contentious, I know; but I couldn't resist. Nothing irks me, I think I've said, like blind piety.

"The millions and millions of born-agains all over the world. Those who've been *saved,* Brian. We can tell because we consult our hearts and God tells us it's so. Isn't there anything you believe because it feels right?"

"Things feel right because they're based in fact, dear, not because of intuition." Mystification my ass; I'm hard-eyed, I'm hawkish, I brook no nonsense — listen to this.

Rosa ignored my gibe. "Then those things aren't theories. Theories are things you have to take on faith. You know them even though there might not be facts to back you up."

"Come on. If you can't confirm it, you don't *know* it."

"That's absurd. How do you know you exist?"

Oldest question in the book, dear wife, and the simplest. *Fallo ergo sum:* I fail, therefore I am. But I didn't give her the satisfaction of an answer; best to let her puzzle it out herself.

"Don't you have any theories at all?"

"Sure I do." Anything to end this conversation. Rosa's vehemence was beginning to weigh on my privates; she kept pogoing up and down for emphasis, with painful results.

"Name one."

I sighed. "Only the person driving is allowed to honk the horn. Feed a cold, starve a fever. Squeeze the paste from the bottom of the tube. On the back at Augusta, every putt breaks toward Rae's Creek."

"Those aren't theories, those are rules. And they're not even *your* rules."

"OK, then . . . never drink wine from a bottle bigger than your head."

"That's a rule, too," Rosa caviled.

I was getting grumpy. "It's my unconfirmable theory that harm will befall anyone who imbibes from a bottle larger in volume than his or her noggin."

Rosa kept pushing. "That's just a rule putting on airs. Don't you have any honest-to-goodness theories? Don't you believe anything because it makes it easier to get up in the morning?" She paused here; her eyes widened. She'd stumbled upon it, the ultimate weapon: her homespun doomsday machine. A smile of schadenfreude spread across her face. "Don't you believe you can, on a given day, beat anybody in the world at golf, even though you haven't proven it yet?"

"Look, Rosa," I said through clenched teeth, "I've had more than enough of this discussion. It's silly, and it's over. There's no reason to believe that God worked a six-day week or that Noah could crowbar two of every living thing into a boat the size of our kitchen or any of a million other Bible stories."

"You think you're so smart; you think faith is dumb, and it makes you feel good to ridicule it in other people," Rosa accused. "You have no instincts at all, no intuition. None."

"Look," I said, "that's enough. What am I *supposed* to think about intuition? Look at my father. All the cockamamie faiths in the world: ten thousand hopes, ten thousand chickenshit failures. He never wised up. Every time he hit a good shot, he thought he had put the bad ones behind him forever. And look at his son, product of his theories — go ahead, take a look at *me*. And tell me honestly how much I should trust intuition."

"That's so unfair, and so mean," Rosa protested. "Your father is a wonderful man, and he has the greatest gift of all — he knows how to make himself happy and how to make those around him happy. Your mother loves him, and I love him, and —"

"Speak for yourself," I snapped. "Don't drag me into that."

"That's horrible, Brian. You love him, too."

I didn't reply. We *had* been happy together, once, but that was on the false ground of golf, back when Dad could put his big hands under my arms and swing me over the fence into the pasture, and we'd set off together through the cow pies. I believed in my mastery then. It was a matter of time, practice. And what's left? Tainted memory. A marriage turning sour. A sheaf of unpaid motel bills, a fan of maxed-out gasoline cards. And in Lamartine, a patch of linoleum, dulled and scuffed by Dad's spikes when he danced in, night after night, to report fruitless "discoveries."

"I know," said Rosa, getting a grip on herself again, "why you don't have theories."

Oh no. And every woman a sage.

"You're afraid you'll pick the wrong thing to believe and something will come along and prove you wrong and you'll have been living a lie. You'd rather throw up your hands and say it can't be figured out than accept something on faith and work through it because you know deep down it's right. But you *do* know deep down, you can't help that. You don't have to listen to it, that's up to you; but you can't not know."

"You're talking about God again."

"No, I'm talking about us. I love you, and I'm not going anywhere. Isn't that enough? Can't we make that into happiness? Can't we make that into a family?" The endpoint of every discussion. The furtherance of the species: a new generation of bafflement and pain. More ducklings, more Schwans.

"Sure it's enough," I said, and kissed Rosa behind the ear. "Sure it is." But I knew it wasn't . . . and her being right only made things worse. You can't build a life on guesses, even if guesses are all you have — isn't that, itself, a theory?

Rosa bristled. "Don't you try to weasel out that way," she said. "I worry about you, Brian. There's something in you that hates happiness . . . there's something in you that can't stand joy."

"I have a theory now," I said wearily. "If I don't get some sleep, I'll be snitty all day tomorrow. And if you don't get off

my lap now, you'll never be a mother whether we want you to
or not."

"See what I mean," sniffed Rosa, trying to laugh at my futile
little joke but coming up short, far short, in a way that made
me shiver. "Do you see what you put me up against?"

As we lay in bed that night, I thought back to my boyhood.
Rosa slept in a wrathful half hitch, her back to me. I couldn't
sleep — instead I watched the blue numbers of the bedside
clock change, listened to the fridge's hum, the baying of the
neighbors' penned dalmatian. There was, after all, one theory I
could remember completely — which felt, while I watched
Rosa's twitches and tremors, as present and real as when I'd
mulled it, years ago, among superhero sheets and stick-on ceiling stars. Its durance as memory pained me; in some way it
meant I still believed. I'm a fool, of course. Rosa's right. When
has she not been?

I wondered whether I should jostle her and say I'd hunted up,
at last, a theory of my own. But it was too late. The sun had
fled; her angry sleep had gone on too long. So I ran the old
thing through my mind, trying to take belief apart.

When I was a kid, I figured every person was allotted a certain number of heartbeats. This number composed a lifespan,
and you could save or spend your pulses, salt them away or
squander them — it was up to you. You wandered from shop
to shop, nose pressed foggingly against the glass, admiring the
available experiences, sampling, weighing prices and risks as
you decided whether to swing open the door and spend a pulse
or two. As you got older, I thought, you'd grow shrewd and
frugal; and ultimately you'd hoard heartbeats like ration chits.
Longevity was the goal. If you spent wisely, you lived long. It
was simple.

As I grew older, saw the way my father's foibles wore on
Mom, saw the way her half-swallowed melancholy — at being

an Upcountry wife, at being a Charlestonian dispossessed —
ate at him, I realized that no heart beats in a vacuum, and that
therefore each moment of anxiety or anger I caused was a kind
of incremental murder: parricide by dribs and drabs. Whenever
I sent my mom's pulse soaring, I shortened her life. "You're
killing me, Brian," she kept saying, twisting her grimace into
the familiar semi-smile of indulgence. "You're killing your poor
mother with all this mischief. Now sit still. Hush. Be good. Be
a gentleman."

I knew full well what I was doing to her . . . and the knowledge was killing *me*. Guilt would bleed me dry someday. God's
arithmetic required that conscience dun two heartbeats from
me for every one I robbed Mom of. I'd be dead by eighteen at
this rate.

I couldn't help myself; knowing the wages, I sinned, offended, misdid. The usual kid stuff. I sizzled grasshoppers with
a lens; from behind a screen of hollies I beaned passing cars with
balls of mud; I touched myself; and now and again I slipped
through the chickenwire into Dantzler's Orchard, scooped up
windfall apples, scarfed them down, and left the cores where
Mom could find them.

That was the strange part — I always deposited the cores
where my mother would happen upon them. Where they couldn't
be missed. It was the most complicated element of the theory. I
knew deception was expensive; guilt exacted a premium for
fear of discovery, and if I didn't provide for the detection and
punishment of my thefts, my heart would pound right through
my chest with its message of shame, shame, shame. Wandering
around the house with apple flesh in the gunwales of my
mouth, brushing my teeth between meals to remove a shred of
skin trapped there like a scarlet *A*, sitting down already gorged
to a dinner — my favorite, cooked especially to please Mother's
little Renaissance Man — and not being able to join the Clean
Plates Club: Exposure was unavoidable, might be lurking anywhere. A giveaway rip in my pants, fructose on my breath, granules of fertilizer stuck like homely blue bangles to my shoes, a

stray maternal glance through the window as I spread the wire: anywhere.

The anxiety wasn't worth its price; better to be busted right off and spared a few heartbeats. When Mom came across the cores, she would deliver a pulse-quickening lecture, so the crime would cost her some of the heartbeats it would — had I not been caught — have cost me. She must have thought I was an unbelievably lazy evildoer. But I was a step ahead, struggling with high math and higher philosophy. I wasn't ready to have my devilment kill me, so I spread the death around a little.

The worst confession I can make is this: Knowing how heavy the blood beat in Mom's temples, knowing what it was costing, I enjoyed hearing her yell. When she sent me outside to tear off a switch, I was never sent back to find a stouter one; I went straight for the big boys, looking for a stick as big as my sin. I even liked the Calvinistic whish the hickory made as she brought it down, tearfully, on my backside. Spankings marked a terrible complicity — Mom and I were dying conjointly, of the same disease, the same sin. We were in it together. Whether she knew it or not, this really *was* hurting her as much as it was me.

There is, they say, no intimacy like that of murderer and victim. I was a boy. I did the best I could: I loved Mom, and I kept on killing her.

Eventually, counting heartbeats got too complicated and too self-conscious; I reached the point where I depleted my store of pulses by counting them all the time, like a purse-proud king who's too busy stacking and restacking his ducats and baubles to make any use of them. The math was consuming my time, and Mom asked panicked questions about the pages of numbers she found in my room: "What are you figuring on so hard, Brian? This doesn't have anything to do with gambling, does it? You're not mixed up with some sort of *sharks,* are you? I *told* your father golf was no pastime for a child." So that even my innocent counting was sucking away at her store of pulses, and every contact I had with another human being — every contact I would ever have — was bloody murder.

I hated God for having let me in on the awful secret. I hated Him for giving me the knowledge that set my heart to fluttering every minute. He was sloppy. He hadn't thought things through. In His edenic pique, He'd underestimated the damage guilt would do if set loose in the world. He was rash, dangerous, a hothead. There was only one way out. I had to kill Him, too.

It was easy. His fatal mistake was original sin. It was bad enough to divvy the heartbeats capriciously, to give some folks half a billion, others ten times that, and stillborns or preemies maybe none, maybe a few hundred thousand: faint, shared, underwater, dark, to no good end. I could see clipping the sinner for his own mischief; it makes a certain sense that if you burn the candle at both ends, your fuel dwindles faster. But original sin was absurd. Purity of heart avails you nothing; did you ask to be the same species as G. Gordon Liddy, Idi Amin, George Steinbrenner? But you're guilty by association, awash in it, convicted for all time. This was clearly, like the Stamp Act, taxation without representation. Jehovah was double-dipping, taking a commission — why should He be so impatient to run us out of pulses? Is it a game?

I killed Him. Who wants a God with His hand in your pocket all the time?

I quit cold turkey. I threw out my pads of numbers, emptied the shavings from my sharpener, gave up my calculations: I no longer tried to figure what percentage of my life might be lost while I waited for Mom's soap opera to end so she could take me to the course, didn't tick off the steps back to school after lunch, didn't record how long it took Dad to lace his shoes in the evenings and multiply it, half in disbelief, by the weeks, months, years; I stopped dividing class periods into two hundred quarter-minute segments and marking them off — the gradations, in trustworthy black and white, of frittered time, wasted life — as they passed. Most of all, I quit numbering heartbeats. When you stop counting, I reasoned, you kill God.

With Him out of the way, it was easy to discard my theory of pulses. Unless someone was up there doing the allotting, there could be no explaining the children who died sixty years before they should, or the accident victims, or even the heart attacks: What if the victim had had one pound less to lug around? What if his rest pulse had stayed one beat lower? What if he hadn't pushed himself those last twenty yards? What if, at lunch, he'd ordered the broiled chicken instead of the Double Chili Frito Pie with extra sour cream (and he was deliberating, he was right on the edge of doing just that)? Mightn't he have lived another thirty minutes, or another thirty years?

Blind, pointless accident entered the world, and took the pressure off me.

I fidgeted next to Rosa until after two, running things over in my head, remembering my struggle during the last days of The Counting: how I'd thought the purpose of math was to allow subtler and subtler calculations of your lifespan and of your culpability in the shortening of other people's lifespans; how, trying to kick the habit of murder, I locked myself in my room for a whole Saturday until I realized, hearing Mom's panicked whispers and Dad's threats, that my absence was killing them faster than any malignancy I could have conceived.

I remembered the way I held my hand to my ribs all the time, felt the palpitations there, the ebbing away of my life — before I was even *started,* before I'd had a chance to make something of myself, of my golf, before I'd laid an eye on Charleston or even a naked girl — and heard my father say, in that tone he has that's halfway between captious and joking, "Madeline, the boy's pledging allegiance again. You don't think he's a Unionist, do you? What would old Jeff Davis say?"

Every sin an enormity. Every pulse accompanied by the tinkle of the register. By the time I finally exhausted myself the other night, I was afraid again, and Rosa went unkissed. I stared into the blank wall of her back, thinking about the years I've shaved off her life already, trying to rally myself to be better. And —

the best, worst proof of my selfishness, my indifference — eventually I crossed over, without a throe or a pang, without so much as a twinge, into a deep and thoughtless sleep. My pulse slowed, my jaw went slack, and I forgot.

It's five till eleven now, and the two epicures are still in there, howling at Country Luke's yarns about pig-poking in Clementine, where the banjos are always dueling and everyone is uncle to himself. Yee-ha. Maybe I should take a walk, get the blood flowing; I'll need to have the blood flowing when they finish. They're probably through the first sorbet now, into the tenderloin; but there's dessert yet to come, coffee, the quitting of accounts. Or maybe I could get a little shuteye, a few minutes. There's an hour yet to wait, and like I said, I need to be sharp when they come out. Just a few minutes. I am so tired.

I awake to the sound of my passenger window being shattered by a Louisville Slugger. Glass lands on me and I feel an itch on my cheek and I see the bat — a heavy, big-barreled thing like Gates Brown used to use — hovering there, unmoving, like the guy who swung it is watching his home run arc through the night sky. Then I see a Brooklyn Dodgers jersey through the jagged windowframe, and another; I'm being attacked by Andy Pafko and Duke Snider.

"What the fuck!" I yell, sitting up, and two heads appear at the window, two identical faces, white, young, acne-ravaged, framed with lank, long, pine-straw-colored hair. I shake my head, thinking it's double vision — but my eyes aren't deceiving me, it's twin Dodger bandits.

"Jesus," says one, "didn't you fucking look in there?"

"What would I do that for?" asks the other. "What kind of peckerhead sleeps in his ride in *this* neighborhood?"

"Don't look at me, shit-for-brains. Ask *him*." He points at me. They lean in the window, give me a rancorous look, and for a minute I think they really expect an answer.

"Ah, fuck it," they say in loopy unison. Then they turn away and amble off, slowly, sluggers swung over their shoulders. There will be other at-bats.

I've added a few powder cuts, not very serious, to my kidney injury; fortunately, none of them is near my eyes. Once I pick away the debris and mop the blood, I notice that the street is deserted. I check my watch: 3:15. Bird and Ellen are gone.

What now? There's no way to find them, of course. It's too late. Ellen's address and number probably aren't — because she's a "public figure" — listed, and even if they were, what could I do? She and Bird have been at her place, if that's where they've gone, for three hours. Busting in on them is likely to get me sued, or shot. And it seems more likely they'd go wherever Bird's staying; he has to be at work long before she does, and she may have roommates or jealous ex-boyfriends or other complications at home. So short of trolling through every motel parking lot between here and Georgetown, there's nothing I can do.

My helplessness comes as something of a relief, to be honest. I've wrung every failure out of this day that it's going to yield, may as well get back to the Ibis and get some more sleep. But I can't . . .

And then I notice there's a note pinned under my wiper blade. I crank down my window, grope along the blade, snag the folded scrap. It's from Bird: "Sleep tight, Lancelot," it says. "And be careful. This isn't a swell neighborhood."

It doesn't seem worthwhile to wonder how he knew what Wass called me at Hawg Heaven, the day I met my wife. It's not productive to guess whether he knew I'd be clouted by the Gemini Dodgers. As I once ceased to count, I have now ceased to question. He knows; he just does. No need making more of it than that.

Most of all, I don't want to think about the adultery I'm

committing, maybe right now, maybe this very moment. I don't want to think of the nervous negotiations about contraception, lighting, position; I don't want to hear mewls or gasps. Don't want to. Don't.

So I take refuge in details. What should I do? I can't go back to the Ibis without having to answer a battery of questions from Hatch: Do you know what time it is? Where the hell have you been, and what happened to your face? Don't you know Rosa's been worried sick about you? What happened to my toaster-oven?

So — the decision comes instantly, as though it's been made for a long time and just waiting for me to see it, to take it in hand — I crank the car and point it toward Fort Moultrie. It's there I'll find the courage to go on . . . if courage it is, if there's any to be found. It's time for my assault. The troops are weary, injured, far from home — but on the move. Finally, on the move.

CHAPTER EIGHT

Friday, 6:35 A.M.

THE PAIN IN MY HANDS IS THE ONE that wakes me. My palms, when I drag them from under my cheek, are striated with scratches. Glass flecks the floorboard; a coil of seatbelt prods my kidney; my face prickles; my head's been stuffed with cotton. My weight has settled between my thighs and my ribcage, and the stench of sleep, slaw, and chicken wings ballasts my breath. Ah, clean living. Ah, morning.

I sit up, find myself in my backseat. Alone on a vast parking steppe, in a lot newly asphalted and empty. I gather my bearings. I vaguely recall coasting in, headlights out for reasons of stealth, relying for navigation on dead reckoning and reflective paint. My car was a matchbox, easily maneuvered; my motor skills were undiminished by the trials of my organs. I was a survivor: I could take any blow Bird could dish out, and finesse remained. I felt a flush of DaVincian pride.

Another letdown. I *am*, I can see now, securely in the space, well between the lines. My bumper lightly breasts the stripe; no magistrate could fault me. But the sidelines are six feet out on either side, and they extend several car lengths beyond the trunk. I've parked in a space drawn for the swankiest motorhome, one as spacious as a duchy.

Over the dunes ahead I see the sun inching through sea oats toward open sky. Outside the broken window I hear the surf's rumble, the ribald laughter of gulls. My mirror reveals a cheek pocked with cuts, a bloodshot eye. The time is . . . 6:37. But where am I? Who is this wretched apparition? And what on earth has happened to my hands?

To the right, beyond a squat coppice of redwood tables, are the answers to my questions — not good ones, to be sure, but all I have.

One thing, first of all, has to be clear: I disbelieve anyone who claims to suffer a memory lapse due to drink or drugs. "I passed out" is the shoddiest excuse I know. Every time Hatch seduces a barfly poet or C&W cowgirl on the road, he slithers out of her arms and bed in the dead of night, pulls the door silently shut behind him, drives back to our motel, scrubs his crusted prick in the shower for a half hour or more; then he awakens having "blacked the whole night out." When he makes this claim (usually while he's watching *Today* and fishing balata out of the toaster with oven mitts), Hatch chuckles and tosses up his quilted green clown hands in what's supposed to be perplexity. "I had a couple of belts," he says, "and then a couple more, and then I met up with this babe who took a shine to me" — he sketches a curvy amphora — "and after that everything gets fuzzy, and now I'm here. Whammo. The big wooze." He begins to juggle the balls he's plucked from his incubator, three, four, six of them, pretending he's doing it not to show off but because they're too hot to handle: "Ooh, ooh, ouch, oh, ooh, OUCH."

OK, OK. I have no doubt — to give all parties equal time — that the woman Hatch has slept with feels the same: She awakes hungover and alone, wonders who the fast-talking doughboy with the big bankroll was, wonders what possessed her to invite him home; and since memories crowd in of his farmer's tan

and his tallow-colored feet clapping against hers (could someone please pluck out my mind's eye? where is the merciful darkness *she* had?) — because there are no good answers to the
questions morning puts to her, she tells her friends the night is
an alcoholic blur, she wishes she could remember, she really
does. She'll wrinkle her nose and flush the toilet for him. As for
the cottonmouth, the saddlesoreness, her memory of the truth:
They'll pass soon enough.

Though I see their necessity, I hate lies like those. I wake up
knowing exactly where I am, what accident or idiocy landed
me there. My head is clearest first thing in the morning —
troubles are best inventoried when the world is made of light
pastels, before the sun has a chance to bake hard color into anything. In those first few minutes of wakefulness no stain seems
indelible, and there's no blunder you can't make good again.

In college I saw a slide of a painting whose artist now escapes
me. It was a frightful thing, Prometheus on a cliff in chains, an
eagle hunched over him like a myopic surgeon, shredding with
its reddened beak. (My professor was Giambattista Lalumia.
While we watched from the darkened orchestra, Lalu jumpily
scoured every slide from corner to corner, beat insights out of
the screen with a riding crop given to him, under circumstances
he never explained, by a grateful jockey at Pimlico. Lalu's taste
ran toward the purple; he preferred *incarnadine* to *reddened*.)

I often think of Prometheus, facing the day with raw scars and
a replenished liver. Even he must allow himself optimism in the
morning. Maybe Zeus has tired of the sport; maybe the eagle
won't show for work; maybe *this* liver will last. Until he glimpses
the circling bird, dark against the sun, Prometheus must hold
out hope. He spends his waking moments falling in love with a
new liver and the day that brought it. It's all there is to do.

The upshot of this is that when I examined myself a minute
ago, I wasn't doing anything so silly as pretending to "discover"

the mess last night made of me. Instead I was trying to make a list of my woes while the cataloging could still be blithe, to take an honest look before the light got good enough for despair.

So I knew beforehand what my hands would look like; I expected the scabby, foul-breathed Grendel who confronted me in the mirror; I found the sun, as always, in the eastern sky. And I knew, long before I let my gaze slide rightward — to the grassy escarpment and the flapping state flag and that hand-mangling fence — that my car was parked at my beloved Fort Moultrie, *né* Sullivan; that I was in one piece, if barely; that I was, once again, Brian Schwan; and that my day of reckoning had arrived.

None of this bothered me. I filed the data with perfect indifference: the dawn, the dunes, the chop out there where the great British fleet was undone. I noticed that the fence I cut my hands on — was it only three hours ago? — which seemed at the time an impregnable thing made of dragon's teeth or pales of steel, turns out in sober daylight to be not even part of the fort, just variety-store chain link surmounted by three outward-tilted strands of wire: The battlements that repulsed the Union Jack back then can't, today, do the trick on glandy teens with spray cans.

I glance at the flags, the ruins, and the sea beyond with the same affable incuriosity I feel for bowling or bluegrass or other people's children. What a nifty spare, what a mean banjo, what a pretty baby. Good fort, good harbor, good morning.

Moultrie can do nothing for me now. It's only another run-down historical site: roped-off munitions stores where you can read glib legends off plaques, glass-cased mannequins in mothy uniforms, a cartoon filmstrip introduced by dead-eyed rangers. Visitors: it is not permitted to remove anything. Our gift shop, on the right as you exit, offers facsimile wheels of the palmetto bark that saved a civilization: Be sure to get yours. Feel free to picnic in the north lot. And if you present your ticket from the fort at any Jasper's Flume Water Park, they'll knock three dollars off admission.

Last night, having made it over the razor wire, I roamed the
battlements in the dark. I was bleeding, exhausted, couldn't see
much: a sickly moon, crisscross of sidewalks, the black roil of
the ocean against a still-blacker sky. It was impossible to get my
bearings. I tripped over a stone coping and landed hard. I heard
a sudden series of clicks, a brief mechanical screech, and an actor's voice rose, crackling, from a hidden speaker; I had, in
falling, set off a recorded paean to the palmetto. I lay in the
dirt, listening to a practiced voice extol the "tricks of density"
performed by these "stout yeomen trees" and waiting for the
inevitable footsteps, the watchman's bobbing beam. But no one
cared; no one came. When the hired baritone signed off, I took
a final sniff of fertilizer and cigarette ash, then climbed to my
feet and headed back the way I had come. I didn't look back.

I'm accustomed to anticlimax. There's even comfort in it. It's
not an end; you always go on to another. You press on . . . in
miserable circumstances, perhaps, but yours, the muddle you
know, the bed you've made so lie in it. What do you want with
a climax, anyway? Do you really wish for a day when there's no
new liver, no cliff, no eagle? You can't. You don't.

I shimmy over the seat, brush away pebbles of window, slip
the key into the ignition. Only minutes to get rolling toward Ile
de Paris before my resolve cracks — before hope becomes in-
supportable again. The engine catches on the first try. Good car,
I think. Good car. Now go.

I'm nearly off Sullivan's and onto the Isle of Palms when the
sun breaks over the treeline. Bit by bit, reality sets in. I cross the
bagatellish "bridge" between the barrier islands — three slabs
of concrete, two measly seams, over it in five seconds — and all
at once I'm a Brit soldier in late June of 1776, on the away
shore of the Atlantic, up to my redcoat in brine. Across the
channel, a hundred yards away, a heron wades in water barely
above its feet, fishing. That close. I see the soldier in front of

me, a boy, take one more tentative step and vanish. His fur cap
bobs on the swells to mark his place, and I turn to the man
grimly following, who won't meet my eyes: *Did you see that?
We're in too deep.* A jellyfish floats spinelessly between us, the
first I've ever seen — a translucent sac, maybe the brain of a
drowned man, blood sucked away by the sea — and the soldier
behind won't look at it or me, but steps closer anyway, staying
in formation. And where is the boy ahead? Gone. Without so
much as a ripple, a bubble; his cap bobs above . . . nothing.
The man behind is at my heels now, eyes still down, breath hot
on my neck, and always stepping, stepping.

It's 6:45, and my tee time's in an hour and a quarter. I have at
least fifty minutes of driving; I'll have no time to warm up. Why
go at all? I banish the question, concentrate instead on logistics,
leaning on them the way, at home, I rely on routine — if you've
showered and shaved and dressed, if there's a cup of inky coffee
in your hand and you're pointed toward the door having been
kissed as a sendoff, what's to stop you from going through with
the day? Too late to turn back. The easiest thing is to wade on.

So I'm working out the details, one at a time. First: suste-
nance. In Mount Pleasant I stop by Hardee's for a steak biscuit
and gravy. At the drive-thru I wait while an aged Byron Nelson
lookalike in a brown smock and a headset nukes my breakfast.
He's evidently come out of retirement to man a register, part of
some new trend: keeping in touch with youth through ground
meat. As the oldster hands me the bag, I hear molten gravy
bubbling inside: The steak will be chewy as a loafer. I thank
him, wedge my coffee between my thighs (having gouged out
the lip-shaped trapdoor in its lid), and drive. Good biscuit.
Good coffee. Good lid. A good start. Check food off the list.

With every minute, every mile, comes a starker realization of
the folly of playing today. One side of the ledger is overloaded.
I always start sluggishly, and I can imagine what'll happen if I
can't loosen up; I have no chance of making the cut; Dad will
be there, Bird, Hatch — Rosa's troika of unsecret agents, here
to smother me with shame and then strip the wreck of usable

parts. And that's just the beginning. What if Ellen, fallen baux-ite over hemoglobin for "Brian," comes to cover the second round, and he and I have to swap identities again? If so, how to tell your father that you're glad to see him, you believe you have your game and your life well in hand now, honestly you do, but by the way could he call you "Bird" today, no special reason, just for . . . luck, that's it, for luck?

And I look like hell, which will put me doubly in dutch with the powers-that-be. I'll be strung up high by the professional-ism board, or whatever that kangaroo court is called, for my charade of yesterday. (The silver lining of running late is that those prigs won't have a chance to call me onto the carpet be-fore I play. And afterward their calls will go unheeded. No need now to fear the street-shoe boys. I'll flip off the douchebags as I squeal out of the lot.) When you throw in the fact that my hands are so tender that I'm having to steer — and eat — with cupped wrists, the further fact that I'm not sure I can manage a shoulder turn around the knot on my back, there seems no rea-son to keep aiming up Highway 17.

But I keep driving, with growing anticipation. Why? It's a beautiful morning. Inertia holds my foot to the pedal, keeps my car — "the Buffoon Ape," so nicknamed when Hatch, pulling down the vanity to check his throat for thrush (which he'd heard on the radio was a common first sign of HIV), set loose one of Rosa's Easter eggs: "Next her the buffoon ape, as athe-ists use, / Mimicked all sects, and had his own to chuse" — in-ertia keeps the Buffoon Ape on the straight and narrow.

By the time I've rehashed the reasons to stick my tail between my legs and slink away, I'm nearing McClellanville. Too far gone. It may even be (admits the sneaky id) that the point of listing the agonies ahead is not to dissuade myself from playing, but to make sure that I *do* . . . to pass the time until I get too far along to call off the day. I've been over the arguments for pack-ing it in a thousand times, and they're not, apparently, enough to keep me away. I suck on them like friendly stones dredged from my pockets, and I'm too happily occupied to think up newer, better reasons to turn toward home with flowers in hand, apology on tongue, sorrow in heart.

The most unexpected incentive for going ahead is that I'm absolutely bursting this morning with the urge to get out on the course and bury my problems. *I want to tee it up.* On mornings as crystalline as this, you play golf; your worries can wait. It's always been that way. I finally have what I want: nothing at all to lose. Tomorrow I go home to be a husband, a father, an ex-golfer. Today I play.

At 7:38 the Eiffel looms up like a promise of landfall. I let my eyes linger on it a bit too long, have to swerve to miss a puff of fur and entrails in the highway. After I've let the thing (a red-coat's shako and its mutilated feather?) slip between my wheels, I recognize it, with a sorry shock, as the remains of the poodle I saw yesterday at the club. She'll never snuffle maypops again, not in that condition. The poor thing won't ever, I think, be the same.

They're mounting up, my animal familiars: the pomo pig, now the steaming nautilus that used to be a poodle's guts. And I do recall that dog — I've seen those innards before, smelled that blood. I can't believe it didn't register yesterday. When Rosa and I were hauling furniture into the new house: all day I'd been trailing her from room to room with loveseats or easy chairs on my back, staggering in a crablike crouch with a brass planter between my knees, or carrying bookcases on my head the way they used to cart water jugs — looking for the elusive place where each would seem "most at home." It was late, and I was beat and thirsty and not a little hostile. All day, under my millstone of the moment, I'd watched Rosa tap her teeth with a meditative finger, get that clouded-over look, and say, "Not here. This doesn't *feel* quite right." I wasn't sure what had put the quiver in my legs, weight or rage.

So when I backed the moving truck out to collect the last

load from her parents', I didn't get down on my hands and knees first to check whether someone's mongrel pest had crawled under to inspect the treads. I felt a bump, almost imperceptible, and I would have let it go, but Rosa shrieked from the porch.

I sighed, cut the radio, settled my cap over my eyebrows, and climbed down from the cab, wondering what the commotion was. Given the outcry, I was happy to see that I hadn't squashed somebody's mother or run over my golf clubs or something: As far as I was concerned, Emma was a better place without that pint-sized beast, which had been yapping and cadging scraps and getting underfoot all afternoon. Rosa managed to divine my attitude, I suppose, and as I stood there tiredly pretending to grieve ("It's a sad thing, all right, but we've got couches to move, you know, and the van's due back at eight or we pay a penalty"), she bellied herself under the truck.

I was dumbfounded; Rosa wears gloves, kneepads, and an allergy mask to help my dad in his garden, for fear she'll swallow a microbe or dirty her jeans. She's not the kind of woman to dive under a rental truck unless she means it. Yet there she was, up to her beam under the rear axle: I could hear sporadic sobs, and between them grunts and pants of exertion. The muff of blood and fur was wriggling, as if under its own power, as she tried to wrench it from beneath the tire.

With a series of gyrations, Rosa worked her way out. She rolled into a sitting position, then gathered the pulpy ex-pet in her right arm and stretched her left hand, which was stained with blood and asphalt, toward me. I pulled her to her feet.

She presented the lifeless body to me like a wrong I had done. Blood dripped along her arm; tears streamed down her face. She lifted the poodle slowly, gripping it by its broken back, until it was chest-high. Then Rosa spread her feet and locked her knees and glared into my face and shook the dog at me and yelled, "Brian! Do you have no more regard for life than this? Is there nothing you care about?"

What chilled me, terrified me, was the formality of it. The elocution, the sniffy grammar, the hint of a script: I wanted to think of this as an end-of-the-day, hormonally triggered, out-of-nowhere tantrum, but it sounded like a . . . well, like a well-drafted censure, ghostwritten by PETA or Eugene O'Neill. I frowned, tried to gauge the evidence against me. The poodle had been split open like a wet sack, and I could see its toylike viscera looping around my wife's upraised hand. Every time Rosa shook her fist, the dog's head flopped against her forearm.

The tears were flowing like a silent cataract, from someplace deeper than simple sympathy; Rosa was crying, I realized, not for the animal — which sagged over her wrist now like a party wig — but for me, for my carelessness, my indifference, my self-obsession.

I'd like to say I felt awful, worse than ever before, worse than ever since; but I didn't. I felt vague and empty, like I'd been left out of something it would have been nice to be part of. I felt awkward in my body: Where to put my eyes, my feet, my hands? How to mold my face to an expression of thoughtful sorrow? How to melt my posture down to the dark stoop of the bereft? Come on, I thought, this turns out to be — for reasons I'd best not worry about now — important to her, so let's make the appropriate face, the called-for sounds, let's get this show on the road.

I realized the last load would have to wait until morning, totted up the cost of another day's rental. I made a note to hose the wheels before I returned the truck. I'd have to get takeout pizza while Rosa bathed; would she consent to jalapeño and onion? I'd need to retrieve the keys from the ignition, close the driver's door. I didn't want to run the battery down. And I noticed, with a guilty flush of lust, that loose gravel had grabbed onto the crotch of Rosa's jeans, that a wisp of hair had escaped her bandanna and was creeping along her cheekbone. I didn't know what to feel, or how. Rosa kept her eyes on me, judging, pitilessly, the quality of my mourning. Maybe thirty seconds had passed, and still no answer to her question.

And then I looked at Rosa — really looked at her, standing in the driveway cosseting someone's ruined pet, late-afternoon sun lighting the panel of truck above her — and I was over-come by a wave of love as helpless as it was unforeseen. At least I ought to have been, and maybe I was. It can be hard to tell the difference between what you feel and what you feel you ought to feel, and this was one of those times. I was tired; I lost track. I threw myself into Rosa's arms, felt the corpse clamp stickily onto the back of my shoulder. There was blood seeping onto my shirt; I'd have to treat it with cold water before I washed it. We hugged, the three of us. *Here's where I'm most at home*, I told myself. *This is the place.* I couldn't tell how deeply I be-lieved this: I was weary; my emotions were another piece of fur-niture I was sick to death of lugging around. Here. Looks good here. This must be the place.

"Of course I care," I told her, kissing her ear and hoping for a lugubrious tone, "of course I do."

"No you don't," said Rosa, pulling back, suddenly dry-eyed, "no you don't. But at least — at least you wish you did. And that's a start."

To Rosa's annoyance, the owner — a widower weary of his dead wife's shedding, shitting legacy — wanted nothing from us but to be spared the sight of the carcass. He could barely conceal his glee, Rosa said. He'd been afraid his laissez-faire policy would have to give way to more direct action: strychnine? dropping the dog over the fence into a neighbor's pit-bull pen?

Rosa had me bury Bartlett in our new backyard. (When I heard the pooch's name I felt, absurdly, a first twinge of sym-pathy — an old lady's lapdog, trapped for most of his life among her musty skirts and named for a clergyman or a pear.) I had foolishly boxed up our flashlight, and we didn't own a proper shovel, so it had to be a low-tech interment. Bartlett's remains sat on the brink of the growing hole in a plastic freezer bag; and as I knelt, troweling out dirt, I turned my back to the door, where Rosa was watching through a doubled veil of tears and screen mesh. I had to turn my back because I didn't want her to see my smile, to hear me whistling "Taps." Because I was, despite it all, enjoying myself immensely — the day had been a riot of inappropriate emotions, and they hadn't stopped yet. I liked the click and whoosh of the tool as it sunk into our new earth, the surprised pink wriggle of the earthworms I bisected, the soft twilight, the hum of the neighbors' pool pump; I made the hole far bigger than it had to be.

I was, all in all, grateful to the ball of fluff in the freezer bag. Before I dropped him into the grave, I ran a careful finger along the seal to make sure he'd be safe. I hoped that would suffice for sorrow. Good-bye, Bartlett.

Peace of mind is too fragile — who knows when some fool pup of a thought will spring up and knock it off its shelf? Drive, Brian, drive, and play golf. There's the tower, right there. Above the trees: a cheapo souvenir blown up to rival God. Drive to it. Stick your tee in the ground. Pursue that ball. Settle accounts with your alter ego. Clap your father on the back, tell him how glad you are to see him, you'll talk after the round. Fail again, for fun this time, maybe make a few birdies along the way. At eighteen shake Dad's hand, tell him it's been a nice run, a good long childhood, but you know it's over. Then go home to Rosa. What could be simpler?

At 7:40 I cruise past the tower, weave around the immovable oak, speed down Champs Élysées Trace (a delightful hybrid, that, of Français and Gated Subdivision). At 7:43 I park beside the crape myrtle nearest the clubhouse, flip open my trunk — and my gas cap, which I relatch in passing — then yank out clubs and cleats amid sheared blossoms and unsteady bees. I replace my snapped putter with a reserve, a flanged Arnold Palmer from my salad days. I run in sockfeet, shoes in hand and wincing all the way, to the pro shop.

The counterman eyes me like I'm a lump of shit escaped from

the bowl. He's a prissy kid, about nineteen, wearing a white shirt buttoned to the neck, an argyle vest of pollen and navy — and to round out his ensemble (I see through the display case), pleated charcoal plus-fours. His whiskerless face and low, knobby chin make him resemble Francis Ouimet. This is one young swell who won't suffer fashion gaffes gladly. Clothes make the man.

A bubble of malice bursts in my chest, and it's all I can do not to voice it: Brummel here probably can't bust ninety, Daddy landed him this sinecure because Junior can't hack college — and he's looking down on *me?* The punk.

Ouimet glowers, speaks: May he, pregnant pause, help me, comma, with anything?

I injure my credibility further by demanding two cadet-medium gloves, any color, one for the right hand, one for the left. As Ouimet digs through the tray of Sta-Sofs, he keeps an intermittent eye on me. Doesn't want the turd to swipe a packet of tees or a handful of water balls or a magnetic four-leaf-clover ballmark. Opportunity may be knocking: They haven't fully trusted him yet, but one collared shoplifter and he's on the fast track to assistant manager. He stalls shamelessly, like a bank teller who's touched off the silent alarm and is trying to burn time till the cops arrive.

"I'm in kind of a hurry," I say, tapping the face of my watch. This doesn't help: I must be an ambidextrous drifter or escaped con posing as a touring pro. Ouimet's going to rifle through that tray of cowhide hands until the chief straggles in. The kid may find my having asked for two gloves less appalling than that I'll settle for mismatched colors, like some kind of lowlife carnival acrobat. Meanwhile, time's a-wasting.

So when I catch him looking my way, I lift my palms in explanation: "Bad hands," I say. "My car got broken into last night, in Charleston."

The dandy rolls his eyes. He finally digs out the right-hand glove, lays it atop the more prosaic lefty — sure enough, they're both beige — then snatches my fifty by its most distant corner. Returning from the register, he drops the change next to my outstretched hand. Don't, he's been warned, touch the animals. Safety first.

"If you're looking to clean yourself up," he volunteers, his tone turning soft in the pitying way it would for a legless vet vending pencils, "the locker room's through there." It's 7:48. "But you better be out of there in ten minutes."

I slick my hair, rinse my cuts, do a few knee bends and hip rotations, spray myself with a not-quite-empty can of deodorant I rescue from the wastebin, and tug the wrinkles out of my pants as best I can — having donned my new gloves to avoid picking up splinters of glass. It's 7:52 when I scurry through the shop again (giving Ouimet a gloved double wave), sling my sticks over my left shoulder to protect my ailing kidney, and jog across the practice green. The bag crashes against my back like surf on some puny jetty. As I hopscotch over practice putts, ignoring catcalls, it occurs to me that at this point it's useless to warm up, and I have eight minutes before it's time to sign in at the tee. I pause at the scoreboard. Reconnaissance: the reason for mornings. Get your bearings. Know thine enemy.

The tour's scoreboard man, a failed artist and gifted drunk everybody calls 20/20, is sitting, lotus-style, on the green shelf at the base of the board, his back to me. Against a backdrop of his multicolored calligraphy, he's chattering on one of the walkie-talkies SGCT officials rely on to seem big-time. They're a bunch of deputy sheriffs in beltless slacks; they need two-way radios like a hacker needs a toe-weighted, titanium-shafted persimmon driver that sells — "wholesale," swears the pro — for nine hundred dollars.

"Roger, that's a big 10-4," I hear him say.

I study the board, relive my putrid round, have my eyes drawn to Bird's bright red row of threes like a bull to a shaken cape. Unbelievable. I check the central panel, the "storyboard" — it contains a list of the leaders, the projected cut, and any news or information we might need. There are 55 scores at 70 or better, and 20/20 predicts a cut of 141. There's a banquet tonight, available daycare, the club-repair truck will be here this afternoon, don't abuse your beer privileges you know who you are, pro-am checks can be picked up at the scorer's tent. And "Congratulations to Jim Soulsby, whose fifty-nine is not only a great, great round of golf but a shot in the arm for our *tour* — *Sports Illustrated* and *USA Today* are expected this weekend. Three cheers for Jim . . . and behave, gentlemen." Nothing about me, at least. Maybe no one but Bird noticed; maybe I'll get off yet.

Ripper didn't post a score. Next to his name is a bold, black "NC" — No Card. If he'd turned in his card and then withdrawn, there'd be an eighty-two there, and his wallet would be heavier by a hundred bucks. But Ripper, God bless him, is of the old school — it doesn't matter how much they milk you for, you don't sign your name to an eighty-two. Your name is all you have. There are things a man draws the line at.

So it'll be just the two of us today, and the first group off. Which is OK by me. Given Bird's speed of play, we may be done by eleven. I'll slip away before the tour director and his minions can finish their doughnuts and convene my lynch mob.

20/20's walkie-talkie crackles. "Hey, Pablo," the tour director says, "keep your eyes peeled for Schwan. Let him know he's got a date with destiny."

The news doesn't rattle me; in fact, I kind of like the sound of it. The dignity-of-the-game sticklers, the defenders of professionalism, the tightass powers-that-be — they can't touch me now. I sidle around the board and toward the first tee just as I hear 20/20 promise, "Don't you worry, Chief. I'll track the little putz down for you. Main board out."

◌

"Behold the man!" Bird greets me as I mount the little hummock that serves as the first tee. Seven-fifty-six: four minutes to spare. "I was afraid you wouldn't make it."

I almost ask, *Did you?*, then think better of it: There'll be time for that. Bird's in a folding chair under the starter's awning, vetting a pin sheet. On the table at his side is the preround paraphernalia: a start list, a rubber-banded bundle of score-cards with players' names typed on them, a box of pencils, local-rules supplements, the starter's terry-cloth hat and megaphone, a stack of pin-placement sheets like the one he's perusing. The larynxless ferryman must be away on an errand.

"Morning, Jim," I say, and I'm caught off guard by my tone — it's *dégagé,* edging into friendly. For some reason my bitterness has dried up and been replaced by that species of bonhomie that, when winners show it, gets called "grace." It's as easy to be friendly to Bird as it will be for him, on the seventy-second hole, to pump the hand of his playing partner and say, "Nice tournament. I didn't deserve to win any more than you did. These things even out . . . eventually."

The painless noblesse of winners. I feel, in retrospect, like last night was a twelve-shot victory: no reason to despise my stand-in, understudy, overlord. For one thing he saved me a couple hundred, counting tips. He delivered me from another three hours of clubfooted conversation. I didn't have to hear knee-slapping "hick stories" about Lamartine (what else could "Clementine" really be?) from a highbrow escapee. If asked, I can still report that *this* is a palate that's never in all its days been cleansed with sorbet.

Most important, though, Bird spared me the mortifying choice, after dinner, of either undressing or unmasking. Though there *was* no choice, really: I couldn't have gone through with it. I must have known that all along. And — face it — the evening wouldn't have come to that. Truth be told, Ellen wasn't terribly fond of me, and maybe I didn't want her to be. Maybe, to save my marriage, I threw a wrench into my own machination. I'm not truly that clumsy, am I — I mean when I want not to be clumsy? No . . . no. I wanted out. So when Bird put an end to the courtship, he wasn't far shy of a savior; and what I feel for him this morning has a measure of gratitude in it.

The starter scurries up from the direction of the practice

green, buries his cigarette-pack voicebox in the skin of his neck, and says, "Eight sharp group. Soulsby, Schwan, West. First of all," he croaks to me, "congrats on your round yesterday."

I look at Bird. Not again . . . this is supposed to be over. I'm weary of masquerades, just want to play golf. Who would have guessed, really now, that acts continue to have consequences even once you've set them aside? How do other people get mixed up in *your* self-pity, *your* confusion? Your life may be a vacuum, but there are always fools who rush to fill it. I remember reading once that Oliver Wendell Holmes's first principle of jurisprudence was this: "My right to swing my fist ends at the other man's face." That seems easy enough, but how is it that everywhere you flail, someone's contrived to set a jaw there? What do you do then? Do you stop swinging?

I meant nothing by it, didn't know anyone was paying attention. These are the minor leagues, only a training ground for real golf, real interviews, real life. Bird's right: This is a game, only a game. And I've never claimed to be anything but a clown, a nobody. How was I to know that people would get tangled up in my masquerade? I don't want the responsibility, again, of being someone else; I never wanted it.

But Bird winks. In fact, he looks tickled. And in an odd way I owe him — it boils down, now, to me owing him. So I put on the mask one more time. "Thanks," I mumble finally to the starter. "Thanks a million."

The old man hands me Bird's card with a pin sheet tucked inside. "My wife and I were mighty impressed with what all you said on the TV. You ought to write that down. 'The secret is there is no secret.' That's a hell of a tip, if you chew on it a minute. Deep stuff. It's — what's that religion with the yaller robes? — it's zim booty, kind of." Hearing the starter use a buzzbox to amplify that phrase makes me realize something: I'd expected him to be quiet, wise, the kind of man who, knowing the cost of words, portions his out stingily — like his predecessor, the clean-eared upside-down man who wrecked his car in the desert. I should have known better. It's amazing how careless we are, how much trouble we take to say nothing; what makes zim booties opt for a higher consciousness, I imagine, is recognizing that people are full of shit, that the only way to avoid causing harm is to find a quiet place where you can let your fists fly without worry that faces will get in the way.

"Which one are you?" the starter asks, turning to Bird.

"Schwan," Bird reports. He's having fun now; this must be what cahoots are like.

"Well, I'm supposed to tell you" — he rummages through his pockets, produces a slip of paper — "the tour director wants to see you in the Tuileries Banquet Room immediately upon the completion of your round. He's got that *immediately* underlined pretty good, so I think he means it." He thrusts my scorecard across the table to Bird.

"Uh oh," I say, beginning to enjoy our little conspiracy. "The director. Been naughty, Full Fathom Five?" Another nickname my exploits in Mississippi got me.

"She says she's eighteen, she's eighteen. The law doesn't make me check ID. I'm a trusting soul."

The starter wags his voicebox at us. "Keep the dirty jokes to yourselves," he warns. "I suppose West isn't going to show."

"He took a powder," I tell him. "Poof."

The starter nods. "All right, then, because of the storm damage you can roll her six inches in the fairways, no nearer the hole; embedded ball rule is in effect. White stakes are out of bounds. Painted circles are ground under repair. It's eight on the nose, so let's get started." He gathers his terry hat and megaphone. "Luck be a lady, fellows."

I don't see why they can't dispense with player introductions on Thursday and Friday, the way they do without forecaddies, standard-bearers, and so on. Until the weekend, there are no fans to speak of, and we know who we are, presumably; but the introductions are one of those formalities that every club likes to observe. They all think it's a touch of class, like at the Masters, and what retired exec doesn't like to have a bullhorn in hand? Remembering back to when he could make the wage slaves step lively; those were the days.

The starter is either in especially fine voice today or has discovered a bleeding-ears setting on the megaphone, which is tucked beneath his chin. It's bizarre to see his mouth move and hear his neck speak, like watching a trumpet played by means of ventriloquism. He caws his way through the Brian Schwan spiel of yesterday, and before his Barrymorean "Play away please" has faded, Bird stripes one down the gut of the fairway about two-sixty. Behind me there's a ripple of timorous applause. What?

I turn to find twenty or so people standing along the cart path at the base of the tee. At first I assume the gaggle of onlookers is made up of time-sharers whose morning jogs have been disrupted by our low-rent circus; of tennis players short-cutting to the courts; of greens crew guys waiting to zip out to a remote corner of the lot for a morning joint. But there are no running shoes, no racquets, no Cushmans — just a score of polite-looking Middle Americans, mostly men, dressed to the nines in rayon shorts and golf shoes.

The clothing is a giveaway. Veteran galleryites don't dress as tackily as their idols, and only a tyro would wear cleats to watch a tournament; but of the twelve sets of feet I can see, ten are stuffed into FootJoys. Bird's round has yanked vacationing hackers off neighboring courses. They skank it around in fifty-nine a side, and they're tired of coughing up a C-note in fees to spray twenty bucks of Top-Flites all over the place and thus to lose — most galling of all — a two-dollar wager. They're tired of having to toss bashful hand wedges out of bunkers after four or five gouges at it; tired of worm-burner tee shots; tired of measuring their scores by bogey, with ninety as the gold standard. By God, they've come to see the *pros* rack up some *birdies*. And if it's a show they want, it's a show they'll get.

The starter, playing his bullhorn like a herald blowing the king's flourish, begins a bio of Jim Soulsby — only it comes out more like a canonization speech. He embroiders the info he has (tour's leading money winner in the young season, etcetera) with stats from yesterday's round (eight birdies, two eagles, eight pars), bits from my tube interview, and a few flat inventions ("the most charming young man you could ever want to meet, despite his accomplishments — this is one boy who speaks soft but carries a whuppin' stick"). Oh, Lord.

During the introduction the herd of fans has been inching forward until they're beside the tee. When the starter finishes, there's a smattering of applause that quickly escalates (peer pressure at work) into an ovation. "Attaway, Bird," says one man.

"Whoo," another yowls. "Whoooo."

"Pound that baby," tries a third.

"You the man," somebody yells, prematurely.

It takes me longer than I'd like to get both gloves back on, and it's clear that this ritual is inflaming the passions of my public. There's a flurry of stage whispers behind me: *Two gloves. Two gloves? Two gloves.*

I wrap my hands around the bouquet of shafts and swing all three of my woods, still in their headcovers, to warm up. I drape them behind my neck to loosen my shoulders and upper back; I bolo them over my head to work my bi- and triceps. My kidney's finally loosening up, and I don't feel too bad, considering. My hands sting, but they'll function.

"Willie Stargell," I hear one guy say enthusiastically. "Willie Stargell used to do that in the on-deck circle!" He turns to his kid, a sullen little Fauntleroy in plaid shorts and miniature spikes. "Remember 'We Are Family,' Brandon?"

"No," says the kid, miserably. "Can't we just go play somewhere, Daddy? These guys suck, and their autographs aren't worth doody." Amen, Brandon: Amen.

My back is still stiff, but I can see the 8:08 group down on the practice green shouldering their bags and making their way over, so I sink my tee and step up to the ball. The crowd hushes. Halfway through my downswing there's a stabbing pain under my ribs, and I spin my left hip out of the way too quickly: I drop to one knee in pain. The shot sails over the stand of trees I was in yesterday, still rising, bound for oblivion and in a hurry to get there.

"Re-tee," one fan announces to his friend, who's likely come to the same conclusion. It's not a tough call.

"O.B.," sighs another.

"Choke," hisses his companion. "I'll give over-under on seventy-five right now. Any takers?"

"I think he's hurt," says one woman. She's sitting on a folding field chair, and she has one of those cardboard periscopes they hand out at the Open: must have expected that SGCT galleries would also be ten deep. She's wearing pompon anklets, and there's a minicooler beside her.

Then the first guy says, "Hell, Bernie, I knew we should run up to Georgetown to play Heathergorse Linksland instead of watching these bums. Lightning don't strike but once." Golf fans think the players are deaf, that we play in a trance of money-lust or pure concentration.

I stand up, trying to work the kinks out of my back. Then I look at Bird, touch a clenched fist to my throat. I'm already having fun. "Fu-u-u-u-ck," I croak. "You may not make the cut, Soulsby."

My second swing isn't nearly as stiff, and I hit the ball flush on the screws, airmail the fairway bunker out there about two-fifty; it's a three-hundred-yard clout, all told, and I'll have barely a hundred to the green. When the applause begins, I smile and wave. The best players laugh at adversity, you know. Then I pluck my tee up and we're off.

I wedge to within fifteen feet and graze the lip with my bogey try. The fans, behind the green and still in a cluster, ooh and ahh. I tap in for six.

Bird drops a birdie putt from eight feet. "Hey, what'd that guy shoot yesterday?" asks someone. "Maybe he's the one to watch."

"I think that's Schwan," says Bernie. "The guy Bird mentioned last night on the news. He shot a wad."

"Seventy-seven," the whooer interjects. "I checked."

"That sucks," says Bernie. "That guy's gonna spend his weekend at home no matter what he does today. This time tomorrow the little woman'll have him up on the roof with a bucket of tar." They guffaw. They've been there.

I haven't seen my father yet, though I've been keeping an eye out. His truck (he traded in the convertible a few years ago) wasn't in the lot when I arrived; I didn't find him in front of the scoreboard, where he doubtless would go — gathering information, ammunition — before he set foot on the course. I've searched for him all the way down the fairway: I even peeked into the cart-storage shed tucked behind a hedge to the right. Dad thinks I don't know he's here; he might, as a result, get careless . . . besides, stealth is one of those skills that deteriorates with age, isn't it? He's out there somewhere, a hunter in his blind, waiting; and I don't want him to loom up in front of me, big and sudden and wrathful, gun blazing. I want a little warning.

On two I hit a decent drive, but a heel-cut seven-iron second leaves me on the grassy downslope at the back of a greenside bunker. Deadsville. I've got to lift the ball out of wiry rough, fly it forty feet to get over the trap, then stop it on a slope running hard away from me. The pin's only twenty-five feet from the edge of the sand. It's an impossible shot, and normally I'd bail out: pitch safely across the bunker to a flatter patch of green, leave myself a thirty-footer, take my bogey and run. But today there's nothing to lose, as I keep telling myself, no reason not to roll the dice. I could make six this way, but what's six to a man who's not himself, who will never be this self again?

I take a sixty-degree wedge, a club so steep I can see every groove at address. Not daring to ground it (if I tamp down the knotweed and crabgrass, the ball may move), I hold my wedge above the Titleist. There's a healthy tremor in my grip, and beneath my gloves I can feel my wounds tingling. I pick the club up vertically, strike the ball a downward blow to pop it up in a hurry. It drops about two inches beyond the bunker. Perfect. When it begins to roll, it spits up a stream of sand that other players have displaced with blasts from the bunker.

"Bite!" I instruct. "Bite! Hit a house." The ball rolls out of sight, and I hop onto the mound behind me to see where it finishes. Gathering speed, the ball ticks the pin, pops out to the right. Six inches. Golf can be thrilling when you play it well.

Still I make a show of howling in disappointment, stab myself in the heart with the grip end of my wedge — like I was planning to can the shot. The fans groan gamely, then clap. The portly whooer whoos. Someone says, "Thataway, Birdie baybay. Stick it in there."

A perfect shot, and it would have run twenty-five feet by if it hadn't rattled the stick. Lucky. Ill-advised. But it stopped the bleeding. I get my par.

Bird makes routine four.

⌣

On three my old nemesis, Bird's pet stork, is resting on a haulm of marsh grass five feet from where he was when I shaved the perch under him yesterday. I turn to Bird to point it out, but he's already huddled over his notebook, scribbling perching-pattern data. So I tell the fans, "That's a wood stork down there, *Mysteria americana*. A rare bird."

They don't know how to take this. I've crossed the invisible gallery ropes: Is that good? Several people bob their heads, waiting to see how others respond. One man claps and then, when nobody takes his cue, stops short and pretends to inspect a ballwasher. The pompon-and-periscope woman pipes up, "Thanks, Mr. Soulsby. Would you like a banana?"

"Call me Bird," I tell her, flashing my winningest grin. "And no, thanks."

"Gentle Ben and the Golden Bear don't talk to the gallery,"

grumbles Fauntleroy, whose father has nudged him as though to say, *Isn't this cool? The pros here talk to us just like regular folks . . . well, if regular folks talked about birds.* The little shit. Hey, Brandon buddy, who dressed you?

A family of white birds, roused by the noise, flap disdainfully across the inlet. "There we see," I say, "the egret in action."

When he finishes his ornithological chores, Bird — who's marked my mimicry of him with a sly half smile — hangs a five-iron over the slough and hooks it back through the wind toward the pin. This is probably the best play for a right-to-left player, but it looks audacious, dramatic. The ball hangs over the marsh for the longest time, then takes an abrupt left turn to safety. It lands fifteen feet right of the hole, and sidespin shoves it up the hill to within two putter lengths. A brilliant shot.

There's respectful applause from my claqueurs: If only Brian had played this way yesterday, they're thinking, we might be pulling for him instead. If only.

I tunnel a four-iron low through the wind, on a string. Once it lands, it slides slightly to the right, ends up eight feet below the hole. It's the best shot I've hit in two days, and the fans go wild. My first deuce of the tournament.

As we walk off the green, Bird turns to me and says, in an uncharacteristically somber tone, "There's something you might want to know."

"If it's about Ellen, that's between you and her."

"And you."

"Not and me. I'm out of it." Don't ruin the day, the mood, what's shaping up to be an enjoyable round. Please don't.

"Look," says Bird, "I just wanted you to know that I didn't sleep with her. That was never in the cards."

I don't want to know this. That crusade is over, failed. Ellen's an adult. If she wants to fall for a periodic table of coal, home-made wings, and a split-level ranch stripped of love and shower curtains, it's her problem. Her fall, not mine. I say nothing.

"We didn't sleep together."

I don't care, Bird. Not anymore. It's over. You've won. It

doesn't matter how the other Schwan whiles away his nights. "Well, how about that?" I say, trying to convey a complete lack of curiosity.

But the point is strangely important to him. "Want to know why not?" he asks, eagerness in his voice, self-justification, a quivery earnestness I've never heard in him before.

I sigh. "She didn't want to?"

Bird shakes his head, almost sadly — that's not it.

I try again. "You didn't want to?" Fat chance.

Last guess: "That time of the month."

"None of the above," says Bird, already walking toward the next tee, flashing his most transcendental smirk. "*You* didn't want to."

I'm left standing alone on the apron. The spell is past, all traces gone: Nothing dissolves awe like bad theater. Our roles really are reversed now; Bird has no power over me. Now I'm the one who knows who he is, what he must do; Bird's the fraud. That "savior" stuff a while ago was just me blowing smoke. The questions have disappeared: *How did Bird happen to see the interview with Ellen? What was he doing at the market? Of all the gin joints, etcetera, why did he pick ours? Why didn't he look surprised to find me there? Whence the hat? Why did he come on so strong — not, it seems to me, his style — with Ellen? And, lastly, at what point of the evening did he know his efforts at seduction would go for naught, that he couldn't see it through — could he have understood all along? Was it part of some master plan?*

Poof. The answers are clear. I told him I was going downtown, and he tripped into the right place; I was making an ass of myself with Ellen, so he stepped into the breach; what do I know about his sexual aggressiveness or lack of it? He knew the seduction would fail when she said no and not before. Several times in the last few days I've thought his insight has bordered on aeaeae, glamor, gramarye, *magic*; several times now he's seemed to cross a border that simple smarts can't get you over. But he's not some cut-rate avatar sent to watch over me, and I was wrong to hold him in awe: He too is just a muddler, a fake. I didn't realize it until he tried, just now, to let on that his moves on Ellen were part of a plan: gallant, sexless, heroic.

It's a put-on. He's embarrassed I saw him executing the full-court press, embarrassed he revealed himself to be nothing more than an operator — better read and more magniloquent than Hatch, but of the same species: muskhound, scuzz, lady-killer. The disclaimer this morning is a version of Hatch's oven-mitt juggling act: *I held back, Brian. I abstained. I did it for you. When you were impaired, I took your keys. What I did last night is no more, really, than a brand of designated driving. Could you expect any less of a friend?*

But this theory, too — how to derail a train of thought? — has its rough spots. Some details can't be boiled away by coincidence, lust, or even friendship. There's the emotion in his hymn to flying. There's the hat, an inconceivable relic of Wass and Hawg Heaven. There's *sub rosa.* Mortals don't shoot fifty-nine, unravel Latin phrases, swipe symbolic headwear from rednecks' attics, invent sciences, revisit the fates of Faustus and Leonardo, set alter egos to sleep and then dispatch avenging Dodgers wielding bats — not all on the same day. Could it be that Bird's act is itself part of the plan, to throw me off the scent? Could he be giving me a taste of superiority, of the feeling that I know who I am and have someone else's number? And this improbable gallery of fathers, sons, whooers, empathetic women: Why are they here? Did Bird summon them, too, so we'd have to trade places again, to give me a few minutes of success before I retire to private life? Only a true messiah would cover his tracks by making a transparent pretense to divinity, right?

And despite that transparency I saw through the charade only because of Bird's advice last night. Here's where the theory gets complicated, Rosa. Maybe he gave me that interpretive nudge because he didn't trust me to see through his act without it. Wouldn't true mystery, whose status as mystery depends on its staying inviolate . . . wouldn't it try to pass itself off as mystification?

Because he knew, somehow, what I'd think of his ridiculous "confession." He knew. Despite felt puppets, fakey voices, a cardboard proscenium, his little skit has me elated. Ellen deserved better than me — better even than a glib, witty, charming ex-husband-of-a-Nobelist version of me — and I'm glad she was spared both Brian Schwans, honestly glad. Bird understood better than I did that I didn't want to sleep with her; he knew I couldn't do anything to betray Rosa. He knew it. And that's the one irreducible mystery in Bird's behavior, the issue that can't be resolved by theories: How could he know what Rosa means to me?

I look at him, drifted down the slope to his bag, scrubbing a grass stain off his ball with a wad of spit and a motel bath towel. He's prone to on-course fits of sneezing; two of his fingernails are clubbed by fungus; his sideburns are uneven, and he stuffs the toe of one shoe with toilet paper because his feet don't match: Is that some kind of a god down there? Could he have come to save my marriage?

Having finished his ball-cleaning, Bird calls me back to golf: "Let's go, Birdman. Let it fly. You've got honors."

He's right. Today there's golf to be played. I have a lifetime to sort things out, but today I have only to whack and chase.

I get into a groove. At four I smoke a drive over the corner of the dogleg and stob a wedge to within twelve feet. Another birdie. At five I hit a six-iron twenty-five feet and run the putt in over a swale the size of a small house. I make a scrambling par at six after driving into the woods, and two crisp three-woods and a nice lag putt give me a two-putt birdie at the par-five seventh. Despite the double-bogey start, I'm two under.

The sun is shining benevolently now; every footstep kicks up glimmering spokes of dew. This is fun, and fast. Bird's pace is infectious, and the caliber of our play helps us rip through the holes in no time at all. After a while I'm in a daze; I leave both gloves on, stride from shot to shot without a thought, smack it, acknowledge the jubilant gallery. My aches have ebbed away, and my mind is gloriously empty now.

On eight, a 210-yard par three, I make yet another birdie. I burn a one-iron off the tee, high and with a light control fade, and it nearly rips the pin out of the hole. Six inches from a one. As I saunter between the yawning front bunkers, twirling my putter and counting the sets of raked-over footprints, I hear a galleryite telling the old one-iron joke: What do you do if you're standing in the fairway, exposed, and it starts lightning?

Before he delivers the punch line I see the first concrete sign of my dad — a line of bent branches snapping back in the woods to the right, at the speed of an anxious father. He's here, following along in his unobtrusive way, paying attention. He's watching this. He's watching me.

*You hold up a one-iron, Dad. Even God can't hit a one-iron.*

On nine I have a tight lie in the fairway, so I decide to punch a nine-iron for extra spin. I move the ball up in my stance, hood the clubface, hit down. It's the kind of shot that sets injured hands to wailing, but the result is worth the pain. The ball lands fifteen feet behind the hole and geetah sucks it back, like a yoyo, to within four feet. It's the sort of thing Sunday golfers just eat up, though spinning one back isn't that hard to do on a soft green. But the applause is frenzied, adulatory. My public loves me.

Another kick-in birdie, and I've taken a snappy thirty-one strokes to turn.

"Goddamn," says Bernie's friend, who wanted to play Heathergorse this morning, "except for that spasm on the first tee, he might do it again today. They need first-hole mulligans out here."

I sidle up to them. "I've played Heathergorse, fellas. Dog track. Only good thing about it is the tram that gets you there. And the Scotsman who tucks you in."

"Yeah," says the whooer. "I heard that tram is *awesome,* and totally authentic. Just like the original."

"They got trams in Scotland?" asks someone else.

"Hell, yes," the whooer says. "Europe ain't as backward as it used to be. They got rid of the commies, and they're about to get Disneyland in there. Europe's on the way up."

I nod. "There's a monorail planned for St. Andrews. A people mover. They've got big-time crowd-control problems, you know."

"I think I heard Dave Marr and Peter Alliss talking about that last year," chimes in Brandon's father.

"Here," I say, "a round for everyone . . . on me." I hold out a twenty and a ten. "And make sure Brandon gets a Coke and a hot dog. I adore kids; they're the future of the game, you know. He may be right about our autographs, they're not worth doody, but you won't find guys in the Big Show willing to spring for wienies. They can flat-out play, but they're robots for the most part. Stiffs. Take my word for it. I know 'em."

Bernie's friend accepts the bills. "You got it, Mr. Bird," he says. "Thanks a million."

There are other murmurs of gratitude, and Brandon's father gooses him. I hear the kid whisper fiercely, "But I hate hot dogs, Pop." Pop glares. "Thanks, Mister," the kid mutters, his father's hand wrapped around the back of his neck.

"Make Brandon's a cheeseburger," I tell Bernie's pal. "He doesn't cotton to redhots." I wink at the boy, who finally manages a weak grin.

"With double pickles?" he asks.

"Double pickles," I instruct. Fifty-nine yesterday, thirty-one to turn, and still one of the guys. Loves trams, beers, surly kids. Special orders welcome. This is the stuff legends are made of.

I shortcut across the lot to the tenth tee. It's 9:20. An eighty-minute outward half, maybe a tour record for speed. It helps that Bird and I together took only sixty-four strokes. I feel fantastic, like I can do no wrong. At moments like these, golf is heaven.

I spot Dad's pickup. Though there are plenty of available spaces, he's parked in the grass next to a half-finished paddle-tennis court (one of the dreamed-of facilities that had to be given up after Hugo: no one plays it, but "paddle tennis" has an unmistakably upper-crust sound in a brochure). Dad's backed up to the fenceline of the court, facing out. He has to be positioned for quick getaways, easy access; rules don't apply to him.

I allow myself to wonder if my six birdies have triggered one of his flip-flops of opinion, his sudden enthusiasms. Maybe I've won him over, and he's beginning to doubt whether fatherhood is the right game for me after all. He came as Rosa's mouthpiece, but he may leave as mine. The tide is turning. I can tell it is.

I wouldn't be surprised to see him step out from behind a yucca, wordlessly, and flash a high sign. Cigar in his left hand; cheeks ruddy with pride; tongue stolen by emotion. Then he'd turn and crash back into the woods like a yeti. Misunderstood. A father full of love. A father whose ambitions for me need only to be shaken awake again.

My spikes grind into the macadam. Since I was a boy, when the scrabble of cleats against linoleum heralded my father's latest discovery, that sound has been triumph's accompaniment. And now, turning at four under, striding through the parking lot with a crackle to announce me, I feel like I have the secret, I can play this fucking game. For the first time it occurs to me that another nine like my first will get me off the chopping block — through the cut. Maybe it's *not* over yet.

On the back Bird keeps to himself, grinds along making mostly pars. He shies from my rowdy boosters, keeps his mind on his

round. And though he's not sharp today, he's playing cleverly
and efficiently: He takes advantage of his good shots, mini-
mizes the damage of his bad ones. He hits nifty pitches to salvage pars on ten and twelve, and on fifteen he manufactures a
magnificent save. After a detour into the trees, Bird extricates
himself with a one-iron turned over and hit left-handed. He
makes a surprisingly limber swing and, keeping the ball under
the lowest cordon of branches, shoots it through a gap no more
than five feet wide. By squeezing 120 yards or so out of the
shot, he leaves himself no more than a flip wedge, and he sets
his third inside the grip. Par.

A birdie on eleven, the first of two par fives on the back, gets
him to three under through sixteen.

Meanwhile I'm still on fire. I'm eating up real estate with my
driver; my iron shots are crisp, high, beautiful, and I'm produc-
ing Platonic divots, flawless exclamation points; when I putt,
the hole looks as big as an oil drum. The gallery, depleted by
heat, previous plans, and the lure of the beach, has dwindled to
eight diehards (six men, the periscope woman, and Brandon,
whose double-pickle burger has turned the tide: he's hollering,
jumping up and down, cheering me every time I so much as
tend the pin or clear my spikes of grass cuttings). Brandon's
mood is catching, and the group, though small, is raucous;
every shot produces a hail of slightly asynchronous *You the
man*s. In part their enthusiasm is because I'm playing well, but
I'm inclined to give more credit to the round of beers I bought
and to the bottle of Jack Daniel's and the cooler of ice the
whooer pulled out of his Tahoe at the turn.

I par ten, twelve, thirteen, and fourteen; birdies at eleven, fifteen, and sixteen get me to seven under for the day. Parring seventeen and eighteen will give me 141, but I need one birdie to
remove all doubt; cut estimates are often intentionally high so
that everyone with a glimmer of hope will play hard.

Twice on the inward nine I've spotted my father, both times from afar. On twelve I glimpsed him from the back, at a service shed behind the green, examining massive iron blade attachments for fairway tractors. His hands were clasped behind him, and he seemed, in the distance, to be almost shaking with fascination. When we crept within a hundred yards he vanished between two spike aerators into the dark of the shed.

What I saw him do on fifteen was even stranger. The bourbon had done wonders for my gallery's *esprit de corps,* but it had taken a toll on muscular coordination and on taste: They were lagging behind, doddering down the fairway in a shapeless pack, telling Helen Keller jokes. Bird had driven into the right rough, so he'd forked off to starboard.

I could see Dad standing below a sloping, built-up yard way down the right side of the fairway — staring up the incongruous slope at the condominiums beyond. South Carolina's coastal plain is flat and sandy, yet this hill was loamy, deep green — obviously man-made, at the cost of a lot of planning, a lot of dirt, a lot of money, and a lot of work.

Dad approached a pine at the base of the slope and held his hand to a low branch, measuring it against his height. He climbed the rise, leaning forward so far that his knees nearly touched his chest with every stride. Then he racked his visor on a photinia at the top, upside down, balanced his cigar on the underside of the hat's brim, and hitched up his pants. He descended the slope about a quarter of the way, three or four steps. Then, using his hands as a brace, he lay down on his belly in the grass, across the hill, face turned toward the pine. After he'd pressed his cheek into the turf there for a few seconds, as though trying to corkscrew an eye into the ground, Dad struggled to his feet — more laboriously, I noticed, than ten, or even two, years ago — then moved up a couple of feet and gingerly set himself down again. It was only when I saw him pace from his mark on the slope to the guide tree — caddie-style, with close attention to the length of his strides, the way he taught me — that I realized what this queer pantomime meant . . . and it dawned on me, with a shudder, how awful and wonderful it was that I'd lived on such intimate terms with this man that I could translate his maniac putterings into something sane, even something sensible. And I could.

Simple: my father was figuring the slope of the hill. He'd seen this hillock and wanted, immediately, to measure it — to know the angle of declivity or the runoff or the cost of the topsoil the builders had to haul in. He had to know. "Men measure things," Dad's told me many times, in his sage-motto mode, "but we don't let ourselves be measured *by* them."

And seeing him taking the measure of something that way, just like old times — it stopped me in my tracks. I stood stock-still, not wanting to come too close: You don't spook a figuring man. My heart leapt to my throat, and I realized how much I still needed his approval. I wanted reassurance, one more time, that golf is my destiny. *You can play this game, son. Goddamn, you can play! Make you quit? MAKE you quit? Hell, I wouldn't LET you give it up after what I've seen today.*

We were getting close: thirty yards, twenty. I drew next to Bird, who'd stopped to watch, silently. It was my fans' chari-vari that brought Dad to his senses. He gave us a panicked glance and scrambled up the slope, snatched visor and cigar off their redtip rack, and lit out for the safety of trees.

☙

The slope calculations augur well. He's acting out math prob-lems because he's anxious; he's never seen me play like this, and he fears it'll fly apart. And his nerves have made him careless. It's not like Dad to be sneaked up on like this. Usually he's as flighty and vigilant as a deer; and, bucklike, he would have left his feet anchored where they were and turned only his head, would have given us a regal look of disdain before he bolted. But I saw the ashen face, the unwonted flash of fear. He doesn't have the heart to tell me.

Like me, my father's prone to count under pressure. Numbers are certain; numbers are unfickle; numbers can be manipulated. So we reckon. (If I implied earlier that I'd kicked the habit cold when I gave up charting heartbeats, it wasn't true, quite. I still pace off drives, calculate a course's acreage, estimate tree heights by comparative shadow lengths, try to guess slope ratings by a method that may look less laughable than my dad's but is no less eccentric.)

The day before we got married, Rosa and I had — at our mothers' mutual demand — a rehearsal. My father balked: "It's not like if I mess up and go down the side aisle, the thing won't take," he said. "Come off it, Mad."

"You're the best man, Russell," my mother told him, "at your only boy's wedding. You'll rehearse, and your mouth will stay shut about it."

The church was booked for another wedding ceremony — there was an epidemic of them that year — so we held our practice at a ballroom in the Holiday Inn. It was pouring outside, and Dad's mood seemed to match the weather. During breaks he kept making a beeline to the smoky window that ran the length of the ballroom. All the meeting rooms at the inn were named after explorers; ours was, honest to God, the Salle de La Salle. A squally rain pounded the glass, and my father spread his feet and stared into it.

During the fourth or fifth break I followed him over, worried. "Pop," I asked, "is something wrong?"

"How come we're wearing those goddamn blue-boy costumes?" he asked.

"I can't remember," I answered. "Purity, or maybe chastity. They symbolize something or another. I can get you a xerox if you like."

"We'll look like D-troit sugar daddies. What does *that* symbolize?" But his heart wasn't in the sarcasm. Dad kept his eyes on the window as I swallowed, shrugged. There was a long pause. "See that swimming pool?" he asked finally, pointing through the condensation and the rain toward a barely visible peanut shape. "If we had three inches of the wet stuff, how many gallons would fall in there, do you reckon?"

"Dad," I probed, "is everything all right?"

He talked through me, his voice a bit quavery. "I figure if you straighten out the pender, we've got a thirty-by-sixty rectangle. That's eighteen hundred square feet. Help me out here, boy."

So we worked it out together, at the window, multiplying and converting while Rosa and the mothers negotiated seating, wording, the allocation of flowers in the sanctuary. "Hang onto this number for me," Dad said, coughing up a preliminary figure and racing off to pin another variable. When we came up with a plausible answer in gallons, he translated the figure to weight, as though someone was going to ask him to haul the accumulated rain away.

Finished, my father turned to me. He had a slightly stunned look on his face. He reached out, touched his fingertips to my ribcage, then tugged at a seam there, pretending to yank a wayward thread. "I admit I'm just a bit antsy," he said. "You're . . ." He stopped. It was the closest to public affection I'd ever seen him come, and I knew better than to try to prime the pump or touch him back or even acknowledge what he said. Dad squinted at his shiny black shoes, sucked his teeth. I stood there, my side tingling, thinking back to the days when I pleased him best: remembering our trips home from tournaments in the convertible, the sparse, shouted conversations, the clicks of his eight-track deck, the way the wind whistled over and through my trophy in the back. Sometimes the flimsy little club in the golfer's hands would be a blur, vibrating fast as a hummingbird's wings.

"That's a hell of a lot of water," I told him at last, turning again to the rain and the pool, from which — the storm had been going on for hours — you could now see a steady seepage: overflow. Together we peered through the watery window at the swimming hole that was, for the moment, the best vessel we could find. We're not good at this.

"You're right," Dad said after a moment, his posture relaxing, "that sure is an ass of water. Let's work out capacity in gallons . . . no, let's test ourselves, *imperial* gallons. With math skills, son, it's use 'em or lose 'em."

◎

"Did you see that old gent slithering on his belly?" Bird asked after we came off the green. "He looked terrified when he realized how close we were. Must be a nut."

"He's my father," I replied, as though that answered the question. "He was figuring."

◎

One birdie is all I need, one more in a round when they're a dime a dozen. One.

It's strange what a new day will do: In the light of my birdie barrage, my problems seem manageable. I've won Dad over, buried the hatchet with Bird. The busted car window's not my fault — I may even be able to parlay the urban-violence angle into sympathy from Rosa. If I throw myself on the mercy of the court, the director will let me off with a minimal fine (maybe fifty bucks) and a bit of community service (a clinic or two for kids in tour towns).

For the moment even the home front seems winnable. Maybe I can get a seasonal job and play the circuit half-time; surely Rosa can't be so selfish that she'd veto that. If I don't make the big tour by the end of next year, or maybe the one after that, I'll give up and go to work with Rosa, making Junior. Sixty-three will buy me another season or so; she'll listen to Dad. When he tells Rosa how I've routed the Ile de Paris, she'll relent. She loves me. She knows that golf makes me happy, in a manner of speaking. She wouldn't deny me the pleasure.

One birdie. I'm one birdie away.

And the seventeenth is a par five, long but easy. It's not reach-able in two because of a shallow green guarded by a creek and a deep bunker in front, but a decent drive and a middle iron will give you a wedge third. If the pin is set anywhere reason-able, you'll need birdie to keep up with the field.

I hit a solid drive and then bunt a five-iron to the hundred-yard marker, trying to give myself a full sandy in: This is no time for touchy half shots. The pin's atop a knoll at the back of the green, an easy position. It's a question of getting the ball all the way up the slope, giving yourself a short roll uphill. I figure I'll hit my wedge a little low, let the ball skip up the rick, then settle.

But I play it too fine, and I skin the motherfucker — the first really rotten shot I've hit since the second hole. The ball squirts into the front bunker, and I'm left with an eighty-foot sand shot up the knoll.

Long uphill trap shots are the undoing of pros. It's impos-sible not to spin the ball hard with an explosion, and it's just about impossible to fly one eighty feet out of the coarse, heavy beach sand Ile de Paris uses. Worse, there's no margin for error. If you're going to fly it eighty feet, you have to hit the ball a little thin, take a little less sand than usual. Chances are you'll either fly it over the green (in this case, an automatic seven) or pop it into the lip of the trap and leave yourself the same shot you had before. Russian roulette. You spin the chamber, pull the trigger, and hope.

I try to imagine sweeping a dollar bill out from under my ball, very shallow, and I swing. The ball skims over the lip by about an inch. It lands ten feet short, skips once, and curls to a stop — six feet from par. After Bird's drained a midsized putt to go four under for the day, I bury my tricky sidehiller right in the cup's heart.

"Nice putt," Bird says. My tipsy fans whistle and hoot. But I still need a birdie.

So it's come down to eighteen. Four hundred fifty-eight yards, to be negotiated in three strokes. Wind right to left, helping a little. Fairway bunkers to the left, boondocks to the right. I check the pin placement on my sheet — front right, the easiest location if you put your drive in the proper half of the fairway. This is it.

Bird hits a wonderful teeball, a high draw down the right edge of the short grass that takes a big kick down the hill; he'll have an eight-iron left. I readjust the velcro seals of my sweaty gloves, noticing the tiny map-lines of blood that have soaked through the leather from the crusting cuts on my hands. I take a deep breath, stab my ball into the turf. OK. OK.

At the top of my backswing, I think "Be aggressive," and I lunge; I hit the ball squarely on the clubface, but catch only its bottom quarter — a moon shot. The drive hangs in the air for an eternity, then plops back to earth . . . in the fairway, but barely two hundred yards from the tee. Disaster.

"Splashdown," says Bernie, laughing. "You copy me, Houston?"

"Roger, good buddy. Houston hears you loud and clear," answers his friend, and they all laugh.

Yardage book in hand, I find the nearest sprinkler head and pace off my distance: 252 to the front. I'll have to do something I never dare, hit a driver off bare ground in the fairway, and even that may not be enough. If I do by some miracle fly the shot all the way to the green, it'll surely roll over the back. My only hope is to aim between the front bunkers, which are only fifteen feet apart, and hope I get lucky. It's a slender thread to hang one's hopes on, but where's the choice now? I have to make birdie. Have to.

The clubhead looks unnaturally big behind the ball; my hands are soaking, smarting. One good shot, I think. One more good shot.

I hit it solidly, a low hook that starts at the palms to the right of the green and bends gently back toward the opening. "Get up," I yell, "get *up!*" The ball disappears over the white sand of the right-side bunker, and I don't see it emerge. After an agonizingly long split-second, I see a blur at the left corner of the trap. The shot lands inches outside the sand and takes a big kick. "Stop!" I yell now. "Sit!" Obligingly, it snags in the deep cut of fringe, hops onto the front edge of the green. In the fairway I close my eyes and drop the club: Yes. Two hundred fifty yards away, I have a twenty-footer for my career.

"YOU . . . THE . . . MAN!" goes the tumult. Ahead, Bird puts his iron in the crook of his arm and claps. My father is nowhere to be seen.

Bird's indifferent nine-iron ends up thirty feet past the hole; he'll go first. As we approach the putting surface, the players warming up on the range and the practice green take notice: It's only 10:45, so how could we be nearly finished? They're also watching our boisterous fans follow us up the hill like a gaudy posse. For some murky alcoholic reason the boys are singing an off-key but heartfelt version of "Bringing in the Sheaves." Several players wander over for a look.

Bird lags his putt within a foot, taps in for 67 and a phenomenal thirty-six-hole total of 126. The applause is polite, nothing more.

I study my putt from every angle, trying to get my breathing under control. I clear every stray wisp of grass out of my line, curse every quisling spike mark that might do me in. I eyeball, stoop, plumb-bob. The putt's going to break about six inches to the left, I figure, if I start it off high enough and firm enough. It's downgrain, slightly downhill, so it'll be fast. The read is solid.

I step up, fold my gloves into my putting grip. The blade is midway between my feet, glowing dully. I choke down a little more than usual, trying to get as close to the action as I can: I could count the dimples from this range. And I draw the putter back, swing it through — "like a pendulum," I think, remembering my first putting lesson, Dad standing behind me, his hands over mine, his breath on my forehead as he taught me the rhythm and pace of the stroke — "like . . . a . . . pendulum." The line is perfect. But as the ball rides across the hill, I see that I've hit it too firmly — too fucking hard. I can only hope that the hole gets in the way.

It does. The putt pounds the back of the cup, pops a full two inches into the air, and rattles back down. Birdie.

I leap and punch my fist into the air. Sixty-three, boys, sixty-three. Come chase it. I'm *back.* My fans are whooping it up like it's V-J Day, clapping one another on the back and giving high fives all around. The whooer's neck is swollen and purple, with Saturn-like rings of fat; he sounds like a stuck siren. By the time I get to Bird to shake his hand, the chant has gone up: "Bird! Bird! Bird! Bird! Bird!" The guys on the practice green gape at the weird spectacle up here. Three or four people spill out of the pro shop to see what the clamor's about.

"I enjoyed it, Bird," I say through the din, "and sorry about yesterday."

He smiles. "No harm done," he says. "That was a phenomenal round. You should be proud."

"Thanks. You played well, too."

"And thanks for taking the crowd. I couldn't have stood the extra pressure." He's bullshitting, but it's nice of him.

We duck into the scorer's tent. It's cool and dark in there, and loud. The gallery has massed behind the tent, continuing its chant at high volume. I can see their bulky shadows moving along the candy-striped wall like a lynch mob in the movies. A few curious kids and bystanders have swelled the ranks.

The scorer is a tour employee, one of the director's toadies; he's known by the players as Pink Man for his bizarrely rubicund complexion. Right now, sitting behind his table, he looks startled. When I stoop to tie my shoe, I spy a skin magazine near his feet. He wasn't ready for us. "You guys done already?" he yells over the noise. He keeps shifting in his chair, quelling that unprofessional erection.

"Ready or not," answers Bird with a smile.

While we total our scores, the chant dies down, and Pink Man recovers his senses. "Schwan," he says, "the director wants to see you *immediately* in the clubhouse. Do you hear me? Pronto. Post-haste. Now."

"Immediately," I repeat. "OK." I flash a smile. Nothing can ruin this day.

He picks up his walkie-talkie. "Chief, this is Main Tent. I've got Schwan here. Come in, please." Glee in his voice. He's got me in custody. The sheriff will be pleased.

Within ten seconds the director's voice crackles over the air. "Send him up. And Soulsby with him."

I look at Bird guiltily. I never meant — I've said this before, and now I mean it — for him to get dragged into my disaster. Bird grins at me, shrugs, and recites: "He seems to snare our feet with magic, weaving some future bondage thread by stealthy thread."

"Hey, cut that code shit out," snarls Pink Man. "I'm onto you jerks. I know what you're up to, smart guys."

Bird snorts. "What's that you're reading, Captain? *DDDDe-licious? Muffin Man? Whoppers?*"

You'd think it would be easy for a pink man to blanch, but this one's color adjusts only in one direction: He's gone right through royalty and is heading for aubergine. My father's color.

We sign our cards and shove them across.

"Someday, Pink Man," Bird says, speaking for me, "you'll have to pull your nose out of the bossman's bum." As we leave I can hear Pink Man calling for the boss on his walkie-talkie. There's a new charge to be added.

Behind the tent our fans are gathered, each carrying a score-card swiped (apparently) from the box by the tenth tee. They surround us, asking for autographs. Bird and I wade through the minicrowd, signing. I tell them all I've enjoyed it, hope they'll come out again. Bernie says he'll be watching my career in the papers. Periscope woman has me hold up one of her bronzed legs so I can sign her pompon sock. A couple of the guys ask me out for drinks, but I demur. "Thanks anyway," I say. "I'm not feeling quite myself. But I appreciate the invite."

On each card I write *Memories of a great day. Bird Soulsby, 59–63.* I save Brandon's for last. I'm tempted to sign it *Best wishes, Brandon. Yours, Ben Hogan,* but that would be a lie. It's wrong to lie to a child. Finally I opt for simplicity: *Best wishes, Brandon. Your friend,* and then I append my name. *My* name, mine . . . but I can't take chances, so I make a flourishing *B* and *S,* leave the rest illegible.

When Bird and I have finished our autographs and good-byes, we walk toward the clubhouse. Our compatriots have stopped putting and chipping, and as we pass they give a mocking round of applause.

This is when I expect to find my father behind an azalea bed or a stucco column, giving me the old thumbs-up. It's time he broke his silence. I have a lot to tell him. But he's nowhere to be seen.

"Bird," I say, "I need to call my wife before we face the music." I have to talk to Rosa, tell her what's happened, let her know what a changed man I am. I'm different. We'll be different. I love you, Rosa, and I can *play.*

"Fine by me. I'll drop my sticks in the Pacer and meet you here in five minutes."

"Thanks," I say. "Five minutes."

I collect my keys and wallet, head to the clubhouse to call Rosa. I feel like singing.

CHAPTER NINE

Friday, 10:55 A.M.

THE NEAREST PAY PHONE IS UNDER the portecochere off the pro shop. It's not an ideal place for a telephone, because every footfall in the passage reverberates . . . but I can't imagine, for the moment, a more pleasing sound than cleat clicks and their echoes. I've never felt better.

It's true that Rosa may have a bee in her bonnet because I wasn't at the motel last night to field her calls; Hatch may have riled her more with his sniveling about the slain toaster-oven, about my "erratic" behavior. I can't deny that I've said and done some hard things, and there *is* explaining to do. But once Rosa hears the number — "Sixty-three, sweetie. You heard me right. Sixty-three, my best round ever in competition" — she'll be happy for me . . . for us. Like me, she's above all a lover of concord, and we'll make peace, as we have so many times before. This time when I insist that things will be different, she'll have reason to believe. There's no arguing with numbers, and sixty-three speaks more persuasively than I ever could.

The electronic operator thanks me; the phone rings in Rosa's office. She's probably picking through swatches of upholstery this morning, popping peanut M&Ms from the beveled-glass dish next to her picture of me. Her shoes are off, and with pantyhosed toes she's gripping (a secret pleasure) the cherry-wood dowel that undergirds her desk. A not-good sample book, an uneventful morning, a comfortable roost — she'll be glad to hear from me.

The things I'll say tumble through my mind, each begging to be first. I've beaten golf, dear; after being roughed up for four years, I've kicked its ass at last. Dad'll be here in a second, you know what a doubter he is — I'll put him on to confirm it. I've got a new lease on golf, Rosa, maybe even on life. I'm sorry I've been such a jerk lately. Things will be better, I promise. By the way, I've pieced together that sea-turtle dream, the one where the stork confiscated your shovel and gave you a piece of his mind. If you play your cards right I'll let you in on the allegory. Of course I mean it, sure. We'll talk, Rosa. Honestly. I'm ready to talk it over. But it'll have to wait — and this is the real *news* — it'll have to wait until Sunday. I have two days' work left here. Sunday, OK?

But there's no answer, and after four rings I hear the extended bell that means my call's been shunted to the secretarial pool.

The phone gets picked up: "Merchandise Acquisitions, how may I help you?" It's no one I know. I ask if I might speak to Rosa Schwan, and the officious voice asks me to hold. When I catch up to Rosa, I'll find out who this new recruit is. She's got phone hauteur down pat, has mastered the audio sneer: She'll go places in the debutante-eat-debutante world of department-store buying.

While on hold I listen to the bedlam of background noise around me: jabbering employees, humming carts, the hollow pop of low-compression range balls across the way, muzak whenever the pro-shop door swings open, an ambulance bleating its way to some faraway disaster . . . and over it all, the grind of spikes on gravel. At last, Rosa, the news you've been waiting to hear. Pick up. It's me.

Finally the secretary releases me from limbo: "I'm sorry, sir," she says, "but Ms. Schwan called in sick this morning. Can anyone else help you?"

"No." She's the only one. "Are you sure she's out?" Sick? Rosa? Since we've been married, she's never been ill. Not one day. She must be playing hooky for some reason. I'll have to call her at home.

"Yes sir, I'm sure. Good-bye." It occurs to me to ask why she took so long to find out that her boss, whose desk must be all of fifteen feet away, didn't come in this morning. And why didn't she ask my name, take a message? Could Rosa be ducking me? Could this woman, whoever she is, have been warned against me?

But she's hung up already, and as I replace the receiver my train of thought is cut short by the sound of rapidly approaching footsteps. Street shoes. It's my father, I think, and about time. Dad, come to congratulate me, to bestow his blessing. I turn to greet him, but it's not Dad: Nobody's where he ought to be this morning.

What confronts me instead is a red-bearded man in green coveralls and a tar-stained Masters cap. "Schwan?" he asks, breathing hard.

For a moment I'm flustered. Who is this? Friend or foe? Who am I to him? We goggle at one another. I finally ask, "Who wants to know?" What's this about? Another interview is out of the question; another autograph might cramp the old biscuit hook, and I've already taken care of every member of what became known, during an unfortunate back-nine discussion of Arnie's Army, as "Bird's Flock." I'll get to the director's inquisition when I get there and not before. No shove is necessary. Lay off.

"Look, if your name is Schwan, they need you in the parking lot, right away. Hurry." The man hustles back the way he came. I walk after him, but when he breaks into a run I follow suit.

When I reach the lot I see, behind my car, the ambulance I heard a moment ago. Its lights are pulsing, but the siren is silent, and a small crowd, including several members of the erstwhile Flock, has massed around its back end. As I near the gawkers I can make out a gurney, a white scoop of chest exposed among the shreds of a ripped-off golf shirt. I glance at my car, see the familiar remains of a black cigar, still smoldering, on its roof, and I have no choice but to recognize that chest: its slight sag, the oblong areolae ringed with spokes of silver hair. My father.

I shove through the ghouls, and Bird grabs me, digs his fingers into my sore kidney, holds me back. "It's OK, Brian," he whispers, "he's going to be fine." Already the paramedics are trundling Dad into the ambulance, a mask over his face. His forehead wet and ghastly, eyes shut tight in a grimace. I can feel the heat bleeding up from the asphalt at my feet. My father has lain there. He may be dying, may be dead already. I break away from Bird.

"I'm his son," I say, too loudly. "I'm Brian Schwan. Is he all right?"

Despite my panic I can hear clearly the whooer's gasp, a shocked inversion of his usual noise.

"Be calm, Mr. Schwan," orders one of the paramedics, hopping down from the bumper. He's wearing an orange jumpsuit and wraparound shades. "Your father has had a mild heart attack. He's not going to feel too great for a while, but he'll be fine." Fine, fine, everybody says fine. Why are they all saying fine? I can't see the EMT's eyes to know if this is the truth. Can they know how severe it is already? Could the danger be past so quickly?

"Don't reassure me with shades on. I want to see eyes," I tell him, and he removes the glasses. Behind me I hear a restive chatter building, hear Bernie suggest that something sinister is happening here, something shifty, something positively *bogus*. "That's Brian," he accuses, and I know he must be pointing to Bird. I hope Dad can't hear this; I hope his last memory isn't of this murmurous affray about who's his son and who's not.

"He'll be fine," the EMT reiterates, impatiently. The glasses have left dark pinch-marks on his nose.

"Can I talk to him? Can I ride with him?"

"Sorry." The attendant is curt. "He's on oxygen right now, and he's not ready to talk. We're transporting him to the hospital in Mount Pleasant. You can see him there." Deliberately he replaces the shades and then looks past me to the mob, whose attention is now fully diverted from my father: Fuck the old geezer. False alarm, give or take. More to the point: Who's who? What's going on here?

I nod to the technician, who's no longer paying attention. Through the open back door I see the crouching form of the other medic, fiddling with machinery, and the white bulb of my father's chest cinched tight under a strap. I think of his troubled heart under there, looking to recapture its rhythm, and I realize my own heart is pounding in my throat, my ears, beating its life out triple-time. Rosa's at home, heartsick; Dad's in an ambulance, semiconscious; the news of his stricken ticker will set my mother's to palpitating. I'm killing everyone I love, again.

The paramedic I spoke to slams the hatch and jogs to the driver's door. In a few seconds the vehicle pulls slowly away. I follow it with my eyes, mesmerized like a child by its lights. I watch the dancing strobe for as long as I can, and when I can't see it anymore I imagine the ambulance's progress up Champs Élysées Trace, around the fallen oak, to the tower. When it reaches Eiffel I hear the siren begin, finally, to wail. It occurs to me that Dad, when he comes around, will be most concerned about blowing his cover; for a man obsessed with stealth, he's been awfully exposed of late.

I fear what I'll find when I turn around. The noise has dispersed, as suddenly as smoke, but the crowd is still there. I can hear them, waiting. There's a question pending, an answer coming. The silence of expectation. I have a nightmare vision of Brandon, horror in his eyes, looking up at me and pleading, "Say it ain't so, Bird, say it ain't so."

Then I feel the real Bird's steady hand grip my shoulder, start to turn me. I let myself be turned.

And amid this turmoil, at perhaps the most confused moment of my life, I know. Nothing's ever been more obvious. I won't be back this afternoon to look at my score and bask in the insincere praise of my peers; I won't tee it up tomorrow; the tournament next week in Savannah, and the ones that follow, will go on without me. My work here is finished.

How could I have thought otherwise? The hopes of the last few hours, the joy I'd dreamt was for once pure — they're stupid, absurd. My round today is easily explained: a fresh identity, a few lucky breaks, the once-in-a-lifetime voice of the swan in song. Golf is over. It's an unbearable relief to know it now, to know it without a doubt. What's breathtaking about this feeling is its utter clarity — like when something you've momentarily forgotten pops back into your head, some simple fact you've known forever, the name of your third-grade girlfriend or the color of your mother's eyes or the love of a wife, and when it slips your mind you try to summon it but can't, and then you give up and resume your life and it returns, out of the blue, and it hardly seems you could ever not have known it. My father is hurt; golf is past; my life is with Rosa.

With that it falls into place, a theory all my own. Every human contact costs pulses: of course: no exceptions. But they have to be spent, these heartbeats, and it's not my fault that my dad's sunk his into me, or that Rosa has, or Mom. It's not even a question of fault; I should be glad. Because what can you do with a lifespan but invest it in those you love — parents, wives, golf, children? There's no mystery in that. That turns out not to be a mystery at all.

I raise my eyes to see the director and his minions — Pink Man, 20/20, the shelf-bosomed nymphet lecturer we saw Tuesday — scurrying this way. Despite their reluctance to abandon pre-round routine, players are fleeing the range and the green to get in on the show. I notice, among the multitude, the clouded faces of several of Bird's fans: the whooer, Bernie and friend, periscope woman, an Ohio chiropractor named Gil . . . though fortunately, Brandon and his father appear to be gone. There's a maintenance cart bouncing toward us from the front nine,

and Ouimet has stepped onto the veranda to see what the un-
seemly fuss is about. The man in coveralls is filling in the arriv-
ing greenskeepers, mechanics, gardeners. The only people absent
from the unmasking are those I care about, those who know
me: Rosa, Dad, Mom. Hatch, I suppose. Even Ellen.

There's only Bird, and so I look to him. His hand, warm and
weightless, is clipped to my shoulder like a tether. He's wearing
a wide, inexplicable smile, as though he's about to introduce
the man of the hour. The crowd grasps, somehow, that Bird is
an impresario, helpmeet, famulus, but not a codefendant. They
know who's who, what's what, and their attention is undi-
vided: It's on me. This is my gathering. This is *my* gallery.

What I want most of all — and Bird understands, I can read
it in his face — is to turn and run. I have nothing to say. I have
to go now. My father is in distress. My life is elsewhere. But
Bird clamps down firmly on my arm: not yet, not yet. He'll
help.

Soon he'll raise his hands to quiet the throng. They'll fall
silent, sentences cut off, thoughts let slip, everything forsaken
but this scene, this exposition. Bird's hands will flutter for a
moment above his head. We will be all they see. "Ladies and
gentlemen," he'll call out, holding the pause until those watching start to question themselves, wonder if they've drifted off
and missed the announcement or if the problem isn't his timing
but their own: gone awol, gone haywire . . . "Gentlemen" —
he'll gesture toward me — "this is Brian Schwan."

And then, after all my dithering, I'll let go; I'll leap from the
back of the bigger bird. Gravity will make short work of me,
and when it's finished I'll dust myself off, check for bruises, get
used, again, to the feel of the ground under my feet. I'll draw a
long breath. I'll nod at Bird, my assistant, my friend. Maybe I'll
even smile, wink. And after that I'll turn and, still in my spikes,
click one last triumphant time down the row to my car.

Brian Schwan. Yes it is.